Praise for Noué Kirwan

"Noué Kirwan crafted an emotional and lovely journey. Come for the witty banter between Lanie and Ridley, and stay for the swoon—y longing this novel evokes. I couldn't put it down! _Frequ..._ r wanderlust in the best way possible."
of Plot Twist

"A heartwarming story about fi_..._ _..._d with unlikely people."
nd & Begin

"Heartfelt and romantic, Noué Ki_..._ _..._crafted an authentic love story about family—both born into and created—and the power of forgiveness that will stay with you long after you've read the last sentence."
—Tracey Livesay, author of _American Royalty_

"Realistic and relatable from the start, _Frequent Fliers_ introduces us to people who are trying to find their place in the world, hoping that spot might hold a little romance, a little love. As the story progresses, Kirwan's characters become friends. You hope for them, laugh with them, cry for them, and ultimately rejoice in how their stories unfold."
—Loretta Nyhan, bestselling author of _Digging In_

"I loved the way Lanie and Ridley's relationship evolved from annoyed seatmates on a plane into a swoon-worthy romance."
—Synithia Williams, author of _The Secret to a Southern Wedding_

"Kirwan's excellent debut brings charm, complexity, and plenty of heat... This mature, steamy romance will have readers swooning."
—_Publishers Weekly_, starred review, on _Long Past Summer_

"[D]eveloped with skill and empathy.... This fast-moving novel spotlights a smart woman's journey to find what she wants."
—_Kirkus Reviews_ on _Long Past Summer_

"[A] deftly written and engaging novel... Readers of angsty, drama-filled storylines will enjoy this love triangle, second-chance romance."
—_Library Journal_ on _Long Past Summer_

"Noué Kirwan deftly traverses decades to tell the story of New York City attorney Mikaela Marchand's intertwined relationships with her best friend and her first love.... A sizzling love story you won't want to put down."
—_Essence_ on _Long Past Summer_

NOUÉ KIRWAN

FREQUENT FLIERS

CANARY STREET PRESS

CANARY
STREET
PRESS™

Recycling programs
for this product may
not exist in your area.

ISBN-13: 978-1-335-42745-8

Frequent Fliers

Canary Street Press
22 Adelaide St. West, 41st Floor
Toronto, Ontario M5H 4E3, Canada
CanaryStPress.com

Printed in U.S.A.

Also by Noué Kirwan

Long Past Summer

Visit the author at nouekirwan.com!

To Dad, for being the original writer in my life and my sounding board when the writer's block hits hard. Love you.

And to Tanisha, my OG CP, for never letting me give up, fall behind or flame out.

one

Lanie

■ 25-AUG ■ Trans-Continental Airways ■ Flight: 5866 ■

JFK-John F. Kennedy Int'l Airport ► LHR-London, Heathrow

Seat Assignment: **12A/12C**

Every summer since she was ten, Lanie Turner ran away from home.

It was sanctioned, of course, her destination known and carefully planned. Despite that, it never stopped being a thrilling adventure and daring escape from the humdrum of her regular life. For years, it remained the only thing about Lanie that made her interesting to peers: the number of stamps in her passport. Really, the fact that she had a valid passport at all, unlike 63 percent of all Americans. But this year, technically her eighteenth annual escape, for the first time Lanie didn't really want to go.

It didn't help that she was out of practice, having spent eighteen of the past thirty-six months housebound—*like most everyone on the planet.* As a result, Lanie hadn't set foot on any conveyance more complicated than New York City's Metropolitan Transportation Authority in forever. Truth was, she'd barely reaccustomed herself to being out and about again. It was a lot, being in her office more than occasionally, making brunch plans with friends, going out on dates. Basically, seeing anyone besides her mother day in and day out. Her mother, who had trouble letting Lanie go down the street to pick up groceries these days, never mind board a whole plane without supervising via phone.

"I'm sorry?" Lanie said into that phone.

"Pining is a recipe for loneliness, honey."

Lanie grimaced at those words before flashing a nonthreatening smile to the blank-faced gate agent standing at the Jetway and showing him her electronic ticket.

Even after thirty-five years in the United States, the slightest musical lilt of a Caribbean accent occasionally threaded through her mother's faster New Yorkese, with its nasal intonation and rolling vowel sounds—particularly when she reverted to her more plaintive "gentle" voice. The same one she'd used, once upon a time, to convince Lanie to eat all her peas and carrots.

"Melanie, you hear me?"

"Yup." She nodded in exaggerated fashion though her mother couldn't see it. "Uh-huh, got it."

Her mother sighed like she knew what Lanie was doing. She probably did.

"I think I'm doing the opposite of pining. If I didn't go it would look like I was—"

The wheels of a hard-shell suitcase ran over her foot. Lanie yelped as the accompanying man raced past her down the Jetway.

"Ouch, we're all going to the same place, buddy!"

"Excuse me!" he called over his shoulder belatedly, on his own more contentious and animated phone conversation.

"What happened?" her mother cried.

Anything and everything related to flying filled Ryan Turner with anxiety. Even when she wasn't the one traveling—which was always, since her mother never ever flew anywhere—Ryan believed flying was a catastrophe waiting to happen. So it didn't take much to make her hysterical.

"Nothing, Mommy," Lanie soothed. "Just some *asshole* who doesn't realize he's only gonna get on the plane a millisecond before I do!"

Sure enough, three people ahead of her, there he was, a tall drink of water waiting his turn to step onto the plane like everyone else. Lanie shook her head.

"Melanie, honey." Her mother continued the unending mild reprimand that had begun a month ago, when she first heard Lanie was buying a ticket to attend her cousin's upcoming engagement party in the UK. "No one would have blamed you if you had chosen to stay home."

"We both know that's not true. And that's why I'm going," Lanie reiterated for the umpteenth time. Her eyes were inexplicably riveted to the back of Mr. Rude Businessman's head as he shoved his ticket at the flight attendant directing people to their seats. It startled the poor woman, but he was still too focused on his call to notice. "To make sure everyone knows I'm happy for them."

"You cannot always be a pushover, just suffering in silence."

"Who says I'm suffering?"

Her mother went quiet, which Lanie knew wasn't good. "I don't think this is healthy."

It wasn't the first time her mother had expressed this sentiment, but it was the first she'd framed it in this way, like a mental health issue. Which got Lanie's hackles up.

"What did Narcisa say?" Ryan asked.

"You remember that just because Narcisa's *a* therapist, doesn't mean she's *my* therapist, right?"

"But she's one of your best friends and she's a psychologist... she must have an opinion? She can't think this is a good idea."

"Sounds like you already know what she said. So what's the point in asking me?"

Lanie took the phone from her ear to show the smiling flight attendant her e-boarding pass.

Finally on the plane and moving down the aisle, Lanie saw Mr. Rude Businessman standing right in front of her row—she checked her pass against the numbers above the seats to be absolutely sure...twice. She groaned. He was still on his call, arguing, white earbuds protruding from his ears. Now, however, he spoke in a strained whisper as he shoved his roller case into the overhead compartment, then dragged his coat off and stuffed it inside too.

Which reminded her.

"Hello? Melanie? No, this girl did not hang up on me!" her mother groused as Lanie brought the phone back to her ear. "Melanie Francesca! Are you still there?"

"Yes, Mom. I have to find my seat."

Lanie watched as a petite older woman stretched and struggled to push a tote into the overhead bin in front of her. At five foot nine, Lanie knew her tall-person duties. With a quick exchange of silent gestures, she juggled her own bag and phone to offer the woman some help. As she situated the bag in the bin, the woman thanked her profusely in one ear while her mother harangued Lanie in the other.

Mr. Rude Businessman plopped down into his seat and Lanie sighed. *Of course.*

The overhead bin above her row—*their* row—was almost full. Her obnoxious seatmate had put his case flat in the compartment with his large cape-like coat on top of it. There wasn't any space left for her carry-on. She glanced around. Every other nearby bin was either full or soon to be. Her shoulders fell. She hated touching others' belongings.

"Is that what I'm supposed to say to the Institutional Review Board when they ask me what the fuck happened?" the man growled. He was in the aisle seat but turned toward the window facing the tarmac. "You know this could put the entire trial in jeopardy? I am the only investigator who can collect consents. We all sat down and agreed. Everyone knows this! It's not new. And if it happens again—I don't give two shits that he's your mate—he'll be sacked!"

"Who is that person shouting?" Ryan cried. "Is he in your row?"

She'd forgotten her mother was still there.

"Mommy, relax… Now, hang on." Lanie took the phone from her ear and cleared her throat just as her row mate was throwing another agitated expletive at whoever was on the other side of his conversation.

His crisp diction wavered somewhere between an American and an English accent. Which gave the cursing a particularly scathing air that must have been especially withering on the recipient's end. It definitely made Lanie wince. His shoulders were hunched like that could prevent anyone sitting within two rows from hearing him whisper-shouting at his colleague.

What an unenviable job that poor person has, Lanie imagined.

"Uh, sir?"

He was a big guy. Even in their larger, premium economy seats, he seemed cramped and, in his irritation, barely confined. Just the way his inoffensive oatmeal-colored cable-knit sweater strained across his broad bowed back suggested agitation as he leaned over the armrest. People glanced their way while stowing luggage and taking seats all around them.

"Excuse me?" she tried again, tapping him on the shoulder with a single finger.

His back eased, head rising. She took a half step back as he twisted to look up at her. Fierce and narrowed dark eyes regarded her behind tortoise frames from an angular, dark brown face, sweeping from her face to her midsection questioningly.

"Lanie! Be careful! Where's the air marshal?" Ryan's tinny voice called out as Lanie pressed her phone to her chest, praying her ample bosom might muffle the noise.

His eyes rose from her squawking phone, unfortunately nestled between her breasts, back to her face.

"Can you tell? Look for a white man who looks like he's going to a ball game…"

His brows shifted inward, eyes squinting even more, before the forbidding expression eased into light amusement, his lips pursing to keep from laughing.

Lanie groaned, shoving the phone into her back pocket. "Um, sorry. My mother. You know how it is."

He didn't respond. *No, apparently, he does not know how it is.*

The amusement that was briefly on his face slipped back into its fetters, returning to whatever place a clearly joyless guy like him kept it caged.

"Yes, um, can you shift your case for me so that I can put my bag in there too?" She pointed a finger upward at the bin and his eyes finally left her face to follow it, comprehending.

"Dash, hold." He turned fully toward her, examining the carry-on at her feet before returning to her face once again. "Is there some reason you couldn't do that yourself?"

The words came out of his mouth in a velvety bass. But his tone was as icy off the phone as on. She got flashes of Mr. Spock, *Star Trek*'s emotionless Vulcan.

"If it needs shifting, then. Shift. It."

Lanie rocked back in surprise, nearly bumping into the person in the aisle seat behind her. Her mouth closed, before opening again. "I—I didn't want to…"

Down the aisle, a man took a suitcase from the woman standing beside him and set it in the compartment above her head. But the jerk in front of Lanie only followed her gaze, waiting for her to finish speaking.

Typical. Lanie didn't know why she even bothered. She shook her head. But then surprisingly, he sighed, unbuckling himself to rise.

"I—I just didn't want to touch your stuff. I'm sorry," Lanie stammered as he moved.

"What are you apologizing for?" he snapped in the same brusque manner he'd said everything else, like her explanation was as ridiculous as her request. He shifted his items and then reached down for her carry-on.

"No, I didn't need your help with that, I just wanted..." Lanie began to object before trailing off as he cut her a glance that made her feel like a child speaking out of turn. She stroked her earlobe and watched silently as he picked up her case and placed it neatly beside his own, snapping the bin shut with finality and an aggrieved sigh. "Wait," she said far too loudly, startling him as he began to sit back down.

He paused, brows raised, clearly at the tail end of whatever limited patience he had. "There's something *else* I can do for you?"

"Yeah, you could get the hell out of my way so I can sit down," she muttered.

"Excuse me?" he asked, but he'd heard her alright. The smirk was back.

"Um, I said, this is my row too. I've got the window. Sorry."

He stepped to one side, holding out a hand and ushering her in. Still, it wasn't what anyone could mistake for polite or chivalrous despite appearances to the contrary.

Lanie stepped past him into the window seat with a quiet groan.

"Right," he restarted his conversation, dismissing her. "Dash? You still there?"

This was going to be a very long flight.

two

Lanie

Once Mr. Rude Businessman reclaimed his seat, it was like the bars of a very tiny jail cell closed behind Lanie, trapping her inside. His big body radiated hostility as it blocked out some of the light coming from the aisle. She shifted toward the window, fastening her seat belt. Only then did she remember her mother, still in her back pocket. She eased up, elbowing him accidentally as she retrieved her.

He winced but ignored her.

"Sorry...hello?" Lanie said into her cell.

There was a pronounced exhalation of air on the other end of the call. "Oh my God, I was going to call the airport police! I thought that man had done something to you."

Lanie rolled her eyes, thankful her mother couldn't see. She meant well but her mother's intense aerophobia was possibly worse when it was Lanie flying. "I'm fine. I am on the plane, in my seat," Lanie reassured.

"Next to that man?"

Lanie cut a glance in his direction, lowering her voice. "Yes."

"Call me as soon as you land."

Lanie took a page out of his book, leaning into the window, speaking softly. "If he killed me on the flight, Mom, how would he escape? By parachute? Over the ocean? You watch way too much true crime."

Her mother chuckled.

"Welcome aboard." The flight attendant walked by, closing all the overhead compartments. He paused, bending forward into Lanie's row. "We're going to have to ask you to turn off all your electronic devices in preparation for takeoff." An identical message came over the PA system and he gave them a saccharine smile to go along with the unspoken warning.

"Mommy, I gotta go."

"Fly safe, cupcake."

"We're in a very fragile spot now and have to pray this thing doesn't blow up in our fucking faces!" the man beside her said as if the attendant hadn't spoken. "Given everything, we'll be lucky if they don't launch an inquiry."

He sighed so heavily Lanie felt a smidgen of sympathy.

"I was hoping to cut down on the number of times I had to come to this damn city."

The sympathy was short-lived. Her city deserved better than this guy. *Good thing he's heading home.* She just wished he wasn't sitting next to her as he did it.

Lanie took out the emergency landing card from the seatback, following along with the attendant gesturing with fake drop-down masks in the front cabin.

Her seatmate's shoulders sagged. "I promised Bea." His voice softened. "I promised her I would be home for her birthday, but the study cannot fall apart because we picked the wrong coinvestigator in New York." He paused, sounding pained. "And that's precisely what will happen if David is unable to follow the simplest of instructions."

Beside her, his voice rose and fell, morphing from enraged chuffing to more resigned sighs. Lanie tried to engross herself in the same illustrations on the laminated card that she'd looked at a million times before. But she caught the moment the flight attendant spied her neighbor, still on his call.

"He's gonna come back." Lanie leaned over, whispering the warning.

"Bea will absolutely murder me if I do," he said to his caller, ignoring her.

The flight attendant wrapped up the safety briefing with his eyes fixed on Lanie's seatmate. She didn't know why she cared other than she had visions of him being escorted off the flight in handcuffs. Flight crews had zero tolerance nowadays. She'd seen it with her own eyes. She didn't always blame them either. And those people didn't just get arrested anymore. No, now you got put on "no-fly" lists. Despite everything, she couldn't let a fellow Black person go out like that.

She nudged him as the flight attendant wound the long plastic tubing of the sample drop-down mask around his elbow and started down the aisle in their direction. She did it again, sharper this time.

"Ow!" He turned to regard her with annoyance just as the flight attendant arrived.

"Sir?"

"Yes?" He looked up in surprise, like he'd been called out.

"Federal Aviation Administration regulations state that all electronic devices must be powered down and stowed before we can depart. As I stated previously." The flight attendant glanced at Lanie.

She flashed him the blank, black face of her phone before placing it back in her lap. He nodded.

"Is your phone off, sir?"

"It is."

Lanie bit her lip at the lie.

"We were having a conversation," she corroborated, thumbing between them.

Her seatmate plucked the earbuds out of his ears and made

a show of putting them into their little white charging case as the attendant watched.

"Have a great flight. Sir." The flight attendant smiled peaceably, tapping where his arm rested against the overhead bin, before walking away.

She and her seatmate exchanged the brief smirk of coconspirators. Lanie watched out her window as the plane pushed away from the jet bridge and began taxiing toward the runway. After a while, the plane began its jaunty acceleration down the runway and Lanie's fingers dug into the armrest as it sped up. Adrenaline-fueled fear and excitement shot through her veins in equal measure, causing her heart to beat wildly as g-forces pushed her back into her seat.

She smiled a little to herself.

It was always like this. Ever since she was a kid. Ever since that very first flight she'd taken at ten years old, to see a grandmother she'd barely remembered and cousins she hadn't known. Armed only with her Rand McNally atlas, little plastic airplane wings pinned to her chest like a member of the flight crew and the "unaccompanied minor" tag that hung around her neck, Lanie began a love affair with travel that had never ended. She held her breath as the nose rose first, looking out the window as the incline grew. Her smile grew as the back wheels left the ground. And then she whispered her goodbyes to her mother and her friends and, most importantly, her New York as the city spread out beneath her and the plane rose into the clouds.

"Thanks."

It came very softly, a whisper over her shoulder. Lanie turned to see her seatmate looking directly into her eyes. She gave him a lopsided, closed-mouth smile, before averting her gaze.

"And...I guess, sorry?" he continued.

"For what?" She returned to his rather handsome face. "Running over my foot? Being rude? Or saying the f-word so frequently my ears might need a pregnancy test?"

A stunned silence unfurled between them. The man's eyes widened, and the corners of his mouth lifted. Then a second later, a big barking laugh cut through the air, attracting the attention of their nearest neighbors. Was there anything that this man did that was small and quiet? Lanie kept up her crooked smile as he sobered.

"Was I really that bad?"

"I mean..." She shrugged. "I might have to go straight to Boots to get some Plan B just in case and, you know, bandages for my injured foot when we land, but..."

That got her another round of chuckles, which she enjoyed. Lanie was at a loss. This guy had been as mean as a mangy dog a minute ago but had now somehow morphed into an easily amused kitten.

He sighed ruefully, shaking his head at himself. "I am not at my best today. I got some very bad news. I'm sorry if you bore any of the brunt of that." He sank against his seat, deflated.

"Thank you." Lanie nodded, graciously. "But you probably owe that apology to your colleague on the phone."

"Dashiell?" he scoffed, waving that idea off. "MacGeraghty's my friend. He's accustomed to it."

Lanie frowned. "More's the pity for him."

That got her another smirk. "So, not your first time in the UK, I take it?" he asked after another extended silence that Lanie had used to look at the pillowy cumulus clouds out her window.

"Oh?" She spared him a brief glance.

He leaned in a little. "Since you know about Boots Pharmacy."

"No, not my first time," she conceded. "And I do love me some Boots."

Lanie had spent most of the summers of her life to date in London. But she wasn't ready to share that. An awkward silence grew between them again until she relented.

"My grandmother lives in Balham."

She waited for talk of either rough neighborhoods or recent gentrification to commence. Lanie had learned those were two of the most foolproof conversation starters for city-dwellers the world over.

His eyebrows rose. "South London, is it?"

"Yup. You?"

"Oh, I'm from London too."

Lanie smiled to herself, noting the small evasion. "East, West, North?"

"Uh, West," he said, still oddly coy.

Lanie briefly nodded, poking out her bottom lip, impressed, she supposed.

"Notting Hill."

Nice. Now her eyebrows rose. *Talk about gentrified.*

So, he was probably rich. But from the vibe of him, his muddled British-meets-American accent and all, she could have probably guessed that anyway. It was like saying you lived in the Village in New York—once upon a time it could have meant anything; now it definitely meant money.

"I love that movie."

"*Everyone* loves that movie," he replied, rolling his eyes. "If I ever meet Hugh Grant, I'm going to sock him in the eye."

Lanie laughed, longer and harder than the joke probably merited.

"It's all the damn tourists," he finished by way of explanation.

"Yeah, I think I got it. Since, you know, I'm from…"

"New York City," they both said it at the same time as she nodded and he chuckled again, mildly.

"Well, if I had my way, Times Square would be erased from the map," she admitted.

He pursed his lips and nodded before whispering, "And I think Leicester Square is an eyesore."

"Don't get me started on the Empire State Building, I mean 34th Street in general. Ugh." She upped the ante.

"The Eye. I cannot stand it."

"Now, hold up, I like the London Eye! Never been on it but it looks fun. Next thing you know, you'll be marking the Tower of London for demolition."

"Tourist." He shook his head in disappointment.

"Watch it now," Lanie warned, but a smile broke across her face.

"What? Let's call it what it is—a giant Ferris wheel. What's the appeal?"

"I like Ferris wheels?"

"That makes one of us."

"So, you've never been on the Wonder Wheel?"

"In Coney Island? I rarely have a chance to leave Manhattan."

"My God, who's the tourist now?" Lanie teased.

"Listen…" He dragged the word out as if taking umbrage to that. "I go to New York to work. That's it."

"No wonder you think NYC is the pits."

He grimaced. "You heard that, did you?"

She nodded. "So, are you afraid of the outer boroughs, the subway, taxicabs, heights, what?" Lanie giggled at the absurdity, but then paused when he stopped blinking. "Wait? *Are* you afraid of heights?"

He didn't answer. Lanie closed her window shade abruptly and turned in time to see his shoulders drop a little with relief.

"I'm so sorry! You could have asked me to close it before we took off."

"I don't usually have to." Her seatmate shrugged. "I usually request the window so I can control the shades, but this was a rushed ticket. I was only in town overnight. And now I've found out I have to be back in a week." He sighed.

"That's what the yelling was about?"

He blanched about as much as a cocoa brown man could

then nodded. He reached over, very officiously, offering her the massive mitt he called a hand. "Ridley."

Lanie eyed this hand with reluctance. "They made me check my hand sanitizer. The bottle was too big. Sorry."

"No, I'm sorry." He withdrew his arm swiftly. "You'd think after almost three years I'd be accustomed to that." He shook his head.

"Honestly, that's one of the things I'm glad hasn't made a comeback." Lanie let a visible shiver run through her. "Handshakes. All those germs, yuck."

"I know." He shook his head. "And as a doctor, you'd think I'd know better."

"Doctor, huh? Well then, you probably should," she teased as he again looked chagrined.

She nodded, twisting at the waist to offer him an elbow. "Lanie."

He brought up his own to bump hers awkwardly.

"That's not really better, is it?" he conceded.

"Hmm, no," she agreed. "It's really not."

They both laughed.

three

Lanie

"Five of spades," Lanie said as her eyes ran the length of Dr. Ridley Aronsen while he, in turn, watched her closely. They faced each other in competition, each taking the other's measure.

Lanie's tongue pressed against her front teeth in consideration. In that moment, Lanie squinted, wondering if he knew precisely how fine he was. Particularly since he seemed so consciously and boringly professorial in his carriage and dress, she was beginning to suspect that it was a put-on. Like, perhaps he was deliberately trying to downplay his looks to be taken seriously. As if a simple boring sweater, dark slacks and the tortoiseshell-colored, brow-line glasses could somehow obscure those intense matinee idol–esque eyes and enviable bone structure. Though truthfully, she did appreciate his "cover" a little. Because she feared he'd have been a little too intimidatingly handsome otherwise.

"C'mon, then," Lanie groused, all but pouting at the handful of playing cards she held on to tightly.

Whatever his motivations, Ridley was terrifically unsuccessful in hiding his charm. Because in addition to being visually appealing, he was attractive in other ways too. Lanie felt an almost instant rapport with him. Like they'd known each other for years instead of hours, telling stories and sharing jokes. Over the duration of the flight, she'd discovered that she enjoyed him, this perfect stranger. And she recognized quickly that kind of chemistry was something she hadn't experienced since childhood.

Not since Jonah.

Lanie's heart gave a faint but pained kick at that thought. The ease with which she and Ridley had shared anecdotes and embarrassing foibles already felt like the stuff of lasting friendships… or possibly even more. Her cheeks warmed at the prospect of it.

"Bullshit!" Ridley declared, startling her out of her contemplative silence.

"Damn. You're good at this," Lanie grumbled, eyeing the two cards remaining in his hand. "Or you're a low-down, dirty cheating cheater."

"Or, counterpoint, you're transparent, totally easy to read." The corner of his mouth rose slightly.

"No, you're definitely cheating." Lanie dropped her cards on the discarded stack sitting atop Ridley's tray table anyway. "I fold."

"Smart decision." He winked.

"I know when the jig is up." Lanie's smile lost its luster as their final round of "Bullshit" gave way to the topic they'd been discussing over their playing cards. "Well, usually."

"So, your friend and your cousin, huh?" Ridley crossed his arms, returning to their subject of discussion. "And you're *not* happy for them?"

Lanie shrugged, reshuffling the deck to return to the flight attendant.

When she'd finally, and with great reluctance, unburdened herself, Ridley was surprisingly understanding and nonjudgmental. Lanie had spent the last hour recounting her reasoning for this trip: the engagement celebration of her favorite cousin,

Gemma, to one of Lanie's closest friends, Jonah. A surprise engagement at that. Lanie still wasn't sure why she'd decided to
confide that, other than that Ridley looked like a safe person
to tell. More than likely though, he'd just mesmerized her.
Ensorcelled her with those warm and inviting cognac-brown
eyes of his. And his scent. Ridley smelled really, *really* good,
like summer campfires—spicy, woodsy and clean. Ultimately,
whatever it was, the story had fallen from her lips with ease
and alarming candor.

"Supposedly being a captive audience for over a year had
given them a chance to really get to know one another."

"Makes perfect sense."

Lanie bristled. "The thing is, they've already known each
other their whole lives."

"Ah well," Ridley reasoned in the same breezy manner he'd
displayed for the past few hours. Long gone was the uptight
and caustic Mr. Rude Businessman. "You must admit, the circumstances of the past few years have made for a lot of strange
bedfellows."

Lanie groaned.

"Poor choice of words. Apologies." Ridley caught himself
but smirked slightly.

Lanie couldn't completely marshal her frustration. "As a result, they'd gotten very close, they said."

"Sure." Ridley's expression remained sympathetic.

"I think what really gets me is they don't actually have anything in common. He's a lawyer and she's a hairdresser."

He didn't respond to that, pushing his glasses up his nose, a
slight frown forming as if he was trying to decipher her meaning.

"Don't look at me like that. I'm not being some classist jerk.
Gem's my favorite cousin, she's beautiful. I love her. But she
hated school, dropped out at fifteen and refuses to read anything more challenging than the features in *Glamazon* magazine.

Whereas Jonah memorized the Declaration of Independence *on a dare*."

"Was it you who dared him?"

Lanie smiled without comment. "Point is Gemma's a *Corrie* addict. She likes reality TV and soap operas. Unless there's a drag queen, top model, housewife or paternity test involved, she doesn't want any part of it. Whereas we like action movies and anime, for God's sake!"

"So, they have different interests." He nodded. "Got it."

Lanie got the impression Ridley was humoring her; he'd heard the "we" she'd let slip but didn't remark on it. She shook her head. She was doing a bad job explaining this.

It was more than differing interests. It was different circles, different lives, different choices. When Lanie was ten and Jonah was twelve, Gemma was fourteen. That was like residing on entirely different planes of existence. As kids, that age gap might as well have meant Gemma was ten years older than both of them. In fact, really Gemma only ever associated with Lanie because she was like the little sister Gemma'd always wanted.

"But," Ridley said, cutting into her thoughts with another one of his own, "other than *Coronation Street* and RuPaul, I don't really have any idea what you're talking about either. That doesn't mean we aren't still having a perfectly good conversation, does it?"

Aww. She liked that he was enjoying himself too.

"Yeah, but we also aren't about to fall madly in love with each other and get married, are we?" she shot back sarcastically.

"Touché."

She sighed, her quick little fantasy-bubble popping for the umpteenth time. Lanie was fatigued with her own peevishness about this whole thing with Jonah and Gemma.

"My point was that things change. People evolve," he clarified.

Lanie nodded; she knew they weren't children anymore, of course. Still, it didn't make sense.

Lanie's lifelong close relationship with Jonah was based on shared goals, shared interests and shared experiences: collecting trading cards when they met at ten and twelve; charting Pokémon evolutions at twelve and fourteen; winning a multiplayer game competition during an all-night, Red Bull–fueled, transatlantic binge at fifteen and seventeen; quizzing each other during his intense GCSE revision at sixteen then her SAT prep at seventeen; standing in line for hours at the first midnight screenings of the latest Star Wars movies in their early twenties. They had each other's backs through both their college admissions processes. And he guided her through the challenges of her college years, sometimes trading dozens of emails and texts with her a day, then they supported one another through the trials and tribulations of being people of color in predominately white graduate programs.

She and Jonah had history, even across borders and oceans. Tons of it, *years of it.*

What did Jonah and Gemma have?

Proximity? They had Lanie's grandmother's church fellowship with Jonah's family for years. They had the neighborhood and one or two mutual friends. But at the heart of it they were still two people who had barely interacted, except to say "hi" and "bye" and occasionally sit in the same pew at church. Until two and a half years ago, when somehow everything had changed. And now they were getting married. *Make it make sense.*

"So…" Lanie took another cleansing breath, pretending she wasn't still stewing. "Anyway, that's the story. I'm headed to their engagement party. Gotta represent for the North American contingent of the fam. Like a good sport."

"Commendable, since having just played 'Bullshit' with you, I know you're hardly a good sport," Ridley said, tapping the tip of her nose with his index finger.

Lanie was so stunned she whipped back in surprise and banged her head against the window.

"I'm sorry!" Ridley was as startled as she was. "I don't know why I did that!"

Lanie rubbed her head, feeling awkward about how forcibly she'd pulled away. "It's fine. Misjudged the space is all." Suddenly she was aware of how small their row was and how close Ridley sat to her. She cleared her throat. "Mind if I head to the restroom?"

Ridley nodded.

Lanie dug into her backpack for her toiletry bag before getting to her feet. Ridley rose with her, crouching until he cleared the overhead bin and following her into the aisle.

She spun on him with a raised eyebrow. "You planning on following me into the bathroom?"

He stopped short, stunned.

She only belatedly thought of the "mile-high" implication of the question. Lanie covered her mouth with her hands. "I—I didn't mean that." She shook her head vigorously, dying a little inside. "I didn't mean it like that!"

A small grin threatened to crack the placid façade of Ridley's face. "Well, um, I was actually planning to use this opportunity to head to the bathroom myself...if that's okay?"

She nodded, unable to speak.

"Thataway," he added, thumbing aft, in the opposite direction of where she was headed.

Lanie bit her lip but continued to nod, face boiling hot. Ridley shook his head. Then, a deep, rumbling chuckle emanated from his chest that made Lanie feel lightheaded yet forgiven for her faux pas. They shared a brief, knowing but nevertheless awkward look before turning away from each other.

A minute later, Lanie pushed the lavatory door closed and then leaned her head against it. She smiled hard, until the apples of her cheeks flamed, her mind swirling with ideas.

She shook off the highly involved love fantasy she'd already begun constructing, letting go of the "how I met your father" story forming in her head to examine her very real face in the large mirror. Her large, thick-lashed, almond-shaped eyes and high cheekbones accentuated the small bags forming underneath them, made worse by harsh mirror-mounted lights. Her usually honeyed and freckle-dotted complexion was a little sallow. The recirculated air had dried her out and red-eye flights were known to be rough on a person's general constitution. She dragged her fingers over her face then rummaged through her beauty bag for something to do about it. Thank God for Gemma, who had insisted she get a ton of products to deal with it.

Lanie pulled a moisturizing spritz out of her bag. Then she plucked at her cheeks a little, hoping to get some of her golden-brown color back. She dabbed her full lips lightly with some tinted lip balm and then rebrushed her thick, tightly coiled, hickory-brown hair into something approaching its original do. That was the extent of her makeover abilities when in an airplane lavatory, so she decided it would have to do. She swept a paper towel across her underarms, then reapplied her deodorant and smoothed down her rumpled shirt. Then, taking a last look in the mirror, she stepped out of the bathroom.

Ridley was already standing in the aisle waiting on her. He leaned against his seatback with his eyes closed, his arms crossed over his chest, head resting on the overhead bin.

Good God, she realized again with a quiet groan, *glasses or no, he is an inordinately attractive man...*

Lanie tried to keep her composure but even looking at him made her heart gallop. It didn't make sense since they'd only just met. Of course, it didn't hurt that standing there, tall, dark brown and sharply angled like some preternatural combination of mahogany and statuary marble, he was a sight to behold.

No, no, we are merely plane pals, more ephemeral than pen pals.

Which she'd had plenty of hopping back and forth across the Atlantic over the years.

Sensing her approach, Ridley's eyes opened and he stiffly straightened to his full height as she came down the aisle. Lanie was certain she was grinning like an idiot, but he wasn't.

Not at all.

He moved out of the way so she could shuffle into the window seat again. Ridley glanced at her briefly before refocusing on the screen that activated the in-flight entertainment system. Neither of them had found use for it before because they'd been having far more entertaining conversations and a lively game of cards with each other. But now he pressed buttons, opening his mouth before hesitating. He eyed her again, almost guiltily, yet still without comment. Then he gave up, searching around himself for something Lanie couldn't identify.

Why did it feel like they were back where they'd started six hours ago? She looked him over, feeling like she'd missed something. But she hadn't been in the bathroom *that* long.

"I'm sorry," he said at long last.

For what, she wasn't sure.

He reached over her for the book he'd abandoned hours ago, tucked in the seatback pocket in front of her.

She leaned back reflexively so that he wouldn't be close as he did it, since even his smell enthralled her.

But then Lanie noticed a new thing on his hand as he stretched an arm across for his book.

"No, I'm sorry," she muttered, taking in the wedding ring that had materialized on his left hand.

four

Ridley

Ridley stopped at the greengrocer and the bakery on the way home. He wasn't above admitting, if only to himself, making a welcome-home dinner—even though he was the one returning—was intended as a bribe. His way of breaking the news to his daughter, Beatrix, that this trip was not to be the last of a few as promised, but the first of many.

The plan was to make a lasagna with his grandmother's legendary Bolognese sauce and his own special creamy garlic bread recipe—*courtesy of Martha Stewart*—that was Bea's favorite. Both recipes required fresh ingredients and a few hours in the kitchen. But fresh off his flight, all Ridley really wanted was sleep and his grandma's authentic sauce. And this recipe, gifted to her as a teen by an Italian *nonna* that had lived next door, required a couple of hours to simmer. Better, he had decided, to get the grocery shopping out of the way now while he was still on his second wind.

So, in addition to his travel gear, his arms were full when he finally got to his home. And that was probably fortunate considering who was waiting on his front doorstep.

"Dr. Aronsen."

He'd always only referred to Ridley by his last name, as a

sign of contempt. Usually, there was no goodwill, kindness or even respect in the words, which suited Ridley just fine.

"Gavin." In a single word, Ridley addressed Bea's biological father with the same amount of disdain.

Gavin Dorrence could live a hundred lives filled with good works and deeds and still never earn the right to use Ridley's first name. They'd known each other since their days at Harvard and had loathed each other since then too. Still, Gavin's use of the word *Doctor* did give Ridley pause, as it possibly indicated some kind of overture toward civility.

So, Ridley checked his hostility and tried again. "I believe our solicitor told yours we'd be in touch."

"Yes, but that was not supposed to mean I don't get my regularly scheduled visitation," Gavin said.

So, Bea didn't go to Gavin's while I was away? Ridley thought, mildly peeved. Ridley kept his reaction to that information off his face, yet knew he would have to have a conversation with his in-laws, Clare-Olive and Philip. Bea's grandparents loathed Gavin as much as Ridley did, but according to the solicitor, no one should do anything right now to poke the bear.

But Ridley still wouldn't throw them under the bus.

"Considering you've missed the past three visits, maybe you have your dates wrong."

Gavin didn't respond to the accusation. He sighed as he rose to his feet, pulling an elastic out of his shoulder-length copper hair, and then pulled it right back up into its untidy, stupidly pretentious man-bun. Ridley fought the urge to quite literally kick the man off their doorstep—his Ferragamos didn't deserve that sort of ill treatment. Still, it irked Ridley how comfortable Gavin was there, sitting on the stoop of a house he'd never lived in.

Ridley could tell by the way Gavin hovered on the steps leaning against the wrought iron railing that he was waiting for an invitation inside.

"Bea has athletics this weekend and revision next."

Gavin's eyes widened. "Is she struggling with something? Because of the..."

"No. Not struggling." It irritated Ridley that that's where Gavin's brain went first. "We want her prepared for the GCSE next year. Math is hard for her."

"Maths? Really? You'd think with three doctors for parents—"

"Dyscalculia is a learning disorder, it wouldn't matter what we did for a living!" Ridley's response was more of a rebuke than he'd intended. But the resentment he felt at Gavin considering himself one of Bea's parents made his words caustic.

Gavin's mouth twisted.

"Anyway." Ridley collected himself. Gavin had at least acknowledged that Ridley was one of her parents too. Perhaps that would bode well for their upcoming legal matters. He calmed. "Bea has a lot of testing anxiety, so we have to do a lot of preparation with her before she sits any exams."

As much as it killed Ridley to think it, Gavin would have to know these things if he intended to share custody or, God forbid, was granted full custody of Bea.

They were still standing on the front steps, which was pointless. Ridley groaned with acquiescence, then came up the remaining steps past Gavin to unlock the door. Juggling all his bags precariously, he pushed their Crayola-blue door open with a creak. He'd been promising to oil the hinges since Thyra asked him to do it four years ago, and now the sound was an embarrassing reminder.

Ridley propped his roller case against the coatrack and walked through the narrow hallway, through the living room and dining room toward the kitchen. Depositing the full-to-overflowing brown grocery bag on the island, Ridley turned to see Gavin right behind him looking around.

He tried to see the space as Gavin might. A large and airy open floor plan kitchen took up the entire rear of the house, facing a teak deck through a glass-paneled wall. Pivoting, iron-framed glass doors faced a lush rear garden, flooding the entire space with light. Sleek modern appliances and minimalist countertops lined the walls and a small dining space separated the kitchen from the living room. It was his wife's dream space, Ridley knew.

"She redid the kitchen. And the living room too?" Gavin asked as if he read minds.

Putting on his company manners, Ridley put the last of the groceries in the refrigerator before turning to him. Gavin was leaning with his hip against the kitchen island, looking far too comfortable, waiting. In all these years, Ridley had still not managed to work out what precisely Thyra had liked enough about her ex to not only date him throughout secondary school and university, but to also follow him across the Atlantic to Boston.

"Yes, a long time ago," Ridley answered.

Gavin was like every odious incarnation of white male privilege personified. As the owner of a bio-tech start-up, he was the embodiment of Silicon Valley tech bro smugness by way of UK public school, and spoke with RP-accented pomposity. Publicly progressive, Ridley guessed Gavin still voted Tory in private and that all of Gavin's "anti-racist" books retained uncracked spines on dust-covered bookcases. Though Gavin always looked and dressed like an underemployed, undernourished hipster grad student, it was all a carefully curated lie. From the obligatory yet pristine Doc Martens on his feet to his hundred-thousand-dollar Audemars Piguet Royal Oak watch on his wrist and that Reiss cashmere scarf wrapped around his neck—perfectly placed to be used as a garrote—the guy was the definition of an absolute poseur. The real truth was his entire wardrobe of "casual separates" and "street wear," like his lifestyle, cost more than the GDP of some small countries.

What does he know about our remodeling? Ridley wondered.

Once upon a time, Gavin could barely drag his ass to the curb to have a conversation with Thyra, let alone come inside

to see his own kid. Ridley bristled, attempting to keep his annoyance in check.

"She did a great job." Gavin's eyes and hand swung around
like a curator explaining an exhibit. "It needed better flow...
and a bit more light. I'm glad you opened the space up."

Ridley squinted at him, adjusting his glasses with irritation
as if that would help him understand the words coming out of
Gavin's mouth better.

"I haven't seen the inside since my grandmother died when
I was a kid. Before I gave it to Thyra, of course," Gavin explained, reading his face.

Gave. Ridley bristled at this. This house, that he'd long
thought was Thyra's, had in fact been gifted to Bea, to be held
in trust until she turned eighteen—because Gavin would never
have given Thyra herself anything so valuable, up to and including his last name. And it was clearly meant as a payoff—no
revisionist history now would change that. Payment to keep
Thyra quiet and not embarrass Gavin's family. The technical-
ity would have been moot if Ridley hadn't only recently found
out this truth, after Thyra died. He'd hated knowing that he
had it all wrong—or worse yet, that Thyra had lied. He also
hated that after all these years, Gavin knew something he didn't
about his own life and wife.

"Gavin, why are you here?"

Gavin took a breath like the windup to a pitch. "I'd like to
have Beatrix for Christmas."

"No." Ridley said it so quickly that the word came out like
a bark.

"Would you let me explain?"

"I don't need an explanation. It's a no now and it'll still be
no a few minutes from now when you've finished talking."

Gavin sighed, his shoulders rising and falling dramatically
as if the words wounded his woebegone soul. Then his more

somber expression broke into the smug, butter-wouldn't-melt manner Ridley was accustomed to seeing.

"I recently bought a place near Vail and I'd love to bring Beatrix over to see it," Gavin bragged anyway as if Ridley hadn't said anything. "Ten bedrooms, she can pick whichever one she wants. She can even bring one or two of her friends to visit for a week. It could be great fun."

"No. Gavin." Ridley struggled to rein himself in, even as his agitation grew. "Did you not hear me? There is no way I'm letting you take Bea out of the country—"

"Now, now." Gavin tutted as Ridley opened his mouth to tell him more pointedly that this wouldn't be happening. "Hold on. As you said, I've missed the last four visits with Beatrix."

"Due to your own negligence!"

"Due to the fact that my business and, frankly, my life right now is in America. When I have business and meetings to attend to, being in London is not conducive."

"Have you not been on the planet for the past three years? Remote is a thing. Zoom is practically a sacrament now."

"Sure, but with most of my business being on the West Coast we're talking an *eight-hour* time difference. Staying here is not practical."

"Not even for your daughter? The girl you *claim* you want a better relationship with?"

"That's what I'm attempting to do!" Frustration threaded through Gavin's voice. "I'm taking time off and making an effort to do something she'll enjoy."

"In a way that's convenient for you! That's not parenting, Gavin. Parenting is sacrifice, making concessions. Understanding that your daughter's life is here on this side of the Atlantic and moving heaven and hell to be here! For her."

Gavin's blue eyes darkened, his lightly tanned face turning pink, the already plummy accent getting obnoxiously posher, the diction crisper, haughty now. "Don't do that. Oh, Aronsen. You do not want to go there."

"What does that mean?"

"You know where Beatrix has been every time I've called her recently?" He pinned Ridley with a chilly glare. "At her grandparents' house. Because you've been in the office. Or at a meeting...or in New York." Gavin let the last part of that slide out of his mouth slowly to make sure the words stuck to Ridley like a stamp. "And rumor has it, you'll be there even more in the coming months."

How the hell does Gavin already know that? Moving in the upper echelons of the medical community, Ridley supposed that someone could have spoken to someone who knew Gavin eventually. But to be aware of the inner workings of his trial so quickly spoke to something else. Something a tad more unethical.

"Point is, we're both doing the best we can."

Ridley rolled his eyes so hard they hurt.

"And since I haven't had my agreed-upon and mandated visitation in quite a while, I don't think it's unreasonable to ask for an uninterrupted two weeks now."

Ridley began to object.

"Particularly since the Baker-Smythes did not make Beatrix available when I arranged something really lovely for our last visit."

"Oh, is that so? What?" Ridley was dying to know what Gavin thought was "lovely."

"A ride alone on the London Eye. For her and all her school friends. I hired one whole capsule, all to themselves."

Ridley pulled his glasses off and pinched his nose before dragging a hand down his face. *What is it with people and that neon-colored monstrosity?*

"My solicitor thinks I'm within my rights to ask for some small concession."

Ridley bit back the urge to tell Gavin where he could stick

his "small concession." He could see the self-satisfied smirk playing at the corners of Gavin's mouth but at least he had the good sense to hold it in check. At the moment, Ridley needed little provocation. Ridley was now sure Gavin had made himself unavailable for the previous visits to build up all this "owed" time precisely to pull this stunt. And then, poor Philip and Clare-Olive played right into his hands by refusing his most recent visitation. Ridley would ask but he already knew what his solicitor would say: play nice.

But all the way to Colorado, on her own? With Gavin, which was as good as being alone. There was no way Ridley could allow it. If Thyra had been alive, she'd never have allowed it either. *Although that is the basis of the problem, isn't it? She's not alive.*

Thyra was gone and Gavin had all the leverage. To come and go in their lives as he pleased, to demand his parental rights, rights that he'd never relinquished no matter how much they'd pressed him to and how many times Thyra had begged him to allow Ridley to adopt Bea. So here they were. At the mercy of Gavin and his army of solicitors on retainer just waiting to make Ridley's life a misery.

For at least the tenth time in his life, Ridley imagined burying Gavin in the back garden and planting some sage, angelica and garlic over the plot to seal in the evil.

"I will not allow Bea to go alone. She must have someone with her."

"Of course, I said she can bring her friends."

Ridley sighed, praying for some divine intercession on Bea's behalf and patience on his. "No, Gavin. Her fourteen-year-old girlfriends are not what I meant. I mean Philip and Clare-Olive." Ridley knew he couldn't go for various reasons, one being a possible homicide charge if Gavin was going to be there too. He just hoped he'd be able to convince Thyra's parents to disrupt their holiday plans and uproot themselves to spend Christmas in a different country for their granddaughter's sake.

It was clear this wasn't what Gavin was expecting. He sputtered a bit before nodding his agreement.

"And." Ridley lifted a finger. "This is all contingent on Bea even being willing to go. I'm not forcing her to spend Christmas with you if she doesn't want to."

Gavin nodded again.

The truth was Ridley needed her to be willing. The more recalcitrant Bea and her grandparents were now, the worse it could end up looking for them in court.

"Oh, she'll want to come."

"You think so?" Ridley leaned back, arms crossed.

"My neighbors are featuring a couple of those boys from that K-pop band the kids are crazy about now at their annual Christmas party, and I also have it on good authority that T. Swift is attending."

"T. Swift, huh?"

"That's Taylor—"

"I know who she is, you absolute git." Ridley stood, at his upper limit of bullshit. His sigh was bone-deep. He needed to get this guy out of his house and get some sleep. "So, if that's all, you can get the fuck out now."

Gavin smiled, as relieved to be back to their normal state of relations after that brief détente as Ridley was. "I'll have my assistant call you with all the details. He'll make up a tentative itinerary that you can share with Bea and her grandparents."

He stood straight then too, headed back toward the front door. Ridley followed at a distance, still slightly nervous about what he might do if he were within grasping reach of the ends of Gavin's scarf.

"Like I said, I have to talk to Beatrix first. And then arrange things with Philip and Clare-Olive. So do not have your assistant call me before I call you."

Gavin grinned. "Fair enough."

five

Lanie

Lanie made sure that Merton Road was empty before retrieving the key from the clay pot that held her grandmother's marigolds in the summer. Stealthily, she unlocked the entryway door and eased it open with a quiet pop of the latch. She slid in soundlessly, but silence greeted her on the other side anyway. Hanging up her coat, she left her carry-on bag next to the wall.

Where is everyone?

It was still a little early for night owls like Gemma and her twin brother, Leslie Junior. But Gran was normally up with the birds, moving around, humming Catholic hymns under her breath at dawn. Still, as she pushed the frosted glass door to the kitchen open, Lanie was greeted by continued silence. Lanie checked the time on her phone. It wasn't that early. The red-eye from New York had gotten in slightly ahead of schedule, landing them at Heathrow at 7:25 a.m.

Lanie shook her head. It was currently nine a.m. Maybe Gran had gone to market on the high street?

She turned to try upstairs just as whispering voices came up the hall. Giggles and shushes preceded them loudly. The dining room door opened. Her cousin Gemma, looking more like her own wayward mother, Elliot, than Lanie had ever noticed before, stepped inside. Her cousin's eyes went wide, settling on Lanie, pronounced cheeks riding even higher on her delighted face as she let out a squeal.

"Mel-a-nie!"

At the sound, the lanky man behind Gemma pushed through the door, alarmed. He eased back smiling when he saw Lanie there.

Jonah.

"A wah-gwan!" Gemma bellowed in a faux-Jamaican patois, pulling Lanie's attention back.

She stamped her feet in place as Lanie approached with open arms. The two cousins met in the middle, both screeching and wrapping excited, flailing arms around one another. It was as if they hadn't seen each other in thirty years instead of thirty months.

"Gemma!" Without warning, Lanie's voice broke as she brushed back her cousin's hair to place her hands on Gemma's shoulders. "Oh, Gem!"

"Hello, darling!" Gemma said, with her brilliant South London accent, holding Lanie's face between her hands. She pulled it down to plaster her with kisses as Lanie laughed. "Oh, Big Cuz!"

"Little Cuz!" They both broke into laughter at the old joke. Though Gemma was the older of the two of them by four years, Lanie had outgrown her older cousin by seven inches at thirteen. Looking her over now, Lanie marveled. She'd forgotten how tiny Gemma was. And with her bare, makeup-free face and hair in its natural state for the first time in years, she looked even younger. Her long, loose sandy-brown ringlets cascaded over her shoulders and were pulled back on either side of her heart-shaped face by two simple clips. There was strain in those normally mischievous, now slightly weary eyes that hadn't been there the last time Lanie saw her almost three years ago. But Gemma was still effortlessly lovely, maybe even a little more luminous now that she was in love.

"Ya look *good!*" Gemma pronounced, deepening her voice and putting a further accented emphasis on the word *good* to indicate this as high praise.

"You too," Lanie replied sans the generic Caribbean accent. She'd never been a particularly gifted mimic of her Antiguan relatives, unlike seemingly every child born to Caribbean parents in the UK…and even some Africans and British whites besides. So, she never tried, leaving the patois to her family.

"We've missed you, Mel."

Jonah's soft voice and her name on his lips still did things to her. The words cut through the cousins' laughter and sheared Lanie's heart to tatters like sharp scissors. The world stopped as Lanie's heart floundered like a bird with a broken wing.

Feeling things she'd never admitted before and now never could, Lanie swallowed, clearing her throat and forcing her lips into a wobbly smile. "Jonah."

Gemma watched, stepping aside so that Lanie's childhood best friend could get his turn.

"Hey, Mel."

Lanie smiled up at her friend then brushed an errant curled lock of his raven hair from his face before going into his arms. She steeled herself against how right he felt in hers, but still her eyes slipped closed. Jonah smelled like his usual spicy mix of sandalwood from his preferred Imperial Leather soap and the warm chai scents, like honey, cloves, star anise and ginger, that permeated his mother's kitchen. There was now something else too, something floral, like roses or ylang-ylang… Gemma.

Lanie's eyes popped open. She patted him quickly, using her other hand on his biceps to break away and step back. This was wrong now, her natural inclination to lean into him, she had to remember that.

Clearing her throat again, she caught the tail end of an exchanged glance between Jonah and Gemma. Lanie's heart tugged at the sight, cheeks burning, stomach clenching. But she knew she couldn't allow herself to be anything but happy to see them together.

"Hey!" She tried for nonchalance. "And where were you two coming from?" She turned on Gemma, a small genuine smile trying to appear. "Where's Gran?"

"Did you check upstairs?"

"No?" Lanie frowned. "I hadn't gone up yet."

It was Friday morning. Normally, if she wasn't puttering around the house, off at the market or visiting a sick friend, their gran would have been sitting in the reclining chair off in the corner watching the morning "chat shows," her daily dose of *This Morning* or *Loose Women*.

Gemma exhaled, her shoulders relaxing. "Well then."

"She couldn't still be upstairs, could she?" Lanie was incredulous. "Doing what? Cleaning?"

Gemma crossed Lanie's path, placing herself under Jonah's arm, splaying a hand across his flat abdomen possessively. Gemma was so short she didn't even reach his armpit, Lanie noted before dragging her eyes away. Gemma looked like she was preparing for something.

"Mel," Jonah started.

"What aren't you guys telling me?" Lanie began a chuckle that fell away as she watched them watch her.

"We're…" Jonah said, rubbing Gemma's shoulder, bracing her, fortifying themselves.

Lanie followed his action, pursing her lips. Maybe her mother and her best friend Narcisa had been right. Maybe this was going to prove too much for her. If this was what she had to look forward to for the next four days, she would have done better to stay at home.

"We're moving the wedding up," Gemma finally blurted out.

"You are?" Lanie's stomach sank, but she was immediately

engulfed in guilt for the jolt of sorrow that information gave her, and the underlying desire that it laid bare.

They nodded. "June. We don't want to wait."

"A-and we'd really love it if you'd be our best mate?" Jonah asked.

"Your best man?" Lanie asked, unsure of what to think of this. It made sense as she was one of Jonah's best mates, male or female. But still it was a bit of a surprise; she'd assumed she'd be enlisted into Gemma's bridesmaid corps.

"Maid of honor," Gemma added, clearing that up and adding to the confusion simultaneously.

Lanie frowned. "Huh?"

Jonah smiled. "Our best mate of honor. Both of us."

Gemma looked up at Jonah again and a palpable exchange of ideas happened. They were really going to have to stop doing that or Lanie was sure she would lose her mind before the day was out.

"We argued about who would get you," Gemma explained to Lanie's confused face. "Each of us had very valid arguments. But we've decided to share you. Best man plus maid of honor. Best mate of honor."

They smiled proudly. Lanie wondered where she had been during this deliberation but affixed a Plasticine smile on her face anyway. "Oh really?"

"She hates it. I told you," Jonah fretted.

Gemma patted his stomach. "No, she doesn't."

Yes, she does.

"Give her a chance to speak."

They stared at her expectantly.

"Melanie?" Gemma prompted.

When she opened her mouth, no sound came for a moment. Lanie's diaphragm constricted. "I—I guess I'll go up and say hi to Gran." She turned and headed to the narrow, carpeted staircase.

"Mel?" Jonah called out.

Lanie was surprised to find Gemma on her heels. "Well, Melanie? What do you think?"

Gemma had always been this way. Spoiled, pushy and intent on her own way. Ryan said it came from being raised by their grandmother. But their grandmother had spoiled Lanie too, during the few short years she lived in the United States. She wasn't like that.

Lanie shrugged. "You seem to have already decided."

Gemma sighed as if with forbearance. "This is a big deal for us, Mel."

Ya think?

"I know that." Lanie sighed then paused. "Wait, are you following me?"

"You've got me wondering if Nan's up here now, so, I want to see too," Gemma lied transparently, clearly hoping her continued presence would impose her will.

Classic Gem.

They navigated the narrow upstairs landing as they had as kids, trying to edge each other out of the way, which devolved into a silly slap fight in front of their grandmother's door.

"Gran?" Lanie said. Gemma took that last second to stick a wet finger into Lanie's ear like she used to back when she was more technically the "Big Cuz" of the two of them. "Ugh!" Lanie glared and slapped her cousin's hand away as Gemma stood there innocently and knocked lightly on the door.

"Come in. It's hard to believe you are both over thirty," their grandmother admonished, tsking. But there was a smile on her face as she did it.

Lanie smacked Gemma a final time then turned back to her grandmother, seated comfortably in a recliner situated catty-corner from a flat-screen television that took up so much space in the small square bedroom that it looked like a theater screen.

Lanie nearly gasped. "Gran, what happened?"

Gemma stepped into the room, seemingly perplexed about what Lanie was referring to. Lanie rushed to her grandmother's side as the older woman brought the recliner back to its upright position and rose slowly. Her normally statuesque grandmother was gaunt, the large Turner eyes lost in a now hollow-cheeked face.

"Eh-eh, yuh forward," her grandmother declared in her thick Antiguan patois, affronted, then code-switched fluidly into the more enunciated and British-inflected voice she generally used around Lanie. "I don't look okay?"

Lanie modulated her tone of alarm at the rebuke.

"Nan's been on a whole health kick. Smoothies, low calorie, vegetarian, the whole bit," Gemma announced, beaming.

Their grandmother smoothed down her housecoat and raised her chin with pride. "Down three stone already."

Over forty pounds? Lanie knew their grandmother had been a diabetic for the past decade, but it had always been well-controlled. Forty pounds didn't seem under control.

"Are you planning to lose more?" Lanie gave a panicky exhale before she could stop herself. Both women fixed Lanie with a glare she withered under.

Tulip Turner had always been a full-figured woman. Legend had it, it's what her husband, their grandfather, liked most about his far younger wife—that, and her green eyes. At nearly six feet tall, she was a big woman in that way too. Taller than anyone else in her family, male or female. And coke-bottle curvy even when, after two kids, the bottle became exaggerated and bottom heavy. That, her height and her pronounced cheekbones were the ways Lanie resembled her grandmother most closely.

However, all that was gone now, and in its place stood this stick-figure version of Tulip. Lanie looked between them, confused as to how they could not see what she saw. Their grandmother didn't just look thinner—she looked emaciated. Jowly in places that used to be plump and round, sunken in places that used to be ample and full. Lanie was stunned...and maybe a little bit scared.

"You're not done?"

Their grandmother straightened further. "I don't know. Perhaps."

"I told her she's trying to get back into her own wedding dress just to show me up!" Gemma said.

They both chuckled at that while Lanie still stood aghast.

"Gran," she started again.

"She looks great!" Gemma cut Lanie off firmly, brooking no dissent, brows gathering like storm clouds.

Tulip's light brown skin flushed an actual red like a delighted schoolgirl.

Lanie, pulled up short, closed her mouth and allowed it to curve upward into some semblance of a smile while her cousin and grandmother tittered.

"So that's it? 'Granny, yuh maaga now.' But no hug, kiss? Nuting?"

The words startled Lanie back into movement. She laughed, reaching for her grandmother, remembering they hadn't seen each other in nearly three years. Outside of semiregular phone calls, they had been out of touch. Gratefully, her grandmother's hugs were still the same. Smothering Vise-Grips that could choke the life out of you.

"Well, I'm off, then. I'll leave you two to catch up." Gemma dropped her shoulders with a sigh. "My fiancé is waiting on me. Gah! I can hardly believe it!" Gemma gushed, still marveling at a development that was already two months old.

She paused at the door. "You'll do it though, right, Mel?"

Their grandmother's arm was still draped across Lanie's shoulders as Gemma spoke and she gave Lanie two sharp squeezes. Lanie knew what Gemma was still asking but refused to give her an answer, only smiling in a brief contest of wills. Gemma finally gave up and retreated from the room.

Gran gave Lanie another squeeze as Gemma closed the door behind her. It was the kind she used to give Lanie as a toddler back in New York when she fell in the playground and was encouraging her to walk off the pain.

"So, how yuh been keepin'?"

"I'm okay," Lanie muttered.

"Are you?" her grandmother asked, sounding like Lanie's mother, Ryan. Even the pitch was the same, condolences and concern threaded through the words.

"I am," Lanie lied, forcing a smile onto her face.

"Save that for tomorrow night when your cousin will need you. How are you now?"

Pressure built behind Lanie's eyes. She prided herself on the fact that she'd never once cried about this, not even when she first heard the news. But it only took a moment to be back there, sitting in her kitchen in the Bronx with her hands on her knees, composed. That morning, two months ago, she'd been totally unprepared to see both Jonah's and Gemma's faces appear on the same Skype call, sitting together when she opened the link. Still, she feigned delight. Then listened patiently as they announced through excited giggles and overlapping statements that they were getting married.

Then she cracked.

"What?" Lanie squeezed her eyes shut before reopening them in a new reality where Jonah was marrying someone other than her. "How could you have possibly been dating for over a year? We couldn't even go anywhere for most of it!"

Lanie hit them with a barrage of questions that they could barely answer before she asked more.

After a few minutes, Gemma laughed nervously before tipping her head to the side, muttering something to Jonah that Lanie couldn't make out. He replied in another whisper, before addressing Lanie out loud.

"Mel, we live across the street from each other." Jonah's smile was strained but his voice was a low, soothing mellifluousness. Calm and quiet...as was his way, always.

Lanie took a breath before speaking again. "No, your *parents* live across the street from each other! You live in Brixton!" Lanie could hear her pitch rising but was unable to stop herself.

"I was sheltering-in-place with my family to help out. You know my dad got sick last year."

"I know, but..." Lanie sighed at the logic; she did know this. What she didn't know was how that translated into a marriage proposal to Gemma.

Gemma!

Right then, Lanie felt a hand squeeze painfully tight around her shoulder. Her mother's face dipped low from behind to appear beside hers on-screen.

"Did I hear good news?" Ryan asked loudly, as if they were on some old-school overseas call with an ocean of static between them.

Her smiling face on-screen nearly pushed Lanie's out of the frame. Lanie, remembering herself, continued robotically through the requisite congratulations before ceding the entire call and the computer itself to her mother and shutting herself in her bedroom.

It took a few days, but Lanie issued profuse apologies to Gemma and Jonah even though her heart wasn't in it, feeling like it was collapsing in on itself.

And that pain still lingered, suddenly as fresh as it had been that first day she heard. For whatever reason, here, given permission by her grandmother to feel the feelings, it became too overwhelming to bear stoically any longer.

"Dammit!" Lanie chided herself. Her lip began to tremble as hot tears started to slip from her lashes, streaking her face. "I am okay. I am. He never promised me anything."

God, I'm pathetic.

Hadn't she said the exact same thing to herself about Ridley, just this morning? Albeit with far lower stakes. It never failed. This was a pattern with her. She kept constructing these elaborate fantasies seemingly out of thin air. Departing on her very own flights of fancy that left her falling alone. Idealizing men who never wanted from her what she wanted from them. Was she so love-starved and desperate that she took even the tiniest crumbs of a smile or a kind word, a little attention, and spun whole love affairs?

The answer seemed to be yes. *And how stupid of you to think it could be otherwise.*

The tears of self-pity came faster after that. A viselike grip surrounded her heart. No one ever liked her, loved her, wanted her enough to make any sort of an effort, offer any semblance of a commitment. She was never important enough. She made herself easy, didn't ask a lot. Only to love and be loved by one special someone. And she still couldn't manage to find even that.

Lanie's shoulders shook as the tears came from all the little places she'd secreted them away over these past weeks. Her grandmother moved her to sit on the bed when she began to shake.

"Ooh, Sec," her grandmother cooed plaintively as they sat side by side. She unearthed an ancient nickname from Lanie's toddlerhood that to this day, Lanie still didn't know the meaning of. "There, there, now. You'll find your one."

"Did you know?" Lanie asked once the crying jag subsided and she could finally speak again, sniffling and hiccuping.

"No," her grandmother answered her question with a sigh. "Not until it had been going on for over a year. Not until he'd moved back to Brixton and it became more obvious she was seeing someone. Not coming home nights. Back to living on her phone."

Gemma was always seeing someone, always out late, always

on the phone. Lanie couldn't blame her grandma for missing it. Normally, that would be wholly unremarkable.

"But this time I could tell something was different," her grandmother continued, smoothing her dressing gown over her knees. "When he had been across the street, she was never far. But once he was gone, so was she. She refused to say, so I spoke with Syreeta and Nishan—"

Jonah's parents, who must have been as shocked as Gran when this all came out.

"They reported Jonah had been odd with them too. But since whatever was happening was making them both so happy when everything was so sad, we didn't pay it any mind. Like a fleeting thing."

Lanie's heart ached anew at that. She truly wanted Gemma to have everything she wanted. *Just not Jonah.*

"But she's good, Sec. And they are so happy. I've never seen Gem like this. And I think he's a very good influence on her."

Lanie's next tears, a fresh set, were of joy for her cousin and friend who had managed to fall in love amid everything. Lanie smiled at the thought. "Yeah?"

Her grandmother nodded, a small smile ghosting her lips. For a single moment, Lanie empathized with her grandmother's awkward predicament, having to walk this silken thread between the elation of one granddaughter and the heartache of another.

"Then I'm glad. I really am." It was the first time Lanie said it that it even slightly resembled the truth.

"And if not now…" Her grandmother knew her too well. "You soon will be. I promise you."

Gran pulled Lanie into her side, giving her another squeeze and a kiss on the temple. She nodded decisively, as if settling the matter.

"Now." Gran sighed. "You'll be staying in Les's old room. Go take a nap, I know you're tired. I'll go make some lunch for us. And make sure you fix your face before they see you again. No more of this." She flicked Lanie's quivering chin with a long finger.

The tone of that last part was less the soothing words of a consoling grandmother and more a directive coming from a family matriarch set on peace in her midst.

Lanie nodded back, heaving another tremulous, cleansing breath, hoping to shake this all off.

six

Lanie

"Why are you more nervous than me?" Jonah slid his arm over Lanie's shoulders and she relaxed into him. Her eyes opened as he smiled down at her. "Breathe…you're not the one due to get married here in nine months. I am."

"What? I'm great." Lanie played it off as her heart galloped and wave after wave of nausea crashed in her stomach like a tide. Still, she didn't think she looked that bad, standing in the mouth of the nave at Our Lady of Divine Grace, her grandmother's church family for the past twenty-five years. Lanie's hand gripped the doorjamb, shaking slightly.

A moment before Jonah appeared, Lanie had been practicing the breathing technique her friend Narcisa had given her. But her belly breathing, as Narcisa called it, was less effective when she kept having to move to avoid people as she did it. She'd begun at the house in Les's room, but time got away from her, necessitating a full-on sprint down the lane in her dress to catch up with her gran and Gemma. Then she'd tried again in the last stall of the ladies' room, until an obnoxious neighbor—talking with one of Jonah's cousins about how lovely Gemma looked beside Jonah and how unfortunate her American cousin was—made that room unusable too.

At that point, Lanie moved back outside to perch on the stone bench in the churchyard to catch her breath. She'd promised her grandmother no tears tonight. She had fully intended to make good on that, forgetting that what she'd been dreading about attending Gemma and Jonah's engagement party was not the happy couple, *but everyone else.*

The churchyard hideaway proved short-lived anyway as Lanie learned that what Gemma and her grandmother were outrunning in leaving her behind was not time but rain. Lanie barely made it back inside before the downpour began. Which left her standing quietly behind the stained-glass doors separating the vestibule from the nave, precisely where Jonah caught her.

"You mean the wedding isn't today?" she shot back at him. "Then what's with all this, then?" Lanie tried to maintain a calm façade, faking it.

Dozens of well-dressed people milled around the sanctuary waiting for the special Vespers service to begin.

"You know this wasn't us. We didn't even want an engagement party."

Lanie leaned away and shot him her most skeptical side-eye.

He chuckled. "Okay, Gem wanted an engagement party, but not all this."

Lanie's mouth flattened as an eyebrow rose.

Jonah gave her a full-on belly laugh for that. "Fine, Gem wanted all of this, *except* for the church portion."

Now that *sounds like Gemma.* The ache growing in her chest eased slightly. Chatting normally with Jonah was soothing her anxiety, as it usually did. She suspected he knew it. He always had before.

"But Amma insisted. As soon as I told her and my dad I proposed, the engagement party was a foregone conclusion."

"I can't blame them, I guess." Lanie smiled finally. "You must be the Sri Lankan version of an 'old maid' by now." It felt like all the blood in her body had finally begun returning to its rightful places.

"Hardly, I'm thirty-three. In my prime." Jonah puffed his chest theatrically.

"False! Aachchi has come and lit a candle for this one every night since he turned twenty-five." Jonah's sister, Charitha, walked by with a fruit platter, taking it toward the multipurpose room next door where the buffet would be happening. "She was afraid she would die before she got to see her great-grandchildren."

Lanie snorted.

"Oy, shut it," Jonah called after her. "Please ignore Charity, she understands nothing."

"There he is!"

Both Lanie and Jonah jumped, turning around to find Our Lady's curate, Father Gary, flagging him down.

"Duty calls?" Lanie lamented the end of their little interlude.

"Apparently. And I should probably find out where my fiancée is too, yeah?"

Lanie challenged herself to find the humor in hearing them call each other that for the umpteenth time in a little over twenty-four hours.

"You're okay though?"

"Everything is tickety-boo." She deliberately said it with the amusing awkwardness of any American using British slang.

Jonah shook his head, amused. Lanie pushed the corners of her mouth upward. Her smile lasted long enough for Jonah to head off.

"And please, Dear Lord, shower Your abundant blessings upon our very own Samara Jonah Perera and his charming bride-to-be, Gemma Sade Adu Turner, and their families at this time of great joy..." Father Gary droned.

Lanie surreptitiously lifted her head and opened one eye. A

glance to her left and right unsurprisingly revealed a row of heads dipped in solemn prayer with eyes closed as Father Gary spoke. But Jonah winced at the public use of his first name and Gemma did also; she hated anyone using her full name. Lanie suppressed an inappropriate smile at the clearly uncomfortable couple, holding hands beside the parish priest in the center of the church's small multipurpose room. They were the sole focus of this ad hoc prayer circle.

Jonah, ever the altar boy, caught Lanie out of the corner of his eye. He looked directly at her and made a show of closing his dark eyes, his message coming through loud and clear. But luckily, miracle of miracles, Father Gary finally concluded his expansive blessing.

As heads rose and smiles broke out across the room, Lanie noticed her grandmother's head remained bowed for a beat longer. But when she rose finally, like clouds parting across her face, the sunniest smile shone through.

"Well then, yes. Thank you for the lovely blessing, Father Gary," Nishan Perera, Jonah's dad, intoned in his best baritone-in-the-church-choir voice. Mr. Perera glanced piously around the room at everyone, but Lanie could swear he'd narrowly avoided giving a stretch and a yawn. "Shall we?"

He didn't have to say it twice. Hands around the room unclasped as the circle broke into disparate groups.

"Hey you!"

Lanie spun to see someone right behind her. "Fatoumata!"

"Wah-gwan, Big Cuz?" Even this Ghanaian's patois sounded better than anything Lanie could have attempted. Lanie lamented her unskilled tongue yet again.

"How are you?" Lanie threw herself into Fatou's arms, hugging the woman tightly around the neck.

Even though she was technically Gemma's best friend, Fatou was one of Lanie's favorite people in England. Though they would only "like" and comment on each other's posts on Twitter and Instagram these days, their relationship went back years and it was always as if no time had elapsed whenever they saw each other.

"I'm good, babes," Fatou said as Lanie released her, restraightening the stylish melon-colored hijab on her head that matched the tan wrap dress, silk drape and sherbet heels she wore.

"You came alone? Where's Arash?" Lanie asked, looking for Fatou's dashingly handsome Iranian husband. Lanie stuck her bottom lip out in a pout. She could have used some gratuitous eye candy right about now.

"At work." Fatou shook her head. "He sent his best wishes tonight. He'll be coming to the wedding though."

Lanie nodded, though she knew it was more than that. Arash was far more serious about his religion, about most everything really, than Fatou was. How they'd made that work between them when she was at her wildest was anyone's guess, but they'd been madly in love and on-again, off-again since university.

"Well, tell him, 'Lanie said hello and that her offer to be a side chick still stands.'"

"Don't threaten me with a good time, eh?" Fatou laughed, swatting Lanie's arm. "Besides, he knows I'm the only one allowed a side-piece in our house!"

Lanie giggled until Fatou paused and leaned in. "This was a bit of a shocker."

So, this was a surprise to Fatou too? Lanie frowned. "You didn't know about them?"

"Oh." Fatou put a consoling hand on Lanie's arm, face solemn.

Lanie bristled a little at yet another sympathetic look but hid it.

"No, babes. They thought they were sneakin' about, but I knew from the start. 'Cos neither of them is exactly James Bond, innit?" She chuckled. "I just didn't realize it had gotten this serious."

Lanie turned to the couple, still standing at the center of the room and fielding congratulations. Composed in a long-sleeved pullover, dress shirt and tie, Jonah looked every bit the mild-mannered, studious barrister he was. Dutifully, he shook every hand and hugged every auntie, uncle and cousin—real or honorary—that pumped his hands, smacked his back or pinched his cheeks.

Meanwhile, standing beside him, looking as gorgeous as ever in her hot pink and black bodycon dress, with sky-high heels that still didn't put her anywhere near Jonah's shoulders, Gemma clutched his elbow. Her greenish-brown eyes wandered around the room longingly. But except for a restless leg that tapped to and fro, Gemma was trying hard not to look bored.

They look good together. Lanie felt a stab of guilt for even briefly wishing otherwise.

"So, when's it your turn, eh?" Fatou asked from Lanie's side, sounding like another auntie and accompanying it with a good-natured little nudge to the ribs.

"Listen, just 'cuz you snagged yourself a good-looking..." Lanie started to whirl around on Fatou until she caught the woman's face.

Fatou burst out laughing. "Hoo, you was ready for me, bwoy!" She covered her mouth with her fist and howled, nearly doubling over.

"Har, har. Don't joke," Lanie said dryly, shooting Fatou a blink-and-you'd-miss-it pout as she continued laughing. "It's been rough."

"I'll bet. These biddies don't spare anyone their grief."

"Would that it was only them," Lanie lamented.

"For true?" She patted Lanie's shoulder. "My girl is getting no rest?"

That was the Mona Lisa of understatements. It was more like she was being given no quarter. Thus far, Lanie had fielded three *You're next*s, four *Don't worry, sweetheart, your turn will come*s, five *Ah well, there's other fish in the sea*s, two very kindly proffers of an introduction to some distant American relative and one entertainingly progressive offer of someone's female cousin.

And if only her sexual orientation hadn't been so specifically Jonah Perera for so many years, Lanie might have even considered it.

After the final well-wisher had been dealt with and the long receiving line disbanded, the happy couple were finally free. Yet after a brief, chaste kiss on the lips, the couple split too, with Gemma making a beeline to Lanie and Fatou as Jonah sought out food.

"Oy." Gemma nearly stomped over to them, catching herself before she shouted it out for the whole room to hear. "Ya 'ear 'im give out mi 'hole dam' government? Shame, see?"

They laughed. It was no secret that Gemma despised her middle name. She was given the full name of '80s British Nigerian R&B/Soul goddess Sade Adu. And in one of the few conversations Lanie ever had with Gemma's mother, the woman took umbrage at the question of why, explaining that Gemma had been given the additional name "Adu" because it sounded "pretty and French."

At least she's not named after the imaginary sons her father wanted but never got, like me and your mother, Aunt Elliot had snapped anytime she received the criticism.

"Just ask Father Gary not to say it in the ceremony," Lanie stated the obvious.

Laden with full plates, and in one woman's case, a small child in tow as well, Gemma's other girlfriends closed in on their group. Lanie knew them all vaguely: two high school chums whose names eluded her; then a bottle-blonde Barbie named Marissa, who was Gemma's former coworker at the salon; and Shanice, a friend from primary school, the one with her toddler son and a brand-new "lockdown" baby girl off somewhere with her father.

"I'll ask Nan to talk to the priest. Just in case." The words were accompanied by a heavy sigh. "So, you want to see it again?" The group all converged around Gemma, beaming in delight at being the center of all this attention. Not waiting for an answer, she extended her left hand to show off her big sparkling rock of an engagement ring. The way it caught the light could have blinded someone. "I still can't believe it!" she squealed, her decibel level ever increasing. "I'm getting married!"

Lanie fought to stop rolling her eyes at the subsequent fawning. It seemed like Gemma was more excited about all the getting-married attention than the actual being-married part.

"Speaking of which." Gemma sobered, taking up Lanie's and Fatou's hands then squeezing them both. "I have a question to ask my sistahs—"

"Ah, no," Fatou said flatly before Gemma had finished.

Not for the first time Lanie wished on her best day to be as no-nonsense as Fatou on any given day. Despite her jovial demeanor, the woman gave no fucks and tolerated less.

Gemma dropped their hands and propped her fist on her hip, skewering her friend with a scathing gaze. "You don't even know what I was about to ask."

"I do. And no," Fatou insisted, nodding. She propped a hand on her own hip as well.

It looked to Lanie like she was about to witness her own private reenactment of a scene from *R&B Housewives*. The others seemed to think so too. Eyes bounced back and forth like they were watching a match at Wimbledon.

"There's no reason you can't. Lolade was in Allison's Catholic wedding last May."

Lanie groaned. She'd artfully dodged answering Jonah and Gemma's question all weekend only to be put on the spot now. *Well played, Gem.* Personally, Lanie couldn't think of a more expensive, thankless and frequently infuriating time suck than bridesmaid duties. She still remembered sitting on the front room couch with Gemma years ago and cackling at those unfortunate sods on episodes of the old TV show *Bridezillas*.

"And why do you suppose Lolade isn't here today?" Fatou teased.

"Oh, c'mon, Fatou!" Gemma whined. "Arash won't mind."

"As if what Arash *minded* informed my decisions," Fatou said, affronted.

In their teens and early twenties, Fatou and Gemma had been wild women, clubbing and drinking as hard as anyone. But when she'd finally agreed to marry Arash a few years ago, Fatou mellowed, deciding to take her religious practice more seriously. Lanie quietly suspected Gemma had never completely forgiven or stopped giving Fatou a hard time for it.

"I didn't mean it that way. Don't be like that!" Gemma pouted, giving her foot a little petulant stomp against the linoleum under their feet.

While they argued, Lanie glanced away in boredom. Jonah stood by the buffet tables. As he laughed with his sister, his wavy, jet-black hair fell into his oval face, making him look boyishly handsome. His white teeth gleamed against his warm olive skin, making Lanie want to smile. His midnight eyes wandered across the crowded room, falling tenderly on his fiancée's back as she fussed—there was no mistaking the adoration and desire in them. Lanie stomach sank. She nearly looked away, embarrassed to have witnessed that. But he caught her watching him and winked. She smiled back weakly before he returned to his conversation.

Yet again, Lanie recognized that she had to excise these feelings from her heart like the debilitating cancer they were becoming. But where was it all to go? What did she do with all the hopes and dreams she'd clung to and nurtured for so long?

"Now that the rain has stopped, I'm gonna step out for two

seconds," Lanie interrupted the ongoing squabble, struggling to keep the tears out of her voice, clearing her throat.

"You alright?" Gemma and Fatou exchanged a look.

"I'm not fragile, Gem," Lanie barked, now sullen. "You don't have to keep handling me!" The frustration of the past day and a half finally exploded out of Lanie.

Gemma recoiled while Fatou's eyes widened. Shanice, Marissa and the others all glanced at each other. That had been entirely too loud. Eyes from all corners of the room fell on them. Even Jonah and Charity looked their way. Lanie's chest ached. She'd probably just created some juicy new grist for the Merton Road gossip mill. Shanice, for one, never shut up.

"I'm sorry," Lanie said urgently. "I didn't mean that."

"We know, darling," Fatou said.

Gemma laughed with the other women, seemingly bewildered by Lanie's outburst. She patted Lanie's arm lightly. But the accompanying smile didn't meet her eyes.

"You're right, Mel. It is getting stuffy. Go get some air," Fatou added, her eyes going soft in a way that made Lanie feel both undeserving of her sympathy and yet resentful of it nonetheless.

Still, Lanie squeezed Fatou's arm in gratitude, muttering a tense "excuse me" before scurrying out the exit door.

Lanie sat cross-legged on the stone bench in the churchyard with her back as straight as she could manage. Pursing her lips, she inhaled through her nose, counting to four, holding it for seven seconds before releasing it. She exhaled deeply through her mouth, the air making a hollow whistling sound as it pushed up out of her lungs, past her teeth and through her lips.

She had to admit, Narcisa was not wrong. She did feel calmer, more centered. Steadier, and most importantly, in better control of the emotions that, for a few moments in there, had been so overwhelming her chest felt like it was being crushed.

But then, the shame flooded in.

Looking up into the night sky, Lanie sniffled, bracing against the cold. At this time of the evening, only the lights illuminating various windows of the sanctuary lit the churchyard. And pervasive light pollution meant she could only see the crescent moon and a handful of stars, Orion's Belt among them, piercing the blue-black of the London sky.

"You out here crying?" a voice asked through the darkness.

"No," she said, quickly wiping her nose with the back of her hand.

It was the brisk dampness and the fact that she was sitting on a wet bench that had her like this. She sniffled again.

"Sounds like tears."

"Well, it's not," Lanie insisted, peering into the darkness at whoever was approaching. She squinted as a shadow came closer, lowering her feet to the ground in case she needed to make a break for it.

"Leslie Junior?" she asked incredulously when the figure stepped into the light and she could finally make out the hints of a face. Lanie let out a relieved sigh, sitting back down on her sweater-covered bit of the bench. She patted the seat beside her. "Careful, it's wet," she warned as he approached.

Gemma's twin, Les, brushed a hand over the coarse surface as if to test it then sat anyway.

"Where have you been? Why didn't you tell me how Gran looked? I'm staying in your room. Why aren't *you* staying in your room?" Lanie tore through all the things she'd been dying to ask since she arrived.

Les chuckled. "Whoa, whoa, Big Cuz. Breathe between words."

"Les, where have you been?"

"A bedsit in Peckham."

"What? Why?"

Lanie looked at her cousin closely. The resemblance was

uncanny as usual. Les and Gem as fraternal twins had always looked more like male and female versions of the exact same person. But with a stronger jawline, the sharper cheekbones of Les's café au lait face and those big, bright, fully green eyes, unlike Gemma's slightly browner ones, Les was the more striking twin. And in winged eyeliner, with purple-black shimmer on the lids that matched the ink-blue suit he wore, and a slick, deep plum lip gloss, Les looked as fetching as his sister tonight.

Lanie smiled, thrilled to see him.

"I'm thirty-five, Mel. Eventually I needed my own space." His shoulders fell a little. "Plus, there were too many big personalities in that tiny house."

Living with her mother for all her thirty-one years, she certainly understood that.

"Had to get out to protect my peace of mind, you know? But I've missed you."

Lanie looked her cousin over. He appeared happy and content, so apparently the personal space agreed with him. She envied him the bravery to just finally do it, yet she kind of wished he was still at home. She desperately missed the fun they usually had when she was here in London. But she also knew that to find it, she'd have to shake off all this morose self-pitying and just enjoy being back in the bosom of all these people she loved. Maybe finally seeing Les was the first step?

"Melanie! Are you out here?" The loud voice of Father Gary ruptured the easy quiet, cutting through Lanie and Les's light-hearted catch-up.

"Father?" She stood. Les stood with her. They looked at each other in bewilderment as the pastor's tone grew frantic. "Is everything okay?"

"Come quickly! It's your grandmother!"

seven

Ridley

Ridley looked angrily at his wedding band still sitting on his ring finger days later. He'd finally given himself permission to try to take it off again. But because after almost three years alone, he'd become so entirely inept at dealing with anyone of the opposite sex, he'd returned it to his hand, then embarrassed a friendly young woman into believing she'd gotten the wrong idea.

She had not.

Deliberately…just to get her to back off. Yes, he'd done that. What a jerk he'd been.

Too much time spent with those Brits, his old mentor from Harvard liked to tease him during their annual check-ins.

As if he hadn't had to be this way for his entire life. To become insensitive and desensitized. To harden himself enough to absorb the numerous disappointments and shocks a life in STEM doled out for a person of color. From his high school biology teacher suggesting he join the basketball team rather than the science Olympiad, to the college adviser who told him molecular genetics might be too difficult for him. Still, there was no denying Ridley had picked up enough British brusque aloofness over the years to rub some people the wrong way.

So, could he say that's what happened?

Deep down he knew it wasn't. He'd run Lanie off because... she made him nervous.

"Earth to Dad, come in, Dad."

A steaming kettle whistled in front of him. "Oh, sorry."

"What's the point of keeping that antique on the hob if you can't even hear it when it's right in front of you? Maybe we need to reassess."

"Reassess, really?"

Bea smirked at him, quite pleased with herself.

"With a vocabulary like that at least I know my tuition money is being put to good use."

When had their little Bean become this incredibly astute and witty creature? It felt like just the other day she was having total meltdowns when they turned off *Gigglebiz* on CBeebies. Now she was arguing the merits of electric versus steam kettles...and shaming her father for his inattentiveness.

"Oh God, now you're getting the look."

"Look?" He raised an eyebrow as if he didn't know exactly what she was talking about.

"The 'what an incredible tiny human creature you are' look."

He knew the one. Her mother had patented it when Bea first learned to walk and it had been a parental staple ever since.

"But you are incredible." He couldn't help himself. Ridley chuckled as she rolled her eyes at him, pouring the piping hot water into two cups for tea.

"So? What's up?"

"With me? Nothing," Ridley deflected. "But I'm sorry I have to go back so soon."

Bea's expression darkened at the mention of his upcoming trip so fast on the heels of the last. "I understand."

He could see by the way her mouth tightened that wasn't true.

When Ridley thought of the next few months he was now

expected to spend traveling back and forth to New York over-seeing the American partner in his joint clinical trial, his blood boiled. He was the principal investigator. The big-picture person. The chief scientist. It was ridiculous that he should have to play parent to adults at the expense of his own child because people couldn't follow simple directions. Directions they'd literally signed their names to. He wanted to rage, and looking into Bea's disappointed face, he almost did.

"But that isn't it, is it?" she asked cannily, cutting through his thoughts.

She wasn't his little girl anymore. And these unnecessary days away would be lost time with her. Losing Thyra had taught him how precious this time was—and how he couldn't afford to miss a second of it.

"Of course it is," he insisted. "But I promise, come hell or high water, I will not miss your birthday party."

"I'm canceling that."

"What?"

"I don't care about it. And I'm too old for a party anyway." Bea shrugged, pushing her spoon around in her yogurt cup.

All the baby fat was disappearing from her formerly chubby, sable-colored cheeks, giving way to the same elongated face with strikingly sharp cheekbones and large, deep-set eyes as her mother. The realization was like a shot in his chest. And like her incisive mother, Beatrix would no longer be so easily appeased by simple evasions.

Ridley debated what to tell her as he brought the rest of her breakfast—the tea, buttered toast and a bowl of fruit salad—to the breakfast table. He retreated behind the center island, racking his brain. "Have you given any more thought to Gavin's offer?"

"The Eye?" Bea made a face, stabbing a square of honey-dew with her fork. "How old does he think I am? A class outing, seriously?"

"I don't think it necessarily needed to be with your class-mates."

Bea shot him a look of annoyance that seemed to say the same thing he was thinking. *Since when do I defend Gavin?*

"Look, Bean, sweetie, if you didn't want to do that, you should have told him so. Hiding from Gavin in your room and telling your nan to run interference was not a great idea."

Her brows furrowed, anxiety beginning to flood her features, returning her to the little girl Ridley saw in his mind's eye. It was a glimpse of who she still was underneath the tinted lip balm, light foundation and sculpted eyebrows she now sported. "Did I mess something up? Is that why I have to go to America for Christmas?"

Ridley sighed. More than anything he wanted to shield Bea from all the legal wrangling that had followed her mother's death. But truthfully, the lockdown that necessitated his continued custody of her may only have delayed what might, in fact, be inevitable. Perhaps, however, if they were cooperative, some livable arrangement could be possible. Because he knew he could not—would not—live without his daughter.

"Of course not," he lied. "You don't have to go to Colorado if you don't want to."

Bea cut her eyes at him. *We're going to have a conversation about her new tendency to do that...later.*

"I'm not a child—"

"You are," Ridley replied, rapid-fire.

Bea scowled but corrected herself. "But I am old enough to understand the truth, Dad."

"You are that too." He sighed with resignation, pausing to take a breath. "Okay, so Ada says it would be helpful..." It pained him to even repeat the solicitor's words. "If we appeared to be a bit more willing to work with Gavin."

Accommodating until it physically hurt were Ada's exact words.

Ridley's heart broke seeing the way Bea's little face fell. "Bean, you said you could handle me telling you the truth." *Or at least some of it.*

"I can!" she retorted with indignance. "It's just that...that this means things aren't going well. Doesn't it?"

Ridley didn't know how to answer this. Bea was so perceptive; lying further didn't make sense.

"No, it means that I need you to consider spending Christmas in Vail with Gavin. Nan and Granddad will be there, I've already discussed that with Gavin. And he also said that Simone and Yvette can come visit too, provided their parents agree."

Bea was unmoved.

"Taylor Swift apparently lives next door, or something?" he offered, feeling as stupid as Gavin looked when he said it.

She shook her head, huffing a breath. "I haven't been a Swiftie since she copied Beyoncé's Coachella performance, Dad!" Bea pushed back from the table so forcefully that the chair legs screeched against the hardwood floors. She grabbed her uniform's navy blazer off the chair back and picked up her book bag. "Whatever."

Ridley stood silently gaping. He'd have known what to apologize for if he'd understood any of the words that had come out of Bea's mouth. To him, that had just been *Blahblahblah Beyoncé blahblahblah Coachella.*

"Bea."

"It's fine, Dad." She came around the island and rose to her toes as he bent, to kiss him on the cheek. Then she paused, leveling him with a version of her mother's skeptical appraisal. It was scarily accurate. "You're sure that's all?"

"Get going. You're going to be late." He placed a kiss on her forehead nestled among her heap of downy walnut curls. Then Ridley promised himself that he'd find a way to shake off the creeping unease about everything in his life right now.

Bea headed down the hall to the front door, audibly dissatisfied. In a matter of just a few days, he'd managed to seriously upset two women.

His week was going great.

eight

Five days later, Gran's GP, Dr. O'Hara, sat at his desk, his mouth downturned, as Lanie and Gemma flanked their grandmother. Lanie had rescheduled her flight home to be there.

Dr. O'Hara's face was grave as they sat across from him. "So," he started, settling further into his wingback chair and flipping through pages in a file. "Tulip told us that she has one that's getting her PhD and one that's getting married?"

Lanie grimaced. Her grandmother never stopped bragging about her or hoping she'd change her mind even a full five years after Lanie stopped pursuing her studies.

He looked between the two cousins, clearly unsure of where his eyes should land. "So, who's getting married?"

Yes, because that one is the real achievement.

"That's me." Gemma raised her hand tentatively, like calling out an answer in a class.

Lanie kept her hands in her lap because she wasn't doing either of those things.

"Congratulations are in order, then!"

Gemma giggled like a pageant queen appreciating her audience. "This June."

A June bride. What a cliché. Not to mention the wedding vendors that would be seeing dollar signs because they weren't waiting the pre-scribed year.

Lanie sealed her mouth shut, having already made that argument...and lost.

"Lovely." Dr. O'Hara gave a perfunctory smile as if the exchange was part of a script and he could now check that box. "A very nice thing to look forward to, yes?"

Gran nodded, reaching out to pat Gemma's hand. "Yes, our Gemma is marrying a nice boy. A barrister."

Gemma beamed at their grandmother's clear approval. And Lanie bristled. There was far more to Jonah than his job, and not for the first or second time she hoped that her cousin realized that.

"Oh, lovely," Dr. O'Hara said again, absently.

As Lanie had become begrudgingly accustomed to over the years, doctors here spoke to her grandmother alternately as if she was a hard-of-hearing, doddering old woman or like a three-year-old that had gotten into a cookie jar before dinner.

"Well, we're here today for some test results, aren't we?" He flipped through more pages, then frowned.

Gran and Gemma nodded as Lanie shifted uneasily in her seat.

"They're a bit more concerning than we thought, I'm afraid."

Gran clutched her purse straps in both hands. "What does that mean? Exactly?"

"Well." He puffed out a sigh, laying his forearms on the desk before him in a way that made Lanie's heart skip a beat and her stomach sink. "Originally, we were concerned about your kidney function. Your creatinine levels are a bit high. While you were in hospital, they did a twenty-four-hour urinalysis. And now we've received the results and found that your albumin to creatinine ratio—we call it an ACR—is elevated."

"Is that *very* bad?" Lanie's stomach continued its roll. Her mom was a nurse; she knew enough to understand that those words didn't mean anything good.

"Well, it would have been infinitely better if we'd recognized it sooner. Mrs. Turner, you and I have spoken over the phone, but I believe this is our first face-to-face meeting since you joined our surgery. Isn't that right?"

Lanie cast her grandmother a sidelong glance. The older woman looked shamefaced. She should. They weren't supposed to be there. Her grandmother used to be conscientious about her health.

"Had we," Dr. O'Hara went on, pressing his point, "we might not be here today."

Gran wound her purse straps around her fist, her polite smile faltering. Lanie frowned at his tone but caught herself. It wasn't as if he was wrong.

"We haven't even had all our televisits, I'm afraid. Have we, dear?"

Lanie refrained from rolling her eyes at the condescension and laid a supportive hand on her grandmother's forearm. But that seemed to startle Tulip, like she only just realized that they were still sitting beside her.

"After your collapse this weekend, we became concerned about your insulin resistance and wanted to rule out renal failure."

Lanie felt her grandmother tense up.

"No worries there though." Dr. O'Hara glanced up from his papers to give them an unconvincing smile. "What a relief, yes?"

He has to be fucking kidding with this. Lanie groaned audibly.

Gran gave her the same look she used to give them as children cutting up in the church pews during mass. Lanie tried not to fidget.

"However, that doesn't mean we're in the clear," he continued as Lanie's knee began to bounce. "Unfortunately, through further testing, we've discovered some serious trouble with your liver."

Lanie's grandmother gasped, a short but loud intake of breath that might have included a sob. Lanie grabbed one of her hands as Gemma took hold of the other. Then they glanced at each other, the animosity of the past few days momentarily forgotten.

Lanie was grateful. Admittedly, in the emergency room, she'd been bossy, taking charge and making decisions on her grandmother's behalf as if Gemma wasn't even there. But it wasn't because she'd previously believed her cousin couldn't do it; it was because Gemma had shown herself to be doing a terrible job of handling things now. Judging by the fact that their grandmother had gotten sick and no one noticed anything until she literally collapsed. So, Lanie had said that.

Just that way.

In front of the ER doctor. And a room full of people. Including Jonah, his parents, Fatou and Les.

Naturally, afterward things had been tense. Lanie chose to keep to her room while Gemma, when she was there, moved in a disgruntled cloud, leaving a thunderous wake in every room, the televisions blaring, doors slamming, shelves buffeting bureaus and a cacophony of cabinets banging to give voice to her displeasure. The aggression could hardly be called passive in any way, save Gemma's refusal to speak. So, Lanie was surprised to see Gemma, coat on and ready to go to their grandmother's appointment with them that morning.

"Your chart indicates that you've previously told us you are not a smoker or drinker, is that right?" Dr. O'Hara continued as Lanie reflected on her terrible behavior this week.

"Yes. That's right, Doctor." Gran nodded. "Except a sip of Communion wine on Sundays and the occasional snifter of brandy for Christmas. Is that bad?"

"The Communion wine is grape juice, Nan," Gemma said softly, patting her grandmother's hand.

"Is it?"

"Don't listen to her, Gran. Next thing you know, she'll be saying that the Communion wafers are really Time Outs too," Lanie quipped.

Gemma let out a single "Ha!" before catching herself. "Nah, those things are rubbish. The body of Christ is tastier than that."

Lanie snickered.

"Girls," Gran snapped at them both. "Blaspheme another time, please." And in Pavlovian style, they were instantly back onside, sitting up and silent.

"Uh, yes." Dr. O'Hara conferred with his notes again, confused by the left turn his very serious discussion had taken. "I mean no, I'm talking about habitual alcohol consumption, yes?"

"No, absolutely not." A dark exasperation traversed Gran's face. A look over at Gemma's face revealed a virtually identical fatigue.

Gran barely allowed alcohol in the house. Lanie knew little about it, but she had gleaned that her late grandfather had been an alcoholic. A mean one, who had made every family member who'd had the misfortune to follow him to England miserable.

"Very good, we gathered that when we spoke to you in hospital, didn't we?" he said before embarking on a detailed review of the results of Gran's most recent blood work.

So then why ask again? Lanie bristled. "The diagnosis, Doctor?" she finally demanded, unable to deal with the suspense or polite dithering any longer.

"Yes, yes, of course." He nodded. "We believe this to be a case of nonalcoholic fatty liver disease."

"Sweet Jesus, mi cyaan manage!" The words tumbled out of Gran's mouth in one long exhalation of air, before she grabbed her chest.

Gemma burst out crying. Lanie glared from the other side of their grandmother.

What the hell? When had Gemma become this emotionally over-wrought person?

"Ladies, ladies!" Dr. O'Hara warned.

Non-what? Liver? No, this doesn't make any sense. Is Gran dying? The idea of it unmoored Lanie. She wasn't like her grandmother and cousin; when she panicked, she got stoic, turned inward and fell into a part of herself no one could reach. But not now. Right now, she needed answers.

Lanie put up a palm, barely wheezing the words out of her diaphragm. "Wait, what—what is that?"

Dr. O'Hara looked stricken, eyes wide. "Well, it's a buildup of adipose tissue in the liver…"

"Adipose?" Lanie focused on the words coming out of the doctor's mouth instead of Gemma's hysterical weeping and her grandmother's muttered prayers. Hanging on to every word and parsing them acted as a distraction from her growing anxiety.

"Just tell me, how serious is this?" her grandmother, who was not crying but was morbidly grim, finally asked.

"Very, I'm afraid. It's incurable."

Lanie felt the word like a knife but remained quiet while Gemma howled like she was the one being diagnosed as terminal. Even their grandmother regarded her older granddaughter with surprise then.

Lanie decided to take this apart like the scientist she supposedly used to be.

"What does 'adipose' mean?" she repeated.

"It means fatty tissue," Dr. O'Hara replied.

"And can this tissue be treated?"

"No. It's not possible to reverse the damage with medication."

"Okay, so what are our next steps?" Lanie asked.

"We have diets that can potentially prevent this from becoming a far more serious problem like cirrhosis or liver failure." He spoke over Gemma's sobs. "There are a few more tests we'd like to run. But we're confident that we're onto the correct diagnosis. So right now, all there is, is just to treat it."

Just treat it? Lanie was in a state of disbelief. *Couldn't he have started there?* If for no other reason than to prevent the histrionics in his office?

"Don't worry, Mrs. Turner, we will have you put to rights in no time, sound good?" Dr. O'Hara said, returning to his obnoxiously patronizing tone.

"Yes, see? Nothing to worry about." Gran digested that while whispering and gathering a sniffling Gemma into her arms. "I'll be fine."

From the doctor's face, you'd think he'd told them they won the lottery.

nine

Lanie

■ 1-SEP ■ Trans-Continental Airways ■ Flight: 602 ■

LHR-London, Heathrow ► JFK-John F. Kennedy Int'l Airport

Seat Assignment: **4C/11A**

It was midday by the time Lanie took her grandmother back home. After hearing her grandmother's diagnosis, it was clear they'd dodged a bullet, but Lanie hoped she wasn't the only one who recognized that or the next time it would be a barrage. At least in those first hours postappointment it seemed like they'd all grasped the gravity. She, Gemma and Gran barely exchanged twenty words on the tube back to Balham. And upon arriving on Merton Road, Gem went to the Pereras without saying a single thing. Lanie watched and wondered if Jonah was even there, this being a weekday. It was more likely he was at the High Court.

"Gem and Charity have become quite close," Gran explained, reading Lanie's face.

"Jonah's sister used to think Gem was an airhead," Lanie muttered.

"Melanie."

Lanie braced herself. It was her grandmother who had originally dubbed her "Lanie," so her full name automatically meant trouble.

"In case you've missed it, a lot has happened since you last visited."

Lanie huffed a little breath of annoyance before the magnitude of that statement fully hit her. Her grandmother glared and Lanie straightened her back and cleared her throat remorsefully. "Sorry."

"Jonah has been a very good influence on Gemma," Gran continued. "Encouraged her to think about what she wanted to do."

"Gem already knows what she wants to do. She's wanted to be a hairdresser since we were kids and she's already doing that." Lanie snorted.

"Yes, but what she really dreams about is opening her own salon and marketing her own line of products. Did she ever tell you that?"

Not in so many words. Lanie shrugged. But based on the number of mayonnaise, avocado and coconut oil hair and face masks Gemma had created and Lanie had endured over the years, she could have guessed.

"You know all that trouble before made her drop out of school."

Lanie nodded. In the kitchen, her grandmother set the electric kettle in the base and turned it on.

"She'd told herself she wasn't smart enough for school or for her own business. It took a while, but Jonah convinced her to get specialized tuition for her dyslexia and focus on taking business classes. She finally enrolled last term and now she's doing really well."

"He did that?"

Gran nodded. "So don't make her feel foolish because school has always been easy for you."

Not really easy, Lanie thought but didn't say. *Just a different kind of hard.*

"At least she's trying to go back when it's hard for her. You won't even try. You just gave it up."

At her Gran's rebuke, Lanie felt about a foot tall. She didn't bother mentioning that she hadn't given up, she'd been pushed out.

Only now, standing on the sprawling shopping concourse in Heathrow Terminal Two among fussy children, fatigued businessmen, giddy tourists and other travelers, did Lanie find herself more at ease. The change in mood buoyed her enough to send Gemma a message.

LANIE:

I'll do it.
Best mate of honor it is

Lanie wasn't sure she was right to accept, especially considering she was still having trouble wrapping her head around Gemma and Jonah as a couple. But she needed to show everyone she supported her people—the pity she'd endured over the past few days proved that much. And she *was* over Jonah. *Completely.* She would tell herself that until she believed it.

Gemma reacted to the message with a string of hearts. Lanie exhaled; that was as close to a makeup as they could manage before she left anyway.

"Lanie?"

She was off-loading the last of her pound coins to a barista at an airport coffee shop when she heard her name enunciated in a deep and incredulous timbre. Sweeping the room quickly, she found Ridley Aronsen standing there in all his tall, dark and disarmingly attractive glory looking down at her.

"I can't believe I found you."

"That's creepy." Her even tone belied her own surprise. "You were looking?"

"No, I just mean I thought you would have left days ago. What are you doing here?" he asked.

Lanie took her receipt with a smile, then moved down the counter to wait for her latte before replying, "It's an airport."

His face fell, mouth flattening.

At his look, Lanie relented. "Something came up. I had to reschedule my earlier flight."

"Everything okay?" He frowned with genuine concern in his eyes.

Lanie fought the easy familiarity that had allowed her to speak so freely with him before, the instant camaraderie that had clearly been one-sided. Still, the impulse to unburden herself gripped her. Then she noted the wedding ring still firmly affixed to the fourth finger of his left hand.

"Should be fine," she replied coolly.

Lanie sought some bit of indifference standing before him again, instead of this heart-quickening thrill at seeing his face. That Ridley was here in front of her after she'd spent seven days reconciling herself to the idea that she'd somehow imagined him was almost comical. She battled to keep her expression a blank mask, focused on getting her coffee.

"Did I make a mistake approaching you?" There was that forthright primness of his again, burrowed into the question.

"It depends on why you did." She raised her eyes to his. "Why did you?"

They watched each other, in a standoff of sorts, each daring the other to acknowledge what had happened.

"To apologize," he stated plainly. Lanie's eyebrows rose. "Scratch that. No, I don't owe you an apology."

"Oh, okay."

With a nod of thanks to the barista, she retrieved her cup of coffee and walked over to the table with the condiments.

Ridley followed her, his infamous toe-mauling roller case right behind him. Placing her cup on the countertop, Lanie pulled out brown sugar packets, then the shaker of cinnamon. As her hands busied, Ridley stood at her side, watching. He was hard to ignore but Lanie was trying her damnedest, only peeking at him out of the corner of her eye.

He frowned at her cup as she stirred. "Is there any coffee in that?"

She regarded the cup. "A little."

"What is in it?" He eyed it with suspicion as she brought it to her mouth to taste.

Perfect.

She swallowed her sip. "Whole milk, three pumps of syrup: caramel, toffee-nut and cinnamon. With whipped cream and salted caramel candy bits on top." She licked away the small whipped cream mustache that sat on her upper lip. "Oh, and a double shot of espresso."

Ridley watched her, his eyes fixed on her mouth as it curled into a satisfied smile, while his own did similarly but possibly in revulsion, as if she'd admitted the cup contained nuclear sludge. It was preferable to his other expression, the imperious "resting blank face" he'd first introduced her to on their flight the week prior. Though what she really would have appreciated was the less dry version of Ridley that had made his welcome appearance later that flight.

"That's easily three days' serving of sugar in a single cup," he remarked. "Hope I don't find you collapsed in the aisle when the sugar high fades."

His words stunned Lanie out of her revelry. Her face fell. She looked down at her cup, as if it had betrayed her. Like she didn't know where it had come from or how it came to be in her hand. It had cost her six pounds fifty, but a flash of her grandmother collapsed on the floor of the church stopped her from taking another sip.

She put it back on the counter, abandoning it, and walked around him.

"What happened? Did I say something?" He spun, asking as she brushed past him toward the exit.

"No."

"So, you are aware that you left that thing you were calling coffee behind?"

"My apology? That you don't plan to give me? Where is it?" she snapped, prompting Ridley as they crossed the wide concourse.

"You misunderstand."

"Do I?" Lanie turned on him. They stood in the middle of the busy concourse as travelers walked by on all sides. "You just said you don't owe me an apology."

"I don't." Ridley's jaw set, a muscle jumping beneath his smooth ebony skin. He seemed to be recalibrating. Where was the cool, fun guy she'd been getting to know on the plane?

Why is this killjoy back?

"Well, I agree, by the way." She'd surprised him with that admission, she could tell. He unclenched for a moment, eyes widening. "Owing me an apology would imply hurt feelings. My feelings aren't hurt."

It was the truth, though it felt like a lie. Her feelings weren't hurt...*exactly*. She was confused by his hot and cold behavior, embarrassed that she'd seemed to read something into it that wasn't there and resolved never to do that again *ever*. But yeah, she wasn't hurt, she was annoyed...with herself.

"I'm surprised to hear that. You seemed hurt." He amended it. "Seem hurt."

"Were you *trying* to hurt me?" Lanie stepped over to a half-empty row far away from the gate entrance. She would still be able to hear them calling her flight at the gate from there. She was always so paranoid about missing an important announcement. She sat.

Ridley dropped his satchel on the carpeted floor at his feet, propping the hard case against a pillar beside him before sitting down in the more crowded row facing hers.

"No, of course not. Why would I want to deliberately hurt you? I don't know you," he scoffed as if affronted. "But it seems as if I might have."

"Well, like you said, you don't know me well enough to make that determination either."

Ridley cleared his throat. "Fine, we're agreed, then. I don't owe you an apology and you don't feel owed one. But might I offer an *explanation* of my behavior, at least?"

"I can't stop you, but I certainly don't need to know," she said firmly. "It's your right to decide who you want to be friendly with…and for how long they hold your interest before you get bored."

He balked audibly, his mouth falling open for a moment. "You're overstating things."

Lanie cringed inwardly. Her mouth went sideways sometimes, as if it ran on its own autonomous motor, and her impulse control varied. And now it was too late to take it back. "Am I?" Lanie crossed her arms over her chest and her legs over each other to take it all in, take him in.

Sitting there in another one of those inoffensive, neutral-toned, cable-knit sweaters that strained over his chest, with a dress shirt beneath it and dark slacks, he looked ready to commence a lecture. And she could see her closed-off reflection in the lenses of his tortoise-framed glasses, like seeing herself through his eyes. She uncrossed her arms and legs, trying to loosen her tightening mouth, attempting a small smile, waiting. She owed this man nothing, but as they'd already established, he didn't owe her anything either.

"You didn't get any coffee." The non sequitur came flying out of her mouth as she tried to restart their conversation.

"From there? God, no." Ridley scowled, leaning in on his elbows to say, "And I hate coffee."

"Then why did you come into a *coffee* shop?"

"I saw you inside."

Easy, Lanie said to herself before she got any more stupid ideas. She considered the bustling concourse for a moment to gather herself. She'd probably have done the same with someone she'd shared even a particularly meaningful cab ride with. It meant nothing. *Melanie, don't start picking out your china patterns. Especially since...*

"I'm sorry. Go on," she refocused.

"Uh, yes, our conversation was entertaining." He paused. "Probably one of the more enjoyable conversations I've had recently." He lowered his voice as if admitting that only to himself. "It would have been a long flight to sit in absolute silence during."

"We could have."

"But we didn't."

She nodded reluctantly.

"And I felt..." A deep line bisected his forehead as his brow furrowed. It was as if he couldn't understand something. "Odd...about how we'd left things."

"How we left things?"

"I, well," he stumbled. "Well, I had more fun talking with you than any adult I've spoken to in months."

"Adult?" That was a strange distinction.

"I have a daughter," he explained. "Bean, uh, Beatrix. She's upbeat and engaging...like you. She's thirteen."

Lanie's heart sank in despair. It was as if she'd been found out. Whereas the world saw her as a woman, she suspected the truth was that she was merely an overgrown adolescent masquerading in an "adult suit." Still, it was hard to hear it confirmed that others saw her that way too. "I'm so happy to have reminded you of your daughter..."

It was obvious Ridley was older than her and except for his smooth, line-less skin, everything about him screamed curmudgeonly eighty-year-old. But Lanie had gotten a glance at his passport as they'd filled out their landing cards and he was only eight years older than her. And physically, he didn't even look thirty-nine. Square-jawed, with whiskey-brown eyes in a narrow face with a full nose, he had wonderfully plush lips that Lanie had shamefully imagined feeling pressed against her own—

"Lanie?" Ridley said, frowning at her.

"Hmm?" Lanie murmured. Her face heated. Was she staring at his mouth? *Oh God.*

His cheek twitched in obvious annoyance. "I did not say you reminded me of my daughter. What I said was that my daughter was the last person with whom I'd had such an entertaining conversation."

"Same difference, but whatever."

Ridley exhaled a frustrated breath.

Lanie did too, wondering if it had only been their proximity and the inescapable nature of their eight-hour flight that had made them so crackling good together before. She wanted that back.

"So, I misunderstood you?" she conceded.

"You did. Again…"

This was getting tiresome. Surely, he couldn't have lived this long without realizing his priggishness was off-putting? But the gate was too crowded, and getting more so by the minute, for Lanie to get up and move. Her row had filled in with travelers. She dispensed with any further pretense.

"I'm sure your *wife* understands you fine though, *right*?" It was an accusation, not a question.

His face fell.

"Or is she not 'engaging' and 'entertaining' enough?"

"Lanie, I'm a widower," he explained.

Lanie's head throbbed, face reddening. *Oh no. No, no!*

"My wife died two and a half years ago."

"Ridley. Oh God. I—I'm so sorry."

"Complications due to lupus." He paused. "It was something

of a surprise." His eyes darkened behind his glasses. For a moment Lanie felt as if she'd lost him to a memory.

"I am so sorry. Shit, I said that already." She strained for something better, more meaningful. "I wish I'd never brought that up."

"It's fine." He came back to her then, shaking his head. "She was only forty-one, far too young. So I've gotten over the impertinence of it. Mostly."

That didn't necessarily make Lanie feel better about her blunder but she understood it wasn't meant to. It was the truth and Ridley seemed to be blunt, she'd already noticed.

"And since then," he continued to her surprise, "it's been me, my daughter and her grandparents in a little bubble. Since the bubble finally popped, it's been nothing but work: getting my clinical trial back off the ground, getting Bea back into school, getting everything back to normal. Or the 'new normal,' you know? So I'm...let's call it shit at talking to random women now," he said in a halting manner.

"*Random?* I see..." Lanie said to herself and nearly laughed before realizing how deeply and horrifyingly inappropriate that would be. It was the impulse control thing again.

"I mean, really talking to anyone not related to me anymore. Then last week I got, I don't know, uncomfortable with how familiar speaking with you became."

"Familiar?" she asked. *Familiar?* She mulled the word further. *A bit clinical but maybe it fit.*

"So, when you went to the bathroom, I suppose I wanted to reestablish our boundaries?" Ridley sat up straighter. "I had only just decided to take my wedding band off, you see."

Lanie almost smiled. It wasn't her imagination. He *had* that ring on.

He shifted uncomfortably. "I certainly didn't expect that doing that would put me on the radar of quite so many women... or at the mercy of so many unwanted advances."

"I didn't realize I made an advance?" Lanie asked, eyebrows rising.

"Not you! Not you, specifically. I meant in general," he corrected himself. "Even my neighbors try to set me up. But I certainly didn't expect that putting it back on would alienate you either, or I might not have done it."

"Me?" she cried, indignant. "You alienated me?"

"What? You don't think that's what happened?" His face was guileless and smooth, the hallmark of an honest man.

She wanted to smack him upside the head. "No! I think I went into the bathroom and the person I thought I'd met disappeared while I was gone."

He shook his head. "We cannot see ourselves, so I understand that you might not realize how upset, borderline angry, you became." The high-handed bearing and sanctimonious tone that had finally begun to recede threatened to return.

Lanie's nostrils flared, her cheeks flushing. "I wasn't angry then," she said. "But I am getting angry now."

"Why?" He seemed genuinely puzzled.

"Ooh, you are right, you could use some reeducation on how to speak to women—"

Just then, overhead the boarding call for first class, business class and premium economy came over the PA. Lanie grabbed her bags and rose. Ridley did too.

"Are you *still* following me?"

"Of course not. I'm going back to New York."

The minute she'd said it, Lanie felt stupid...*again*. Why would he be at this gate otherwise? *Duh.* "That's what you were complaining to your friend on the phone about, right? Having to turn around and come back to New York so soon." She deflated.

"Dash? Yeah." Ridley nodded, hefting his satchel onto his shoulder.

Why did he hold on to this for six days, to the point that he feels compelled to apologize, er, explain himself? Still, that went both ways. *Why do I care?* she wondered. And why did she feel at times assuaged and yet still annoyed?

"You back in premium?" she asked, an olive branch of sorts.

He took it with a smile. A real one. Bold and surprisingly sexy. But also achingly brief. Lanie blinked, short-circuiting the somersaults rolling through her stomach at the sight, and it was already gone.

"Business," he answered.

"Lucky dog." They both moved toward the gate, Lanie in the lead as they merged with the line forming.

"Lanie?"

She was coming to like hearing her name in his buttery-smooth bass.

"Hmm?" She turned to him, stepping into line behind a woman whose arms were laden with duty-free bags.

"It occurred to me that I—ah, I should have given you this before." At that, he flipped something between his fingers at her.

"Your card?" Lanie stared at his hand. "Okay?"

She took it from him.

"I wanted to give you my card to—" Nervousness looked peculiar on him.

She smiled knowingly. "To start your reeducation?"

He struggled. "No, I, uh, thought maybe we could have lunch while I'm in town?"

She slid her finger across the smooth, clearly expensive card stock, peering at it as if she couldn't decipher its use.

RIDLEY P. ARONSEN, MD PHD MRCP (LONDON)
ST IGNATIUS NHS FOUNDATION TRUST, UK

"You're kind of the only person I know there," he added.

"I doubt that," she scoffed. "Well, I don't know about my availability."

"Should I ask for it back, then?"

"No, thank you." She pulled her hand away, suddenly suffering from an inability to look directly at him, splitting her focus between him and the card. "Upon further consideration, I may be free."

His mouth hitched in the corner. "Okay. Well, I'm over there." He nodded toward the first-and-business-class line that had only five people in it, compared to her twenty. "So, you'll call me, yeah?"

"Sure." She gave him a half-hearted smile. "Uh, thank you, Ridley... I mean, Dr. Aronsen." Lanie smirked as he rolled his eyes at the self-correction. "It was a pleasure to meet you." Lanie offered her hand for him to shake.

He looked from her face to that hand, aware of the significance.

"The pleasure was mine," he said with sincerity, but a formality had returned to his tone.

"I found a smaller hand sanitizer this time. Yay, Boots and their two-for-one on travel sizes." The cheer was painfully awkward.

Ridley slotted his large hand into her slightly smaller one. *Odd.* She didn't expect it to be so soft. Her mother's hands were rough-worn from all the harsh soaps and astringents she constantly had to use in the hospital, going in and out of patient rooms all day. Lanie wanted to pause a second longer to bask in the warmth of his hand surrounding hers.

They looked into each other's eyes. Lanie knew that she had not imagined it; something had happened between them—was happening.

Nope. She let go.

She couldn't rightfully ask the universe for more than this. This was a decidedly better ending than they'd had last week. Better to leave it right there instead of calling him later with "Wedding Bell Blues" playing at top volume on a loop in her brain.

Right?

ten

Ridley

Ridley didn't see Lanie when he got off the plane. That wasn't a surprise, as he was one of the first people off—*other perks of business class*—and a driver sent by the university was waiting for him on the arrivals concourse. Standing with a placard featuring his name, the driver didn't see him until they were standing face-to-face.

"D-Dr. Aronsen?" He was clearly not what the driver had expected. *Typical.*

Ridley nodded anyway.

He was never what people expected to see when they were meeting with a "Dr. Ridley Aronsen." He blamed his mom's affinity for horror movies for some of that. But he knew what the main reason was—because he looked more likely to be a point guard for the Celtics, or even the guy driving the car as opposed to the man being picked up by it. Most often when people saw Ridley, they didn't see the principal medical investigator of an important clinical trial, or a doctor who was a member of the Royal College of Physicians, or even a good father or son, just an intimidatingly big Black man.

"Oh, okay." The older driver bent to grab his suitcase.

Ridley slipped it behind him on its smooth wheels. "It's okay, I can handle it."

The driver snapped back in surprise.

Ridley got his back up far too easily. He eased a little. He was projecting. "Why don't you lead the way."

The man shrugged and led him toward the revolving doors of the exit.

Inside the car, Ridley fished his phone out of his coat pocket. It was incredibly soon to expect to hear from Lanie but she'd said she'd call and that could literally be at any time. *Best to be prepared.* He didn't know why he wanted her to call. There was more than one moment sitting in that terminal with her when he'd wondered why he was bothering at all. He didn't owe her anything and she certainly hadn't made any effort to be pleasant.

"No hard feelings about that thing earlier?" the driver asked, breaking into Ridley's thoughts.

"Sorry?" Ridley had no idea what the guy was talking about but wished he would stop turning his way as they flew down the expressway.

"Not realizing you were the doctor."

"Oh. Don't worry about it." Ridley shook his head.

Ridley's mind pulled back to thoughts of Lanie and he ran a finger over the business cards tucked into the pocket of his phone case. Maybe he liked that she was smart and snarky, and clearly unafraid to be unpleasant or prickly. And he was... intrigued? Some of his colleagues saw him that way too. But he had this soft underbelly that few got to see, that he was constantly protecting. He suspected she did also. So, maybe Lanie was a kindred spirit and perhaps that was why he wasn't put off by it or her?

Is that why?

"So, what kinda doc are you?" The driver spoke again after long minutes of welcome silence.

"Hmm?"

"Your specialty?"

"Oh, I'm a nephrologist, by training. But I'm a physician-scientist in actuality."

Through the rearview mirror, Ridley could read the blankness in the driver's eyes. "Is that like, a special type of doctor?"

"Uh, it only means I'm not in direct clinical practice. I don't see patients generally, I do research."

"No, I meant nef-rolist? What kind of specialty is that?"

"It's kidneys," Ridley explained simply. "I specialize in kidney function."

"Oh." The driver nodded. His eyes, draining of interest, returned to the road as they crossed the suspension bridge from Queens over the East River into Manhattan.

Ridley looked from the city streets whipping past his window down to his phone again. He did hope she would call. Maybe they could have a drink. He didn't know New York that well and considering he was set to be here frequently, it wouldn't hurt to know someone in the city. To get out of his rut. A little practice before his interpersonal skills got too rusty. And getting to know someone like her—*like him*—might be exactly what he needed right now.

eleven

Lanie

When Lanie let herself into their apartment, her mother was stationed in her regular evening spot, nodding off in front of the living room television. On-screen, an old episode of a reality crime show watched her, instead of the other way around. But Ryan Turner stirred at the sound.

"How was the flight?" She yawned, stretching awake.

Lanie stood there and exhaled before answering, happier than not to be home. Their living room was bounded on all sides, save one, by African art and posters for old art shows featuring African American artists. Overall, the design scheme was all browns and beiges with earth-tone textiles, beads and the indigenous art of numerous cultures. In their living room, Lanie and her mother could travel the world—*circa 1975*—without leaving the house, all thanks to Pier 1 Imports and World Market…just the way Ryan liked it.

"Flight was okay," Lanie whispered. "No turbulence."

Her mother sighed with relief. An actual aerospace engineer came through her ER once and explained to Ryan that turbulence rarely brought down planes. Still, her mother remained wholly unconvinced.

"And, Mom?"

"Much better."

"That's good." Ryan had called her mother as soon as Lanie informed her, but there had never been a question of whether she'd buy a plane ticket and find out for herself.

"Gem's still pissed?"

"She was hot as a .45 on Sunday night but she might be over it." Lanie sighed. "Especially since I agreed to be her maid of honor."

"You did?"

"Yeah. Well, technically, I'm Jonah's best man too."

Ryan frowned. "How's that going to work?"

"Not sure." Lanie shrugged. "But it'll give me an excuse to see Gran a little more often."

"Great idea."

"Maybe you should think about, I don't know, doing that yourself? Go visit your mother. We got lucky this time, we may not the next."

Her mother's mouth was a grim line and she nodded in agreement. But Lanie still doubted that would amount to anything.

"When was the last time you saw her?" Lanie abandoned her bag in the hall and collapsed on the couch across from her mother.

"When Les brought her for a visit. Goodness, was it ten years ago already? Maybe you're right. Maybe I can plan to go to Gem's wedding? When's it again?"

"June." Lanie smiled encouragingly.

"Anything else eventful?" her mother queried as if she knew Lanie was humoring her.

"No, not really."

Lanie eyed her mother's cello sitting in its stand in the corner. "You practice while I was gone?"

Her mother's eyes followed hers to the instrument. "I need to take it to a luthier, have the strings tightened and have them look at the fingerboard." She shrugged. "Maybe next week."

"You've been saying that," Lanie muttered.

It was one of the only things Lanie missed from being cooped

up together during lockdown. The times when even after gru-
eling, thankless shifts at the hospital, her mother would come
home and work out her grief and stress by playing, filling the
house with music for hours. Now that things were back to "normal," her mother hadn't touched her cello in months.

"Another envelope came for you from that professor in California." Ryan glanced at Lanie, cannily turning the conversation toward something Lanie didn't want to talk about. "I left
it on the bed for you."

"I met someone," Lanie offered up to circumvent that discussion but regretted her attempt at diversion almost immediately. It definitely gave the wrong impression as evidenced by
her mother's eyebrow quirking as her attention swung away
from the television. "I mean, I met the same person both coming and going," Lanie amended quickly. "We were on the same
plane both times. Isn't that...funny?"

"Wow, that is a big coincidence."

"Yeah, I thought so too," she conceded, relieved her mother
was clearly disinterested in hearing more. "Especially since I
had to change my flight."

But Ryan surprised her daughter then, her mouth lifting in
the corners like she was slowly coming to understanding. "So
what? You sensed fate at work, felt sparks?"

Lanie chuckled, rolling her eyes at the hokeyness of the question. People only felt "sparks" in the rom-coms she and her
mom binged on Saturday nights. "No." She snorted.

Her mother's amused eyes returned to the television then,
dismissing it. "Well then."

Although Ryan desired grandchildren theoretically, she'd
always maintained a very casual attitude toward Lanie's love
life and marriage prospects, making no secret of her desire for
Lanie to be careful. Probably because she and her sister, Elliot,
had both made their own mother a grandmother quite young.

Perversely, Lanie was annoyed by her mother's level of disinterest. She never really believed Lanie might have met The One, in part because Ryan didn't believe The One existed anymore. Lanie's father had disabused Ryan of those notions years ago. Lanie felt foolish now. This whole fanciful line of conversation was of Lanie's creation; she couldn't blame her mother for taking her cues from her.

"Like I said, not a big deal. A funny coincidence, that's all." Unable to help herself, Lanie continued, "He was very cute, in a crotchety old man kinda way." Lanie smiled to herself. For someone who was supposedly disinterested in giving her mom the wrong idea, she didn't know why she wouldn't shut up about it.

Her mother's eyes fixed on Lanie. "Crotchety? How old was he?"

"Mom."

"What? I can't ask?"

"I don't know, thirties?" She wasn't sure why she lied.

Suspicion ghosted across Ryan's face. "Okay, well, what's he do?"

"Ah, he's some kind of doctor, I think." Lanie attempted to gloss over it, watching her mother's face, realizing finally that she'd gone wrong. Lanie's father was a doctor. Ryan's expression leeched any joy out of their small moment. She knew she should have waited to tell Narcisa. "No big deal. Just a cool coincidence. It's doubtful I'll ever see him again."

The business card in Lanie's back pocket practically singed her as she said this.

"True." Ryan nodded absently, glancing back at her TV program, her interest again waning. "You'd do well to aim lower anyway."

And with that, their conversation was over.

Lanie sat there for another few minutes before grabbing her bags and heading to her bedroom.

twelve

Lanie

Aim lower.

It was an otherwise quiet day at her office, but Lanie's mom's admonition still rang in her ears even days later, thwarting her. Luckily, Lanie's job as the administrative assistant for Empire University's chair of the Psychology Department wasn't a particularly challenging job.

Of her brain's capacity, Lanie had once estimated she only used about 30 percent of it day-to-day, managing the chair's budget and expenses, coordinating departmental and educational meetings. And being in a small department at a top-rated research university meant perhaps even less since their department was under the radar, under-enrolled and underfunded. All of which was right up Lanie's alley. After imploding spectacularly in her own academic career, it was possibly even what appealed to her most. What comforted her. Here in the Psychology Department, despite her boss's recent attempts to coax her back into academia, she felt appreciated but otherwise unbothered, allowed to blend into the background.

So, it was easy in the middle of the day to, say, pick up her cell for possibly the fifth or sixth time and attempt to make a personal call. Her mind had wandered repeatedly to Ridley's card all week. But working up the courage to finally contact him and take him up on his offer still proved difficult.

LANIE:

Hi Dr. Aaronson—

Delete Delete
Lanie checked the business card for the millionth time this week, running her thumb over the embossed letters before trying again.

LANIE:

Hi Dr. A-r-o-n-s-e-n.
This is Lanie we met—

Delete Delete Delete Delete Delete Delete Delete Delete

LANIE:

Hey Ridley.
Just texting you like we disc—

Delete Delete Delete Delete Delete Delete Delete

LANIE:

Hey! It's Lanie

Delete Delete

LANIE:

Hey!

Send.

Lanie's stomach rolled like the three little dots that appeared on her screen after long minutes of waiting. After a whole sixty seconds of staring at them, undulating like unceasing waves of punctuation, Lanie placed the phone face down on her desk, going back to the expense report she'd been working on.

Finally, an additional minute later, her phone pinged. Lanie dared herself to try waiting to finish the rest of the department chair's report. She wrote exactly two more lines before her nerves got the better of her.

RIDLEY:

???

LANIE:

It's Lanie

RIDLEY:

Seriously? Lanie's cheeks burned. She flipped the phone over again, slamming it on the surface of her desk so harshly she had to pick it back up immediately to inspect the screen for damage.

No, I have not been torturing myself for four days over a person who couldn't care one way or the other. She felt so stupid.

The phone pinged again. She snatched it up.

RIDLEY:

Hey Lanie. It took you long enough

She smiled.

RIDLEY:

Seriously. I leave tomorrow

Oh shit. Had it really been that long? Well, for the first three days, recalling her mother's words, she was adamant she wasn't going to contact him. So, yes, that made sense. Her frown disappeared abruptly, replaced by the wish to bang her head against a desk. What had she waited all these days for?

LANIE:

Sorry. Next time?

She pressed send before realizing how presumptuous that was. *Next time? God, girl, for real? What if he isn't coming back for months?*

RIDLEY:

That's okay, we can still meet up.
Tonight?

Lanie's lunch threatened a return visit. She slapped a hand over her mouth to discourage it. She bit her lip. She was wearing a well-worn baby blue twinset and black slacks, her usual business casual wardrobe. Not great for going out after work.

RIDLEY:

Short notice. I know

LANIE:

No it's my fault.
You told me to reach out

RIDLEY:

So dinner?

Lanie blinked.

LANIE:

Didn't you say coffee?

RIDLEY:

I don't drink coffee

That's right. She remembered him saying that.

RIDLEY:

Do you drink coffee for dinner?

LANIE:

 I don't

RIDLEY:

Am I being forward?

Yes.

LANIE:

No

RIDLEY:

Are you busy?

Lanie's stomach lurched again. Was he really asking her out? She looked around her small office to make sure she was still alone before glancing back to her phone.

She tried to ignore the nerves and excitement bubbling up inside her. Her dating history told her she didn't have a shot, but she couldn't help picturing a cozy booth in a restaurant, soft lighting, Ridley's knee bumping hers under the table…

RIDLEY:

Are you still there?

He's impatient, she thought. Until she checked her computer screen—it was a full two minutes later.

LANIE:

RIDLEY:

Ok. So?

Lanie held her breath after typing the three little letters. Her heart thumped wildly in her chest. But the next words popped up without the warning of dots before she could press Send.

RIDLEY:

Lanie, relax. It's not a date.

She deflated. She knew that but still, it was a kick in the crotch to see it written there in sans serif font.

Why would it be, Lanie? The man isn't interested like that. He's getting his feet wet again. You're his method of reentry.

She blew out a breath and hit Send.

LANIE:

RIDLEY:

Pick the place. Text me the address.

Lanie frowned. *Well, okay, boss.* She nearly saluted.

thirteen

Ridley

Ridley tapped his fingers along his crossed upper arm and checked his watch again.

It's been almost an hour. Am I being stood up?

Perhaps he'd come on a little strong? Maybe he shouldn't have asked her to come out so late? Now that he'd thought about it, meeting at six, the earliest he could get out of the hospital, did seem more like a date than a casual dinner between acquaintances. He was so out of practice he didn't know anymore. He hadn't been a single man in over a decade. Or maybe his tone had been a smidgen too reproachful when she finally reached out. He hated to admit it even to himself, but he'd been so eager to hear from her. Every night as he took the car back to his hotel, he looked at the bustling city passing by his window and could clearly see how he was squandering his time here. Back when he and Thyra would travel for business, they always carved out at least one night to go out and wander during their visits. Things were different without her. *Everything is different without her.* Now, for this trip, it was hospital to hotel and back. Of course, he knew he could go out alone; he just didn't want to.

The food smelled good, at least. He was fascinated by how excited that made him. After all these years, he was still afraid to admit out loud how much the food in the UK did not appeal to him. So much so that, if there weren't other brown people cooking it, he wanted no part of it. Luckily, Thyra's mother, Clare-Olive, still kept their refrigerator at home fully stocked with the same Caribbean dishes her daughter had. Plus, there were solid Nigerian, Indian and Moroccan options within a stone's throw of the house; otherwise he and Bea would have starved. If his mother-in-law couldn't make it by and it was left up to him, it'd be Pizza Hut and Chicken Cottage every night. It wasn't that he couldn't cook; Ridley just rarely had the time anymore.

He sighed, drumming his fingers against his knee now. The scent of savory spices filled the air, along with the stronger, more pungent smoky aroma of charred meat. Ridley's stomach grumbled in outrage at the wait.

Lanie had picked well. Daebak Grill was trendy but comfortable, with a rustic vibe. The dimly lit but surprisingly spacious dining room was set among seemingly identical storefronts in Koreatown. Flickering candlelight set a calming mood. Shiplap walls made of reclaimed wood held ledges filled with hundreds of wine bottles and surrounded a dozen small pods separated by timber support beams. Each pod could accommodate between six to eight diners on low red leather sofas around a small charcoal grill built into an even lower dining table at the center. White twinkling lights dotted the ceiling of the room, adding to the ambience.

"Ridley?"

He looked up to see Lanie enter breathlessly.

"Sorry. They said there was some kind of signal problem on the train." The words flowed out of her mouth like a torrent. "The Q had to run on the local track. We were being held between stations. We waited for an hour but then when it pulled into the station, there were cops waiting on the platform. Turns out it wasn't signal issues after all. They were holding the train to give the NYPD—"

"Lanie," Ridley stopped her, totally disinterested in this story. He held out a hand as she dropped down onto the sofa bench opposite him, before stopping himself. Last time he'd touched her, she nearly jumped out of her skin. Probably best to avoid that. "Breathe. You're here."

She paused.

"That's all that matters, I mean," he added quickly. He couldn't believe he'd almost stepped in it again already.

She blinked as if reanimating then nodded. "Yes. Sorry."

"It only matters that you came." He meant it.

Seeing her there, out of breath and in a slightly rumpled plain blue sweater and black pants, it was clear she hadn't gone home to change. Which was okay because he hadn't either. He nodded, hoping that was understood.

The server arrived with a smile, a water glass and a menu for Lanie. But she only glanced at it for a moment before setting it and her purse aside. It was Ridley's turn to be stunned when she looked up at him. She looked like one of those huge-eyed anime characters Bea used to draw. He'd forgotten how much he enjoyed her face. Just the pleasant symmetry and elegant shape of it, with her cute nose and the solar system of dark brown freckles that crossed its bridge and continued over her round cheeks, up over the lids of her expressive light brown eyes. He suspected she didn't even realize how much could be so clearly read in those slightly upturned Betty Boop eyes of hers.

For instance, the fact that she was a little annoyed with him right now.

"Thanks," he stated, to break the ice and make up for shutting her down a minute ago. "For coming out."

She took a deep breath and settled into the seat. "Thanks for inviting me."

She crossed one leg over the other and began tapping her foot with…impatience? Irritation? Nervousness? He only knew how *he* felt: self-conscious.

Have I already bollocksed this up?

"You come here often?"

Lanie cracked a smile. Ridley almost smacked himself in the forehead but exhaled when she didn't comment on his use of the World's Most Tired Pickup Line.

"It's just that you look like you already know what you want when you barely looked at the menu."

Her grin broadened, cheeks reddening as if she'd been caught. *How many million times had Lanie probably heard she had a great smile?* Her mouth, cheeks and eyes brightened simultaneously like what he'd said genuinely tickled her.

"I love this place and their bulgogi is delicious. I usually have the beef. I've figured out exactly how long to keep it on the grill to get it exactly right. Tender, not chewy." She kissed her fingertips. "Perfect. And the marinade…" She closed her eyes as if in ecstasy.

Ridley watched raptly. Her enthusiasm animated her whole body. She leaned forward, her elbows on her knees as if sharing a secret. "I had to finally ask one of the waiters, Hyun, 'cuz it's that good. He said, instead of the typical way, the secret to it is the pineapple juice. Apparently, it sweetens the marinade and ten—"

"Tenderizes the meat, yeah." Ridley nodded.

"Really, you knew that?"

"Well, I assumed. Acidic substances like pineapple juice break down chemical bonds by digesting the proteins in the meat, making it more tender."

"I'm sitting here with Bill Nye the Science Guy." She beamed at him. "You cook?"

"Not much anymore."

She gave him a quizzical look.

"Before medicine, my first love was food science. And I've

done a bunch of little weekend science experiments with my daughter."

"I'm impressed. So, you *are* Bill Nye. Saturdays must be fun at the Aronsen house, huh?"

"They definitely used to be." Ridley laughed with a twinge of bitterness, sharing all the times they had to wipe experiments like Mentos and diet cola off the ceilings, or oobleck from… everywhere, after they read Dr. Suess's *Bartholomew and the Oobleck* and decided to make their own. There'd been plenty of misadventures over the years, but he'd had fun introducing Bea to the easy home science of non-Newtonian fluids, like ketchup and molasses.

He could see wheels begin turning in her head. "I love non-Newtonian fluids!" Lanie enthused. "There's just something about a fluid that can become more liquid or more solid depending on the amount of pressure applied."

Her sudden geeky excitement was entirely sincere. This woman was full of surprises. He tried to hide his.

The server returned to place metal bowls filled with squares of tofu in chili-sesame sauce, separate plates of pickled radish, soybean sprouts and cucumber salad on the table around the grill. It all looked delicious. Ridley realized he hadn't looked at the menu since Lanie walked in the door. He hadn't looked at anything else since then either.

His cell phone beeped, clattering loudly as it vibrated across the wooden tabletop. "Excuse me."

Lanie nodded, leaning back to recline against the red leather, watching.

BEAN:

Mom loved me more.

Ridley quirked an eyebrow as his fingers began typing out a reply.

RIDLEY:

Excuse me?

BEAN:

Mom loved me more.
She would never have forced
me to take Classical Civilizations.

RIDLEY:

She would have, but
YOU chose it anyway.

Ridley glanced up at the waiter, ready to take their order. "Sorry. Gimme a sec to pick something."

Lanie shrugged.

BEAN:

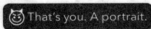 That's you. A portrait.

Ridley snorted before glancing at the menu again, trying to multitask. But the menu suddenly seemed made up of all gibberish where English words definitely used to sit next to the Korean characters. He looked over the top of his menu at Lanie's expectant face. "Barbecued meat?"

"Yes." She chuckled, relaxing, head propped up on her arm. "Do you have any preferences?"

BEAN:

Dad, where are you?

Ridley's heart unexpectedly picked up the pace.

RIDLEY:

> New York

BEAN:

> Haha. No. Where in NYC?

"Nope," he answered, distracted and weirdly still drawing a big fat blank.

Lanie looked up at the server, who was still standing there, with remarkable patience considering the circumstances. There were only around ten patrons in the entire restaurant; still, the server sighed audibly, eyebrows raised, as she looked down at him.

The phone buzzed again in his hand.

BEAN:

> Dad?

"I am so sorry." It was as if Ridley was a juggler thrown too many balls to keep aloft. Had his social ineptitude really become this bad? He glanced from his phone in one hand to the menu in the other again. It was definitely an English-language menu. *Make a decision, man!*

RIDLEY:

> How do you know I'm not
> in my hotel room?

"Pick for me, would you?" He gave up, smiling apologetically at Lanie. "It's my daughter."

"We'll have the beef combo," Lanie said to their serenely tolerant server. "Ah yes, the thirteen-year-old that I remind you of?" Lanie then asked him.

BEAN:

> Because you didn't ask me WHY
> I'm up at midnight. ☹ Neglect.
> Abandonment. Dejection, c'est moi

He checked his watch. She was absolutely right. It was 1:30 in London, on a school night.

RIDLEY:

> Your French is coming along I see

Ridley sighed heavily, finally registering Lanie's words. Opening his mouth at the same time he pried his eyes away from his phone screen, his gaze grazed the length of her, sitting in quiet repose in front of him. He drank her in from the ballet flats on her feet upward, then said, "There is no planet on which I could *ever* confuse you with my daug—"

He stopped at her face, as one of Lanie's eyebrows rose. His eyes returned to his phone.

RIDLEY:

> Why ARE you still up at midnight?

Wait, what did I just say to her?

She was smiling. She'd been teasing him. Ridley shook his head. The phone's vibrations tickled his hand.

BEAN:

> CLASSICAL CIVILIZATIONS DAD!

RIDLEY:

> Goodnight Beatrix Olive Baker-Smythe.
> Go to bed NOW!

BEAN:

> My whole government,
> Dad? Really?

Ridley nearly threw the phone away from himself in an effort to concentrate on his company. He took a deep breath. "I, uh… What were we saying?"

"So, you're headed home tomorrow?" Lanie asked, seemingly amused by all of this.

"Yes." He sighed. "But I think I'm considering running away with the circus right this second. Is that still a thing?" He leaned back in his seat. "Or maybe joining WitSec?"

"I think you have to have witnessed a crime for that one."

His phone vibrated yet again on the seat beside him. "In a moment, I think I might commit one. Will that count?"

He picked it up, typing quickly.

RIDLEY:

> BEAN TO BED!

BEAN:

> I'm not 5 anymore, Dad.

RIDLEY:

> TO. BED. NOW!

BEAN:

> Nite Dad.

RIDLEY:

> Night love. ♥

Ridley exhaled, finally casting the phone aside. "So, what did you order for us?"

Lanie narrowed her eyes. "The beef combo."

Ridley didn't have the heart nor the intestinal fortitude at that moment to tell her he tried to severely limit his red meat intake. And he'd already indulged in bacon and a burger this week.

"Looking forward to it." He rubbed his hands together and then his stomach in a circle instead as she smiled. He really did like her smile.

"If you don't mind me asking, who watches your daughter when you're away?"

"Her grandparents. Her mother's parents." He didn't know what he would do without Clare-Olive and Philip. Particularly in the years since they'd lost Thyra.

"And your parents…?"

"Are retired civil servants from Massachusetts, that are now living their best life as Disney Adults in a condo in St. Cloud, Florida."

"Seriously?" Lanie laughed.

Ridley nodded. Washington "Wash" Marcus Aronsen the Third and his wife, Rosetta, were by far the oldest pair of teen-age lovebirds Ridley had ever met. He adored his parents but after growing up with them, Ridley still counted himself lucky that he and his siblings managed to get to school ever and never lost all their teeth to cavities or burned their house down. *Self-involved* was the word he most often euphemistically used to describe them, while *neglectful* might have been more accurate.

"You've heard of Forever 21?" Ridley asked.

She nodded.

"Well, they're kind of forever fifteen."

Lanie's brows creased. "Have you managed to see them recently?"

"Oh yeah." He waved a hand. "They took Bean to Disney not long after it reopened."

"Wow. That's dedication."

"You don't know the half of it."

It was the only way he or any of his siblings saw their parents anymore. But that wasn't fun get-to-know-you banter.

"And you?" He turned the tables, interlacing his fingers over his knee, getting comfortable.

Ridley could swear he saw something in her face shutter at his words. Lanie's smile didn't exactly disappear but certainly lost wattage.

"Far less entertaining," she said in a voice a little above a mutter. "Mom's here in NY, Dad lives in Connecticut."

Lanie looked positively relieved as the servers arrived, carrying platters of raw meat and sides to their table. The tension that had appeared out of nowhere eased marginally.

"So, Massachusetts?" Lanie laid a few pieces of thinly sliced brisket, from the myriad assortment of meats they'd received, directly onto the brazier with her chopsticks. The searing meat sizzled.

"Born and bred."

"No wonder."

"No wonder what?" He watched her flip the assortment of meat and vegetables on the brazier with meticulous care, only allowing them to brown, not burn or smoke. The scent was heavenly, the sizzling sound a melody his stomach burbled to.

"No wonder your accent is all over the place. One minute you sound like a bloke from Merry Ole England." She put on a cockney accent so thick and horrid it made Dick Van Dyke's accent in *Mary Poppins* sound like Meryl Streep's in *The Iron Lady*. "The next, I swear you sound like my neighbor Jamal from up the block."

Ridley threw his head back, laughing so hard and long that his sides hurt. He'd heard constantly from his family and American friends that his accent had gotten muddled, the implication almost always being that it was affected. This was the first time he'd heard it framed like that.

Which delighted him.

No, *she* delighted him.

fourteen

■ 27-SEP ■ Trans-Continental Airways ■ Flight: 988 ■

JFK-John F. Kennedy Int'l Airport ► **LHR-London, Heathrow**

Seat Assignment: **18C**

The late-afternoon sun was setting in a grayish haze behind the Gothic Revival spires of the Royal Court as Lanie waited inside a small café across the street. Jonah tapped lightly on the window next to her shoulder as she sat leaning against it, responding to work emails on her cell. She startled, both at the unexpected disruption and at the sight of him in his suit. He gestured for her to come out rather than coming in.

She checked the time. They were running late.

"Hey! Look at you, suited and booted. You look great!"

In a slim-fit, European-cut gray suit with a checked black tie and a stylish brown leather satchel slung over one shoulder, he was more rakish and quite frankly sharper than she'd ever seen him. Lanie had always known Jonah was brilliant but she'd never believed he had the temperament to duke it out in a courtroom. He was the diffident and studious type, better suited to a solicitor's life seated behind a desk, buried in legal paperwork. But this suit with his hair swept back in midnight waves told a different story. Like he was a shark that prowled a courthouse.

"Yeah, thanks," he said bashfully, giving her an odd, one-armed hug that Lanie wondered at.

She'd realized only after she'd been asked to join him today that all their recent interactions had been filtered through Gemma. In fact, they hadn't really spoken alone since he and Gemma announced their engagement.

"Sorry I'm late, we were in chambers. It ran long."

"No worries." She tagged him awkwardly on the arm. "Let's hit it. Your appointment starts in twenty."

Thirty minutes later, they stood inside Neville and Co., a high-end menswear shop just off Savile Row in Mayfair. Walking in, Lanie gasped, taking in the celebrated clothing store that still occupied the same town house it had for the last hundred and twenty years. Even the spiced-vanilla-and-tanned-leather scent that filled the air felt rarified. Lanie was always out of her depth in luxury stores. There was no way she would've ever dared set foot inside a place like this without the appointment scheduled by Gemma or the credit card supplied by Jonah.

The whole store exuded money but the upstairs atelier—where their personal tailor, Richard, stood waiting patiently to begin taking Jonah's measurements for his morning suit—was especially sumptuous. The walls were indigo blue, inlaid with picture frame moldings and decorated with vintage game animal illustrations. Edison bulbs highlighted massive built-ins that held racks of clothing, artfully arranged by color with suits, jackets, ties and pants of all kinds. Dark reclaimed wood side tables and navy club chairs dotted the space. It was as if the place was suffused top to bottom with testosterone of the aged, white and male variety.

"So, how's work?" Lanie asked as Jonah undressed in an adjoining dressing room. She drummed her fingers along the supple arm of the brown leather nailhead chair she sat in, waiting.

"Stressful." Jonah sighed. "New promotion, and then this wedding stuff?"

"Can I get you and your fiancé something to drink?" Richard leaned forward to ask.

Lanie's stomach made a quick revolution. It wasn't by any means the first time that someone had confused them for a couple over the years. But it was the first time since she knew definitively that that was never to be. Air whooshed out of her lungs, making her voice thin and reedy.

"H-he's not my— I mean, we're not a—" Lanie shook her head. "I'm the best man."

Her words were idiotic, spoken to Richard's befuddled face. "My apologies, Ms. Turner."

"Um, a Tom Collins for him, and you wouldn't happen to have any wine?" She cleared her throat, whispering.

"White." He nodded. "Riesling?"

Lanie forced a smile and nodded, taking a moment to gather herself. Richard walked away with their order.

"Mel?" Jonah called.

"I'll bet it's been tough," she commiserated then, wondering exactly what "stressful" wedding stuff Jonah was referring to. She and Les planned to go to Deptford to possibly hire a DJ friend of his. She and Fatou were frantically calling around for still-available June venues. She and Gran were the ones vetting prospective caterers, proofreading the save-the-dates and choosing invitations. It seemed to be all-hands-on-deck so far, *except* for Jonah's and Gemma's.

"These accelerated Pre-Cana classes are doing my head in," Jonah continued.

"Oh. Who knew there would be so many rules to deciding to share the rest of your whole life with someone? Am I right?"

"You're a real barrel of laughs today, Mel," Jonah said drolly.

"I certainly try," she snarked. "Um, have you given the rings any thought yet?"

"I have," Jonah answered from behind the door. "They're on order."

Lanie dared to put her feet up on one of the ottomans but immediately dropped them as Richard reentered the room.

"Already?" Lanie took the two glasses from Richard's tray and set Jonah's aside before taking a sip from her own. "And?"

"Gem wants a carat, channel-set in platinum."

"Oh, of course she does." Lanie rolled her eyes before remembering the tailor was standing right there watching. She cringed theatrically, hiding behind her wineglass, but Richard only smiled.

"I'll be getting something in titanium. It's sturdier."

Lanie sighed. *And cheaper.*

Jonah made a very good living—Syreeta and his *aachchi*, Leela, made sure everyone on Merton Road knew that. And, as Gran had always said, Jonah never spent a bad penny. Ever since they were kids, while Lanie would come home from excursions broke, Jonah returned with most of his allowance intact. He'd always been frugal but, where Gemma was concerned, it seemed to Lanie he was hemorrhaging pound notes. Lanie hoped he knew he didn't, or shouldn't, need to buy Gemma's affection.

"I only hope you can keep track of 'em better than our Drake 'Assassination Vacation' tickets," she said instead.

"When are you gonna let that go?" He laughed.

"Never!" she groused, melodramatically. "All I know is I saved up for 100-block tickets at O2 and had to settle for scalped 400-block seats."

"How many times must I apologize for that? Oh, that's right, 'The rest of my worthless life.'"

"Ahem, *wutless*." Lanie deployed her only bit of patois. "Yuh wutless life."

Jonah finally emerged from the dressing room in a slightly

oversized deep royal blue morning coat over a baby blue waist-coat. He'd kept on his gray suit pants, original shirt and tie. "I don't know. What do you think?"

"You headed to the Royal Ascot after the wedding or something?"

Jonah groaned, immediately retreating to the dressing room.

"Where's the top hat?" she heckled. "I must go fetch my fascinator."

Richard snickered, trying his best not to. Lanie smirked.

"I hope one of those drinks is for me?" Jonah called over the door. "I sense that I'm going to need it messing about with you."

"It's sitting next to me as we speak."

"Give it here."

They both giggled as she got up and passed it, sloshing messily, over the door to him.

Jonah was pretty sozzled by the time he stood emulating *The Vitruvian Man*, arms and legs outstretched as Richard circled him with a measuring tape. Lanie wandered the room, sipping from her third glass of wine, letting her fingertips run along all the sumptuous and exorbitantly priced clothing. The liquor had finally unwound the tight knots that being in this store wound up in her belly.

"I don't believe you."

"Yeah, well, you wouldn't," Jonah mocked. "You're the one sitting alone at the airport three hours early, still convinced somehow that the plane's gonna leave you behind."

Lanie's face fell. "It's a legitimate fear. I worry I'll fall asleep at the gate and miss the boarding call."

Jonah giggled.

"Don't make fun! It's a real source of anxiety for me."

Jonah knew enough about her anxiety that his hearty laughter petered out somewhat, but she knew it was a joke.

"I think the pants need to be taken up just a little," she stated to Richard, changing directions.

"What kind of break do you want?" Lanie walked up to Jonah, reaching for his pant leg to adjust how the hem sat over his shoe.

He twisted away, stepping back and nearly toppling off the fitting platform.

"Sir!" Richard startled, as Jonah almost tumbled backward over his crouched form.

Lanie recoiled immediately at Jonah's reaction. She'd barely touched his knee with her two fingers.

"I—I was just trying to show him." Lanie's cheeks flamed, her whole chest feeling like it might cave in.

"S-sorry," Jonah stammered. "You just surprised me."

"I surprised you?" Lanie frowned. "What the hell?" She was mortified.

"Mel," he said, reaching for her arm.

"Don't *you* touch *me!*" It was her turn to flinch.

She threw his hand off, slapping it away. Abandoning her wineglass on a nearby table, Lanie grabbed her coat and purse and hurried down the staircase.

"Lanie, I'm sorry!" Jonah called out.

Lanie made for the front door, winding through the elaborate clothing racks, holding back tears that threatened to spill down her cheeks. When exactly had their relationship eroded so much that he cringed when she was near him? She'd thought it was her imagination that he'd become distant, stiffening when she hugged him.

"Lanie! What the hell?" Jonah said, barreling into the street behind her. He caught up just outside the store, still wearing the sample morning suit. "Don't you think this is a slight over-reaction?"

"*I'm* overreacting?" She spun on him, shouting and making air quotes with her fingers. Then she quieted, remembering the tony neighborhood they were in. "What are you talking about, Jonah, huh? And what was that? Acting like I was trying to maul you?"

"I'm sorry," he repeated ineffectually.

It was like her Jonah had gotten brain-napped by Gemma. He never used to dress like David Beckham, he didn't spend like King Midas and he definitely didn't cringe at her touch.

"Look, Lanie…" he started and she rolled her eyes.

"Look, Lanie" was something of an alliterative catchphrase her paramours used as they let her down in variations of the word *easy*.

There was the guy from the dating app who'd said, *Look, Lanie, no offense but you're a lot bigger from the waist down than in your profile pic. And I don't think it's fair to me that you misrepresented yourself.*

And the guy she dated from the university library who'd said, *Look, Lanie, I'm not going to apologize for having needs.* When she refused to give him a blow job on their lunch break.

And even four years later, her chest still burned, thinking of her most recent ex and his excuse: *Look, Lanie, it's for the best. You didn't seem all that interested in getting serious anyway.* He'd been right but that was after informing her of his engagement to a woman he'd been dating for four of the six months they'd been together.

Hearing "Look, Lanie" from Jonah's lips felt like a betrayal.

"I think it makes Gem uncomfortable that we're—"

Lanie held up a hand. He very pointedly didn't edge away this time, closing his mouth. "She said *what*?"

"Well, no, I mean that, she didn't say it, but…"

So, what? This is preemptive?

She forced a smile up from the recesses of her emotional stores. "*Look, Jonah*, you don't need to worry. I wasn't trying to feel you up—"

"I know that, I'm sorry," he interrupted.

"And I wouldn't ever do anything to make you uncomfortable," she continued calmly. "I honestly don't get why you think I would."

"I didn't. I just, I don't know… I just don't think you realize how often you touch me."

Lanie was stunned. "If I've been overstepping, invading your personal space…"

"No, no, it's not that. We're mates. I love you."

Lanie's face heated at that.

"But it's different now. And, I—I just think we need to act like it."

"It's not like I want to jump your bones." *At least not entirely.* "You and Gemma are a couple now. I get it. And I respect it." Lanie huffed out an exasperated breath. "What are you thinking?"

"I don't know!" A gust of wind pushed a lock of his ridiculously gelled hair and flopped it over his forehead, like a South Asian Clark Kent. Lanie balled her hand into a fist to stop herself from pushing it back for him. "I just don't want it to be weird between us."

"Ugh, Jonah! Then why'd you have to make it weird?" Lanie shook her head, disgusted with herself and him. "I'm supposed to be helping you with the suit but now I just want to go home." She could feel the effects of the wine beginning to dissipate, her previous buoyancy abandoning her.

"C'mon, Lanie, I said I'm sorry. I panicked. I thought—"

"That I was going to grab the crotch of *my cousin's fiancé* in public?"

He frowned at that. "I swear, it was just a flinch, Lanie. That's all."

They had always been *them.* Jonah and Lanie. Two peas in a pod. She'd never thought about how much they touched each other or talked to each other or knew about each other. Ever since they were kids, their relationship had always felt appropriate for them. Now she didn't know. Was this what their friendship had to become? Was this their new normal? If so, she'd better start getting used to it.

"Well, I can't believe I have to say this out loud." She counterfeited a believable façade of calm. She hoped Narcisa would be proud of her. "But I respect your autonomy *and* I'm happy for you guys."

"Really?"

"A hundred, thousand percent," she said, trying to convince them both. "I'm helping you two, aren't I?"

And that was it. If this wasn't enough, what would be?

He shrugged. "This is difficult for me too, Mel. Everything's so new, so different now. Between us, with Gem." He sighed. "I think I'm still figuring it all out. Trying to be mindful of Gem's feelings...and yours."

"Me too, Stupid." Lanie took a cleansing breath, not quite believing he gave a shit how she felt.

"Can we go back in now?" he asked hopefully, shivering. "Gem will kill me if I mess this fitting up."

"Yeah, I bet. Since she's apparently dressing you now."

He paused, holding the door open for her. His shoulders drooped. "Lanie."

"What? I'm kidding!" She threw up her hands defensively. "Geez."

"No, you're not," he said but smiled, following her back inside.

fifteen

Lanie

■ 3-OCT ■ Trans-Continental Airways ■ Flight: 278 ■
LHR-London, Heathrow ► JFK-John F. Kennedy Int'l Airport
Seat Assignment: 32A

Ever since Lanie left her graduate program at Empire University and started working there instead, her boss, the chair of the Psychology Department, had been a cantankerous, pompous know-it-all. Five years later, he was still pompous but now he was *her* cantankerous know-it-all. And over nearly two years of everyone working primarily from home, he had become her ridiculously understanding and lenient, pompous, know-it-all boss. His remote work policy was as long as the work got done he didn't particularly care where anyone worked from. Though he liked when you were in for you to be *in*, present and accounted for. So, Lanie made a habit of eating lunch at her desk. Still, occasionally, he did surprise her.

"It's a beautiful day out, Melanie. What are you doing inside?"

She shook her head. "Just being my dutiful self." She gave him a quick salute. "After all those months apart, I thought you'd want to see my pretty face. No?" She batted her eyelashes exaggeratedly.

"Sure, sure, very good. Anyway, I'm off to lunch with Dean Michaels, before my seminar. You want anything while I'm out?"

She shook her head.

"By the way, did you get the application, from Dr. Markham at Berkeley? I had him resend it to your house. You should have received it by now." He raised an eyebrow at her.

Ever since a merit-based raise had necessitated he take a gander at her personnel file, Professor Skinner wouldn't let this subject drop. She didn't know why the old man cared so much. It was like now that he knew she had three-fifths of a doctorate, he was personally invested.

"Yep."

"And you're giving it some thought?"

"Not really," she joked. "I'm content in this department. Taking care of you lot."

"Nice try." The older man smiled. "You're hiding out here. I want you to start thinking about school again. Got it?"

"I swear you and Narcisa are in cahoots," Lanie said, pointing her pen at him, squinting. Narcisa and her wife, Isis, were professors in his department. "But yes, Dr. Skinner, I got it."

And I have no intention of doing anything with it. She'd learned her lesson already. They'd made sure she learned it.

"I won't pretend Dr. Escolástico and I haven't discussed you and your future once or twice," he admitted. "And we agree. You need to move on. You need to spread your wings."

"Yup," she said again.

"I see you nodding but I feel like it's going in one ear and coming out the other." Professor Skinner shook his head.

"I'm trying to clear everything off my desk and get the filing done while I'm in this week."

"Suit yourself. Off to England shortly again, then?"

"Yes, I'm checking in on my grandmother." When he nodded, she continued, "Then I'm helping look for wedding venues with my cousin. But I've rebooked all our meetings so we can see each other virtually—noting the time difference, so don't worry."

"I'm not," he replied and she could tell it was the truth.

"Dr. Skinner, I appreciate you understanding…this is certainly a unique situation."

"No more unique than the past few years." Her boss waved his hand like the accommodation he was making for her was no big deal. "But it only proves my point that you should enjoy the nice weather while we have it," he said as he headed out the door. "Outside, Melanie. That's an order."

"Sure thing," Lanie said, settling further into her seat. She had too many things to catch up on to waste time outside. The phone rang and she waited for Professor Skinner to be fully out of earshot before she picked it up, not wanting to draw him back in for a second lecture. "Office of the Chair. How may I help you?"

"I found you." The voice was smooth and deep like it was dipped in dark chocolate but the sentiment was terrifying.

"Excuse me?" Lanie applied her toughest hard-ass New Yorker accent, conveying to the person on the other end that this was a business phone on which only business would be discussed. She had no time for mouth breathers and wasn't about to be on an episode of those true crime shows her mom liked so much. "This is the Psychology Department. Now, how may I help you?"

The person on the other line cleared their throat audibly. "L-Lanie?"

No one at work called her Lanie.

"Yes?" Despite that, she didn't relent or crack. "Who is this?"

"Ridley."

Oh, shit.

Lanie slapped a hand across her mouth. Sure, they'd been

texting off and on for about three weeks now, but she'd forgotten what he sounded like…and what that voice was liable to do to her upon hearing it. Thank God. She couldn't imagine listening to that voice for three weeks straight without her panties spontaneously combusting.

"Ridley?" She was a little shell-shocked.

"Yes, sorry. I thought it would be a nice surprise to call your work number. Don't ask me why. I wanted to let you know I was in town."

He'd said he'd be there later in the week but Lanie had relegated thoughts of him to the section of her brain designated for all things tentative—and to put it bluntly, unlikely. Like, the very idea of a hot doctor from the UK that she met and texted back and forth with a couple times wanting to see her again. Yet, here he was.

"Something came up at home that I have to be back for. So, this is a quick forty-eight hours in town and I'll be gone by Thursday night. I wanted to let you know because, um…" Lanie could hear a breathlessness, as if he were exerting himself. "I'm worried we're going to miss each other."

Lanie's short-lived surprise curdled into disappointment. "Oh no, I wanted you to see it before it got too cold."

"See what?"

She could hear a car door close amid the traffic noise outside. "The Wonder Wheel?" She winced, awaiting his response.

Ridley sighed heavily. "You're still trying to convert me into a Ferris wheel enthusiast? Even though you know I don't love heights?"

She chuckled at his impatience. She'd forgotten how soothing the cadence of his voice was and how it entered her eardrums, flowing directly into her nervous system. He had the kind of voice that could tuck her into bed at night. Lanie fought her own sigh, just listening.

"There are other things there. Like the Cyclone and the

Thunderbolt roller coasters, the boardwalk, the ocean. There's a Halloween Harvest with pumpkins. Plus, Nathan's. I was planning a no-expenses-spared outing. Dinner included. Really do it up!" She laughed.

"Hot dogs, huh?"

She was pleased to hear him finally laughing too. "*Uh...*as many as you wanted."

"Wow, you were really planning to spoil me."

"I'm trying to put our best foot forward."

"Well, you're certainly doing it with that kind of itinerary."

Lanie kept the smile off her face as one of the professors passed by. She lowered her voice. "I try."

On the line, she could hear Ridley negotiating things with a cabdriver. "Sixty-eighth and First."

Straight to the hospital. He wasn't even dropping off his luggage at the hotel. And so close, she contended with a twinge of inexplicable disappointment.

"You sound super busy, let me let you go," she said, fully aware that he'd called her.

"No, that's why I'm calling. Since I'm going to be east today instead of Uptown, I thought I'd swing by my office for an hour or two, then come get you for a long lunch. I just figured out that my office on the East Campus is literally four blocks away. Did you know that?"

Yes. "Really?" Lanie feigned surprise.

"So, what do you say? Lunch at two?"

"Can we make it one?" Lanie thought about when her boss would be back. *But he did tell me to go out, didn't he?*

"One thirty?"

Lanie rolled her eyes at this horse-trading. "Okay, but then you'll get a half hour less of my delightful company."

"How will I manage to persevere?" As usual, his delivery was as dry as the Mojave.

sixteen

Lanie

Lanie left the chair's office with two sandwiches, chips and soda from the dining hall tucked into her small tote and set off at a quarter after one. To her surprise, Ridley was standing at the massive brick archway and black wrought iron gates at the entrance to her university when she got there.

"Hey!" she said. "How are you already here?"

As she approached, Ridley's face brightened without actually smiling. He pushed his glasses further up the bridge of his nose like he wanted a better look at her. "I think even as I said it, I didn't realize how close we were to each other." He surprised her by leaning in with a hand to her waist, giving her a peck on the cheek.

"Y-yeah," she stammered, unnerved by his sudden closeness. "W-we're practically on the same campus."

"And it's beautiful! It's a real shame I'm not on this side of Manhattan more often."

The tiny arboreal campus was the first location of the original liberal arts school that became her university and it remained tucked into a tranquil, if forgotten, little nook between the affluent old-money town houses of the Upper East Side and the East River. Lanie loved it because it reminded her of how much she enjoyed the hidden-in-plain-sight, *Secret Garden*–esque nature of their "main" campus. In truth, given her less than ideal experience in its halls of academe, she'd have quit years ago if not for the lush, idyllic grounds, her family of coworkers and the general kinetic bustle of student life.

"Can I…?" Ridley held his hand out and it took a moment before Lanie realized what he wanted.

Her heart gave an achingly painful thump in her chest when he didn't reach for her hand, but for her tote. After a moment of hesitation, she gave it over. His eyebrows rose and fell quickly, looking at two large soda bottles jutting out the top.

"I like Italian soda."

"Very much, apparently."

"You're usually Uptown, right?" She ignored his gentle ribbing.

"That's right. West Harlem. Lead the way, Tour Guide," he entreated her.

"It's a little walk but a good place for lunch."

Considering he had longer legs, Lanie could still have left Ridley far behind. Eventually, Lanie paused, waiting for him to catch up, then extended the crook of her elbow to him.

"Too slow for you?" He sounded amused.

"If we plan to get there and back before dark? Yes."

Ridley rewarded her with a smirk, and obligingly took her arm. She clamped down on it, tucking him into her side like walking a three-legged race, and set a brisker pace.

"You New Yorkers. It's obvious why none of you drive. You all have little motors in your backs." Ridley wasn't winded but it was clear he wasn't accustomed to her faster pace as they crossed the avenues, headed west. The further they went, the more crowded the sidewalks became with shoppers, businesspeople and, as they got closer and closer to Fifth Avenue, tourists. As they passed Madison Avenue with its high-end boutiques,

Lanie paused to look at the small cluster of bridal ateliers that lined the block.

"Window-shopping?"

Lanie came to a full stop, glancing between him and a particularly showy strapless dress with a straight neckline, crystal bodice, full skirt and a huge bow at the back. It would be ostentatious for her but exactly the kind of over-the-top style Gemma liked.

She'll be shopping for something like this very soon.

"What?" Lanie asked once she realized Ridley was waiting for an answer to some question.

"Are you getting married sometime soon?"

She supposed he was teasing but since Ridley rarely smiled, it could just as easily have been a real question. But the possibility of that felt further away than ever before. And Lanie didn't know how to feel. Like the question hit ctrl-alt-delete in her brain and she was waiting on the reboot. Lanie hated when she got like this.

"Lanie?"

"Huh?" Her eyes lost focus. He drifted into a haze in front of her. She shook her head, unable to formulate a coherent lie to change the subject.

He gestured at the dress spotlighted in the window with his chin. "Picking something for your cousin?"

"Certainly not for myself," was all she could manage, feeling slightly lightheaded.

Lanie had never been especially fragile or desperate... despite recent appearances to the contrary. But try as she might, she couldn't shake him—the only person she'd ever truly been in love with her whole life: *Jonah. And now he's marrying my cousin Gem.*

She couldn't escape the high-velocity impact of that reality, and it never failed to bowl her over. Shock her into a complete mental shutdown. She was supposed to be over this. She'd promised her grandmother and her mother and Narcisa she would be.

"I'm so sorry," he said.

Lanie blinked. Ridley was looking down at her and holding her arm tightly now instead of vice versa. He was holding her steady, like she was about to pass out. She tried to shake him free but found her legs were a little wobbly.

"For what?" Since she was the one about to wither from embarrassment.

"I'm sorry about your friend and your cousin."

Oh. My. God. "How much of that did I say out loud?"

"Did you not mean to say any of it?"

"No, I didn't." She looked back up at the dress in the window until Ridley distracted her.

"Oh. Well, don't worry," he cut into her thoughts. "I'm like a vault. Your secrets are safe with me."

Lanie was still slightly dazed so she only understood every other word. Revealing her reluctance to attend the engagement party on that first plane ride to London was one thing. Admitting it was because she was in love with the groom once upon a time was completely different, a level of friendship Lanie wasn't sure she'd reached with Ridley yet.

Ridley adjusted his grip on her arm, pulling her gently from the bridal shop window. Lanie didn't resist and realized then she couldn't have even if she wanted to.

seventeen

Ridley

They made the short walk in silence and Ridley correctly guessed that they were headed to Central Park as they walked along Fifth Avenue to the southeast side entrance across from the Plaza Hotel. They followed the small sign pointing toward a zoo.

Only her breathing at his side and the warmth of her body slightly leaned into his arm reminded him he wasn't alone. She hadn't told him about her feelings for her cousin's fiancé before but it hadn't been hard to glean. When they discussed it, she'd been so adamant about the couple's incompatibility that even he began to suspect there was more to it than she'd said.

Ridley gave her a small smile as soon as he saw the ironwork ivy trellises and granite stone pillars. But she patted the arm locked with hers as a gentle signal to stop before they got there. Instead, they settled on one of the benches along the promenade leading to the zoo's entrance.

"How are you feeling?" He examined her face.

Her eyes focused on him as she returned from wherever she'd retreated to.

"I'm sorry," she said, covering her mouth belatedly, horrified.

He shook his head. "It takes a level of intimacy to have confided what you did. Deliberately or not."

She gave him a weak smile for that.

"You're fine," he said. Bea sometimes got overwhelmed too, so Ridley recognized the signs. But he didn't say that because Lanie didn't take it well the last time he'd mentioned Bea. Instead, he handed her the tote and she pulled their sandwiches from it.

"I've got roast beef and grilled chicken." She held both of them out to him and he tapped the chicken.

Lanie appeared more present, but the strained silence remained. Ridley knew the longer it continued the more difficult it would be to salvage their limited time together. He reached for lighter ground. "So, how about those Knicks?"

She snorted. "Pass."

"Whew," he joked, making a show of wiping his brow. "What about the Mets, Nets, Jets? Any opinions?"

"The Mets with their current roster won't make it to the postseason next year, not that I care. I'm a Bronxite, so rooting for them would be heresy," she said, between chews of her sandwich. "Now, the Nets have no rotation behind their current starting center, which is gonna put them in a tough spot come playoff time."

His mouth was agog before the corners rose slightly.

"And the Jets...well, the Jets. What can I say? They are a team of well-paid professional athletes, allegedly."

When she came back, she did it with a vengeance, apparently. He stared.

"What?"

"So, you're not a fan of sports, is what I'm hearing you say," he deadpanned.

"Not really, but my dad was," Lanie admitted. "He took me to assorted games as a kid. For his visitation, it was always a game and dinner. Although we weren't allowed to eat anything at the stadium, only real restaurants like 'civilized people.'" She rose rather abruptly to throw their refuse away.

Ridley scrambled to catch up with her just as she made it to the entrance of the zoo.

"I lost most of my enthusiasm for it all when I realized it was more about him seeing a game and having a nice meal than about me. Haven't had any real love for any of it since then but I learned a lot."

Her father sounded like a dirtbag. Men like him gave Ridley agita. "Yeah, I have a love-hate thing with basketball myself," he agreed, deciding not to pry further. He certainly didn't want to discuss his college years spent hustling up and down a basketball court for scholarship money. Ridley checked his watch and blew out a breath. *Damn.* "Unfortunately, this is going to have to be a whistle-stop tour of the zoo. I have a meeting at three."

"Hold up, I said let's go earlier and you're the one who wanted it later."

He straightened his glasses, eyebrows rising. *Is she angry about that?* "True, so I shuffled things a bit when it didn't work for you."

Lanie's face did a peculiar thing he couldn't read. Then she cleared her throat, but still sounded pitchy. "Oh yeah? Good, 'cuz I'm still expecting to see you in London whether or not you cancel on me here."

"As I fully expected."

After a moment of unseemly haggling—*as if I'd ever allow her to go pay for the tickets when she paid for the lunch I'd invited her to*—they walked briskly through the exhibits of the park.

"How about you? Do you have a favorite sport?" Lanie asked, smiling as they approached the Polar Circle, the penguin and harbor seal enclosure.

"Nope, but I do like football... I mean soccer. My wife, Thyra, and her family are insane Arsenal fans and I inherited it."

Lanie watched him intently like what he said was riveting. It was a little unnerving when she got intense like that. He nearly laughed at himself. According to Thyra and Dash, that would be a bit like the pot calling the kettle black.

"I get it," she replied a second later, breaking into a laugh that he'd come to enjoy immensely. "My cousin is a huge Man U fan while her twin is all about Real Madrid. I stay out of it."

His eyebrows rose. "Champions League must be really fun in their house." He got it. The Baker-Smythes tolerated little dissent in their ranks. It was Arsenal or finding a new place to live.

"Oh yeah… 'And that's why I killed them both, Your Honor,'" Lanie quipped.

She was so funny. But it was often so wry he could understand if people didn't always get her.

She smiled at him, looking pleased, although he had no idea what he'd done. Then her wide eyes moved from his face to the harbor seals splashing and slipping in and out of the water behind the glass

A short while later, he checked his watch. *Shit*, the time was flying and he couldn't keep Dr. Haim, the medical director, waiting. He'd spent over a month trying to get on his schedule only to be told it was this afternoon or not for another five weeks.

"I think I gotta go."

Lanie looked lost in delight, smiling at the seals' antics.

"Lanie?"

"Yeah?" she said absently as if she didn't want to tear her eyes away.

Her joy was enchanting. He found her enthusiasm for small things diverting. He really hated having to leave now. "As much as I love the penguins and seals, we gotta cut this short."

She checked her phone and grimaced. "Oh, okay. Let's go."

They made it back much faster this time. At the corner of First Avenue and Sixty-ninth Street, where their paths diverged, they waited for the light to change. He groaned inwardly. Hanging out with her was quickly becoming something he looked forward to. Ridley supposed he should actually say that.

"Sorry, I wish I had more time," he said instead.

Lanie swiped at the air, as if brushing the words off. "It wasn't as fabulous as Coney Island would've been but I'm sure your daughter will get a kick out of you telling her about this." Lanie pulled out a fuzzy toy from her tote. It was an emperor penguin. She handed it to him as he stood stunned.

"Wha—? Where'd you find the time to grab this?" He was genuinely pleased; Bea would love it.

She shrugged. "When you were buying the tickets, I got it from the kiosk. I thought you might like it. Emperor penguin fathers look after the eggs after the mothers have to leave to forage. They sleep standing up to keep their eggs warm for more than two months until they hatch in the spring. They go one hundred and twenty-five days without food for their chicks."

Ridley turned the little bird toy over in his hands. Most of the time, being Bea's father was gift enough but every once in a while it felt good to be seen. Even by a relative stranger with a gift intended for his daughter.

"If you don't like it, I can take it back?" she said quickly, as if she was waiting for him to shove the bird back at her.

"Thank you." He squeezed it between his hands like an oversized stress ball, as he tried desperately to marshal his feelings over this small but potent gift.

This woman is something else.

"This is great." He swallowed and finally looked up at her when he was certain she wouldn't see the moist sheen irritating his eyes behind his glasses. "This was a, uh, fun little lunch date."

"We got off to a rocky start there but ultimately it was my pleasure," Lanie joked.

"Next time you come to London, I promise I'll do you one better."

"*Do* me?" Lanie gave a weird cough-laugh hybrid, making an odd, almost giddy noise that made him wonder what he'd said, before answering, "I—I mean, I'll expect you to."

He checked his watch using the same hand that tightly held the penguin. "Gotta run."

It was hard to leave.

Ridley touched her lightly as he had before, turning into her and leaning in to give her a kiss on the cheek. But Lanie reached up for a hug then, turning her face into his too. She sucked in a startled breath when his lips accidentally brushed the corner of her mouth. He pulled back in surprise, looking into her eyes and giving a faintly embarrassed little laugh, which she matched, at their mistake.

But wow. What a mistake.

It had been so long since his mouth had been on someone else's and definitely since the last time he'd felt the same voltaic charge he felt now. Almost without his consent Ridley's hand, that had been very barely touching her waist, pulled her closer. Staring into his eyes, Lanie leaned in too and his heart thudded wildly.

Was he really about to do this? Ridley looked from her ridiculously plush and pouty lips to her bright golden eyes. Then she licked those lips.

That's it! Fuck it. Yes, I am.

Insensible to the broad daylight and the very busy, very public street, he slowly placed his mouth over Lanie's. She tasted deliciously of lime Italian soda and cherry ChapStick. But with a herculean effort on his part, the kiss remained just this side of chaste. Just his mouth on hers, his lips capturing hers.

"Get a room!" A cabbie hanging a right around that corner honked, shattering the moment.

Though it felt as if the world quieted for a time, Ridley was sure it had only lasted seconds, because he nearly groaned with need when Lanie pulled back a moment before their tongues touched, startled by the noise.

"Shit," he whispered as they parted, scanning her face as if he didn't know how they'd ended up here.

Lanie pulled back further, shaky fingers pressed to her reddened lips.

Shit. Shit. *Shit!*

They stood there, momentarily stunned. He didn't know who would apologize or if anyone should.

Finally, she spoke. "Fly safe."

Okay then.

"See you soon," he said because he could think of nothing besides her mouth.

My God.

He turned and left, walking quickly down the street.

eighteen

RIDLEY:

Lanie, you up?

RIDLEY:

Can we talk?

LANIE:

Yeah. Talk about what?

RIDLEY:

I know you're joking...

LANIE:

Fine. It didn't happen if
we say it didn't happen.

RIDLEY:

Is that what you want?

LANIE:

Depends

RIDLEY:

LANIE:

Whether or not saying it
happened makes this weird?

RIDLEY:

Weird?

LANIE:

Like between us.

RIDLEY:

LANIE:

Right! It was just something we did.

RIDLEY:

Our version of a secret handshake.

LANIE:

LOL! Seriously?

RIDLEY:

No not seriously

LANIE:

How about an accident
that made our lips collide?

RIDLEY:

Whatever helps us sleep at night

LANIE:

Excuse you, it's only 10pm for me.
If anyone is losing sleep thinking of
my luscious lips on theirs, it's you

LANIE:

Ridley?

LANIE:

Oh Doctor?

LANIE:

Just kidding. Geez.
See what I'm saying? Weird.

RIDLEY:

Not weird. Sorry. I thought I heard
something. Probably just the foxes.
But you're good then? You don't
feel like I overstepped?

LANIE:

What? Is that what you're up late worried about?

RIDLEY:

Maybe.

LANIE:

No! We kissed each other. It was an accident, sure.
We got carried away. But we're two adult people who

don't need to imbue it with any more meaning than that.
Okay?

RIDLEY:

A momentary lapse?

LANIE:
Sure. Now hold on.
Did you just say foxes?

RIDLEY:

It's not nearly as cute as it sounds.

nineteen

Lanie

■ 18-OCT ■ Trans-Continental Airways ■ Flight: 79 ■

LHR-London, Heathrow ▶ JFK-John F. Kennedy Int'l Airport

Seat Assignment: **24J**

Lanie moved through the security checkpoint like a zombie. She was so tired and for the first time in forever she was ready to go home. Spending a long weekend running around London used to be her idea of a good time…in her twenties. She was not twenty anymore, she lamented. Yet despite being bone-tired, she didn't realize quite how close she'd been to collapse. Not just mentally but physically—even the clothes she wore today could have spun completely around her body with her still wearing them.

Heading to the departure gate, she could feel the stress of overseeing all the little details of Gemma's wedding was taking its toll. In recent weeks, she barely thought about anything else—the perfectionist in her, a side she struggled to keep at bay, had reared its uncompromising head. If she wasn't careful, she would barely even take the time to feed herself. In fact, she'd forgotten to eat today, she realized as her stomach growled loudly. It would never be clearer than it was at that moment that she needed to go home. With a convenience store sandwich in hand, she arrived at her departure gate, as usual relieved to be the first one there. She was alone.

Well, not totally alone, it appeared. There was someone else there sitting right by the gate. Almost directly in front of the customer service desk.

Lanie stopped midstride, dumbstruck.

She didn't know how long she stood on the concourse as people walked past, in absolute shock. Now that she was closer, the person was wholly visible, sitting all alone with his roller bag, casually reading a paper and sipping from a paper cup. It was Ridley.

Lanie moved toward him slowly, glancing around, astonished. He was supposed to be in New York. "Ridley?"

He rested his newspaper in his lap and looked up. Pushing his tortoiseshell frames up the thick bridge of his nose, his eyes traveled up to her face like she was the one who wasn't supposed to be there. "Hey," he replied. "You okay?" There was a coffee caddy on the seat next to him with one cup, which he removed then handed to her as she nodded.

She took it, puzzled, and popped off the top to examine the contents. The heavenly scent of coffee beans, hazelnut, caramel and toffee sauce filled her nose. She took a sip. "Ooooh, and it's still kinda warm! Sorcery! Thank you." She exhaled with relief, nearly collapsing into the seat beside him. "What are you doing here?"

"I told you I was coming in this morning."

"Yes, but that was this morning." She checked her phone. "It's twelve p.m."

"Yes, well, I realized that you can get a lot of work done in the quiet of those airline club lounges."

"You got into the Trans-Continental lounge?" It said a lot

about the airline culture she'd already begun to fall into that she was a smidgen impressed by that.

"Apparently, since I flew business class today, I was eligible." He shrugged.

"Ridley, *what* are you doing here?"

"It felt like too much of a coincidence and a missed opportunity to arrive the exact same day you depart and not see you."

Okay, that is sweet. She'd dated men who'd done less. "But three hours, Ridley?"

"What's three hours between friends?" His face was still incongruously serious.

She hemmed while he continued.

"You said it was unfortunate we'd miss each other. You also said you hated being at the airport all alone with nothing to do, right?"

He hadn't told a lie yet. She nodded. In all their back-and-forth texting, she may have possibly said a lot of those things.

"Seriously, Ridley, aren't you tired? Don't you need to get home to your daughter?"

He frowned and pulled back slightly. Lanie hadn't realized until then that they'd slowly begun leaning toward one another, their shoulders nearly touching. She immediately regretted saying anything, wishing she could coax him and his delicious bergamot-and-vetiver scent closer again.

He shook his head. "She has athletics all afternoon."

Lanie wasn't sure she understood what that meant.

His eyes roamed her face. "Track and field?"

Lanie made a small O shape with her mouth.

"So, she won't be home until six-ish," he continued, watching her face as if it could tell him things her mouth wouldn't. And reminding her of the last time he'd looked at her like that. Right before he kissed her.

"A-and your work?"

"Lanie." One eyebrow rose behind his glasses. "Do you want

me to go? Because just saying so would probably be faster than running down each supposed item on my daily schedule."

Lanie was momentarily speechless. Ever so slightly magnified by the strength of his lenses, in the light cast from the giant window right next to them, she could see all the whorls and swirls of his dark brown irises. The rich cognac brown of his eyes pulled her in like a sci-fi tractor beam.

"Lanie?"

"N–no," Lanie backtracked when she could finally speak again. "No. I'm sorry. I just assumed you'd have better things to do than sit in the airport on the off chance you'd run into me."

"Run into you?" His eyes narrowed, examining her face again as if he was trying to decipher something. "I didn't run into you. I waited for you."

At those words, Lanie's heart took off like one of those out-of-control hansom cabs that circled Central Park, galloping wildly like a spooked horse.

He didn't mean it like that, he didn't mean it like that. He did not mean it like that, Melanie!

"You gave me your flight info, remember?" His delivery was deadpan as usual. But then he sat up straighter. "Wait, I just heard myself say that. Was that creepy? It sounded creepy. Oh my God." Ridley put a hand to his face, like this was really just dawning on him.

She barked out an awkward laugh, and sniffled, nodding. "I mean…"

"I just thought it would be nice. You know? I know how much I hate waiting in the airport too. I miss the days when you could sit at the gate with people to see them off. Are you too young to remember back then? Anyway, I thought since I was coming and you were going—"

"Ridley." Lanie chuckled, putting a hand on his arm. "It's okay. I appreciate it. This was a really cool thing to do."

He appeared barely placated by her reassurance. His eyes

closed and his face pinched together. "This is really weird, isn't it? Or inappropriate?"

"For real." She sighed. "This was a very nice stalker-y thing to do." She glanced over at Ridley and from his very somber face she could tell he was taking her very seriously. She laughed to lighten his mood.

"Ridley." She sighed again, realizing this wasn't the time to toy with him. It was important. "Maybe once upon a time you might have been doing the most, but nowadays, no. I have good friends I met on Discord and on online MPGs that I've never even seen in person before. So, we're cool."

"Once upon a time? Is that a dig at my age? I am a millennial too, you know."

Lanie nearly choked with laughter. "You thought I was too young to have waited at the gate with other well-wishers! But I suppose I should expect that from an *elder millennial*."

"Watch it now." Ridley chuckled. Lanie paused to appreciate this rare sign of amusement from him.

His laughter petered out quickly and Lanie already missed it. His voice was a deep baritone and his laughter was like a slide into a silken bath of warmth.

"So, what's wrong?" He frowned.

Lanie shook her head. "Nothing."

"Don't be difficult. What's wrong?"

She panicked. "It would take too long to explain."

Ridley checked his watch. "We have time."

"You don't want to hear this."

"As you just mentioned, I stayed a whole three extra hours in this airport like a weirdo just to say what's up." He wrinkled his nose. "So, I think I do."

Lanie launched in. "Okay…um, I guess it's this wedding. And Gemma's demands. They're getting ridiculous now. *And*, she's changed the wedding date to Valentine's Day but won't explain why."

"Not romance?"

"Do you know how much 'romance' costs on Valentine's Day? It's like they see the suckers coming."

Ridley snorted.

"So, I'm wrangling the details of this new development, plus I'm securing hotel rooms, as well as finding hairstylists and makeup artists for everyone—because naturally we're gonna need two since there's the morning mass and then the evening reception. With outfit changes. Oh, and did I mention there's a luncheon in between? At a venue *I* have to find? Because apparently Gemma's too stressed with her night classes and Jonah's always working, so neither of them can plan their own wedding!"

Ridley clicked his teeth. "Sucks. And that's why my wife and I eloped. Just me, her and the group of friends that could find a cheap ticket for the weekend to Mallorca."

"That's a destination wedding, not an elopement."

Ridley opened his mouth to retort as his phone buzzed. Lanie was disappointed when it looked like he was going to pick it up, but instead Ridley returned the phone to his pocket.

"Po-ta-to, po-tat-o." He shrugged. "Point is, it was done on a week's notice and a shoestring budget and our plane tickets and accommodations were the most expensive part." He shook his head. "A big thing is masochistic. Or in your case, sadistic... no matter how much I benefit from it."

"My status as my cousin's beck-and-call girl pleases you?"

"Anything that keeps you coming back pleases me."

Lanie paused. Quite possibly the planet Earth paused, Lanie wasn't sure.

He cleared his throat, as if he'd just heard what he'd said. "I mean, it's been fun to keep crossing paths...right?"

She dared herself to touch him, grabbing his hand that rested on his thigh and squeezing it. "Yes. This was very cool, Ridley. You don't understand how much it means to me that you waited." She released her grip just as his thumb glided over her fingers. Startled by the realization that his wedding ring was again gone, she slipped her hand away. Lanie glanced at the time on her cell phone and then up into his eyes. "Look at that: an hour gone. That flew by."

"Not bad. See, waiting is better with company."

"Lots of things are better with company." Suddenly shy, Lanie cast her eyes down. But when she brought them back to him after a noticeable silence, Ridley was just smiling at her.

A real honest-to-God smile. An amazingly warm, ear-to-ear smile from a mouth full of beautifully straight, Colgate-white teeth.

Lanie winced internally at the sight as her heart sank. She had a crush on Ridley.

twenty

Ridley

Ridley was at the door as soon as he heard Bea's key in the lock, opening it before Gavin had the opportunity to run away.

"Dad," Bea said brightly, rising to her toes to kiss Ridley on the cheek. "Welcome back!"

"Thank you, Bean," Ridley said, barely able to pull his eyes away from Gavin long enough to acknowledge her.

"Uh, okay," Gavin signed off, flustered, throwing a three-fingered salute at Bea. "This was fun, Trixie."

Ridley blinked. "Trixie? Who's Trixie?"

Both Bea and Gavin paused as if caught red-handed.

"Well, uh," Gavin started but Ridley turned to Bea standing next to him in the doorway.

"Gavin asked what he could call me and I told him 'Trixie.'"

"Since when? Who calls you Trixie?" Ridley asked with irritation.

"I know but—"

"No one calls you Trixie."

"I asked her if I could call her something no one else calls her," Gavin said, straightening to his full height.

Ridley's eyebrow rose. Gavin had an inch or two on him

but he had at least forty pounds of muscle on Gavin. "Bea, hon, can I have a moment to talk with Gavin alone?"

"Dad." Bea's voice had a shade of warning in it.

"Go on. I'm sure you weren't doing any homework while you were out. Head on upstairs." Ridley matched her tone and she understood it was an order, not a request.

Bea sighed and headed toward the stairs. "'Night, Gavin, thanks."

"'Night, Trix." Gavin waved and Bea waved back.

Ridley glared at the man. He waited until he could tell Bea was on the landing of the upper floor before starting.

"Look—" Gavin tried to preempt him.

In a single word, there went all the cool and calm he thought he was going to exhibit when they finally arrived. *Late! On top of everything else.*

"No, *you* look," Ridley growled in the lowest registers of his voice, but still clear enough for Gavin to hear from a foot away. "You call me before you even *think* about seeing my daughter, you understand? You do not come within fifty meters of her without clearing it with me."

Gavin's eyes widened, genuinely surprised. "Mate—"

"You and I know I'm not your fuckin' mate. You let me know beforehand if you want to have contact with Bea. We agreed to that. Your solicitors agreed to that."

"Yes, although in my defense, I did try to call you this morning." Gavin held his palms up in surrender like Ridley was a volatile substance he was shielding himself from. "Your phone kept going to voicemail."

Ridley paused for a second, the glacier of ice-cold anger that had formed in his chest cracking. "I didn't hear any messages from you."

"Then I called your office. Your assistant, Therese, said you were due in from New York by the late morning. So, I called again later."

Ridley gritted his teeth, remembering the call from Gavin he ignored while he and Lanie were talking about her cousin's wedding.

"At that point, I just decided to meet you there and ask. I came early but you didn't show up." Gavin let the unspoken accusation sit there between them.

"Oh." Ridley felt about a foot tall.

"Aronsen, mate—" Gavin self-corrected. "Ah, Aronsen. I had no intention of taking Bea anywhere today. The opportunity just presented itself. Frankly, I'd think you'd be glad someone was there for her. She did really well. Third place overall."

Ridley hadn't thought he could feel lower, and yet there it was, a subbasement of self-loathing, courtesy of Gavin Dorrence. The fight went out of him.

"I am." He was certain he'd choke on the next few words but they came out surprisingly unencumbered. "Thank you."

"It was no problem. When I'm here, I'd love to be another person in Bea's phone tree."

"Phone tree?"

"Of emergency contacts. People she can call if she needs help."

Ridley's heart skipped a beat. He nearly clutched his chest those words frightened him so much. "I, um…" The last time Ridley could recall being this tongue-tied was when he asked Thyra to marry him.

"Just think about it. If I'm around I want Trix—I mean, Bea—to feel like she can call on me."

Ridley laughed humorlessly. "When you're around. You heard yourself, right?"

"That's rather unfair, Aronsen, when you're frequently on a different continent yourself."

"Yes, well." Ridley didn't need a reminder of his hypocrisy. "Her name is Beatrix or Bea. No one calls her 'Trixie.'" The words were snide and filled with the irritation Ridley really felt for himself. "And you won't be the first. Understand?"

Gavin fell back a step on the front stairs, thrown by the abrupt subject change. "Well, she's thirteen years old, I think she can make up her own mind. She told me Trixie—"

"She's fourteen."

"What?"

"She. Is. Fourteen. Her birthday was last month. You forgot those ridiculous London Eye tickets already?"

Gavin reddened. "She didn't like them?"

At Gavin's demoralized expression, Ridley was unexpectedly hit with a pang of remorse. He knew what it was to have no idea what a teen girl thinks is cool. He shook his head. "You want them back?" Ridley offered. "Maybe you could trade them in for concert tickets? She's really into BLACKPINK right now."

"BLACKPINK…so she does like K-pop?" Gavin nodded as if making a mental note. "Thanks. I'll see what my assistant can do."

Ridley bit his tongue…it was not his job to teach Gavin how to be a better father. In fact, as Ridley knew, when he let himself acknowledge it, it was against his best interests.

"I'm really sorry about today," Gavin offered, more contrite than Ridley was accustomed to. "It was a miscommunication. Won't happen again."

"We'll both work on that," Ridley conceded.

Gavin held out his hand but Ridley just looked at it. "Germs," Ridley said after searching for an excuse. "Nothing personal."

"Right," Gavin replied, sticking the hand in his pocket. "I'll go now. 'Night."

"'Night." Ridley watched Gavin retreat down the walkway toward the small silver McLaren parked on the street.

"Oh yes, Aronsen," Gavin called as Ridley was beginning to close the door. "Bea and I were talking and I want to extend an invitation for you to join us in Colorado for Christmas."

If Ridley had been given dozens of guesses for what Gavin was going to say, none of them would've been that. "Uhhh…"

"Just think about it for now. I know Bea would really love it if you could come. And we have more than enough space."

Ridley nodded as if he would actually consider it. "Gavin!" he called out a moment later, rolling his eyes as Gavin lifted open the butterfly door on the ridiculously expensive car. "What about the Eye tickets?" A whole pod could not have been cheap.

Gavin shrugged, stepping into the McLaren. "Keep them. You must know someone who'd enjoy it."

Ridley had just reached the point where the TV was watching him instead of the other way around when he heard the refrigerator open and close. His eyes popped open immediately.

He sat up and looked over the back of the living room couch at Bea puttering around in the kitchen in her pajamas. He checked the time on his phone. After an initial message that read RU up? that received no response, Lanie had sent him a series of GIFs of sleeping animals, cartoons and children.

"It's late."

"Dad, we're out of Wotsits," Bea said, like they were already in the middle of a conversation. Coming around their large L-shaped couch, she collapsed heavily into it. Her fist contained a handful of gummy bears.

"Last I looked, in the larder there was a whole variety pack of crisps."

"Yeah, because you keep getting the variety pack when I only like the cheese puffs."

"Since when?" Ridley muted the television.

She gave him that incredulous look teenagers were experts at that wondered, nearly aloud, whether adults held even a single coherent thought in their minds ever. "Since always."

"No," he insisted. "We've always gotten the variety pack.

You used to eat the other ones too." He struggled for the type since that brand featured dozens of styles and flavors. "What about the…the prawn cocktail?"

"Yeah, when I was ten."

Ridley gave an amused snort. *So the other day.* He almost said it out loud but caught himself, well aware of how important it was to Bea to feel far removed from age ten Bea. To feel like a proper teenager.

"Well, I only like the salt and vinegars," he laughed. "So, someone must have been eating the res—" Ridley ran out of steam hearing his own words. Beside him Bea was completely silent, examining the colorful gummy bears in her palm.

Thyra's name was not forbidden in the house. Pictures and totems of her and the three of them as a family covered many walls and most of the flat surfaces around them. Every door and table, wall and window was infused with Thyra's energy and spirit. Little had even moved since her passing—less because Ridley kept the place like a shrine to her, and more because Thyra had already found the perfect place for everything and Ridley found it difficult to improve upon perfection. Still, the subject of Thyra—and more specifically, the agonizing absence of her—was something of a third rail in the house, zapping all who went near it.

"I'll talk to Mrs. Handa," Ridley said quietly, referring to their longtime housekeeper.

In the silence, vague yips from the fox den at the back wall of the garden could be heard.

"Oh, the Tods are up for the night," Ridley announced to which Bea rolled her eyes.

"Are you ever going to call someone?"

"Why? Those foxes aren't hurting anyone."

"They dig up Mum's plant beds."

"They did until we erected that little fence. Now we're cool."

Bea chuckled, like her father was decidedly *not* cool. "You built it."

"You helped…a little."

"Foxes need to be controlled. They carry roundworm."

He nodded. "Yes, I know."

Bea sighed. "But Mum said you'd never do it."

"I know that too." Ridley echoed Bea's sigh in reply.

Cats carried roundworm too, yet Thyra had no problem letting Bea near her parents' indoor-outdoor orange tabby, Sweetie Simpkins.

"Alright, fine. If Mr. Tod and his family are really cutting into your quality of life, I'll call pest control in the morning."

Bea popped the last gummy bear into her mouth and shifted closer to him. Ridley opened the afghan he'd had laid across his knees and Bea snuggled into his side.

"You don't have to do that, Dad. Honestly, they upset Mum more than me. It was her tomatoes, carrots and strawberries—"

"What are you, rubbing it in? I said, I'd call." Ridley laughed, pushing some of Bea's frizzy hair off his shoulder so he could see her face resting there.

"Maybe a little bit." She smiled mischievously, holding up a tiny space between her thumb and index finger.

Ridley pinched her nose between the knuckles of his index and middle fingers.

"Dad!" Bea screeched, swatting at his hand.

He stopped after a minute of rough-and-tumble where Bea tried to free herself and then there was silence between them. Only Bea's labored breathing sounded in the room. But after a moment, Ridley realized her shoulders were shaking. She was crying.

"Bean?" He sat up from his semi-reclined position across the couch, causing her to sit straighter beside him. "What's going on?"

She shook her head. "It's stupid."

"Nothing you say is stupid."

"It's awful then. I shouldn't be thinking it."

Ridley's stomach rolled. "What? You know you can tell me anything."

Fresh tears filled her eyes, coming even faster and harder than before.

"Bean? Did Gavin say something to you while you were out?" Ridley's jaw set, ready to pull on his clothes, jump in a cab and go beat Gavin's ass in his fancy fucking luxury apartment in the Shard.

"No." She sniffled, taking the tissues Ridley offered. "He was fine. Nice, even."

Ridley's mouth twitched. *Nice?*

"I loved Mum."

"I know you did, honey. You do."

"I love her," Bea corrected herself. "But…but if something happened to you…I don't know what I would do!" She broke into a fresh set of tears. "It scares me."

Ridley didn't know what to do with that. His heart soared but so did his guilt. *God.* Every time he thought there were parameters or bounds to how much he could love this kid, she'd do something or say something and he'd realize he hadn't even reached the threshold. That there were infinite expanses past which he could love her still.

"You would be taken care of. As always, you have your nan and granddad. If something had happened to me instead of Thyra, you'd still have your mom," he said through the lump forming in his throat, remembering all the moments when he'd pled for the universe to somehow take him instead of his wife. Terrified over how Bea would take being left in his care instead of her mother's. Frightened about what the world would look like with just him and Bea in it.

Bea shook her head. "No, but Mum wasn't good at stuff like this. Hugs, and tea, and snuggles when I'm sick, and MCM

Comic Con tickets, and Elephant Toothpaste. Mum didn't do that. Mum packed me off to Lyndhurst."

"We both did that."

"No, it was her school. 'Lyndhurst was some of the best years of my life,'" Bea parroted her mother's familiar line.

Ridley took a breath, trying to gather his thoughts and his excuses. In truth, despite Ridley's vehement objection, Thyra had unilaterally decided to send Bea away in the lead-up to the most serious turn in her lupus that she ultimately died from. At the time, she hadn't even told Ridley she was getting sicker, feeling weaker, as always powering through the pain and fatigue. She just decided to send Bea off to the boarding school she'd spent years at herself. It was one of the worst disagreements he'd ever had with his wife—made worse when she pulled rank and reminded him that Beatrix was "her child." It strained their relationship in a way that they never had a chance to recover from. And even now, Ridley had difficulty restraining his residual resentment toward Thyra for being forced to shoulder a portion of the blame for a decision that he wasn't a part of.

But preserving Bea's memory of Thyra is more important than pride or the correct assignment of blame. Ridley struggled to remember that himself sometimes. *Bea needs to hold on to the best memories of her mom.*

He'd decided that at Thyra's deathbed when she chose to leave Bea in Sussex rather than allow her to come home. And nothing had changed.

"Lyndhurst School is one of the best schools in Britain. And you're a legacy. Your granddad went—"

"I know." She rolled her eyes. "I know. Mum went and so it was important that I go too. All the Baker-Smythes go to Lyndhurst. Just 'cos eighty billion years ago granddad's granddad was the fourth son of a baron or something." Bea pursed her lips in distaste. "Colonizers."

Ridley stifled a snort, looking at his fawn-brown daughter

being haunted by the ghosts of the very white peerage. Particularly since he was an American and almost all of Thyra's family, besides her father, were Black people, the whole Lyndhurst School thing had seemed like class-conscious claptrap they were going to skip. Until Thyra suddenly decided not to. Still, he tried to remain respectful.

"There can be too many viewings of *Black Panther*, I'm realizing."

"Dad, be serious." Her tears had finally dried up.

"Sorry."

Ridley gave Bea a squeeze. "Well, you don't ever have to go back. I know how much you love Hillsleigh Girls' School."

"What if Gavin decided to send me back?" Bea's eyes were platter-sized and beseeching. "He went to Lyndhurst too."

In fact, it was where Gavin and Thyra first met, Ridley recalled bitterly.

"No, that's not his..." He shook his head. Yet as he spoke, what must have been swirling in Bea's head for months finally dawned on him. "Oh no, honey. I won't allow that."

"It may not be up to you."

This plainly spoken truth ran through Ridley like a sharpened blade. Sometime soon, it might not be his decision. His sigh was so deep and long Bea shifted under his arm.

"Will you consider coming to Colorado for Christmas?"

"Huh? Absolutely not," Ridley answered.

"It's important that we play nice. You said that yourself."

"I did." Ridley didn't like hearing his words turned on him.

"Maybe if you're nice to him, he'll stop taking you to court."

"Bea, he doesn't want me there. He was just being polite."

"I don't know, Dad." She pulled out of his arms to turn to him fully. "I didn't suggest it."

Ridley frowned. "You didn't?"

She shook her head. "He said he thought I'd be happier if you were there too, not just Nan and Granddad."

Gavin wants me to come? Ridley didn't know where to file that information away. "I have work."

"Dad, please?" She drew out the words to give them eight extra syllables.

"I don't think I can make it, honey." He didn't say that he wouldn't want to, even if he didn't have to work. "But I'll think about it."

Bea's looked skeptical.

"We'll see, okay?" His resolve to not go under any circumstances wavered under her pleading eyes. "Let me check my schedule. Talk with Therese." He planned to have his assistant make up a conflict if she had to.

Bea nodded hopefully. "Okay." She kissed him on the cheek as he gave her another hug.

"It's super late."

"I'm going." Bea nodded, rising from the couch. "'Night."

"'Night."

Ridley saw her up the steps before picking up his phone. It was two a.m.

He could use someone to talk to. Not about this…not necessarily. He just needed to reach out.

RIDLEY:

You up?

LANIE:

It's only 9:00.
Do I seem like somebody's grandma?

RIDLEY:

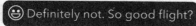 Definitely not. So good flight?

LANIE:

As well as can be expected. Seven hours in a 17 x 32 space can't be good for you.

RIDLEY:

No it's not. But you got home safely?

LANIE:

You sound like my mom. Since my responses aren't coming from the bottom of the Atlantic, the answer is yes.

RIDLEY:

So snarky. 😊 Good

There was a pause Ridley didn't know how to fill and for the briefest moment he second-guessed the impulse to reach out. He had just seen her earlier today, which was a little trippy to think about considering she was three thousand miles away now.

Ridley smiled to himself, settling back against the couch pillows and indulging in their conversation, breathing easily for the first time since…

It stunned him to realize this.

Since he'd seen Lanie that afternoon.

twenty-one

Lanie

"He sounds too good to be true."

Lanie looked at the woman sitting across from her in the faculty dining room and shook her head.

"You have to make sure this guy's on the level," Narcisa said. "Fuckbois come in all shapes and sizes nowadays. Just 'cuz this one has 'MD' attached to his name doesn't necessarily mean anything."

Lanie didn't need to be told that given the father she had… and her mother's frequent reminders.

"Well, he seems to check out. He's a widower," Lanie said.

"You know this for certain?" Narcisa interjected.

"Seriously?"

"What?" Narcisa shrugged. "It's in a New Yorker's nature to be distrustful."

"Yes, I know. For sure."

"Uh-huh." Narcisa sounded severely unconvinced but nodded, and reached for her drink, causing her profusion of silver bangles to jingle.

In direct opposition to the Earth Mother image that she typically projected with her chunky quartz jewelry, healing crystals and constant aroma of essential oils, Professor Narcisa

Escolástico was not a person whose bosom was available to cry into. But she was also not some acid-tongued jerk. What Narcisa was, without question, was a pragmatist. Her advice was always no-nonsense practical and her delivery was unfailingly forthright.

"Just checking," she said, spooling the spaghetti from her plate of cacio e pepe between a spoon and fork. "You know I have my own scars from back in the day when I was still in the penis game. That's how I know to ask." Narcisa sighed. "People should get hazard pay for that shit."

Lanie snorted in spite of herself, nearly choking on a mouthful of pasta. "Girl, his wife *died* a few years ago. Left him with a little girl. I know, okay?"

Narcisa's face remained disappointingly impassive. "Well then, that's even worse."

"How so?" Lanie really didn't like where this might potentially go.

"Then he's rebounding."

"Gee, thanks."

"Because she's dead, honey. Not because there's anything wrong with you."

Lanie huffed in indignation as Narcisa took a sip from her negroni.

"He's just getting back out there after years of wedded bliss. You have to take that into consideration."

"Sure." Lanie didn't really need someone to tell her she wasn't Thyra. She knew that. The more she thought about the woman, the more she knew she could never measure up. And the more she wondered why she'd begun thinking about that at all.

"And it's damn hard to compete with a dead woman," Narcisa added.

"This is getting dark. Can we change the subject? Because I'm not competing with his wife. It's not even like that between us." Although Lanie had begun to wonder if they were lying to themselves. Or she was on her side of things, at least.

"I'm just saying. Take it from me, dating a widower or a man with any significant baggage can be difficult."

"Baggage?"

"Yes. Getting involved with a man who already has kids and very possibly an idealized version of his last partner—alive or not—can be rough. I'm sorry, but it's true."

"You're making it out to be more than it is."

"Oh?" Narcisa's eyebrow rose dramatically as if she was trying to fit it for a monocle. She clasped her hands together on the tabletop beside her drink, waiting. "To hear you talk about him, I thought this guy was serious."

Narcisa was too much sometimes.

"About life? Yes. About his work? Definitely. About me personally? No, I wouldn't say that. I just like him. That's all."

"Lanie, has anything even happened between you and him?"

Lanie had to control her irritation at how far-fetched Narcisa's question made the possibility of that seem. *Who am I kidding? It's Narcisa*, she reminded herself.

"No." It was still too weird to talk about that kiss.

"Do you think something might?"

She was too embarrassed now to admit to hope. Narcisa made Lanie sound foolish for even instigating this conversation. She knew she wasn't just imagining things; she was sure something was happening between them.

Maybe.

"I don't know. He has a real life, with real concerns. Whereas I have a bunch of student loan debt from a half-finished doctorate and a roommate that happens to be my mother." She weighed her flat palms as if to visually illustrate the imbalance of a drastically unequal scale. "It's more than that though," Lanie said, losing her enthusiasm for the topic. Forget wet blanket Narcisa—she was talking herself out of wanting this.

"I'm not going to sit here and listen to you put yourself down, Melanie." Narcisa set her spoon and fork aside to skewer her friend with an exasperated gaze. "Say you have nothing in common, say you don't find each other attractive. But don't suggest you have nothing to offer."

"Sis, we're not even close to being the same." Lanie sighed. "He and I together... Me even thinking about it doesn't really make any sense, does it?"

"According to you, he hasn't said anything besides 'Lanie, let's hang out.' So why are you thinking about his home and family and whether you're good enough for him? Yes, it's giving a bit premature to me."

"We've *been* hanging out." There was indignation in Lanie's voice that she was trying to hide but Narcisa made her feel so ridiculous. "It *feels* like it could be more." Lanie itched to divulge the kiss now as proof, but was more certain than ever it would just confuse things. For Narcisa and herself.

"*Feels*, huh?" Narcisa's eyebrow arched as if Lanie had said she *felt* like the tooth fairy was real.

"What?"

"Lanie, have you ever heard of the term *limerence*?"

She shrugged, shaking her head.

"It's the tendency in some people to seek a happily-ever-after with every person they meet."

"Oh wow, Narcisa! That's really nice." Lanie's impulse was to grab her coat and bolt.

"Now wait, Melanie," Narcisa said. She held out her hand like a stop sign. "Hear me out."

Lanie's irritation ratcheted up a notch just hearing Narcisa's voice slide into the soothing tones of her therapist mode.

"I'm not saying this *is* limerence. I'm saying that this relationship could fall into a pattern of behavior that is *similar* to limerence, if you're not careful."

"I don't see a difference." Lanie took a deep breath to prevent herself from saying something she would regret. She settled back into her seat but folded her arms across her chest like a barrier.

Narcisa sat up straight. "Then that's part of the problem."

"Patterns such as…?" Lanie asked, molars grinding.

"Do you spend a lot of time when you aren't together, thinking about him, obsessing?"

"No. Obsessing? Absolutely not." It wasn't a lie even if it wasn't strictly the truth. They texted a lot, sharing memes and jokes, brightening the grayer corners of each other's day. But that was a mutual thing. She certainly wasn't obsessing.

"Well, I mean, we *are* talking about him now," Narcisa ventured gently.

"Yes, because I wanted your opinion. As a friend." Lanie's voice was prickly. "Which I now regret."

"O-kay," Narcisa said with an air of forbearance that irked her. "But do you frequently wonder what he's doing? If he's thinking about you? Try to decipher the meanings of the things he says? Hang on his tone of voice when you talk?"

Lanie scoffed. "No. But I mean, we also do more texting than talking so there's no tone of voice to hang on to."

Narcisa rolled her eyes. "I think you know what I mean, Melanie. Does a less than optimal conversation with him affect your mood? Are you bummed if things go badly? Jazzed when they're good? Do you spend time replaying things, measuring what he thinks of what you said?"

Lanie's stomach began churning. She recognized the behavior, but not with Ridley. Never. She said what she said, and Ridley took it however he took it. That was one of the most refreshing parts of their relationship and it went both ways. They didn't edit each other.

"No, I do not," she stated confidently. "When I don't like what he says, I turn my phone over and engage the DND button." It didn't happen often. Though his most recent erroneous declaration and tirade detailing why *Die Hard* was not a Christmas movie had gotten him ignored for hours.

"That's good," Narcisa said calmly, apparently reading the peevishness in the set of Lanie's mouth. "And I'm just asking."

Lanie's mouth slipped all the way to one side of her face in disbelief. One thing about Narcisa—she never "just asked."

"I mean, you have had the tendency to fall into these really intense infatuations that don't ultimately go anywhere. Face it, you've got a broken picker."

"Gee, thanks," Lanie barked defensively, trying to clear the thought from her mind. "And so? What does that mean?"

Lanie's love life sounded that much more pathetic coming out of Narcisa's cynical mouth, but she didn't bother disputing the facts. It was true, her relationships did tend to burn hot and fast. But that was only because she didn't take them seriously. Because they weren't ever love. Because they weren't...Jonah.

"You're a serial dater," Narcisa pronounced.

"What's that mean? Is it like being a serial killer?"

"Yes, but hopefully with a smaller body count." She winked at Lanie. "Basically, you fall out of relationships as quickly as you fall into them."

"No, I don't!"

"Okay, what about John, who you planned a Valentine's weekend getaway with but then he went back to his ex?"

Lanie groaned.

"Or Luis, who decided you were too tall for him after you wore heels to his niece's quince?"

"How was I too tall? I wore kitten heels and he was six foot one!" Lanie griped. "I bought a brand-new dress for that."

"That was your own fault. What did you think you were doing meeting his family? You'd barely known him a month," Narcisa pointed out, showing no mercy.

Lanie shrank in her seat and, despite it being midday, guzzled her glass of merlot.

"And what was the name of that guy who worked in Sociology who convinced you to donate some of your sick days to him when he broke his leg skiing?" Narcisa snapped her fingers trying to recall. "Without you, I might add. Darius—"

"But I've never claimed to be in love with any of them!"

"No, you're right. Technically, you didn't," Narcisa conceded. "Are you claiming to be in love with this Ridley guy now?"

"No." Lanie crinkled her nose, voice barely above a whisper, averting her gaze. "Of course not." Lanie tried to keep her tone light. Narcisa examined her closely. "What? I admitted I barely know him! And I've never claimed to be in love with anyone. Only—"

"Right, right, only Jonah," Narcisa continued with a deep sigh, shutting Lanie up.

Jonah was the one who had occupied her life and concentration. The only one whose attitude when they spoke could dictate her mood that day, be it in person or via video chat. The only one who'd had her counting the days every year until her summer vacations to London. The only one she ever obsessed over—the one whose attentions made her feel important and validated.

"But Jonah's never felt that way about you, correct?"

Lanie began to rebut, her mouth opening, before she stopped.

They were the greatest of friends—*up until recently, at least*—and there had been a brief moment when she thought he did. When they would hang out as teens, up until the wee hours of the morning talking. And that one time, which amounted to little more than a night when it seemed like they were finally on the same page. The night she thought he finally felt the same way about her that she did for him. But Lanie would never share that story. Not with Narcisa, not with Gemma, not with anyone.

"No," Lanie answered instead. "Never."

"And that's precisely what limerence is, Lanie," Narcisa explained as if she could hear Lanie's thoughts. "All that love energy expended on people who didn't earn it and don't want it. It's an immature version of love, an imitation of the real thing that is more about your fantasies of what love could be and who you *think* these men are than about the actual person and who they are *showing* you they are."

There was a ponderous silence as the reality of Lanie's clearly imaginary love life bounced around her brain like a pinball. Remarkably there was even the jarring ring of the bumpers inside her head, courtesy of the glass of merlot she'd drunk with her lunch. Still, she reached again for the now empty glass feeling sick.

"Now," Narcisa continued, in her normal bulldog style, not finished making her painful point. "I'm not saying that your thing with Ridley is the same. What I'm saying is, take the time to ensure it's *not* the same."

"How?"

"By being thoughtful. Don't idealize him. How is he as a person? Is he a good man? Is he respectful of you? How is it when you're together? Does he even really like you?"

"Ouch."

"Babe, I don't mean it like that. I just mean stop with the lovesickness. You're a physicist for God's sake."

"No, I'm really not."

"Here we go with the self-defeating impostor syndrome again. Stop! You were making moves in a novel space where they were actively trying to undermine you. As my girl Brittney says, you were an infiltrator. Own that," Narcisa corrected her. She patted her best friend's hand, which sat limply on the table. "Anyway, *mi amor*, if anyone's equipped to consider this logically, it's you. Does the way this Ridley treats you equate with *actually* liking you? Or are you getting mixed signals? Does being with him make you feel uncertain or appreciated?"

"Narcisa, it's too soon for all that." It wasn't. Lanie knew the answers to a lot of that already.

Narcisa nodded. "Okay, that's good that you even realize that."

That was the problem, and it only left her more confused. She bristled at how stupidly immature this whole conversation made her feel.

twenty-two

Lanie

"Next time I'm in town I have to visit my sister Siggy down in Philadelphia," Ridley explained. "I've been promising to visit. And I think she's starting to take it personally that I've been on the East Coast four times in the past three months and haven't stopped by yet."

Lanie lay on her bed talking with Ridley. She didn't know when their text messages had graduated to transatlantic phone calls but now they were talking two or three times a week in addition to the texting. She had learned so much about him in that time. He was an Aries; he'd lived in the UK for thirteen years; he was originally from Worcester, Massachusetts; he was one of four kids; he'd gone to Williams College on an athletic scholarship for his undergraduate studies and then on to Harvard for medical school. And now, because she'd explained how small and tight her family was, he'd decided to tell her a little more about his own.

"You're such a bad brother," Lanie teased.

"I know, I know. I'm just dreading the drive but Sig's convinced herself that I think I'm too 'fancy' now to condescend to spend time with her. Which I find ridiculous, in no small part because she's a tenured professor at Temple. So I wonder, who's afraid to associate with whom in this scenario?" He laughed. "My sister is very class-conscious."

"My dad's the same. He barely talks to his siblings down South, only my aunt Claudia. None of the others have ever even been invited to visit him, that I know of. He lives in Darien, Connecticut, in a six-bedroom house, with his white wife and two point three children."

"'Point three'? Isn't it 'point five'?"

"They have an old Persian named Truffle. And I deducted points because Truffle's a little asshole."

Ridley snorted. But Lanie winced remembering that one of the things he'd told her was that Thyra was biracial.

Why did I mention that Dad's wife was white? Ryan and her resentments were in Lanie's head even when Ryan wasn't physically there.

"My teenage parents could barely handle the four kids they had," Ridley admitted.

"I think I was a handful for my mom too. She ended up needing my grandma to come help her." It was a gross oversimplification but made Lanie feel like she was sharing as much as he was.

"I wish my grandparents had chosen to stay more involved. Maybe then my parents wouldn't have moved around so much or named all us kids after their favorite horror movies."

"Really?" Lanie perked up, lifting her legs and crossing them at the ankle like she was a teenager talking to her crush. "Is that why you're Ridley?"

He paused, then sighed before speaking. "Yep, my mom loved the *Alien* franchise and my dad's favorites were the *Halloween* movies. So, 'Sig' is short for 'Sigourney,' then there's Jamie Lee, Carpenter…and me, Ridley."

Lanie's barking laugh burst forth as she tried to stifle it. "No, no, I'm so sorry. I'm not laughing at you."

"Seems like you are. But I get it. We used to get it all the time, particularly me and Sig. But even Jamie Lee legally changed her name to James in her twenties—"

"Lanie, you okay?" her mother called out. "I'm in the kitchen. Can I make you some lemon ginger tea for that cough?"

"Hold on a sec," Lanie said quickly then punched the mute button and held the phone to her chest.

A minute later, her door opened a crack and Ryan's face peeked in.

Lanie shook her head. "No, thanks. I'm just laughing."

Ryan smiled. "Tell Gem Auntie says hi, and to give you a little break. She's a grown woman, she can make at least some of those wedding decisions on her own."

Lanie coughed out her residual chuckle. "Thank you for lookin' out, Mommy. But it's not Gem, she's been scarily radio silent all weekend."

"Probably saving it all up for when you see her next," her mom said presciently.

"Probably." Lanie looked down at the phone in her hand. "Well, I got to get back to him."

"Him?"

Damn. She knew her mom was curious but after what she'd already said Lanie was reticent to divulge any details. "Yup, him." She nodded, owning it. "Anyway, it's my fault. I told Gem to tell me what she needed." Lanie sighed, and that was biting her in the butt currently. "I am her maid of honor after all."

Ryan shook her head. "There's such a thing as overdoing it."

"What's that mean?"

"Lanie, throwing yourself into helping them won't do as much as you think it will to prove you're not hurt."

"Hurt?" Lanie understood after a moment her mother was talking about her and Jonah. Funnily, she hadn't thought of him. Not in any real way. Not in weeks. *Huh.* The realization was bracing. "I'm not. Just being a good cousin."

"Okay, 'good cousin.'" Ryan closed the door on her way out. "'Night."

Lanie rushed back to her phone. "I'm back. Is that another reason why you're Ridley?" Lanie said, resuming their discussion as if it hadn't paused. "Makes you sound like a white guy?"

"I wish it was that calculated since it would mean my parents had been thinking about it. It would have made a lot of the shit I got for being a Black kid named Ridley worth it." There was a long pause. "But as I said, my parents are…free spirits." He sounded like he was being facetious.

"I think 'James' is pretty cool for a woman," Lanie offered.

"I do too. She's a systems engineer for Raytheon down in Florida and said it makes things much easier because people always mistake her for a white man before they meet her."

"Oh, but that's not…" Lanie deflated. "She shouldn't need a masculine name."

"Agreed."

There was a pause. "Though I do understand the impulse. I think if I'd applied to grad school as 'Mel Turner' I might have done better."

"Bad grad school experience? I get that," Ridley answered, clearing his throat. "Thyra had a lot of difficulties too. Back then, I had thought it was difficult for me, being a Black man in medicine, but seeing how doubly hard it was for her studying emergency surgery was humbling."

Jesus, Thyra was a freakin' surgeon? Lanie thought, hating the twinge of barely logical insecurity the knowledge unearthed, even as she saw the similarities between them both.

"Yeah, I bet," Lanie answered quickly, sweeping a stack of readmission papers from her old grad school off her bed, suddenly angered. Dr. Markham's application from Berkeley was among them.

"She had to work daily, hourly, to show her colleagues she

deserved to be there. Again and again. At the top of her game constantly."

Lanie could hear the second-hand frustration in his voice and she recognized it, having experienced it herself.

"We've tried to teach Bea that she deserves to be in any room she enters, but you know how it is. And I know it'll always be an extra struggle for her. Even more difficult for her because she has dyscalculia."

"Dyscalculia?"

"A learning disorder similar to dyslexia but far less well-known. Bea struggles with understanding or remembering mathematical concepts. We had to take her out of school for a little while when we first discovered it. It took years and a formal diagnosis before any of her teachers took us seriously."

Lanie opened her laptop and typed "dyscalculia" into a Google search. As she read, the urge to share her experience with her anxiety grew, but it felt insensitive to shift the attention away from Bea.

"There were a million tests and assessments and parent-teacher conferences before we could get her help. We had to pay for a lot of it ourselves when going through the council stalled repeatedly."

There was another extended silence. Lanie waited to see what else he would say, not wanting to overstep. "Yeah, that sounds like my cousin, Gem," Lanie shared. "But for her it *was* dyslexia. Diagnosis took some time too and she ended up dropping out of school eventually. She's a gifted hairstylist though."

Lanie found she couldn't talk about how, when faced with the adversities of grad school and the entitled boys' club it was, she'd chosen to give up because of her crippling anxiety. She couldn't admit that she'd allowed all the doubters and detractors who'd wondered what she was doing in their labs, who wouldn't study with her, and professors who'd refused to mentor her and questioned her aptitude, to get into her head. Especially since admitting that to someone like Ridley, who had married someone like Thyra—both of whom had toughed it out and persevered—would only make her seem weak, cowardly or worse yet, like the doubters had been right.

"So, is Bea okay now?" she deflected.

"Sure, she'll always have her challenges. She's not neurotypical but she has strategies now, or as she calls them, 'hacks'—*thank you, YouTube*—to deal with them."

Lanie's stomach rolled. She questioned, for a moment longer, whether or not to share her truth…the fact that the anxiety attack he'd witnessed wasn't a one-off. That her struggle was ongoing. But she decided against it.

As close as they'd become in a few short weeks, they weren't *there* yet.

twenty-three

Ridley

Sting and the Police sang from the small Bluetooth speaker that sat on the corner of Ridley's large desk as he sat hunched over, elbows on the surface, cradling his chin in one hand while scrolling a finger down his iPad screen with the other.

"Hey! Got a minute?" The words were accompanied by a knock on the door frame of his London office. The face of Ridley's oldest friend as well as his study coordinator extraordinaire, Dashiell MacGeraghty, followed.

Ridley nodded.

"Theo says that his calibration guy will be here for the freezer first thing in the morning," Dash informed him.

"And did you tell him that we're getting different readings from the controllers than from the data logger?"

"Yup." Dash stepped fully into the doorway, sticking a hand into the pocket of his twill chinos and leaning against the jamb. "Hence, they're coming tomorrow morning...first thing."

"Sorry, I'm just worried that if it wasn't time for our recertification in New York, we might've missed that little malfunction here in London too."

Dash took a deep breath, his blue eyes narrowing on Ridley. He rubbed the robust brown beard along his jawline with his knuckles.

"We wouldn't have." Dash came further into the room. "Because I don't need an accreditation assessment to tell me whether *my* lab is up to snuff," he said, his Irish brogue getting thicker, as it did when he was getting excited or feeling aggrieved. "Particularly when it's completely voluntary anyway. Only an eejit sets themselves up for failure."

Ridley groaned, taking off his glasses to massage the bridge of his nose. "Sorry, I didn't mean to imply anything. I know that you're on top of it."

"And on the sides and the bottom of it too."

This was undeniably true. If there was anything Ridley could say about his friend and longtime colleague, it was that minutiae, no matter how minuscule, did not get past Dash. When Ridley said to people that he was a scientist, without fail, visions of Ridley as a tall, dark Bunsen Honeydew in a laboratory surrounded by microscopes, centrifuges and bubbling glass beakers, wearing a starchy white lab coat, appeared. But the lab coat was probably the most accurate part.

As the principal investigator of a clinical trial, a good portion of his job involved taking meetings, approving trial participants and overseeing compliance with governmental guidelines, among various other tasks on any given day. It was actually Dash as his coordinator who, generally speaking, dealt with the obvious stuff, keeping all the trains running on time while Ridley was elsewhere buried neck-deep in paperwork. And Ridley loved that division of labor. Normally, he didn't micromanage or stray outside their prescribed realms of responsibility. He just liked to know things were under control.

"You know I'm just paranoid about spoilage," Ridley explained apologetically.

Luckily, Dash never took things personally. It was the bedrock of his relationship with a prickly man like Ridley and as one might expect, Ridley appreciated that more than he ever admitted. "Relax, Granda'. Your cold chain will stay intact, I promise," Dash said, referring to the part their temperature-sensitive cold storage freezers played in ensuring the safe storage and transport of their medicine vials.

Ridley rolled his eyes. Dash only called him "Granddad" when he was being particularly ornery. Which was especially jarring since Dash was six years older than him. Ridley ran a hand over his head, feeling the fuzz on the sides by his ears and the nape of his neck. His low-fade Caesar was well overdue for a shape-up. Just another way in which he wasn't handling business at his usual high level.

I probably look like a hobo to Lanie, he chided himself, then wondered why he was thinking of her again. He was thinking about her a lot lately.

"You know it's probably nothing, right?" Dash rounded the chair in front of the desk and sat in it. "I bet when the tech comes, he'll say that we can account for the difference of degrees with the calibration itself."

Ridley sighed then nodded. He also knew that Dash was experienced enough to be entrusted with whatever the issue turned out to be. Unlike the coordinator in New York—one of Dash's grad school friends, whose mounting incompetence necessitated Ridley's frequent visits to the States to oversee everything and who was on the razor's edge of being demoted—Dash was competence personified.

"Alright, alright. I'll relax."

It was all under control; they both knew it.

"Quarter to six." Dash made a show of checking his watch. He looked at the darkened sky outside the paneled windows behind Ridley's desk. "Time to pack it up, Dr. Aronsen."

As if responding to Dash's pronouncement, Ridley's cell went off, rattling loudly on the blotter covering his desk. Reflexively, he snatched it up, checking it, then smiled.

It was Lanie.

"That Buzz?"

"No."

Silence.

Ridley looked down at his iPad and reread the same sentence about some patients being treated with competing pharmacological interventions to the ones he was studying. *For the fourth time.* But he'd be good and goddamned before Dashiell MacGeraghty outwaited him. He skipped forward, stroking a finger along the screen, pretending to be engrossed.

Dash sat in the chair opposite him, outstretched legs crossed over each other casually, twiddling his fingers.

"So…" he said, catching Ridley's eye before he could resume pretending to read.

"So?" Ridley fought slight amusement as Dash fished.

It was ironic. Dash nicknamed Bea "Buzz" when he was the one who incessantly circled a thing before landing on it.

After another minute or two, his friend's patience had grown gossamer thin. Dash rubbed his furry jaw again. Dash never looked more like an oversized Tolkien-movie dwarf than when he got focused and intractable, frowning furiously with an expression carved of stone.

"Oh, is that who I think it is?" Dash pointed one of his thick fingers at the phone back on Ridley's desk. "The girl?"

Ridley flipped the phone face down as if Dash could see something, checking the iPad again. But it had gone to sleep. "No."

He said it as easily and as devoid of emotion as he could manage. Still, Dash was like a dog with a bone now.

"Liar." Dash's Irish tongue rolled dramatically.

Ridley groaned, wishing he hadn't let Dash in on anything involving Lanie. But that had become impossible after an evening when he and Dash were supposed to be having a "lad's night," hanging out watching football. Instead, Lanie had texted him all evening. And in that flurry of messages, Lanie had proven herself to be an important new wrinkle in Ridley's life. Just by virtue of the fact that each and every time she reached out, Ridley responded, clueing Dash into something without saying a single word.

"Fine, it was her." Ridley fought a rising at the corners of his mouth.

"Oh Jaysus! You like her!"

He supposed there was no point in denying he did. "So?"

Dash's round and ruddy stone dwarf face lit up. "You? The captain of the HMS *Celibacy*?"

Ridley rolled his eyes.

Before Thyra's passing, Dash used to call him the "captain of the HMS *Relation-ship*," so Dash thought this new moniker was some clever wordplay. But looking over Dash's shoulder, Ridley just wished his office door was closed.

Dash clapped his large palms together loudly. Ridley jumped. "So?"

"So, it means you're ready to dust the cobwebs off the ole bollocks and stop being such a dryshite!" Dash rubbed his hands together with relish. "At bloody last!"

"Get out." Ridley pointed at the door.

"What?" Dash held his hands up defensively but chuckled with puckish amusement. "Have you mentioned her to Buzz?"

Ridley's mild amusement was cut short. "No. Of course not."

"Don't get testy," Dash said. "The amount of time you spend on that phone, I just thought maybe—"

"It's not that. She's just…" Ridley shrugged. "Just…"

"Just what? Spit it out, man!"

"Interesting."

"Can I finally know Just Interesting's given name? I mean, you see her every time you're in the States, for feck's sake. You're not just texting anymore, clearly."

Ridley took a moment, imagining her laughing face before giving his friend's question his attention. "Melanie."

"Melanie? Melanie sounds like a felony. How old is she?"

Ridley used his middle finger to shift his glasses slightly on his face. Dash grinned.

"Old enough." Ridley realized then he didn't actually know. He guessed not much past her mid-to-late twenties.

That would make her ten years his junior. *God, am I robbing the cradle?* Ridley kept the doubt in his mind off his face, then shook his head. *Why the hell am I even thinking that?*

"But it's not like that between us anyway," he asserted, oddly confused about whether that was true.

"Okay." Dash nodded, amused, finally beginning to rise. "Well, I'm happy you've finally met someone 'interesting,' regardless. It's been too long, brother."

Ridley nodded, but still wondered—had it been long enough?

twenty-four

■ 20-NOV ■ Trans-Continental Airways ■ Flight: 403 ■

JFK-John F. Kennedy Int'l Airport ► **LHR-London, Heathrow**

Seat Assignment: **15F/15G**

"I don't think I can do these forty-eight- to seventy-two-hour hops back and forth much longer." Ridley yawned, making the words barely decipherable. Lanie walked with him through Immigration at Heathrow after yet another of his practically overnight jaunts to New York. "But I have to say, I think it's impressive how you look so fresh coming off a red-eye."

"I'm a veteran traveler. I've got tricks up my sleeve."

"Oh yeah?"

"A whole bag of them, in fact." Lanie thought about Gemma with gratitude.

"Well, it's working for you."

She could see from the bags under Ridley's eyes that it wasn't working for him so much anymore. And while it thrilled her to be able to occasionally fly back and forth to London with him, she wasn't without sympathy for the strain of his fifth or sixth visit in fewer months.

"Thanks." Lanie's cheeks reddened as she placed her passport down on the glass panel of a high-tech turnstile. "I miss the stamps."

"You can always get back in the line, if you really need one." Ridley thumbed toward the long line they'd skipped past.

"Uh, no."

It was easier to breeze through Immigration now that they'd installed the fancy new electronic turnstiles, but Lanie couldn't help feeling robbed. "How will I know where I've been years from now without my passport stamps?" she sulked.

Back in her late teens and twenties, Lanie could have racked up a million flier miles on TitanAir, a discount airline that offered dirt cheap flights all over Europe. Every summer, for the cost of a pizza pie, Gemma used to drag Lanie all over the continent—Paris, Amsterdam, Lisbon, Frankfurt, Madrid—basically anywhere they could grab a cheap ticket and fly to in under three hours.

"You need your passport to remember all the places you've been?" Ridley said it with judgmental disbelief.

Her chin rose with defiance. "I'll only say we had *a lot* of fun back in the day."

Ridley's eyebrow rose. "We?"

Lanie watched all the bags go around the carousel, trying to identify her massive seldom-used suitcase before pointing it out as it headed toward them.

"What the hell do you have in here? Rocks?" he asked, straining a little to haul the weighty bag off the carousel before it moved away.

Lanie rolled her eyes. "Lady things."

This time around, in addition to her normal travel-friendly backpack and carry-on approved suitcase, Lanie had needed to carry a larger suitcase to accommodate nearly a dozen beaded, sequined, silken and otherwise bedazzled bridesmaids' dresses. Gemma had seen them in an imported wedding magazine someone had left at her salon. And naturally, all the ones she liked were made by designers who either didn't have an authorized retailer in the UK or were similarly obscure. So, in her capacity as the world's best maid of honor, Lanie had rented samples and lugged them across the Atlantic for Gemma's perusal.

"Ladies' parts, you said?" Ridley teased with a perfectly straight face. "Feels like it."

"Haha." She smirked. "Anyway 'we' included me, my cousin Gem and her best friend, Fatou. We were very bad. Every summer was a Hot Girl Summer. Years before Megan Thee Stallion. We were, like, the Three *drunken* Musketeers." Lanie blushed remembering it. "So yeah, I do need my stamps to remember…some of it."

Ridley eyed her, crossing his arms over his chest. "And what did your grandmother think?"

"You're assuming a lot, thinking she always knew. Particularly when we were younger."

"But you left the country."

"Within the EU, baby."

He looked first astonished then a little shaken by the thought. "No," he said, shaking his head. "I don't see it. Not you."

"Absolutely me." Lanie gave a nod, amused by his incredulity. "We were teenagers. We went all over the place."

"No, I mean, Lanie Turner, Miss Aplomb herself, getting blackout drunk in Europe?"

Is that how he sees me? She was flattered. "Believe it. And that's *all over* Europe, by the way. Before I could even drink legally in the States," she gloated. "One time in Amsterdam in Vondelpark, I passed out and when the girls woke me up a couple of hours later, there was this couple near us…"

They had cleared the customs area and were walking through the arrivals concourse to the street.

"The joke was we got kicked out for sleeping there, but that couple didn't for…what they were doing."

"What were they doing?"

She caught his eye and wiggled her eyebrows suggestively.

Ridley's eyes widened. "You're joking."

"Nope. Then one time I lost my passport in a bar on Rose Street in Edinburgh. Some bar. Had no idea which. That was a fun night, trying to retrace our steps." Lanie's head hurt remembering that. "We drank so much back then that I don't even drink anything harder than wine anymore. I figure I've killed enough brain cells. And I need all I can manage to keep."

"You know that's a myth, right?"

"It is?"

He nodded.

"Wow, I was sure I lost some crucial IQ points during college."

"Tsk, tsk," Ridley teased.

"So." Lanie took a deep lungful of the chilled and rainy London air. "How are we doing this? I've got my Oyster card but I suspect you don't want to jump on the tube."

"Nope." Ridley's brows furrowed as he shook his head.

Lanie rolled her eyes.

"Don't give me that look. I take the Underground all the time," Ridley challenged her.

"Okay, when?" She didn't even bother to hide her doubt. "Where?"

"Except for, you know, coming from the airport. But that's because I know they're sending a car." He straightened his glasses, deliberately avoiding the smug look she wore. "Anyway, because of that I can give you a lift to Balham. Won't that be nice?"

"That's on the other side of the river from you. Don't be silly."

"It's a driver. He won't mind the extra cash. I guarantee it."

Ridley wore his own smug look now. "Just hang out here with me. And relax."

Lanie bit her lip, panicking internally. Why, she didn't know. She'd already planned to split the cost of a cab with him. Truth was, Lanie was still just coming to terms with the fact that she wanted to be around Ridley as much as she could. All the time.

A few minutes later, a sleek black BMW honked its horn, startling Lanie as it slid up to the curb in front of them. Ridley bent forward to peer into the lightly tinted windows, looking confused.

"Dash?" Ridley asked, surprised to see his best friend.

Lanie took a step to the side, feeling the need to stand apart from him. She hadn't realized until that moment how close they were to one another, but suddenly there was this pang of guilt. Ridley glanced at her but otherwise didn't say anything, turning his attention back to the driver of the car.

"Surprise! I'm the welcome wagon. Happy to see me?" Dash spread his arms wide as if he planned to give the world a hug, not just Ridley.

Ridley definitely seemed surprised too. *Happy*, not so much.

Lanie gave him a tentative smile. Dash screamed lumberjack with his full beard and broad shoulders. *Are there lumberjacks in the UK?* She mulled over the random thought. *If so, that's what this man should be. Wearing flannel all the time.*

Once Dash had hopped out of the car and opened the trunk with his fob, Lanie noticed he was shorter than Ridley, closer to her height. He slapped Ridley hard on the arm, jostling him. "Let's get these into the boot, shall we?" Dash looked back and forth between them, never losing the enormous smile.

Ridley stood there for a moment longer as if he'd forgotten how to speak. Dash grabbed his bag and Ridley followed his friend to the back of the car.

"Change of plans, apparently," Lanie muttered to herself,

fishing her Oyster card out of her pocket. It seemed that she'd be taking the train after all.

"What are you doing here?"

Lanie could just make out Ridley's words when he seemed to regain his ability to talk. It intrigued Lanie that he was so discombobulated. It might have been amusing if she didn't suspect she knew what had tripped him up in the first place.

"I'm here to take you to work," Dash said innocently. "And maybe I also wanted to see what Just Interesting looked like."

There was a hurried exchange of words Lanie didn't understand and largely missed because they were now obscured by the raised trunk lid. Afterward, both men returned to the curb, looking at her. She smiled awkwardly, waiting for someone, *anyone*, to break the conversational seal.

"Well," Lanie announced, starting to back up. "You've got a ride, so I guess I'll take off."

Ridley snapped out of his daze then, reaching out lightning fast. "No, uh, ride with us." He took her by the forearm, before dropping his hand from her wrist just as quickly. Still, it was enough to pause her midstep. "I already promised you a lift."

Ridley looked over his shoulder at his friend, who merely watched this play out.

She forced a smile. "Ridley, you didn't promise me anything."

"Dash." He turned back to his friend, who brightened expectantly. "Dr. Dash MacGeraghty, let me introduce you to Ms. Melanie Turner."

"So formal." Dash eyed Ridley, and Lanie was certain she caught a glint of mischief there, before regarding her. "Hallo, Ms. Melanie, a pleasure!" Dash gave her a nod that she reciprocated. His appraisal felt slightly more than casual.

"Hi, nice to finally meet you," Lanie said, shaking off any growing discomfort.

"He talks about me, does he?"

Her smile grew into something a little more genuine. "Yes, but it makes me wonder why you still talk to him. Apparently, you do all the real work while he's off gallivanting," she joked.

A spark of amusement finally lit in Ridley's eyes, the corner of his mouth rising slightly to a near smirk.

Dash looked from Lanie to Ridley. "Ooh, I like her!"

Dash's otherwise fairly tame accent really popped on the words *like* and *her* and Lanie remembered how much she enjoyed the Irish.

"Me too," Ridley replied almost reflexively, catching both her and Dash by surprise. He coughed then to clear his throat. "By which I mean, um, you can see what good company I have on my flights sometimes."

"Yeah, I definitely do," Dash said. "Well, in we get and off we go then."

Lanie looked to Ridley, whose expression, as usual, gave her nothing. Certainly not sympathy or concurrence with her plan to leave. Finally, he just shrugged.

"Really?"

"Far be it from me to force you into something you don't want to do, Ms. Melanie, but I guarantee, we're better company than you'll find on the Piccadilly Line at this hour of the morning. And the ride is far smoother." Dash smiled again, pointing with pride to his 3 Series. "Promise."

"Fine." Lanie gave up, beginning to pull her enormous bag toward the car.

"Ah, ah, ah," Ridley finally interjected, tutting.

He stopped her with a hand over hers on the handle of her suitcase. Their eyes met and Lanie's stomach took a tumble as it did often nowadays. Without intending to, Lanie shot a guilty look in Dash's direction and saw his attention was taken by Ridley's hand still covering hers. She slipped it away quickly, hustling into the back seat.

★ ★ ★

Lanie hated to trade in stereotypes but so far Dash was every notion of the jolly Irishman she'd ever encountered. The only thing missing was the shock of red hair. He was expansive, lively and had the singular ability to drag real, actual laughs from Ridley at an alarmingly frequent rate. In front of Dash, Lanie again saw the jovial man she first met on the plane. As they drove, Dash dominated the conversation, regaling Lanie with stories. Of how they met when Ridley was a young American doctor in a fellowship program at St. Thomas's. Of being the best man at Ridley and Thyra's wedding and misplacing their wedding bands. Of practicing the art of the diaper change on Beatrix's dolls in preparation for his own daughter.

Traffic was lighter than it would be in a couple of hours. Between that and Dash's stories, they made it through West London, flying through Hammersmith and Fulham and almost across the river, before Lanie knew it.

"For at least a year, my daughter, Peach, refused to wear anything but her nappies…" Dash said through a gale of laughter. "And the missus and I started thinking, 'Maybe this isn't so bad?' We were saving a ton on wee clothes she was just going to outgrow, right? But then we didn't have any clothes for the next one!" Dash let loose yet another peal of his hearty guffaws, wiping tears from his eyes with a thumb.

LANIE:

Your friend is a trip.

RIDLEY:

He is.

Smiling genuinely as Ridley looked at her through the side mirror, she gave him a quick wink.

"After that, every time we just went to the charity shops to get their things!"

"'Every time'? How many?"

"Three more. Four in all. Peach, Clementine, Plum, and my youngest, a boy, Crispin. Three girls and my wee man."

Moments later, Lanie's phone buzzed.

RIDLEY:

YES. 😑 THEY ARE ALL NAMED AFTER FRUIT.

Lanie snorted loudly. Dash glanced at her through the rear-view mirror. "I can see it now, a house full of little nudists," Lanie recovered quickly.

Dash's boisterous laughter filled the car.

LANIE:

Okay then, so what's Bea named after?

Lanie saw in the side-view mirror the cloud that quickly crossed Ridley's face and she regretted asking. He was hard to navigate; she never knew when and where was too far. But his face told her she'd tripped one of the invisible lines in his mind. Ridley's lips flattened.

"What's the matter?" Dash surprised them.

"What? Nothing." Ridley squirmed, put on the spot.

Lanie pressed her phone into her purse, turning to the window in time to see the verdant greenery and flat expanse of Clapham Common come into view. They were nearly there and Lanie was glad, because the car suddenly felt too small. She was tired of sitting in this confined space too. When her phone vibrated, giving a brief chime a minute later, Lanie ignored it, more embarrassed than upset she'd overstepped.

She gave Dash a forced smile when he checked her out in the rearview mirror. The car fell into silence.

"Okay?" Dash said unconvinced. "How about this then?"

Dash turned the radio to BBC Radio 1. The DJ's mile-a-minute delivery and thick Scottish brogue made her nearly indecipherable to Lanie. So, her mind wandered. The phone chimed again. Lanie sighed.

RIDLEY:

I didn't choose her name.

RIDLEY:

Since her childhood Thyra had always liked Beatrix Potter.

LANIE:

😄 I love Beatrix Potter!

RIDLEY:

Then I need to take you to the Victoria and Albert Museum. Every year we used to do a pilgrimage there to see the Beatrix Potter archive.

"Are you two *texting* each other inside the same car?"

They both looked up simultaneously, as if caught.

"Truly?" Dash's eyes flew from Ridley to her in the mirror. "What are you, children?"

"I swear we weren't talking about you, Dash!" Lanie spat out.

"Likely story," he said sullenly as Lanie looked from one to the other of them in their respective mirrors before bursting out laughing.

"Remind me to never commit a crime with you," Ridley broke his extended silence to say drolly.

Then they all laughed and before she knew it, they were pulling up to her grandmother's curb. Ridley hopped out to get Lanie's suitcase out of the trunk.

Dash turned around in his seat to face her. "So, Melanie."

Lanie startled at the full and sudden force of his attention.

"Don't worry, *grá*. I don't bite." He laughed and Lanie settled a little. "I just wanted to say it's been a pleasure."

"It was really nice to meet you too."

Dash eyed Ridley outside walking the suitcase up to her door, pulling it through the gate as he continued, "Ridley's ma best mate and this has been a rough couple of years for him, he's said?"

She nodded, growing curious where this was going.

"That's why I'm so glad he's found someone to talk to. And he likes you. I just want to make sure you know that, 'cos I love the guy, but uh, he's been absolute minus craic the past few years—understandably—" He put up a palm to stop her, as if she had any idea what he was talking about. "So, it's been really lovely to see him come out of that. Thank you."

"Okay…"

Dash clammed up just as quickly as he'd begun talking when Lanie's door opened.

"You guys planning my birthday party in here or what? Hop out."

"I don't know if I like you enough for that," Lanie teased, taking his arm to help her out of the back seat. "Thanks."

"Me neither!" Dash smiled. "No clue."

"Just talking about me, then?"

"It'd only be fair if we were." Dash leaned toward the passenger window from the driver's seat to watch them both on the curb, giving Lanie a wink.

"You're good from here?"

Lanie nodded, backing toward her grandmother's front door. "Yep. Talk soon?"

"Yeah, I'll call you later. I have an idea I meant to run by you." Ridley got into the car as Lanie turned to walk away.

She paused for a moment, replaying Dash's words. *Ridley likes me.* She knew that she liked him too. But perhaps that was not what he meant. *No, don't do that,* she admonished herself. *Don't go there, Lanie.*

Feeling for her keys, as she stepped up to the front door, Lanie realized she'd left her small backpack in the car. "Oh shit!" Spinning on her heel toward the street, she couldn't see the car on her road anywhere. Lanie pulled her cell phone from her coat pocket and dialed Ridley.

"…her. You could certainly do a lot worse for a little fun," Dash was saying as the call connected.

He could do worse? Than what?

"Dash, I'm on the phone." Ridley's voice bore a sharp edge. "Lanie?"

A little fun?

Dash's words pressed into her, coloring their whole ride, souring their whole interaction, particularly that odd bit at the end.

Was she supposed to be the "little fun" he was talking about?

It definitely wouldn't be the first time, and probably not the last time either, that someone had dated her for that purpose. As a placeholder or for the ego boost or someone to validate them or just when they were between *actual* girlfriends. And she'd been largely okay with it. Nobody was "using" her, she'd insisted for years, because her love was waiting for her. The man she was waiting for just needed to wake up and finally realize it. But the truth was that Ridley had just been using her too.

Lanie sighed. *And now, this.*

If she seriously considered it, it made a hell of a lot more sense that an attractive young widower would be looking for her to help him "get his groove back" than to have anything serious. Why would he have any genuine interest in her? What did they have in common? Ridley was eight years older with a teenage daughter and a real job. He had a real career instead of a nine-to-five, he owned his own home and had real commitments and concerns. A couple of engaging conversations did not a real relationship make. When she thought of Dash's words as some sort of tee up to a proposition, they made a hell of a lot more sense.

"Lanie? Are you there? Hello?"

"My bag is still in the car," she said flatly.

"Do you need it now?" Ridley asked.

Lanie pulled the phone from her ear and looked at it incredulously. She'd just replaced the picture in her phone of Ridley's business card with an actual picture of him very studiously doing some work as they sat by the gate before a flight. Now she wished she could reach into that photo and shake him.

"No, I can stand outside in the cold indefinitely." Sarcasm dripped like acid from her words.

"Shit, you're locked out?"

Technically, no. There was the key under the pot and with her Gran's lifestyle getting more and more sedentary, chances were better than decent that she was at home too. Lanie stepped up from the curb and rang the bell. Almost immediately she heard movement from inside.

"'Cuz we're running a little late for a meeting. But..." There was a flash of hesitation then she heard him say, "Dash, turn around, she left something in the car."

"No," she said quickly. They were running late because of her. And while given what she now knew, she shouldn't care, but she did. "No, I can get in. Someone's home."

"You're sure?"

Lanie took a breath. If Ridley came back right now, it was highly unlikely they would still be friends tomorrow.

"Yes, positive."

"Okay, I'll get your bag back to you as soon as I possibly can. I'm sorry."

"You'd better."

"Call you late—"

Lanie disconnected the call just as the door opened. To her surprise, instead of Gran, Gemma opened the door casually, snacking from a bag of chips in her hand. "Oh, I didn't think you'd be here."

"Why?" Gemma gave her a quizzical look. "Don't I live here?"

"Yeah, but I know you spend a lot of time over at Jonah's," Lanie explained.

"I had to be here when you brought these, now, didn't I?" Gemma stepped into the doorway and reached for the large suitcase. "Cor, it's bloody boulders in 'ere!" Gemma put on the voice of an old cockney man.

Lanie slung the strap of her weekender over her shoulders and then bent to give the large suitcase a shove over the raised threshold of the front door.

"How the hell did you get this here?" Gemma asked between labored breaths.

Grabbing the side handle of the bag to evenly distribute the suitcase's weight between Gemma and herself and lug it further inside, Lanie admitted begrudgingly, "With a lot of help."

twenty-five

Lanie

"What's the matter, Sec?" Tulip asked Lanie, looking up from her episode of the upcycling show *Money for Nothing*. She was in her recliner, with her knit throw over her waist and her word search in her hands. Lanie lay across her grandmother's bed, purportedly hanging out with her, but she was mostly in her own world.

"Nothing," she replied easily, but her grandmother frowned behind her bifocals. "Just nonsense," she continued when that answer was unsatisfactory. "With some guy."

It had been two days, and Ridley hadn't gotten her key back to her yet. After overhearing Dash on the phone, Lanie wasn't sure she wanted to speak with Ridley at all anyway. He'd spoiled what was supposed to be a morning of light—or at least productive—wedding planning with Gemma. The dresses were a pain to haul even with Ridley's help, but Lanie was still excited to see her cousin's enthusiasm—even though she decided none of the samples were quite right in the end.

A little fun, he'd called her. It burned in her gut every time she thought of it.

They were supposed to be meeting at the Bank tube stop

on Sunday to go someplace called the Sky Garden for brunch before she flew out that evening. But right now, Lanie wasn't certain she wanted that to happen.

"Is this the white man you've been seeing?" Her grandmother peered over her glasses to ask.

"Gran!" Despite her general funk, Lanie burst out laughing. "What white man?"

"Gem said you met some white Englishman named Ridley on the plane and you had been seeing him. You disappear for hours, sometimes for a whole day while you're here. I thought to ask Gem and that's what she told me."

Lanie sobered. She hadn't realized anyone had been paying attention to her comings and goings. Between Gemma's classes, her full-tilt wedding prep, Les's absence and Gran's new tendency to hole up in her room, Lanie thought gossip would be the last thing on their minds. Although, knowing Gem, Les and Gran, they'd find time.

"Despite his name, he's not white." She chuckled again thinking about it.

Poor Ridley.

Her grandmother looked skeptical but nodded. Lanie was sure she caught a distinct sense of relief. Her grandmother's father had been white and Lanie knew as far as her grandmother was concerned, being fetishized for their resultant light skin and eyes had caused her and her children no end of troubles.

"And he's not English. He's an American, he just lives here."

"And what does he want with my good granddaughter?"

Lanie smiled. Unlike with her mother, Lanie could feel the affection laden in her grandmother's words.

"Oh nothing, we're just friends."

Gran pinched her lips together and poked them out in the universal old Caribbean woman expression of "if you say so" skepticism.

"Honestly! It's purely platonic." *On his side at least...regardless of what his friend was trying to do.*

"What is going on with your face, then?"

"Huh?" Lanie feigned innocence. She really had to learn to school her features better. She could feel her cheeks begin to burn. "Nothing." *And work on being a better liar overall, apparently.*

Gran nodded. "Well, it's been a long time since I fancied a man, maybe I've forgotten what that looks like."

Lanie giggled nervously at that description. "I do not 'fancy' him."

Her grandmother couldn't possibly know how much time they spent in contact with one another or how many hoops they now jumped through regularly just to make sure they saw each other, spoke to each other. So, if it already looked suspect, wow... Lanie marveled.

"MOH-MOH! Get up!" Gemma burst into the room, startling them.

"I refuse to answer to that stupid nickname." Lanie folded her arms and rolled onto her back to look at the ceiling.

"Oh, but you *are* my little MOH-MOH." She flopped onto the bed beside Lanie. "My darling maid of honor."

"I thought I was the 'best mate'?"

"That too." Gemma plied Lanie with gentle tickles in her sides.

Lanie slapped at her cousin's hands. "What am I, five? Stop it."

They tussled briefly until their grandmother's ancient bed frame creaked in protest, then they both sprang off it in alarm.

"A-good! It serve you right if it broke down under your backsides! You too big to still be doing that nonsense. I warn you from me," Gran admonished, but then a huge smile broke across her face. "My silly girls."

Lanie was grateful for moments like these with her grandmother. Gemma too. Like when they were children. The idea that they'd come really close to losing that made a chill run through her.

"We have to run, Nan," Gemma said. Her voice was pitched high and excited. "I got us in at Kaashvi and Co! Well, Charity did. They had a cancellation and her friend's sister's roommate is one of the salesgirls there. So, she's hooking us up! Get dressed." She pointed at Lanie. "We have to be in Notting Hill by one fifteen." And with that, Gemma rushed back out of the room.

Notting Hill? Lanie's stomach rolled.

"Sec? You're sure you're alright?"

Lanie caught her grandmother's look of concern.

"Of course." She took a deep breath and smiled.

Gran still looked doubtful.

At least she could get her damn backpack back.

"What do you think of this?" Gemma walked out of the dressing room in an ivory tulle saree with embroidered sequins in a floral design. It had a sweetheart neckline that strained against her startlingly full breasts and a sheer sequined sleeve on one side with the loose, decorative fabric end of the saree, called the *pallu*, sweeping the floor on the other. It looked great and complemented her slim figure. "I don't know if I want this much of my stomach exposed," she complained.

Lanie wrinkled her nose, frowning. Though she might have understood since Gemma had recently gotten curvier in the middle, the truth was her cousin had once reigned as queen of the exposed midriff. At one point in their youth, Lanie wondered if Gemma was deliberately cutting all her tops in half.

Still, Lanie agreed, while the dress was undeniably beautiful, Gemma was right to have serious misgivings—though chances were they weren't the same misgivings as Lanie's. For Lanie, the primary concern was that she and Gemma's other bridesmaids were expected to wear sarees at all.

"It's spectacular," the saleswoman, Charity's friend's sister's roommate, Parminder, said.

Gemma rolled her eyes and Lanie grinned behind her hand. Parminder had said the same thing about the last three dresses. Yet it was also true. Each one had looked amazing on Gemma. She had the body for sarees.

"I liked the peach one better," Marissa offered, coming out of a different dressing room wearing a cream-colored georgette saree embroidered with sequins and soft blue and pink flowers along the edges.

"Oh yes, that one was an Amitava Lahiri. He's a really famous Bengali designer. Very in demand. Does all the Bollywood movies. Really superb stuff," Parminder added, walking over to Shanice, who had emerged from yet another dressing room, and adjusting the *pallu* sliding off Shanice's left shoulder.

Lanie leaned forward from her perch on the velvet-damask, Louis the Fourteenth–style chaise longue at the center of the styling suite and whispered, "Is this okay?"

She'd been watching all three women gleefully going through an assortment of different outfits for, according to the time on her cell phone, the past seventy minutes of a two-hour appointment.

Gemma, who spun in a three-way mirror trying to catch a clear view of her bottom, paused. "What?"

"Us wearing sarees. Is this in good taste?" Lanie knew from experience that Gemma could get ideas in her head and not really think of the consequences or implications. Whereas Lanie couldn't even bring herself to try one on for fear of the inappropriateness.

"Do you mean wearing Indian sarees when Jonah is Sri Lankan?" Gemma asked in her regular speaking voice, not catching that Lanie was trying to be discreet. "Syreeta told me herself that Indian sarees were the way to go."

"Oh, technically, a saree is the traditional everyday wear of an Indian woman," Parminder said, coming back to Gemma to again adjust some fabric. "Those are sarees." She pointed to the bridesmaids' dresses, made up of a blouse and one piece of intricately draped, folded and tucked fabric. "This is a *lehenga choli*. Well, to be even more technical, the *lehenga* is the long skirt, the *choli* is the fitted embroidered blouse and the *dupatta* is this long piece of cloth worn with it for special occasions, like a wedding." She smiled and draped the *dupatta* across Gemma's neck.

Lanie smiled tightly at the correction that overlooked her actual point. "Thanks."

Parminder looked the *lehenga* over. "So, what do you think?"

"I don't know. They're all so beautiful," Gemma hemmed.

Beautiful and expensive as hell, Lanie thought.

It was nice that Jonah had given her his credit card and told her to get what she needed, but in Lanie's opinion, Gemma was losing the plot. She had Jean-Georges taste on what should be a Nando's budget. Every *lehenga* she'd tried on topped out at over five thousand pounds. And that didn't even factor in the three-thousand-pound Reem Acra dress she was wearing for the Catholic wedding mass that Lanie had finally found on luxury consignment.

Lanie girded her loins. "Gem."

Gemma looked up from admiring herself in the mirror again.

"Is it appropriate as Black women for us to be wearing sarees—I mean, *lehengas*?" Lanie put it plainly.

Marissa, the lone white woman, just stood there awaiting the answer and Shanice began slipping the fabric off her shoulder, guiltily. They all looked at each other as if this was the first time any of them had thought of this.

Seriously?

"Black people can culturally appropriate too," Lanie reminded them.

"Yes, look at what happened with Rihanna," Marissa added.

"But she snapped in that—" Shanice started.

"But was it right?" Lanie interjected.

"O-kay," Gemma huffed, putting her hands up in surrender. "What do you think, Parminder?"

The saleswoman put a finger to her chin like she was really considering it.

As if she's going to pass up thousands of pounds in sales by saying no. Gemma knew that too, which was why she asked. *Where's Fatou's level head when we need it?* Lanie lamented.

"No, I think this is tastefully done. You are obviously planning on being respectful of the culture. And you said your fiancé is South Asian, right?"

"Yes." Gemma nodded.

"Well then..." Parminder said as if resting her case.

"See? Mel, no problem." Gemma turned back to the mirror. "So, um, sweetie, I don't know about this one. Maybe the first one?"

Lanie sighed, pulling out her phone. But she paused before texting Ridley in frustration as she might normally. This would just be about getting her backpack. *Nothing else.* Let him find someone else for "a little fun."

LANIE:

> Hey, I'm around your way shopping with my cousin. Can I drop by?

There was a pause before those three dots, the bane of her existence, started to bob.

RIDLEY:

> You're in West London?

LANIE:

> I am.

RIDLEY:

I'm not. I had to come into work today.

LANIE:

I want my bag Ridley. Cuz it feels like you're holding it hostage.

RIDLEY:

What if I was?

This dude thinks his ass is funny.

"I'm going to think about this for a little while longer but we'll take the saree Marissa is wearing," Gemma declared.

Lanie looked up. "We will?"

"Yup." Gemma smiled with Parminder. "Let's get them all measured." Gemma pointed at her bridesmaids. "And the other girls will stop by later."

RIDLEY:

Can you come by after 7pm?

LANIE:

We're wrapping up now. We have another thirty minutes tops

The dots again.

RIDLEY:

Damn, I really wanted to get it to you myself. But let me see what I can do.

"Lanie! C'mon."

Lanie looked up again to see Parminder holding a pad and pencil while one of the other sales associates, who had appeared out of nowhere, looked ready to accost her with a measuring tape.

She pasted on a smile for Gemma and stood for her measurements, playing the role of perfect MOH to a T.

twenty-six

Lanie

"You know someone who lives around *here*?"

There were five of them, Lanie, Gemma, Gem's friends Shanice and Marissa and Fatou, who had joined them for a late lunch, who walked like little ducks in a row, down the long line of rainbow-colored terrace houses on Ridley's street. Lanie gaped at the large homes, all decorated in different pastel colors with stark front doors, frequently painted a primary color. Gemma nudged her in the side.

"I do too. My great-aunt Heléne lives three streets over," Fatou said with indignation. "Which reminds me, you never saw me around these parts, yeah?"

They all chuckled.

Lanie looked down at the text exchange again. "We're looking for thirty-five," she announced.

"Well, this is forty, so can we figure out if we're going up or down? My feet hurt and these bags are getting heavy," Marissa said.

"And I have a baby to get back to before my tits explode," Shanice whined.

"Okay, okay." Lanie scanned the tranquil tree-lined street. It reminded her of one of the stately brownstone-lined blocks in Harlem. She dreamed of living in a house like any of these. After three decades of living in a tight two-bedroom apartment, four floors of space was a luxurious fantasy.

"Here!" Fatou said, pointing at a cheerful daffodil-yellow house with a small wrought iron gate and three short steps up to a small portico with an electric-blue front door.

Above the portico hung a veritable jungle of plants and vines, some of which overgrew their pots and hung down, wrapping around the columns as if reaching for the ground, trying to reclaim the house for nature. Lanie wondered absently when last anyone had been out on that balcony to do any pruning.

"Well?" Gemma said impatiently.

"Sorry," Lanie said, dropping her handful of shopping. She rang the bell twice before she could hear any footsteps approaching. Her heart raced in anticipation.

Besides Dash, she'd never met anyone in Ridley's life before. It went both ways, of course; he hadn't met any of her family either. And this would only be his housekeeper, Mrs. Handa, but the idea was still daunting. When the door opened, however, it was not the older South Asian woman she expected.

"B-Bea?" Lanie said, her heart now at a gallop.

"Yes." The teenager smiled at her warmly. "Are you Melanie?"

The girl's brown eyes were so huge they seemed to take her in all at once. Bea was absolutely adorable with a heart-shaped face, high cheekbones, full lips and eyes that were downturned in the corners. Her hair was pulled back in a ponytail and crowned with assorted multicolored clips to keep her flyaways under control. She wore a grass-stained white soccer uniform, complete with knee socks and cleats.

"You're American."

She couldn't be sure, but Lanie thought she caught surprise in Bea's eyes.

"I am." Lanie nodded. "Nice to finally meet you! Your dad talks about you all the time."

Bea gave a frown so fleeting that if Lanie hadn't been looking directly at her, she would have missed it. But then she smiled and looked past Lanie, down to the small gaggle of chattering women on the street.

"My friends. We were shopping in the neighborhood," Lanie explained. "See the one in the middle?"

Bea nodded.

"She's my cousin. She's getting married soon."

It was far more information than Bea needed but Lanie sometimes rambled when she was nervous.

Bea smiled. "She's pretty."

"She certainly is," Lanie concurred. "Well, your dad said I could grab my bag?"

"Sure." She turned and headed back into the house. "Come in. Your friends can come too."

"I'm sorry. All Barbz are middle-aged now," Bea said to jeers around the room. "There, I said it."

Lanie didn't know where the time had gone when she heard the front door opening. She had in no way planned to be still sitting in Ridley's—*spectacular!*—kitchen debating 2010s-era female rapper fandoms with a fourteen-year-old when he finally got home. But somehow, as frequently happened when she, Gem and Fatou got together, things just spiraled out of control to the point that they were all huddled over a picked-over box of pizza two hours after they'd arrived. But Lanie would blame Shanice and her urgent need to pump, if it came to it.

"Middle-aged!" Gemma screeched in faux outrage. "How *dare* you!"

"Nuh-uh! Somebody come get this child!" Fatou demanded.

"Bardis are the wave," Bea doubled down, holding her own surprisingly well for a teenager among five adult women.

"Boogie Down representation. As a Bronxite, I'm wit' it." Lanie gave Bea a high five for their mutual love of rapper Cardi B.

"OMG, you're from the Bronx?" Bea said with a level of excitement and awe that Lanie could honestly say she'd never encountered before.

Naturally, Ridley did know they were there. Lanie had cleared their presence with him shortly after they arrived to find Bea there without Mrs. Handa, who'd had to rush home to tend to an ill Mr. Handa. But still, they hadn't planned to stick around quite that long.

"Hey," Ridley said cautiously as he entered the living room, walking toward the lively kitchen.

It had been two days and yet Lanie's insides felt like they were turning into a gelatinous puddle at the sound. It was hard to remember what so offended her about Dash's suggestion that they have "a little fun" when she turned and saw all six feet three inches of him approaching.

I like fun. I really *like fun.*

He looked a little confused by their group for a moment, before his eyes settled on her and softened. "Did I miss pizza?" Ridley's large palm grazed Lanie's lower back as he circled the table to reach Bea on the far side. Lanie stiffened, resenting how every nerve ending she possessed went on high alert just from that glancing contact.

"Dad, did you know that Melanie has a STEM degree?" Bea quizzed him without missing a beat, as if he'd just been in another part of the house all along. "In physics! From Empire University! It's on my list of American schools."

Lanie had been ready to fall out of her chair when she found out Bea had not only been looking at schools in the United States for college but had heard of EU, specifically.

"Degrees!" Gemma clarified.

"Our Mel is a proper egghead," Fatou offered.

"No, I'm not," Lanie countered.

"Wanted to work for NASA."

"A *very* long time ago," Lanie cut in, embarrassed by how ridiculous that probably sounded to a man of Ridley's achievements. To any real adult, honestly. It was like saying you wanted to be an astronaut when you grew up. Even if her dream was only to work in the Science Mission Directorate there.

"I think I did." Ridley looked at her with uncertainty as he walked up and kissed his daughter on the top of her head.

Lanie shook her head. She'd only told him she worked at EU. He shrugged. *Sorry*, he mouthed to her over Bea's head.

Fatou and Shanice clocked the exchange and looked at each other with raised eyebrows. Lanie groaned inwardly, knowing she'd hear all about that later.

Just then, she caught a stray elbow to the ribs as Gemma looked at her expectantly.

"Ouch! Ridley. Let me introduce my cousin, Gemma. And our friends, Fatou, Marissa and Shanice." Lanie rubbed her side as they all waved at him.

"You have a beautiful home, Dr. Aronsen," Shanice said, smiling broadly, already besotted.

Shanice needs to remember she's already married. Lanie wanted to sulk. Having need of a quiet room to use her breast pump in, Shanice had managed a look around while briefly installed in the upstairs study by Bea.

"I'm so glad I got to finally meet you," Gemma said. "We were wondering where Mel was always sneaking off to."

Lanie's face burned. "I haven't been sneaking anywhere."

"She's been with me."

They both spoke simultaneously then looked at each other.

"You two need to work on your story," Fatou said, winking with a sly smile.

Oh God. Lanie's face flamed white-hot. It was completely

innocent, but Gemma and Fatou had a way of making nothing into something. Which would be bad…in front of his daughter.

Where was a hole to jump into, or better yet, throw them into, when she needed one?

Bea frowned at them all, looking a little confused. Lanie used that opportunity to distract her. "Bea," Lanie said, grabbing her attention. "You should have your dad bring you along on one of his trips to New York. Have you ever been?"

She shook her head, seeming to still be mulling the previous conversation.

Ridley glanced at Lanie but his attention remained with his daughter. "We've been talking about it. Right, Bean? Maybe next summer."

"Yeah," Bea said, her enthusiasm for the topic returning. "I have a list of all the places I want to see. Dad said maybe we'll make it a road trip."

"Or maybe a train trip instead?" Lanie remarked, remembering how nervous he'd said he was driving to Philadelphia. "The less time you spend behind the wheel, the better. Right, Doc?"

Bea gave her another curious look, her smile faltering for another moment, before nodding. "Dad doesn't usually admit he doesn't like to drive."

Lanie didn't know what she'd said wrong, *again*, but Bea's shifting mood definitely felt like a cue. "Anyway, it's after seven, maybe we should go."

Ridley paused in his reach over Bea's shoulder for the lone remaining slice of cold pizza. "Really?"

Lanie looked around at her companions pleadingly.

"I have a six-month-old that I have to get home to," Shanice said, saving them all from an awkward exit.

They all began to rise from the table, nodding in agreement.

Ridley and Bea walked them to the door.

On the stoop, Lanie turned back but avoided Ridley's eyes. "Thank you for being an amazing hostess, Bea."

"Yay, Bea!" the ladies chimed in from the street below, waiting on their Uber.

Bea beamed.

"Thanks for my bag," Lanie added, unsure how to wrap this up with five pairs of eyes on them.

"Sorry again that you had to come all this way to get it," Ridley said. "I've just been swamped at work this week." His arm was draped over Bea's shoulder as they both stood in the doorway, precluding any greater conversation. "And thank you for staying with Bea."

"It was our pleasure." Which was true. Bea was fun, cute and supersmart. The best kind of kid as far as Lanie was concerned.

"For God's sake, just shove the shopping in the boot, Marissa!" someone, likely Gemma, yelled, then there was a honk. Lanie turned to see the others were piling into the car.

"Gotta run." She tried being casual, giving a little wave as she ran down the steps and through their gate onto the street.

"Budge up," Fatou ordered, making room as Lanie gave Bea another little wave before climbing into the crowded cab.

Fatou broke the silence a moment later, as the car started down the street. "He a peng ting, bwoy!"

They all laughed.

"Seriously, that man is proper leng!" Marissa concurred, slapping Fatou's hand.

"And posh." Gemma turned, eyeing Lanie from the front seat. "Um, how is this the first time your cousin is hearing about 'im?"

"I thought you knew, since you were running your mouth to Gran?"

That shut her up.

twenty-seven

Ridley

Ridley and Bea stood in the doorway as the car went down the street, taking a whirlwind of laughter, perfume and boisterous voices with it. And like people who marveled at a tornado that blew through their whole neighborhood but somehow left their house standing, they were both shell-shocked. When the rear lights finally disappeared, they exhaled.

Bea stepped back into the hall. She had a huge smile on her face. Ridley smiled back. It had been a really, *really* long time since that many people were inside their home. In fact, the last time was at Thyra's repast. It had been longer since they'd hosted Thyra's small get-togethers or a lively group of Bea's girlfriends or even had Dash, Maeve and their kids over for dinner. And now, in Bea's exuberance, Ridley saw how much that had affected her.

"They were fun," Bea said happily. "Lanie said you guys are plane buddies."

Is that what she called it? "Pretty much."

They went back into the kitchen to start cleaning up. Speaking of tornadoes, it looked like one had hit his kitchen. There were plates, cups, potato chip bags, food wrappers, soda cans and water bottles strewn everywhere. If he hadn't seen them with his own eyes, Ridley would have thought Bea hosted a party for a gaggle of her school friends while he wasn't home.

"We couldn't figure out what to eat. Melanie's friend Shanice said she was still eating for two. Then it took us a while to settle on pizza," Bea explained, seeing her father's face.

Ridley chuckled, pulling out the garbage bin. "It's okay, sweetie."

He'd been surprised when Lanie called to say she'd found Bea home alone. Mrs. Handa was supposed to still be there for another few hours and Bea wasn't supposed to be home until later from soccer practice herself.

"She's pretty too," Bea said.

"Who?" Ridley couldn't tell if this was a fishing expedition or just an observation.

"Melanie, of course." Bea took an exasperated tone.

"What? There were five women here. Specificity, Bean, we've discussed that before. When you can, be specific." He was being evasive.

"I think Melanie is very pretty, Father."

Ridley smirked with his back to her. He debated his response while washing the dishes. He supposed Bea knew eventually he might start dating again. But a little under three years after her mother's death, was she ready to see it? Shit, was he ready?

"Yes, she is. They all were." He turned to gauge her response.

"Don't objectify women, Dad," Bea said, stuffing things into the bin.

He snorted. "You asked."

She took a long-suffering breath. "You had her bag. Why?"

"She didn't tell you?" Bea shook her head. "She left it in your uncle Dash's car. Remember, I told you he picked me up from the airport? Well, I should have said he picked 'us' up. She was there too." Ridley watched Bea carefully. "She's just a new friend, Bea. That's all."

Bea exhaled, visibly relieved. Ridley smiled at his daughter, and she smiled back.

And that is definitely the truth, Ridley reminded himself. Regardless of how it had begun to feel.

The Sky Garden was like a giant greenhouse five hundred feet in the air. Taking up the top three floors of a thirty-eight-story office building, it was a glass-enclosed public park and restaurant space. Ridley had heard about it but never visited it before. He hadn't wanted to impress Lanie when he very casually suggested meeting up in the breathtaking space. But with a three-hundred-and-sixty-degree view of Metropolitan London out floor-to-ceiling windows, with lush trees, flowers, ferns and succulents inside, it would definitely seem to Lanie like he was. And overlooking Tower Bridge and St. Paul's Cathedral outside, he was eager to see what she thought.

Lanie arrived, dressed in a bulky turtleneck sweater, blue jeans and a pair of sneakers. Looking down at his dress shirt, tie and slacks, Ridley worried that they'd gotten their wires crossed. Watching her marvel at the three-story atrium, however, it was clear he hadn't gotten that wrong. She was impressed. Even if that was only one of the feelings warring on her face.

"Hey," he said after he'd flagged her down. She'd slowly, quite possibly reluctantly, come to join him.

Ridley slid a hand over her shoulder in greeting, pulling her chair out for her. Again, he wasn't sure if he'd imagined it, but she seemed to edge away as she seated herself. He reviewed their interaction at the house again. Though the group of people with them had prevented any real discussion, he realized for a second time that her remoteness might not be his imagination.

"We okay?" he asked as she sat across from him.

The waiter came and poured water into their empty goblets but moved away quickly with a tight smile for Ridley, feeling the chill at the table.

Lanie's usually expressive face was a mask. "What makes you ask that?"

His hackles rose. Thyra would make him guess what he'd done wrong. That wasn't a dynamic he had any interest in revisiting. So, what she wouldn't do was lie in his face. "Playing coy doesn't suit you."

Lanie looked piqued, her already large doe eyes going wider. "Fine, what does 'a little fun' mean? Your friend Dash called me that." Her tone was confrontational.

"When?"

"When you dropped me off."

"Dash said that to you?"

Ridley knew Dash had said something unnecessary to Lanie when he wasn't in the car. He could see that on her face. But if Dash had been inappropriate—something Ridley genuinely had difficulty imagining—a failure of imagination wouldn't prevent him from having words with his best friend.

"No. He didn't say it to me. He said it to you when I called you back. You answered the call and he said 'she's good for a little fun.'"

Ridley had wondered how much she'd heard. "No, he didn't."

Lanie's hazel-brown eyes narrowed and if looks could kill, Bea would be an orphan. "He did. I heard him. He called me 'a little fun.'"

Ridley nearly laughed at her expression but caught himself. Lanie didn't look in the mood to joke. Adorable? *Very.* Murderous? *Even more so.*

"No, I promise, he didn't."

The waiter caught Ridley's eye but Ridley shook his head discreetly.

"Don't lie for him," Lanie said, livid, her face warming to a florid red.

He exhaled, relieved this could be easily cleared up. "He

called *the Borough Market* a little fun. As in, I was wondering if I should take you there the next time you came into town and he said, 'You should. You could do worse for a little fun.'"

"Oh." It was like all the air leaked out of a large and angry balloon; Lanie quite literally deflated. He hadn't noticed it before but now he saw her go concave as if she were decreasing in outraged volume.

Why and how had every permutation of her face and mood become so riveting to him? When had it happened, that even her anger was attractive? "Is that what you've been angry about?"

He warred with a sense of amusement at how irritated she was, but maintained a straight face.

"I wasn't angry."

"Now who's lying? You gave me the cold shoulder in my own house."

She opened her mouth then closed it, pursing those pillowy lips at his challenging expression.

She tried again. "I was wonderfully pleasant there. Just ask your daughter."

Ridley mirrored her when she cracked an arch smile. She had the best smiles, he'd noticed. "I did," he challenged.

"And what did she say?" Lanie asked as if genuinely interested.

"That you were wonderfully pleasant...to *her*."

Lanie let loose a peal of giggles as Ridley waved for their waiter, finally signaling him forward.

twenty-eight

LANIE:

I'm back in London on the nineteenth.
Will you be available?

RIDLEY:

What no Christmas plans?

LANIE:

Sure, but my mom has to work all that week.
So as long as I'm home by Christmas morning,
I'm golden.

RIDLEY:

More wedding business?

LANIE:

We have a cake tasting.

RIDLEY:

Sounds delicious

LANIE:

I certainly hope so. How about you?
Christmas plans?

RIDLEY:

Nothing much. Work.

LANIE:

You know I have never asked you
what your study is about?
All I hear study this, study that

RIDLEY:

You sure you're interested? It's a lot.

LANIE:

Hit me.

RIDLEY:

It's a multi-target therapy study
comparing the use of plankolumab
to azifrotinib as induction treatment
of proliferative lupus nephritis.

LANIE:

Okay.

RIDLEY:

😃 In layman's terms it's a safety and efficacy
study comparing two new experimental
medications for stage 2-4 lupus

LANIE:

Is that what your wife had?

LANIE:

I'm sorry was that too much?

RIDLEY:

No

LANIE:

We can talk about something else.

RIDLEY:

No it's OK. At a certain point I had to get comfortable talking about this. Yes she had stage 6 by the end.

RIDLEY:

Technically end-stage kidney disease is what she died of

LANIE:

I am so sorry.

RIDLEY:

Me too.

LANIE:

Is that why you do what you do?

RIDLEY:

It's definitely a part of the reason.

LANIE:

I bet Thyra would be honored.

RIDLEY:

I hope she was.

twenty-nine

Lanie

■ 19-DEC ■ Trans-Continental Airways ■ Flight: 506 ■

JFK-John F. Kennedy Int'l Airport ▶ **LHR-London, Heathrow**

Seat Assignment: **17G**

Had anyone told Lanie that cake-tasting wouldn't be her absolute favorite part of best mate of honor duties, she'd have called them a damn liar.

Now though, sitting in front of eleven small cake samples, just the sticky-sweet smell of vanilla and caramel essence, ganache, royal icing, fondant and marzipan everywhere nauseated her. She'd thought the best idea would be to come to the tasting on an empty stomach. *All the better to eat you with, my dear.* But, an hour later, Lanie felt distinctly like the Big Bad Wolf at the *end* of the tale—ready to be split open and field dressed.

She pushed back from the table exhausted, marveling at the indefatigability of Gemma and Fern, the pastry chef and owner of this fancy patisserie in Knightsbridge. Even clout-chasing in SW1, where high-end stores like Harrods and Harvey Nichols were, was in its own way tiring and pretentious. There were perfectly lovely French bakeries south of the river.

Gemma and Chef Fern effused over an angel food cake with a berry mascarpone filling and Chantilly frosting as Gemma shoveled the umpteenth bite of cake into her mouth. At a certain point, all the flavors had begun to merge. Lanie didn't know where Gemma was putting it all on her tiny frame.

Her booty, definitely, Lanie speculated with a chuckle; all the Turner women had more than enough to share.

Gemma looked up frowning but continued debating the merits of curds versus compotes with Fern uninterrupted. When the tiny bell above the front door rang out, indicating a customer, Fern made a quick apology and left the kitchen.

Gemma's eyebrows shot up expectantly. "Well?"

This wasn't Lanie's wedding, so it wasn't her decision. "I don't know, what are you thinking?"

Gemma licked the frosting off the fork hanging from her mouth, mulling her decision.

"Gem, we're running over." Lanie checked her watch.

"Don't rush me."

Rush her? It had been over sixty-five minutes of nonstop cake.

"Fern's been nice enough not to say anything but that's probably her four o'clock."

Lanie kept her voice even, though she was dying for a resolution as much as she imagined the proprietress was at this point. They'd sampled nearly every iteration of cake, filling and frosting the woman offered. It was time to decide. Particularly since Fern was allowing for their truncated timetable. As Lanie had come to understand, there were an assortment of vendors who were only too willing to accommodate their last-minute Valentine's Day wedding requests as long as the couple understood there would be a tremendous upcharge for the short notice and the date. So, Lanie was becoming adept at making decisions…quickly.

"Pick one."

Gem dug her fork into a lavender-infused white almond cake with apricot compote.

"Okay, that?" Lanie had liked that one but anything chocolate was usually Gemma's go-to.

Gemma shrugged.

"Gem. C'mon!"

Gemma frowned. "It's a lot of choices."

Lanie agreed. This would have been far easier with fewer options to choose from.

Gemma's eyes began to water. "I wish Jonah was here."

I wish he was too. Lanie struggled valiantly not to roll her eyes. *Instead of me.*

Gemma's chin wobbled. Lanie didn't know when her cousin had become *this* sloppy, emotionally needy mess. She didn't know what to say or if she should even acknowledge these tears at all.

Lanie sighed. "You know he would have if it wasn't a last-minute appointment."

"He should be here. He's the one who loves *The Great British Bake Off.*"

"Jonah loves baking competitions?"

Gem nodded, pinching her trembling lips together in an effort to staunch the flow of tears, even as she ate another sliver of a nearby cake. "He's dying to be a contestant."

Since when? He used to eschew all reality TV as "lowbrow entertainment." *The snob.* Maybe it was the subject matter? Lanie had never tried to get him into a cooking show.

"He loves *R&B Love Lives* and *Felonious Househusbands* too. He says Gizelle is his other boo." Gemma laughed through her tears at the recollection.

"Other boo"? The fuck?

Lanie couldn't pay Jonah to sit still through any of that with her. From *The Real World* to *Love Is Blind,* he'd refused to be drawn in. For her at least. That realization rankled her.

"That cake's good?" Lanie cleared her throat to ask. "Seems like you're partial to the chocolate with the raspberry compote."

"Can't. Need a light color." Gemma gestured at herself, mouth full.

Right. In case of spills.

"But anything is capable of staining a little bit."

Gemma grunted, swallowing a forkful of chocolate cake with Bavarian cream. Lanie smirked at Gemma, childlike and sporting a dollop of cream at the corner of her mouth.

Fern returned. "So, what do you think?"

Lanie had an idea. "How about we keep the chocolate cake but pair it with a white chocolate frosting and a fresh raspberry and Bavarian cream filling?"

Gemma held still as Lanie reached across the table to wipe her cousin's mouth with a napkin.

Fern nodded. "Instead of the raspberry compote?" she verified.

"Can you?" Gemma broke into a smile.

"Of course." The chef nodded.

"That way you get the chocolate flavors you want with the raspberry but it's less of a stain hazard. Sound good?"

"Sounds lovely," Fern concurred.

"Okay..." Gemma said. "Sure."

Lanie hoped all was well with the lovebirds because Gem's response decidedly lacked enthusiasm. But maybe Lanie was just projecting...because she was *definitely* over all of this.

thirty

Ridley

"You do know that I've been to Borough Market before, right?" Lanie said as they walked down the long, crowded aisles of shop stalls in the famous indoor food market.

The real point of bringing her to the market had been to help her with any last-minute Christmas shopping she needed. Borough Market was an eclectic mix of vendors selling everything from fresh and prepared foods to aromatic bath bombs and tartan-print scarves. The enormous art deco market and all the stalls were festooned with lights and evergreen boughs for the holiday season. A gigantic wreath with a red bow and fairy lights hung fifty feet in the air from the metal-and-glass rafters as a centerpiece.

"I've only taken you to new places," she insisted.

Ridley didn't think she was honestly complaining but he indulged her anyway because it was becoming his new favorite thing to do.

He smiled inwardly. "No. Not really."

"What? The Statue of Liberty, the High Line, the New York Aquarium. I even inadvertently managed to give you a five-borough tour…"

"But I've been to see the Statue of Liberty before, and the High Line too."

"You have?" She stopped midrant. "Why didn't you say something? You let me go on and on about it."

Because I love anything you're enthusiastic about.

"Because I hadn't been since they opened the extension. I hadn't seen that Honeycomb thing yet." He shrugged.

Increasingly, he found he'd go anywhere she wanted as long as they were together. Ridley had discovered Lanie was an ideal traveling companion. She was adventurous, willing to try anything once. She was exuberant about the things that caught her interest and curious to learn about things she didn't know. And she was remarkably resilient. When a thunderstorm had driven them indoors the day they finally reached Coney Island, she'd merely shaken off the rain and gone to wait out the downpour in the aquarium with some hot chocolate.

"The Vessel."

"What?" He'd gotten distracted watching her stroll through the market.

"It's 'the Vessel,' not 'the Honeycomb,'" she corrected, as she walked along eyeing various objects.

Over the past few months, Ridley found himself coveting Lanie's pleasure, wanting to be the one who provided it. He didn't know exactly when it had happened that their amicable relationship had begun to change, but increasingly, he felt it.

"When were you last here?" he asked.

She looked sheepish, not meeting his eyes. "When I was seventeen."

"Has it changed since then?"

It was as if he'd teed her up; she rebounded beautifully. "Ah-ha! No! It's Borough Market. It hasn't changed since the eighteenth century."

This woman.

"Now, Lanie," he said, holding in a smirk. "Fundamentally, no. Literally, yes."

"Yeah, well. My point stands. I've been here before."

"Fine. I wasn't aware it was a competition, but you got me."

"Point for me!" She smiled mischievously and Ridley realized he was happy to lose.

They left the market with a few bags, feeling stuffed from sampling various snacks and giddy from cups of mulled wine. Ridley was pleased with himself. They'd made it all the way through the market and onto the Queen's Walk along the Thames with his real surprise ahead and Lanie still unaware.

"I'm getting tired. Can we sit a spell before we head back?" She wandered toward the benches facing the river.

"You're worse than Bea. It's a little further, c'mon."

"What is? Where are we going? We've already passed the Tate and the Globe Theatre. What other tourist spots are left over here?" She looked around with exasperation.

"You're on the verge of whining, FYI." He raised an eyebrow at her, locking her arm in his to keep her from sitting down at any of the very inviting seats along the walkway. "You'll see. C'mon."

They'd done the bulk of the walk and Ridley knew the only reason their destination had not yet occurred to her was because he'd been so adamantly against it. From their current vantage point, it could already be seen, looming large and obnoxious above the treetops.

When they finally arrived, Lanie stopped, craning her head upward to stare. "No the hell you didn't!"

And there was that big, bright megawatt smile that made Ridley's heart physically ache in his chest.

"No," she said again, shaking her head.

He nodded and she screamed. He did not expect that.

"But you said you hate Ferris wheels?"

"Technically, the London Eye is not a Ferris wheel. It's a 'cantilevered observation wheel'—whatever that means," he said dryly. "And I'm sure my acrophobia will appreciate the differences."

"Aww, Ridley, thank you!"

Lanie turned into his arms and hugged him. He settled his chin into her hair, as they both held on a little longer than normal. And with a great sinking feeling in the pit of his stomach, Ridley recognized how right this felt.

"Merry Christmas," he whispered into her curls, as his mouth dried and his throat stopped working properly.

He gave the attendant his name and reservation information as Lanie waited on the landing, watching enclosed observation pods circle slowly on the giant wheel. When he was done, he came up behind her in the relatively long line. Lanie leaned back into him as they waited and Ridley placed his hands on her shoulders, squeezing them occasionally.

As the wheel slowly came to each stop a new group was admitted into the pods stationed at the landing. Finally, the attendant put his arm out to pause Lanie. She hung back as the doors closed on the people before them and the wheel started up again, rotating that pod away.

"I think a couple more people could've fit on that one but whatever," she intimated to him under her breath as she peered over her shoulder.

Ridley just smiled at her eagerness. Despite his own reticence, he'd known Lanie would love this.

When the next pod landed in front of them, the previous occupants disembarked and the attendant let her and Ridley on.

"Watch your step," the attendant advised.

Lanie raced around the oval bench to the far side of the oblong, egg-shaped pod.

"Have fun!" the attendant said as the doors closed and the pod began to rise.

Ridley's stomach was already doing somersaults just seeing the full 360-degree, wall-to-wall windows, even though they weren't yet two feet in the air.

Lanie spun around, only then noticing that none of the other people in line had joined them. Her face was a question mark. "We have this *whole* pod to ourselves?" Her eyes went wide. "For real?" She clapped her hands together and made a quick lap around. "Oh my God! Ridley, thank you!"

He so wanted to take all the credit, but his stupid conscience nagged at him. Yes, he'd been waiting for this since Gavin first suggested it. But ultimately it was still Gavin's suggestion. "Wasn't my idea."

Lanie paused, her brows furrowing a little. "Whose idea was it?"

The answer to this question was far more involved than he'd intended. Against his better judgment, Ridley glanced outside. With floor-to-ceiling windows on all sides and London spreading out beneath them, there really was no other place to put his eyes. It was either Lanie's face or the drop into the Thames outside.

A powerful wave of nausea hit him and he slumped to the bench.

"Ridley!" Lanie rushed to him. "Are you alright?" She grabbed his hand, crouching in front of him.

"I'm fine," he said, but in truth, he felt incredibly woozy and maybe even a little frightened. "This is why I hate Ferris wheels." Even to his ears, his voice sounded shaky. He looked up to the ceiling, but even that was made of glass. "We're in a damn giant glass egg," he whispered to her, feeling even worse now, if that were possible. He panted, opening the collar of his button-down.

I fly on planes all the time, dammit! The last time his acrophobia had been this bad was the last time he rode a Ferris wheel, coincidentally. As a kid, he'd gone up in one with his sister James, then wet himself when they sat helplessly at the top for five minutes due to mechanical difficulties.

"How long is this thing?" He couldn't remember what the website said.

Lanie opened the little pamphlet she'd snagged near the ticket counter, then bit her lip. "Thirty minutes."

Ridley moaned.

"I am so, so sorry, Ridley. If I'd known your fear of heights was this bad, I would never have pushed it!" Lanie's words came fast and flustered. "Y-you fly all the time. I really didn't understand."

He squeezed his eyes shut. The pod moved so slowly that with his eyes closed, it didn't feel like he was going to tip over even though he was seated. "Well, Lanie, I know. I didn't either. So, make that make sense." Lanie squeezed his hand and he opened his eyes for a second to look into hers. "I'm sorry for ruining this for you."

"Ridley, the gesture alone was more than enough." She swept a hand over his face, using delicate fingertips to remove his glasses and close his eyelids. "Keep your eyes closed." She sat beside him and huddled into his arm. "You're gonna keep your eyes shut and I'm gonna distract you."

"Unless you've got a sedative or a tranq dart in your pocket, I don't see how." It felt like there was no power on earth that could erase the image of the river, the Houses of Parliament, Buckingham Palace and the rest of Metropolitan London looming three hundred feet below him.

"Watch me," she said defiantly. "Or you know, *listen.* Don't open your eyes."

Ridley took a deep breath, focusing on that intoxicating jasmine-and-rose scent that constantly wafted off Lanie. It was on her clothes, in her hair, and anytime he was within a foot of her, it filled his nostrils. He used it as aromatherapy right now, breathing it in and out as her curls tickled his nose.

"I'm waiting," he said into the silence.

"For what?"

"The distraction."

"Oh, yeah. Where'd you get the tickets for this?"

"I thought you were supposed to do the talking?" He was being mildly evasive.

"I never said that." She held his arm tighter, her head settling comfortably into the crook of his neck. "Talk."

He sighed. "I got them from Bea's biological father. Guy named Gavin."

Lanie said nothing as he detailed the mess that was his life right now. Including the increasing risk of losing Bea, and therefore the deal for Christmas he'd struck with Gavin. She listened intently.

"Thyra and I, well, it wasn't quite what we let people imagine." Ridley shrugged. "We met in school, but it didn't start as some great college romance. For one, she'd had a serious boyfriend when we met—Gavin. He's actually how I met her. Gavin was a resident on one of my intern rotations." He opened an eye, quickly scoping for Lanie's expression. She seemed impassive, absorbing the information without judgment.

He exhaled, continuing, "I did fall in love with Thyra, yes. And I followed her here to England, yes. But, God help me—" He took a deep breath before starting. "Thyra was extraordinary, you know? Ridiculously pretty, funny, bold, brilliant. Much smarter than me. And I developed a crush on her that grew into something more, the more time we spent together. Gavin and I were, let's call it, 'cool' with each other."

He was rambling, he never rambled, but getting to the nuts and bolts of this was hard for many reasons.

"And essentially, I was always around, offering to help her study or bringing her meals. All it took was seeing everything that Gavin was and being the opposite—which was easy because he's a dick."

Lanie snickered.

"I want to be clear, we weren't together while they were together...*exactly*. I was her friend. But in all honesty, it wasn't for a lack of me trying. And I know how it probably sounds. It's just that I knew he didn't deserve her. That she'd get fed up with him…and, well, eventually, she did." He peeked again. Lanie's nose was scrunched in a frown. Ridley's heart kicked up in panic.

"So, you 'nice-guyed' her."

"You've lost me."

"Basically, you pretended to be her friend, biding your time." She said it frankly, but Ridley felt the sting of reproach in it. Lanie had clobbered him with the blunt force of the unvarnished reality. No matter how he dressed it up, he supposed…

"No! I never pretended… You don't understand."

My God. Was that what I did?

"I mean…" He paused to really consider. "I don't know."

"Don't stop," she encouraged him nevertheless, holding him tightly.

"They broke up and, admittedly with very little space between, we started dating. Then she found out she was pregnant. And reasonably, the baby couldn't have been mine, so I was terrified she'd go back to him. But then suddenly she got sick."

"Her lupus?" Lanie prompted him.

He nodded. "Developed a blood clot in her leg that could have killed her." Ridley took deep breaths, trying not to relive the terror of that time as he recounted it.

"It's okay if you want to stop." Lanie seemed to feel him tense but held him tighter.

"No, it's okay," he continued even as his chest constricted. "I don't know why I'd been so afraid. Because Gavin, of course, did what the Gavins of the world do: abandoned his responsibilities to his unborn child until it was convenient for him to acknowledge them."

"Asshole."

"Yeah." Ridley couldn't have said it better. "I showered Thyra with all the attention and affection I had to give. While he ignored the fact that she was going through this."

"So, you continued dating her when she was sick *and* pregnant with another man's child?"

Ridley wondered at the slightly awed tone of Lanie's voice and thought back to the little she'd told him of her own parents. "Of course."

Perhaps her father is a "Gavin" too? He hated that for her. He'd long ago realized what he did wasn't something every man would do. But it seemed illogical to him that any man who claimed to love a woman could not love and care for her child too.

"It didn't matter. By then, I was already in love with her."

Ridley looked at Lanie. Her cartoonishly large eyes ran the length of him like she was taking his measure as a man.

What does she see? he wondered. The calm, capable, trustworthy man he aimed to be, or something else? Whatever it was, it was less the carefully crafted façade of Ridley Aronsen that most people got. And the idea of that disquieted him some.

"Well, it's good you were there when Bea was born."

Ridley shifted in his seat.

"Not exactly. Thyra left Boston to go back to her parents once she knew Gavin didn't intend to help her. She was all alone in the States. No family, and between the baby coming and the lupus diagnosis, she needed more help than I thought I could give."

"And you?"

"Like I said, we hadn't been dating that long. I was just a kid. Only in my third year of medical school." He shrugged. "So, she broke up with me and I stayed there to finish."

He didn't bother with the sordid saga of Thyra confronting Gavin, only to be bought off by his family with that house—that it turned out they didn't even buy for *her*.

"But immediately I knew I'd made a mistake letting her go. So as soon as I graduated, I followed and begged her to take me back. Bea was one and a half by then. Gavin's parents offered Thyra some financial support but only after she'd done a paternity test and put his name on the birth certificate to force their hand. But sometimes I wish she'd waited for me. Still, I can't blame her for not doing that. She was young and struggling."

He'd never gotten the whole story of what happen before he arrived and, having learned that even the part he thought he knew was a lie, Ridley tried not to speculate or even care anymore.

All that mattered was Bea.

"So, where are Gavin's parents now? Does Bea see them?"

"Devon somewhere. Bea gets a birthday card and a Christmas gift every year. She's never met them."

Lanie squeezed his arm sympathetically. "There's a whole side of my family I don't really know either. That's why my mom had to ship me here to my gran every summer. No childcare in New York."

He nodded in understanding. "I don't know where Thyra and Bea would've been without my in-laws. Where I would be now either."

When Bea was small, Thyra had leaned as heavily on her parents as Ridley did now. Philip and Clare-Olive were angels who were due an immense debt of gratitude…but also overdue for a break.

Ridley's pulse had calmed. And when he finally looked out, they were on the other side of the apex. He exhaled with a shudder.

"I think you should go."

"Go where?" He could tell Lanie was trying to distract him again, but just having her there, leaning against him, made things better.

"To Colorado." She hadn't said anything when he first mentioned Gavin's ludicrous offer; he should have known she was merely formulating her opinion.

Ridley frowned furiously. *That is absurd.* He wouldn't stay under that jackass's roof.

"Seriously, if the custody is such a done deal, maybe this is his peace offering. A way of saying he wants you all to be okay with each other. If he's gonna get at least shared custody then it behooves you to improve your relationship with him…at least for Bea's sake, if not for your own."

"It 'behooves' me?"

"Lanie know many big word."

He chuckled.

"And if he's still a jerk, you be the better person." She pulled out of his embrace and he felt the loss acutely. She took his face in between her hands. "Ridley, listen to me. That animosity in your heart only eats at you. *Gavin?* He's gonna be out here living his best life with your daughter in tow."

Oof. The idea of that burned.

"Choose to extend Gavin a little grace and believe he invited you to Colorado in order to mend fences and not for some other nefarious intent. Take it from a child of divorce: if you're going to have to co-parent with him, you need to bury the hatchet now. For your sake as well as Bea's."

She'd said the magic words that unlocked his heart then filled his vision with her big, mesmerizing hazel eyes staring at him as he inhaled her intoxicating scent. Ridley felt bewitched.

"I'll think about it."

Lanie's palms, still bracketing his jaw, pulled him forward infinitesimally. And his arm, which had remained loosely wrapped around her lower back, tightened. Greedily, Ridley took her all in this close-up, lingering on her pretty bowed lips before returning to her eyes. She searched his face in return, bringing him incrementally closer until his mouth was slotted over hers.

Ridley pulled that bottom lip he was already deeply enamored with into his mouth and Lanie sighed. The blood drained from his brain. He could already feel his pants tightening. His other arm snaked around her too, pulling her into his chest.

As the tip of her tongue traced the line of his upper lip, Ridley lost track of how high up they were. Lanie and her mouth were the whole world opening before him. He captured her tongue and savored the taste of mulled wine there. Inhaling the heady mixture of her floral signature and the spicy cinnamon and oranges on her lips, he bit her lightly. She moved in closer as he slipped his hand into her open coat and cradled her ribs just below the swell of her breast. He relished every sigh she emitted as he rubbed the underside of it with the knuckle of his thumb. Lanie moaned, gripping the back of his neck to steady herself as he dipped his tongue into her mouth. And she sucked on it until he could feel himself hardening.

"Please stand clear of the opening doors," the automated announcer instructed overhead, startling them both.

They sprang apart like guilty teenagers as the doors of the pod opened. The attendant smirked but otherwise pretended not to have seen anything through the glass.

Ridley hadn't even registered the last few minutes of the ride and he rose from the bench like he was coming out of a fog, shopping bags covering his crotch. Lanie's tan skin was flushed red and her lips were kiss-swollen and sexily plump. Looking at her, Ridley's mind ran riot. On one hand, seeing her, brown eyes wide and dazed, lips pink and pillowy from his kisses with her hair slightly disheveled, all he wanted was to push her up against the wall and finish what they'd started. On the other, however, he was deeply embarrassed. They were friends, and she was young and still figuring herself out while he was married with a kid.

Well, not married…not anymore.

"Thank you," he said quickly as they both hustled out of the pod, shamefaced.

"I'm sorry about that." He rubbed at his lower lip as if in evidence, removing the remnants of her lip gloss.

"No worries. I said I'd distract you, didn't I?" she joked.

But Ridley knew Lanie well enough now to see the smile didn't reach her eyes.

thirty-one

Ridley

■ 23-DEC ■ Trans-Continental Airways ■ Flight: 964 ■

LHR-London, Heathrow ► JFK-John F. Kennedy Int'l Airport

Seat Assignment: ~~14J~~ **31A/31C**

Ridley stuffed his carry-on into the overhead bin and sat in the open seat beside Lanie.

Her mouth dropped open, watching. "Wait, what are you doing here? I thought—"

"That I wasn't going to come?" He gave her a playful smile, shrugging. "Yeah, well, a very smart woman with a big vocabulary said it 'behooved' me to join my daughter. And I knew what flight you'd be on, so, I bought a last-minute ticket. And here I am."

"Is that why you're in coach like a pleb too?"

"Pretty much," he lied, and doing that had honestly sucked.

"And just happened to get the seat right next to mine? What's the likelihood?"

"What's a little moving heaven and earth to be here? For someone I love, I'd do anything."

Lanie's face reddened. He liked that he'd flustered her and

suddenly wondered what she'd look like red-faced with exertion too. Then just as quickly he blinked, dismissing the unbidden, totally inappropriate thought. "Bea will love this surprise," he quickly added. Ridley flagged down a passing attendant. "Can I have another water for her and a Bloody Mary for me? Cheers."

The attendant looked puzzled for a moment before nodding as Ridley turned back to Lanie.

"Uh. Isn't it a little early in the flight?"

He checked his watch. As the saying goes, it was five o'clock somewhere. "Nope."

Plus, he needed something to settle these sudden nerves.

"God, you have some real 'entitled white man' energy some-times. Has anyone ever told you that?" She spoke in censure, but chuckled lightly.

"No, I think that's definitely a first."

■ 23-DEC ■ Trans-Continental Airways ■ Flight: 964 ■

LHR-London, Heathrow ► ~~JFK-John F. Kennedy Int'l Airport~~

KEF-Keflavík International Airport

Seat Assignment: **31A/31C**

"Attention, passengers, the captain has turned on the seat belt sign. We ask everyone to return to their seats and fasten their seat belts. The captain has identified a mechanical issue requiring us to make an unscheduled landing."

"Nothing to worry about, folks." The captain's composed voice took over smoothly from the head flight attendant over the PA as passengers looked around, gauging each other's level of panic. Alarmed murmurs quieted. "It's a problem with the oxygen system that feeds into the drop-down masks. Nothing that impedes our ability to fly. So, it's only out of an abundance of caution that we've decided to land at Keflavík International shortly."

"Keflavík?" Lanie turned to Ridley.

"Iceland." Luckily, he could answer in a decidedly calmer fashion than he might have if the pilot had said it was a problem with the engine. But he still gave a short chuckle to mask his growing unease. "I've been before. You'll love it."

The captain continued, "We'll have the ground crew take a quick look-see and hopefully, we'll be back in the air and arriving in New York City ahead of that snowstorm. Happy holidays. Cabin crew, please take your seats and prepare for landing."

"You have, huh?" Lanie searched Ridley's face as if deciphering something written there. "Well, I'm sure I'd love it more if this was a scheduled stop."

A rotation of Christmas classics played in his ear as Ridley watched Lanie slouch against the front desk at the first hotel that had possible room. Her elbow was thrown up on the high counter. He smiled inwardly. She tapped at the surface with the edge of a credit card to a rhythm only she heard. He stood a foot away waiting on a customer service representative from a different hotel to return to the phone. The staff member at the counter looked about as helpful as the person who had him on hold. Which was to say, barely.

Lanie occasionally swatted the tiny ornaments hanging from the miniature tree on the counter, like a cat. She hadn't noticed but every few moments, the hotel rep glanced up from his computer monitor at her.

She has another admirer. Ridley had come to recognize that Lanie was not aware of the attention she and her wild curls, full lips and galaxy of freckles garnered.

As his daughter might say, Lanie was "deeply weird." But in a way that people were drawn to, and was pretty cute. Like her tendency to scrunch her nose, or tap it when she was thinking, as she was doing right then. Or how when she was concerned or nervous, she'd tug on her earlobe. Or how she barely stilled even asleep on a flight, fidgeting constantly.

Ridley smiled to himself thinking about it all.

Any luck? Lanie mouthed when she noticed him watching her.

He snapped out of his distraction, the fleeting grin disappearing from his face. He shook his head as hers fell sideways onto her arm draped across the counter dramatically.

He wasn't surprised that they weren't getting anywhere. Therese, at home, had zero luck procuring them a single hotel room anywhere within twenty minutes of the airport online. Their unscheduled pit stop had become an overnighter, and by the time they'd cleared Immigration, nearly all the flights inbound or outbound from the United States had been canceled. The Big Board of Flights was by then awash in red, thanks to the snowstorm there that had landed early.

They journeyed from airport hotel to airport hotel looking for available rooms. Ridley could have kicked himself. It wasn't like he hadn't known they'd been trying to beat a turn in the weather—it was winter after all. Now, there had been a run on rooms here in Keflavík and between that and the regular holiday season bookings, they were, in effect, nomads.

Five minutes later, after an entirely abortive conversation with the customer service representative, Ridley resigned himself to having struck out. "No luck," he admitted with a sigh as he rejoined Lanie at the front desk.

By then, the early sunset in Iceland had sent the light down behind the horizon hours ago and true night had fallen.

"Anything here?"

Lanie shook her head but it was the hotel clerk that spoke.

"I'm sorry, Dr. Aronsen." He gave a genuinely defeated shrug.

"So, that's it? We're supposed to sleep outside?" Lanie asked, and though she may have been directing the question to Ridley, her eyes remained on the clerk. She didn't exactly bat those long, brown lashes of hers but her tone and expression definitely read as coquettish.

A flush ran up the young blond clerk's neck into his face. He looked back down at the computer screen and punched keys determinedly. She glanced in Ridley's direction then, giving him a flash of a conspiratorial wink.

He stifled a laugh. *Well, maybe she does know she's cute…sometimes.*

"There may be one room available that I can offer you."

"One room?" Ridley's voice pitched upward, sounding more alarmed than he should. Lanie straightened from her prolonged lean against the counter to regard him. "Sorry, if that's all you have, sure."

Lanie's face was unreadable as she turned her attention back to the clerk.

"Unfortunately, it is." The clerk tapped a button. "So, I may have something in about thirty minutes. That is, if they don't extend their stay due to that." He tipped his chin upward.

Ridley looked in the direction the clerk had nodded. A television in the restaurant bar across the lobby displayed a Doppler weather radar image of two large, multicolored, swirling masses obscuring the entire Northeastern US.

Ridley groaned and excused himself to make a call to Bea's grandparents. They'd be sitting, waiting on news from him.

"You sure you're comfortable…with, well, you know…" Ridley trailed off awkwardly twenty minutes later as he followed Lanie down the hall on the second floor. "Sharing one room?"

"It's a suite with two bedrooms. And we were always gonna be in one room unless we wanted to stay in Reykjavík."

He nodded. That was the one thing his unsuccessful calls to various hotels repeated. They could always take the hour-long trek into the capital. There could be hundreds of available rooms there. Unfortunately, if they were rebooked onto a flight first thing in the morning, they'd run the risk of missing it, being an hour away. Lanie couldn't tolerate that and Ridley agreed.

They could have—*would have*—done much worse. So why didn't he feel better?

When Lanie opened the door at the end of the hall, she clapped her hands together in delight as he stepped inside behind her. Lanie walked from one bedroom to the other, feet away, inspecting them before claiming the left one for herself.

"You have the bigger king bed but I'll take the two doubles to have the bigger of the two bathrooms. I need space to spread out my products."

"Sounds fair," he said absently, taking in the space as she disappeared into her room.

Ridley's eyes transited the large space. It was a rather nondescript, utilitarian beige-encased main room with a wide but uncomfortable-looking gray sectional at the center. And an oval, particle board–style, walnut coffee table facing a sizable wall-mounted television.

"You okay?" Lanie wandered back into the main room after she'd dropped her bags.

Ridley nodded, uncertain he was telling the truth.

"You don't like it?"

"It's not that," he fibbed. "I'm worried I might miss Christmas if we can't get on a flight tomorrow."

Lanie's eyes softened. "You'll be there. I know you'll make it." Lanie glanced at her watch, clearly unsure of what to say next. "What I don't know is, the time the kitchen in that restaurant downstairs closes. So, I'm gonna run down and see what I can grab." Lanie turned and ran into the bedroom she'd chosen, climbing onto one of the beds and reaching for something in its center.

"Good idea," he said while trying to banish the single

thought that was running rampant in his head at the view she presented. Ridley's mouth dried watching her ample bottom crawl across the bed in the shaft of light that shone in from the main room. He had no right thinking the things he'd begun to.

"Can I get you something?" she called over her shoulder.

If Lanie knew what he was thinking, there was no way she'd willingly share a room with him. What he needed was to call Bea, then check in with Therese and Dash. He should probably even check his email.

"Uh, no, thanks," he replied, looking away guiltily.

Then he needed a shower. In fact, if they were going to last under the same roof all night, whether or not it was in entirely separate bedrooms, he was going to need a cold one.

thirty-two

Lanie took a deep breath as the elevator ascended.

She'd considered staying downstairs longer to heed the advice she'd been given where Ridley was concerned. Narcisa kept reminding her to be sensible about this. And as she awaited her dinner, she tried to repeat what her mother had told her.

Aim lower. The idea nagged at her.

Ridley wanted her, Lanie knew that. But, what did that mean precisely? It wouldn't require much of him to be merely interested in sex and nothing more. She'd met more than her fair share of those guys. Stupidly slept with some too. Still, that didn't seem like Ridley's style. He respected her. He paid attention to her without keeping his eyes squarely on her tits and ass.

At least usually.

She was pretty sure she hadn't imagined the air in their suite shifting. Ridley's eyes roaming her body and following her around the room the same way her super's cat did when it stalked its prey. But even if he was mildly interested, would she willingly trade Ridley's respect for some meaningless sex?

Yes!

That's the limerence talking, Lanie, the Narcisa in her head firmly shut her down.

Lanie stepped off the elevator with take-out containers from downstairs. She'd picked up a burger for him anyway, even though Ridley was sure to hate it. "Hey!" she called out, coming through the door. "I got—"

He wasn't there but an English-language cable news station played on the large television.

Lanie placed the take-out containers on the low coffee table in front of the couch and broke one open to get at the steak fries, popping some into her mouth.

"Food's on!" she called out, voice muffled by a full mouth.

She went into her room and stripped off her street clothes. Digging through her overnight bag for the T-shirt and shorts she usually slept in, she groaned, remembering that her bra would have to remain on since she had company. The main room was still empty when she reentered. Sighing, she walked up to Ridley's slightly ajar door.

"Oh, Doctor!" Lanie rapped out a short beat using both hands. "Ridley?" His door slid further open on soundless hinges. She took two tentative steps into the darkened but empty room before sucking in a breath.

Reflected in the bureau mirror to her right was an unobstructed view of Ridley through the open bathroom door on the left. He was standing in the glass shower. Lanie froze then gasped upon seeing where his hands were.

Christ on a cracker.

Lanie willed her legs to move, to back out quietly before he discovered her violation. To wipe this unauthorized vision of him from her mind before he turned and saw her standing there. Lanie tried to silently escape, but in her haste to back up, she accidentally brushed the light switch at her elbow. It winked on and off as if she'd been deliberately trying to catch his attention.

"Lanie?" Ridley grimaced through the water running down

his face, eyes snapping to the reflection of the open door just as she stepped out of view.

She spun, fleeing to her own room. Once inside, she closed and leaned against the door, dropping her face into her hands. Panting, she willed herself to shake the mental image loose. To somehow pretend it hadn't happened, if that was possible. But a knock on the door minutes later said that it wouldn't be.

"Lanie?"

She pressed her back into the door as if Ridley might try to push his way in. But the knocking was tentative, like his voice. "Lanie? Were you just in my room?"

Shame flooded her. "I am so incredibly sorry!" The words flowed like a torrent. "I swear to God, I'm not the kind of person who would sneak into someone's room and watch them shower! I didn't see anything!" she blurted out. It was a very obvious lie, made more so by her insistence. "I didn't!"

"Lanie, can you open the door?"

"Are you dressed?"

"At this point, does it matter?"

She groaned audibly.

"Sorry. Yes, of course I am."

Lanie was sure her brown face burned crimson. It would have caught fire, if possible. Still, she opened the door a crack. "I am disgusted with myself. I have no excuse. I brought you food and..." she sputtered into the silence with her eyes still closed, as if to look at him now would scald her retinas.

"Lanie." He sounded exasperated. "Open your eyes, please."

When she dared peek, Ridley was attired identically to her, wearing a T-shirt and a pair of boxers. His face was that unreadable mask she hated.

Is he pissed?

"Oh God, Ridley. I am mortified," she started again, easing the door open completely. "I was knocking and the door just opened and...and—"

"Lanie, calm down." He raised a hand to touch her before seeming to think better of it.

It fell back to his side, balling into a fist. Lanie felt physically sick. Bereft. She'd ruined things, she knew it—whatever this was between them. He'd trusted her and she'd violated his privacy. Tears welled in her eyes, but she fought them back.

This is about him, not me. Crying now would likely result in him trying to comfort me, which is gross.

Ridley frowned, looking at the floor, rubbing his neck. Then he took a breath. Lanie was desperate to know what he was thinking but felt particularly undeserving of his innermost thoughts. If their situations had been reversed, Lanie knew the sense of betrayal would have been so acute she wasn't sure she could have continued to share the suite with him. She would completely understand if he felt the same.

"Do you need me to go?" she whispered, barely able to push the air accompanying the words out of her diaphragm. "I can get my things."

"What?" His eyes flew to her face. He seemed surprised, while this felt like the most appropriate response to her. "No, no, of course not."

"But I—"

"You accidentally walked in on me taking a shower." He finished her sentence forcefully. "That's it."

Lanie tugged at her ear. *So, we're pretending the other part didn't happen?*

"Right?" he insisted.

"Right." She nodded. "No big deal." Lanie laughed it off, feigning a playfulness she didn't feel.

A lengthy silence grew between them as Lanie's gaze fixed on his. Ridley's expression darkened, growing fierce as his eyes raked over her, a hard obsidian behind the lenses of his glasses, his irises indistinguishable from the pupils. Her eyes fell to his mouth when he spoke.

"Okay, then let's eat."

Still, neither of them moved as the space between them became charged.

She didn't know what was happening but after their moment on the street and on the Eye, it suddenly felt ridiculous to keep pretending it was nothing. *Narcisa and Mom be damned.* They didn't understand her relationship with Ridley in part because she'd never truly been honest about it—to them or herself.

"What—what are we doing, Ridley?" Lanie held her breath, praying he wouldn't pretend he didn't understand what she was asking or she would perish from embarrassment. "I mean, what do you want this, us, to be? Friends or...?"

"I don't know," Ridley admitted, surprisingly.

Despite that answer, her heart surged with that ridiculous, continually revived hope as awareness filled his eyes.

"That's the problem. I don't either," she said, the air seeming to thin around them.

They were both lying. And they both knew it.

"But the way you look at me, touch me, kiss me, it isn't like a friend."

"I..." He breathed through the single syllable.

"And I can't bear this in-between much longer."

Ridley's open perusal paused at her full breasts and Lanie's nipples went diamond hard beneath the flimsy cotton shirt and lace bra. His eyes shot back to hers, nostrils flaring, jaw clenched as if holding back.

"Say something," she whispered. "Please."

"I want to—" His already deep voice dropped an additional octave that made her practically vibrate in resonance. He stepped closer as if pulled. "To see you like you saw me tonight—"

Lanie covered her face. "I am so sorry about that."

He frowned. "After what I just said, you think what I want is an *apology*?"

She shook her head.

"Good, because to be clear, I want *you*."

thirty-three

Lanie

Ridley was so close Lanie had to tip her head back to see into his eyes. Warmth radiated from him as her breasts grazed his chest, setting off sparks and igniting the first firework in a cascade in her belly.

He slid his hands across her shoulders but then stopped. Unlike the other times he'd done that, he braced her there, each finger pressing like individual brands, burning into her skin. He scanned her face, before giving a resigned sigh as if relenting. It wasn't a question of stopping now, it seemed to say, just the matter of who would move first.

"Can I?" Lanie reached up tentatively, taking his glasses off his face and placing them on a nearby table. "Can you see?"

He nodded. "As long as you stay close."

She'd rarely seen him without his glasses. His eyes were smaller, darker and more intense. His eyebrows arched naturally, less the censorious judgment she'd assumed than his normal expression. *He really is a Vulcan.*

The thought amused her as she slid her fingers along the slope of his nose, stopping where the glasses made semipermanent divots on the sides. "You're a real stud, anyone ever tell you that?"

He shook his head. "May I?" he whispered.

Lanie nodded. He replicated her motion, pulling the elastic out of her hair before fluffing out the voluminous curls. Her barely tame hair rebelled fully with his encouragement, creating a wild halo.

"And you're stunning," he replied.

"Shaggy." She ran a hand over her hair. It bounced back immediately.

He remained paused in her threshold. "Are we doing this?"

Lanie was afraid to reveal how truly eager she was. She feared her desire might frighten Ridley off as it had all the previous men in her life. But then she shook off the flash of Jonah's face, before it could gain further purchase in her mind, nodding instead.

Lanie's hand moved to Ridley's neck, pulling his mouth down onto hers. She rarely initiated kisses, finding it too awkward and vulnerable a position to tolerate. But she had with Ridley, repeatedly now, she realized, because he'd made her feel that empowered, that safe, like it was both her decision and natural for her to take the lead. Her lips slipped over his, her tongue caressing the seam, coaxing them apart. Ridley relaxed, welcoming her mouth, melting into her and easing into their kiss. Slowly, his arm encircled her waist, drawing her closer as his hand cupped her jaw, fitting her lips more securely to his. And when his tongue finally dipped into her mouth, she sighed with relief.

Soon, Ridley took control, his kiss growing more fervent, stoking the fire igniting in her belly, heating her. He released her jaw to possessively slide a hand under her hair and hold the nape of her neck. Lanie inhaled a startled breath as he pulled her flush against him, revealing the erection growing between them. Grasping his roaming hand, she slid it from the small of her back onto her ass, and Ridley groaned in approval, tightening his grip.

"You really want to do this?" he asked breathlessly, when his mouth left hers to hover right above her ear. "You're sure?"

Lanie nodded vigorously as he ran his tongue along the column of her neck. She couldn't think of anything she wanted more. "Why do you keep asking? Are you?"

He gripped the ass cheek she'd offered him, squeezing, nearly pulling her off her feet, letting her feel every hard inch of him. "Hell yes," he replied. "I just want you to be sure."

"I am."

Ridley entered her room then, backing her into one of the beds inside. He leaned in, kissing her hard again, as he rested a knee on the bed behind her to ease her back onto it. He held her neck, settling his forehead against hers for a moment, their noses touching. But when she wrapped her leg around his calf, clinging to him, they fell onto the bed together awkwardly, laughing into each other's mouths.

Ridley's body covered hers until he pulled back slightly, holding himself up by the elbows to look into her face. He smiled. It was a big one, possibly the biggest she'd ever seen him wear. A small depression more than a true dimple revealed itself in his left cheek. She reached to touch it.

"What?"

"How do you not know how cute you are?" She tapped the dimple.

His eyebrows rose. "Not handsome?"

"Not with that." She slid the finger from that dimple to caress his bottom lip. He bit the tip of her finger playfully, before sucking it into his mouth. "Is that why you don't smile a lot? Because then people would know how cute you were and wouldn't take you seriously?"

He snorted, shifting his body to more fully cover hers, settling between her legs. "I don't smile a lot?"

Lanie clenched, trying not to squirm under him. It was exquisitely torturous; she wasn't sure she could bear added friction. She shook her head. *How can he not know that?*

"Well, I guess..." He paused. She wasn't sure he'd continue, the smile slipping from his face back into its normal hiding place. "There hasn't been much in my life to smile about lately."

The somber response jarred Lanie. It reminded her why they were there, headed to the States and what they were doing. In her admittedly limited experience, having sex with a guy wasn't a great way to get him to stick around. In fact, quite the opposite—and that probably went double for a widowed father still grieving his late wife. Ridley now seemed as vulnerable as she felt and a sliver of doubt edged in.

Was she about to ruin something precious?

"Until you. And this, between us," he finished.

At those words, Lanie's train of thought derailed. All her doubts vanished as Ridley brought his forearms up to bracket her head, dipping his face to kiss her again. He lapped at her lips, his tongue intertwining with hers. She drowned in the depths of his kiss, losing her bearings, only knowing that there was too much clothing between them. She reached for his T-shirt, preparing to pull it off when he caught her hands.

"Uh-uh. I told you what I wanted," he said into her lips.

"What?" She'd already forgotten.

"I. Want. To. See. You. Now." He kissed her eyelids, nose, cheeks and mouth to punctuate each word. "It's only fair."

"Fair?" Lanie's stomach dropped. She'd thought he was being facetious. "You don't want to...to...?"

"Oh, I do wanna fuck you," he clarified.

Lanie startled at the frank tone, filthy statement and dead serious expression.

"*Very* badly, in fact." His lips curled into a wicked smile. "And I mean to."

Lanie's mouth dropped open at his directness, shuddering at the promises in it. "But?"

"But I don't see any condoms, do you?"

She shook her head, unable to form sentences. She never carried them. For her, sex was rarely spur-of-the-moment. And she wasn't even on the Pill.

As he nudged her chin up with his nose, sprinkling kisses along her clavicle, Lanie wondered at the chance of finding Plan B in the hotel convenience store. *Unlikely*, she groaned. Ridley began to grind his hips against her, licking at the hollow of her throat, and for a brief moment, she seriously considered throwing caution to the wind.

"So then, penetrative sex is out, unfortunately," Ridley said, bringing her back down to earth, thankfully.

Despite what was happening, Ridley was his usual pragmatic self. Even as his hands roamed her body, rubbing and squeezing until she wanted to cry out, he remained entirely logical. It was the perfect reminder that it was the real Ridley on top of her and not some fantasy version she'd conjured.

She nearly laughed. *Take that, Narcisa!*

"But we can still enjoy ourselves and each other. Can't we?" As he said this, he slipped his hands up under her T-shirt to cup her breasts.

She inhaled jerkily.

"God, these are magnificent. Has anyone ever told you that?" He squeezed her breasts, gliding his thumbs over the thin lace covering her nipples until they tingled, pebbling against his fingertips. "Moreover, *you* are magnificent. And I want to see you, all of you. Will you let me watch you?"

As he said this, it made the same amount of sense it had the first time. "Watch me?" *Was that his kink? And why did it suddenly sound so oddly exciting?*

His voice was muffled as he dipped his hot mouth to cover her breast over her T-shirt. She gasped as he nipped at her through the fabric, creating a wet spot. *Just like that*, she ached to cry out as the small bites and the enthusiastic kneading with his large palms threatened to do her in. She squirmed beneath him, a small moan escaping her mouth as the intensity built.

"Yes, pleasure yourself." Ridley eased back, breaking their embrace, rising to his knees. "I want to watch, to see the way you come."

She slid a hand down her own body into her shorts in frustration. "You can help me with that!" she whined in protest, but he shook his head.

"No," he said with surprising adamancy. "Not by touching you. I need you to touch yourself. I'm a scientist, observation is crucial."

Only Ridley could say something like that with a straight face.

"I-In front of you?" Lanie faltered. She dragged herself up from her elbows into a sitting position. She didn't even like to touch herself alone in the dark, let alone with the lights on and someone watching.

"Lanie, come here." He crooked a finger at her, voice husky with desire.

After a moment, she crawled across the bed to him obediently. He cupped her face between his palms.

"Want to know a secret?" He brushed his lips lightly across her lips and nose as she nodded.

"I'm not upset that you saw me masturbating." He whispered the words along her jawline, moving his mouth down her neck and across her shoulder, feathering her with persuasive kisses. "Because I was thinking about you while I was doing it."

Lanie's stomach flipped. She was glad to be already sitting on her heels or she would have dropped.

"Your body is so damn beautiful to me." He whispered the words against her throat. She raised her arms, helping him bring her shirt over her head like his voice and delicate kisses were casting a spell, entrancing her. "I got so hard thinking about it. Thinking about you."

With gentle hands, he slid her bra straps off her shoulders before unhooking her bra completely. Then he kissed a trail down her breasts to her peaked nipples, giving them each a swipe of his tongue before continuing down to her soft belly. She sat back so he could access the waist of her shorts and encourage them and her panties over her hips and down her legs. Ridley skimmed accompanying light kisses along her hips and thighs as he tugged them off completely.

"I've wanted to touch you so badly."

He was so close to where she wanted him that Lanie held her breath in anticipation. But then Ridley sat back on his heels instead of burying his face between her legs and she could have cried. He sat transfixed, until Lanie had to fight the urge to cover herself.

"I want you to know, it's not only your body that I find incredible. I find your mind fascinating too."

His eyes remained focused on her as he spoke and Lanie watched the way his lustful gaze trailed over her body. Her face burned at the sight because it was so equally adoring.

"You know, they say the brain is the most important sex organ." Ridley reached for the lamp on the bedside table and dimmed it to a soft haze. A small concession, she knew. Then he sat back, his eyes returning to devouring her whole. "So, I'd like to see how your mind works. What gives you pleasure... so I can replicate it."

With a shiver, Lanie considered his words. She was astonished to realize the idea of an audience of one, if that one was Ridley, did hold a certain sensual appeal for her.

"I've never done anything like this before..." she admitted, embarrassed by her naivete. Closing her eyes, Lanie marshaled her nerves. "Okay."

"Don't worry," Ridley said. "I'll be right here. I just won't touch you."

"That's what I'm worried about."

He chuckled.

Scooting to the headboard, Lanie took a breath. Then slowly, she drew a hand down her body. Her breathing sped up as she moved, her heart thumping a staccato of fear as the pads of her fingers skimmed her skin. However, the sensate pleasure of her hands gliding along the softness of her own body gave her the right amount of encouragement and confidence to continue. Lanie tried not to think of Ridley's eyes, instead focusing inward. Concentrating on her pleasure alone. She brought a hand back up to fondle her breasts, tweaking them until the sharp sting made her let out a faint moan. At the sound, to her delight, she opened her eyes and found something igniting in Ridley also. A flex and jump in the muscle at his jaw revealed how valiantly he fought the urge to join her. And the fact that he wouldn't—even though she desperately wanted him to—made her skin prickle. The idea that no matter what she did he would keep stubbornly away enticed as much as it frustrated. She watched him watching her circle her areola lightly, teasing them both with her fingers, until goose bumps rose across her skin.

He was spellbound.

Lanie let her other hand slide unhurriedly lower, over the curve of her stomach, past her pelvis and toward her thighs, building the anticipation for them both. She licked her lips before letting her hand slide between her legs and Ridley groaned at the sight, reaching for his own groin. Her body bucked at her own touch, unprepared for how sensitive and wet she already was. She played with herself, reveling in the feel of delicate fingertips slipping past her plump, slickened lips.

"Jesus." Ridley let out a low moan. "Lanie, look at me."

Lanie's eyes opened, seeking him out, unaware of when she'd closed them. She caressed her mound playfully as Ridley bit his lips, eyes hooded and intent on the motion of her fingers. His hand slipped into his own shorts, attending to the straining bulge there with languid movements, mirroring hers.

"I've wanted you, *wanted this*," Ridley admitted in a husky whisper as she moved.

The sight of him touching himself too made her whole body

flush with a fiery arousal. "What?" she panted. "To watch me get myself off?"

His grin was feral. "No, to get to be here when you got yourself off." His eyes roamed her naked body with hunger, as palpable as a caress. "Thank you," he groaned, still stroking himself.

She moaned, sliding her damp fingers through her folds, back and forth until her hips rocked involuntarily. Keening loudly, she zeroed in on the web of nerves there at her center and moved faster. All over, beads of sweat began to prickle her skin.

"I bet...you're so wet..." Ridley choked out, moving his hand faster and faster over his shaft, peeking out over the top of his shorts, while keeping his eyes fixed on her. His words were a strangled whisper. Waves of need coursed through Lanie, watching, making her own hand quicken. "And tight...a perfect fit for me."

The sound of Ridley's deepening voice, its barely restrained lust made her skin burn hotter, hot enough to singe. She hissed, adding another finger, her third, dipping them all into her canal, hooking them to hit her G-spot and then pulling out at a wildly erratic pace, chasing her orgasm.

"I wish I could be inside you right now—"

"Ridley!" She cried out his name. "Ridley," she pleaded again. "J-just. Shut. Up!"

He grinned, sealing his mouth shut as Lanie held his gaze. His pupils were dilated to jet-black pools in the dim light and his breathing was as labored as her own. Soon, trying to say more became difficult, whimpering as their movements and moans resounded in the silence.

"Touch me," she begged at last. With Ridley so close, it was sublimely torturous, like they were almost touching but not. And she wanted him so badly that thinking about it sent more ripples of pleasure flowing through her. "Please."

He shook his head.

Opening her mouth again, only for another strangled sob of "please" to escape as her climax approached, the throbbing intensified into a full bloom of ecstasy. Soon, her one hand wasn't enough, since Ridley still wouldn't touch her. Lanie kneaded her own breast with her free hand, teasing and pinching to heighten her own pleasure. She sped up her movements as the rise and peak of her orgasm closed in. Her back arched upward as the first wave of pleasure began to crest.

Ridley approached then, leaning over her. She awaited his kiss but instead, with a flick of his tongue, he swirled her nipple into his mouth, sucking until an involuntary scream tore from Lanie's throat with her sought-after release.

His exquisite but unexpected touch overwhelmed her senses. It was as if it engulfed her entire body in a white-hot flame. Her nerve endings blazed, all firing at once. He bit lightly, licked and then sucked until, overcome by wave after wave, she gasped his name. A moment later, Ridley released her from his mouth, emitting a low groan as he met his own climax. He collapsed onto his stomach at her side, dropping his forehead onto her shoulder.

"What happened to 'No touching?'" she asked breathlessly, only the sounds of their panting filling the space as sweat evaporated from their skin.

"I couldn't help myself," he panted, his hot breath tickling her breast. He stripped off his shirt and shorts, saying, "Lanie, look."

Out her large plate glass window, the curtain of midnight sky was shot through with vivid goldish-green streaks. Lanie marveled. Despite having studied the celestial phenomenon extensively, she still hadn't ever seen it in person.

"Aurora Borealis," she said in awe.

They lay in mutual silence considering the spectacular view, undulating waves of colored light.

"Wow."

"That's what I studied, you know."

"The Northern Lights, really?" Ridley's head, resting on her chest, turned up toward her face.

"Not exclusively. I studied plasma."

"Like blood plasma?"

"Um, mine are ionized gases, positively charged ions and the negatively charged electrons. Gaseous matter..." She stroked his cheek. "Like interstellar particles, stars, solar winds..."

He watched her blankly.

"More physics than blood, Doctor."

"So, not the same, then?"

"Nope." Lanie chuckled.

He considered that silently for a second. "So, you *are* an egghead."

She slapped his shoulder, laughing. "S'pose so."

"Can I ask what happened?"

"Who says anything happened?" She struggled not to shut down immediately as she normally did at the mere question. "Got a master's degree. Well, technically, I'm almost ABD— 'All but dissertation.' Either way, I'm done."

Falling silent, she covered his hand with hers, intertwining their fingers.

"Melanie."

Her mouth flattened.

"I lost my adviser, then my funding." Even in the intimacy of this moment, her face burned admitting this. "I've always dealt with a lot of anxiety. I just kinda fell apart and gave up before they asked me to leave. That's it." She shook her head, leaning forward, kissing his forehead. "Now, we've got an early flight."

Lanie turned onto her side, admiring their wall of lights and pulling Ridley up by the arm behind her. He draped his fore-arm over hers, as she fell asleep dreaming of the glorious light show and feeling Ridley molding his body around hers.

thirty-four

The next morning, Lanie and Ridley had luckily been booked on an a.m. flight direct to New York. Ridley had an almost eighteen-hour stopover, but would still be in Denver by Christmas Day. They spent most of the flight sharing silent glances, but Lanie could feel it wasn't the same as last night. When they disembarked, though only a step behind Ridley, she felt miles away.

Mixed emotions dogged her, effectively ruining the flight home. On the one hand, there was the ever-present relief that she always experienced when she first spotted the New York City skyline rising above the Atlantic through the airplane window. But on the other hand, was this persistent nagging that had gripped her throughout the flight. It whispered that her bubble was about to burst jarringly. That this frangible thing they'd newly created would not have the strength to last past the arrivals terminal at Kennedy.

Ridley hadn't, of course, done anything to encourage the feeling. But his quiet also felt heavy and ominous, like a harbinger of something ruinous. She'd experienced it before, how the lust in a partner's eyes curdled the next day, or with the better ones, within subsequent weeks when she inevitably grew tiresome. When what seemed doting and adorable before became "clingy" and "unattractive." She was by no means awash in lovers but the few she'd had previously had the exact same MO—fickle men with the staying power of tissue paper.

She didn't regret sleeping with him, even if it was a onetime thing. Besides, it wasn't Ridley's fault she felt this way. She was the one who dreamed of the beginnings of a happily-ever-after before last names were even exchanged. And had indulged her imagination with fantasies of some romantic Icelandic holiday—or maybe even joining Ridley in Vail. But Lanie could admit that was pushing things too far, even for her.

Still, it couldn't help but feel like a one-night stand that somehow morphed into an extended, uncomfortable few more hours stuck together postcoitus. Or more realistically and worse yet, two friends who had let a moment's sexual tension get away from them and now didn't know how to live in the aftermath. She'd learned the hard way what came of that.

So, they didn't talk about it, for which Lanie was both grateful and somewhat unsettled. Ridley didn't appear worried, but for his part, he also seemed to have come to his own answer to the unspoken question of what was next.

"This is where we part ways…"

"What?" Her attention shot to him.

"I said, this is where we part ways."

"Why?" She reflexively held his hand tighter as he tried to let go.

He smiled but a flush rose to her face. She let him go immediately, embarrassed.

She was already beginning to do it. *The clinginess again.*

"Um, because I surrendered my American passport five years ago. So, I have to go get in the foreign nationals line." She looked up. They were standing at Immigration.

That's why she'd always lost him when they deplaned separately. She was looking at the wrong line. Her cheeks rose in anticipation of a smile before it faltered again.

"So...?"

That didn't mean this wasn't the end. It just meant he had a perfectly good reason to leave.

"I'll see you on the other side. I'm here for the night." He frowned at her and pushed his glasses up his nose. "Unless you've already got plans? I thought maybe we could get something to eat and then I'd take you home?"

Take me home? Lanie's heart galloped but she maintained her composure, only barely. *Not to his hotel?*

A smile broke across his face that emphasized that strong jawline and infinitesimal dimple.

Another one. Lanie was impressed. *That was two in two days.*

"Yes? No?" He paused, tapping his passport in one hand against the other.

Her honest first impulse was to say no. To try to at least feign some restraint, but those soulful bourbon-brown eyes magnified by his prescription lenses were always so expressive when he wanted them to be. Right now, they seemed to transmit a genuine interest in this idea as opposed to it being a polite and perfunctory invitation.

"Sure." She shrugged, fighting her own smile as if he hadn't handed her the moon and stars.

"You do understand you don't have to do this, right? We can turn back whenever you want."

Ridley nodded. "Yes, but I think it might be nice."

On the cab ride from the airport, Ridley had proposed going to The Bronx first instead of taking her to dinner. Lanie's stomach clenched at the prospect. Lanie knew this might not be the best time. Exacerbated by tales of the mechanical problems of the plane and then the unexpected layover in Iceland, her mother's anxiety had skyrocketed to the point that nothing short of laying eyes and hands on Lanie would calm her. She might not be up to entertaining company. And regardless, it would hardly be Ryan as her best self.

A quick bite and then immediately home to present herself for Ryan Turner's inspection was the best plan. But Ridley had other ideas.

"How about you both join me for dinner?"

"What?"

"You and your mom. Let me take you both to dinner."

Even as the cab pulled up to the curb in front of her building, Lanie still wanted to skip this. But she braced herself for it anyway, stepping out of the car.

After feeding bills to the driver, Ridley followed her. Lanie tried to remain composed, but knew Ryan would read into Ridley joining them at home. Lanie took a deep breath.

Ridley gave her a wide berth as she entered the building negotiating her luggage. She'd rejected his offer of help, wishing to put a little distance between them. She didn't explain herself but he was understanding. She could do without more of her mother's disapproval where Ridley was concerned. And as of last night, being anywhere within ten feet of him meant possibly revealing things she didn't mean to.

Lanie knocked rather than letting herself in. Since she'd already texted her mother to extend Ridley's invitation, Ryan surprised her by answering the door ready to go. She wore a smart navy sweater dress and knee-high boots. Her locs were tied up in a matching cloth and she wore hammered bronze earrings shaped like the African continent. Her coat was already on. It had been so long since Ryan had a date that Lanie forgot how well her mom cleaned up outside of her work scrubs or housecoat.

"Lanie?" Her mom pulled her into a fierce hug. "Oh, honey!"

"I'm here, Mommy. Safe and sound. See?" She stepped aside to present Ridley. "Meet Ridley Aronsen. Ridley, this is my mom, Ryan Turner."

While her heart crawled slowly up her esophagus, Ryan and Ridley exchanged cordial greetings and holiday tidings.

Lanie exhaled. *So far so good.*

Two hours later, the three sat sated and comfortable in Zero Otto Nove, a small family style Italian trattoria on Arthur Avenue, The Bronx's small but authentic Little Italy.

Ridley stared around the restaurant at the vaulted ceilings and Southern Italian piazza-inspired décor. Then he leaned back in his chair, stuffed, rubbing a nonexistent food belly. "That was delicious. If I didn't have a connecting flight to catch tomorrow, I'd have all this wrapped up to take home."

The servings had been generous, and their eyes had far exceeded their stomachs' capacities. As a result, there was enough food for a few additional dinners.

"What's your final destination?" Ryan asked.

"Beaver Creek, Colorado." He wrinkled his nose as if he couldn't believe it himself.

"Never heard of it," Ryan said with a sympathetic smile, folding her napkin and placing it carefully on the table.

"Me neither," Ridley responded with a grimace. "But my daughter is spending Christmas up there with her grandparents and her friends."

Lanie was unsurprised but intrigued by Ridley's omission of Gavin. He didn't owe her mother—or even her, frankly—

an explanation, but he did need to learn to say the man's name without physical pain.

"And you're headed up there to meet them. Is it a surprise or are you a straggler?"

"Bit of both, honestly. It's a surprise *because* I'm a straggler," he admitted. "It's largely thanks to your daughter that I'm even going at all."

Lanie's face flushed at the unexpected compliment. There was a disarming warmth in his eyes. Lanie pushed a mushroom from her boscaiola sauce around on her plate to avoid his gaze. This was exactly what she was afraid of her mother witnessing.

"Oh yes?" Her mother's faded accent resurfaced with those words.

"And despite the delay..." Ridley's normally inscrutable poker face betrayed him for a moment. He smiled—a small, blink-and-you'd-miss-it smile, but a meaningful one. "I think it was worth it."

Then he winked right at her... In front of her mother. Lanie's eyes widened and he seemed to catch himself belatedly.

"Uh, I mean, will be worth it."

She wanted to sink into her chair, her face going beet red.

It was possible that her mother, despite her Sherlock Holmesian powers of deduction, honed by years of reading mysteries and watching true crime, had missed his underlying sentiment. But Lanie doubted it and she knew her reaction probably wasn't helping.

Her mother glanced from Ridley to Lanie as the guilt radiated off Lanie in waves. She was a grown woman and yet she felt like a child caught up past her bedtime.

Normally, Ridley was a stone, as impassive and inscrutable as the Sphinx. But now he might as well have come to dinner in a T-shirt that had "I fucked your daughter in Iceland" written across the chest. Lanie couldn't believe it.

Her mother leaned forward then, eyes narrowing. "So, remind me again, Dr. Aronsen, you met my daughter on a plane?"

Oh no.

Ridley nodded, blissfully unaware of the temperature change as Lanie's stomach churned.

Her mother's assumed posture—elbow on the table, three fingers cradling the side of her face in concentration—boded poorly for the rest of Lanie's night.

"What would you say intrigued you enough to stay in touch?"

"Mom!" Lanie worried the small stud in her left ear nervously.

"What? I'm curious. You talk about the man. I see you texting all the time, I know you now fly together on occasion. I want to know what was so remarkable about my daughter that it made him want to keep in touch."

Ridley's impenetrable visage again dropped like a steel curtain. Lanie didn't even think that he knew when he was doing it. And it wasn't necessarily hostile; it just seemed like Ridley refused to give anyone any part of himself that he didn't explicitly intend for them to have. Up to and including any insight into his emotions at any given moment. So, he didn't look shocked or flustered or even angered by her mother's impertinence. He just looked blank, then pensive.

Still, to Lanie's surprise, as he opened his mouth to speak, he did look at her and smirk. It was a delighted little movement of his lips like he was reassuring her that he had this, before returning his attention to her mother very seriously. "I think Lanie is a fascinating young woman. And I saw that from our first meeting. She's smart and feisty. I was being a real jerk when we met. I believe you were there, in fact, Mrs. Turner. On the phone, right?"

"*Ms.* Turner." Ryan gave him a tiny smile and a nod of acknowledgment. "And I guess I was."

"Well, if you recall, I was in the midst of throwing a wobbly.

That is, until your daughter put me right in my place. She was unexpected. I liked that."

"It did not happen like that! You were flipping out on Dash and I was sitting very quietly next to you, hoping you wouldn't notice me there," Lanie corrected.

"Absolutely not." His Vulcan eyebrow went up. "You gave me the full schoolteacher dressing-down. You got on me for my language and you told me I was being a jerk."

"I didn't!"

"That was the gist. I was being a bit much, I admit."

"You are so lucky that nice man still talks to you…" She laughed until she noticed her mom following them both, going back and forth, with keen interest.

Well, shit. Lanie realized she was apparently as bad as Ridley at being discreet.

"He was very nice," Ryan said, coming back into the apartment later, as Lanie followed, stripping off her winter coat.

"I'm glad you think so." Lanie was genuinely pleased that Ridley and her mother had gotten along so well.

"What happened to his daughter's mother? He didn't mention her."

"He's a widower," Lanie answered pointedly, already annoyed by the question. "His wife passed away a few years ago."

Her mother took in that information with a frown.

Here it comes. Lanie braced herself.

"Is that why the grandparents take care of her now?"

"They help *him* take care of her," Lanie nearly snapped. It was not her job to defend Ridley but she felt compelled to.

Ryan gave her a look. "No, *they* take care of her. They're with her instead of him at Christmas. And with the number of times you've told me he was in town in the last few months…"

"Mom, what does it matter?"

Ryan slouched out of her coat and sat on the couch heavily.

"I'm just trying to figure out what this man with a practically grown daughter of his own wants with mine."

"Bea is fourteen. I am an adult. What he wants with me is my business."

Her mother sighed, sounding very weary. "So, you have already slept with him, then?"

Lanie covered her face, shaking her head. It was very technically not a lie and her mother was being obscenely intrusive. "Mom, respectfully, my sex life is not your concern."

"Oh, I don't care about your sex life, Melanie! I care about my daughter being used and cast aside when the man she's seeing finds a woman more…suitable."

Lanie collapsed in the chair diagonally across from her mother. "That's quite the vote of confidence in me."

"Melanie. You know what I mean."

"No, I don't."

"What happened to me with your father—"

"I'm not you and Ridley is definitely not Dad."

Ryan snorted. "I thought your father was special too. Men like your father, successful men, are good at making women like us feel important to them. But that's only until they get what they want."

Lanie bit her lip. She loved her mother, and Lanie knew how badly her ex-husband had treated her until he ultimately left Ryan alone with a toddler and an unfinished musicology degree. But Lanie also knew she'd never allow a man to treat her the way her father had treated Ryan. The cheating and gaslighting. Not even to save their relationship.

"Ridley has been entirely honorable," she insisted.

"For now." Her mother's mouth set.

"No, period." Lanie got up, heading into her bedroom, tired of the various stanzas of this same old song her mother had been singing forever. She stood by the bed and began unpacking her bag.

"They don't choose us, baby. Not in the end," her mother said from her doorway. "He'll make you love him, give up your life for him, maybe even leave your home, then he'll leave you and just pick someone else. You know I'm right."

And there it was. *Leave your home.* Her mother's real fear. The words were like spiked spider legs painfully crawling up her spine. Lanie shuddered.

"Look at Jonah, after all those years with you right there." Her resentment suffused her words. "What does he do? He chooses Gem. Gem! God knows I love my sister's child, but she's as unchallenging and uncomplicated as they come."

Lanie recognized the ugliness of her own thoughts in her mother's words.

"That's who they'll pick, honey. Ornaments, pleasing women they can control." Lanie had a hard time holding her tongue, not defending Gem or Ridley or even herself as Ryan pushed on. "Or they'll pick women they believe are their equal. They never choose women like us."

Lanie spun on her mother, enraged. "'Women like us,' who? Who are we, Mom?"

Her mother shrank a little at Lanie's raised voice. "No one special."

Lanie was too stunned to speak.

She grabbed her bag and ran from her mother's words, as far and fast as her legs could carry her, out of the apartment, down the stairs and into the cold night.

thirty-five

Ridley

When Ridley's Uber pulled up, Lanie was sitting on the stoop of a storefront church next to her building. It had begun to snow and tiny white crystals dusted her hair, glittering under the streetlights. Sitting there alone, the snowflakes gave her an ethereal appearance, like a snow angel. She was both so beautiful and so sad that his chest constricted painfully at the sight. And when she looked up as his door opened, his anger swelled at her bereft expression. Her large eyes were red-rimmed and her nose and cheeks were rosy and slightly swollen.

"Lanie?" He stepped a foot out of the car but she came up to him instead.

When I left things were fine. He couldn't understand how a half hour later she could be crying on the other end of the phone.

Throughout their meal together, Ridley had marveled at how much Lanie resembled her mother. There were even moments as they ate where, in looking between them, it was positively uncanny. But as evidenced by her extraordinary resemblance to her cousin Gemma also, the Turner genes were clearly strong. Still, Lanie was not, as it seemed she feared, her mother's doppelgänger. In fact, in temperament, Lanie seemed to be her mother's diametric opposite.

Lanie was open, where her mother seemed guarded. She was adventurous and extroverted, while her mother, though engaging in her own way, was very shy. But what he would never have guessed was that Ryan was as cruel as Lanie was sweet. Because it could only have been cruelty that drove Lanie out of her house on Christmas Eve to sit in the snow.

"Sorry. You didn't have to come back," Lanie said as Ridley scooted over in the car so she could slide in beside him. Fresh tears slipped down her cheeks.

"I didn't know who to call on Christmas Eve." Lanie shook her head again as her shoulders began to shake with sobs.

Ridley's heart cracked at the sound. Her face was cold when Ridley took it between his palms and lifted it to him. "What happened?" He wiped away the abundance of tears with his thumbs, then pulled her into his arms.

Lanie shook her head, unwilling to say, instead tucking herself under his chin. She wrapped her arms around his waist as if trying to leech warmth from him.

He wouldn't press her. It didn't matter anyway; he was happy she'd called him at all.

"Do you want to hang out for a while?" he asked, gently. "Find a place to sit and grab a drink until you and your mom cool down?"

"On Christmas Eve?" She lifted her head, looking up at him. "No, I just want to go back to your hotel with you."

Despite Iceland, Ridley was still stunned by Lanie's directness. To him, it was remarkable that after weeks of denying anything was happening at all, they could finally be so open about it. That Lanie could wear her desire so blatantly on her face now. That he could so freely admit how much he wanted her too.

He squeezed her to himself, inhaling the jasmine-and-rose scent that lingered around her like an aura.

"You sure? I have to leave pretty early tomorrow morning."

He mentioned this decorously like a gentleman, as if offering her a pass, instead of giving himself one. His heart thundered, terrified she'd say yes but also desperately afraid she might say no. His performance anxiety from yesterday hadn't faded, and in fact, may have ratcheted up a little.

"I know." Lanie pulled back. "Would you like me to go home?" Confusion began to cloud her face. Ridley knew she would get the wrong idea unless he did something. The same way he'd suspected she had that morning.

It pleased him to think he was coming to understand Lanie, the nuances of the little faces she sometimes made and the things she didn't say. He knew that he would have to be brave now to show her how much he did, in fact, want her to stay the night with him.

In lieu of an answer, he tipped her chin up to meet his mouth and kissed her. Tenderly at first, but then with more insistence. Once her lips parted and his tongue met hers, he wanted to make this connection last. He wanted to taste every part of her soft, maraschino-flavored mouth forever. Lanie slid her hands up to cup the nape of his neck, holding him close, and the traffic and noise and the city itself fell away.

Ridley kissed her all the way into Manhattan. Somewhere in the back of his mind, the thought came to him that his obvious yearning should probably make him embarrassed or at the very least circumspect, but it didn't. He wanted to devour her. To put his mouth on every part of her she would allow. He slid his hand under her coat and sweater, trying to find any small piece of her flesh he could. She moaned into his mouth when his hands rubbed small concentric circles at the small of her back. She bit his bottom lip playfully when he looked distractedly through the windows, searching for street signs or any indication of where they were.

"Don't worry, the driver'll tell us when we've arrived," Lanie assured between kisses.

The amusement in her voice now pleased him almost as much as having her in his arms did.

Ridley laughed too until Lanie dragged his mouth back to hers.

When Ridley came out of the bathroom, Lanie was reclined at the foot of his bed in only a bra and panties.

"I don't have anything to wear to bed. I don't even have my bonnet," she said, her voice low and soft, to his stunned face.

It wasn't seductive—it was just stated as a fact. Had he mistaken what she wanted to do there with him? Had she only needed a refuge for the night from her mother? No, the look on her face, as her eyes traveled from Ridley's feet to his face, was wanton and alluring.

"Uh, you can borrow my Durag, but it's silk, not satin. And I can find one of my T-shirts, if you'd like?" he offered anyway. As if sex hadn't been a part of their unspoken agenda since he'd tried to eat her face in the Uber.

"Good, maybe for later." She twisted her arm behind her back, undoing the fastenings of her bra. The sides hung loose, only kept in place by the straps over her shoulders, which she began to slip off.

Ridley stood there, transfixed. He didn't understand where his nerves were coming from. They'd had sex yesterday. Albeit, more *in front of* each other than actually *with* each other and it was in an entirely different country. Still, it counted. It was still just him and her and her magnificently naked body, with breasts he couldn't wait to sample again, an ass he wanted to sink his teeth into and the prettiest little—

"Ridley, come here."

Lanie was completely nude now and all the swirling thoughts Ridley had flew directly out of his mind.

In clothes that always complemented her, Lanie was like an extremely buxom hourglass, a ten out of ten. But out of them,

Lanie was a marvel of divine proportion and beauty, a Venus. She was statuesque, lushly pear-shaped with full, heavy breasts, thick arms and thighs, and a pleasingly rounded belly.

Ridley shed his T-shirt and boxers hurriedly as he approached. Just her scent was a potent sex potion that addled his brain, making him rock-hard. He wasted no time lowering her back onto the bed then covering her body with his. He kissed her fervently, spending long minutes adoring every part of her like he'd dreamed about doing. His teeth skimmed her ample breasts as he filled his mouth briefly, creating enough suction to make her squirm beneath him, breath hitching.

Lanie watched, eyes hooded, as he ran his hands and tongue over the stretch marks on her biceps and sides, tasting the faint saltiness of her skin. She laughed, tickled, when his lips lightly caressed the pudge of her stomach. And she shivered under him as his mouth lingered along the curves of her hips, mapping the terrain of her body for his future exploration while she stroked the back of his head and neck.

"You make me so happy," he confessed, pausing on his way to her core. "And I want to show every inch of you how much."

Lanie giggled like he was joking…maybe not realizing he was serious. She was phenomenally sexy and it continually astounded him that she didn't seem to know it. It had distressed him how many times in the last few weeks he'd thought of having her in this way. Fantasized about this as she remained oblivious to her effect on him. But here she was now, with him. He came back from his fantasies to the vision of sensual desire before him.

"Ridley?" Lanie touched a finger to his jaw to get his attention. "Did I lose you?" She chuckled nervously and he did too.

He shook his head, backing away, his anticipation building. "No, sorry, I just want to look at you for a minute."

It was true. His eyes roamed her body greedily, laid before him like a feast. He almost didn't know where to begin. Ridley moved from her belly button to her pelvis to her knees, showering extra attention on her hips and inner thighs, covering her with light kisses. He fell to his knees at the end of the bed and reached for her, sliding his hands underneath her bottom. Ridley pulled her toward his waiting, wanting mouth with a jerk and Lanie yelped at the sudden motion, then laughed.

"Sorry," he said, abashed by his blatant lust.

"Now who's saying sorry too much?" Lanie reached forward to stroke his cheek.

She gasped, falling back against the bed, when Ridley lifted her thighs, spreading them and hooking one over his shoulder. Lovingly, he kissed her nether lips before using his fingertips to spread her open under his tongue, lapping at her folds.

"Oh fuck," she exclaimed into the silence as Ridley took his time, savoring her.

He tasted her all over, relishing her piquant flavor. His tongue penetrated her, eliciting small spasms that he captured with his mouth before zeroing in on the neat bundle of nerves that had her weeping his name over and over as he sucked on it. He knew then he could lose entire days doing that alone. Hearing her trembling sighs and feeling her tiny quakes against his mouth. Lanie wrapped her hands around his head, gripping and holding him where she wanted him.

"There, oh God, just there," she instructed.

Luckily, Ridley had always taken direction well, worshipping her with gently insistent flicks of his tongue until her thighs shook. He worked her body, pushing her toward his sole objective, wanting to feel her come against his face. He lost himself to this goal. Inhaling her maddening scent and feeling his hunger grow. At last, a tremor ripped through Lanie, her back arching and mouth opening in a soundless gasp. Then she flooded his mouth and he lapped up his spoils as his own core tightened, seeking release.

"Enough," she pleaded as he continued, finally spent, pushing his forehead away with her palm. "It's too much. Please!"

He lifted his mouth from her reluctantly and smiled. It might have been years since he'd had any practice but he was gratified to know that his skills hadn't abandoned him.

"Stop gloating," she said, panting for breath. "Now, c'mere." She pulled him up her body with little coaxing until he covered her again, then licked the taste of herself off his lips, kissing him deeply.

Ridley braced himself on his forearms, trying to calm down. After what they'd shared, any more of herself she offered would be a bonus, he reminded himself. His reward for a job well done. But just looking at Lanie's luscious body was nearly too much for him. He craved every part of her now like a last meal.

She dragged her hands lazily up and down his back as they kissed, in no rush at all. He stared deeply into her gorgeous eyes. This close, he could see the little swirls of green and light brown that flecked the halo of her irises.

Fuck, he was falling for her. *Had fallen. It's already too late*, he admitted to himself.

Lanie brought her legs up to wrap around his hips, pulling him closer. Ridley reached above her head onto the nightstand, feeling for the condom that he'd retrieved from his shaving kit. And instantly, he was in his head again, afraid like he'd been the day before that he'd embarrass himself.

After a three-plus-year sexual hiatus, Ridley knew he would have been disappointing, not only to Lanie but to himself. So, yesterday he'd lied. There'd been a string of condoms, furnished by Dash, sitting in his shaving kit the whole time. And they'd been in there for nearly a year now, ever since Dash ordained that Ridley's mourning period had officially come to an end. Ridley had vehemently disagreed, though he never actually removed them.

Now Ridley eagerly tore open the condom packet with his

teeth, before covering Lanie's mouth with his as he rolled it onto himself. They continued kissing, tongues passionately intertwined, making out until his erection became an insistent rod throbbing between their bodies. Ridley took another deep breath, trying to slow down, acquit himself honorably, not come as soon as he touched her.

But then, Lanie nudged him, losing her cool.

Entry was urgent, rougher than Ridley intended as his patience frayed entirely. And like opposing pieces of the same puzzle, he exhaled while she inhaled at the moment their bodies joined. His fingers dug into the soft skin of her thighs as he stretched them wide and thrust in and out of her.

"Open for me," he begged, back bowed and hips crashing into hers, frenzied, seeking her channel and pulling almost entirely out before slamming all the way back in. His mouth hungrily explored the depths of hers as she shuddered beneath him with his every hard plunge into her. Ridley had wanted to be gentle, planned to exercise care, but his need overcame his senses. Still, Lanie met him thrust for thrust as he groaned her name between gritted teeth.

Her walls clenched all around him, making him see stars and sending pulses like icicles skittering down his spine. Soon, he felt his release coming, bearing down on him, and he slowed again, trying to find a new rhythm that gave him more time to last but still suited them both. Ridley took subtle direction from her, moving in her, listening to her whimpers, feeling as her legs began to shake around him when he went deeper and deeper, finding the place that made Lanie's toes curl and hitting it again and again until she came.

Ridley continued at that unhurried pace, trying to prolong the incredible feeling of being inside her. But eventually Lanie disengaged to switch positions. She rose over him and stayed there. Lying above him, giving him sweet little kisses as he pressed against her entrance impatiently. It was an excruciating tease as his need to come still dogged him. Lavishing his mouth with the attention of her tongue, Lanie finally eased herself back onto him, adjusting her body until his thick shaft filled her up. She hissed at the snug fit. His eyes rolled up into his head at the delirious, tortured feeling of her sliding down.

He grabbed handfuls of the ass that of late had begun haunting his dreams and kneaded it, encouraging her to ride. Lanie was a quick study and a captivating sight mounted on him, demanding and then taking her own pleasure from his body. Sweat covered both of them in a slick sheen that made her glow in the dim light and he watched avidly as it dripped down the crevice between her bouncing breasts.

Enflamed, Ridley bolted upright and hungrily wrapped his lips and tongue around her areola, licking and sucking until she moaned.

"Oh God, yes." Lanie rested her cheek against his head.

She wrapped her arms around his neck and shoulders, clutching him to her bosom, her hips continuing to move. He ran possessive hands along the sloping curve of her back before slipping them beneath her to cup her bottom, pulling her into his meeting thrusts.

With her undulating furiously on top of him, Ridley couldn't fight off his climax any longer. It hurtled toward him with the power of a locomotive bearing down. The feeling seized his lower back and groin, tightening until his whole body stiffened under hers. His orgasm shook him and Lanie grasped his shoulders, holding him to her as he trembled. He nestled there, in between her full breasts, as the sensation rocketed through him, leaving him feeling sapped of strength and lost to an aching sort of bliss.

He flopped back onto the bed afterward, panting and thoroughly exhausted. Lanie settled down on top of him, still straddling his hips, her chin resting on her hands across his chest, breathing heavily too.

"I think...you were trying...to impress me, Dr. Aronsen."

Ridley chuckled, his heart racing for more than one reason. He brushed the loose brown curls back from her moist hairline, so he could see into her still-flushed face. It was just as bewitching as he'd imagined. "I was."

Why deny it?

"Well," she said with a long luxuriant exhale. "Mission accomplished."

thirty-six

Lanie

"I think you're luminous standing there."

Ridley came up behind Lanie. She stood at the wide window of his hotel room with views of Broadway and the rest of SoHo below. The hotel, a cute boutique-style place on Spring Street, overlooked the shopping thoroughfare. Today though, it was empty of its usual crush of shoppers—because of course, it was Christmas Day.

Ridley had just gotten out of the shower and was slick with water. Still, he wrapped his arms around her for a moment and whispered huskily in her ear. He gave the globes of her breasts an appreciative massage that made her eyes close involuntarily. Briefly, Lanie forgot her unease and let her head fall back against his shoulder. Her problems with her mother were suddenly far away as Ridley kissed the crook of her neck. She nearly moaned.

Catching herself, Lanie slipped from his embrace and hooked the back of her bra together before turning to face him. "You have a plane to catch."

He nodded and moved to his suitcase propped open on the hotel luggage rack, wearing only a towel slung low across his hips. Inexplicably, Lanie turned away modestly when he stripped the towel off and threw it onto the bed to get dressed.

She gave a deep sigh. "This is going to sound argumentative and that's not my intention, but you don't have to say that."

"What? That I think you're radiant?"

Lanie's lips went tight across her mouth as she pulled her shirt over her head, struggling not to roll her eyes.

It wasn't Ridley's fault she didn't believe him. As much as Lanie didn't want to acknowledge it, she knew this was it. This was the point when she discovered what kind of relationship she was in with Ridley and where it had always been headed. This was the point where it would all begin to end. *Like it always did.* Historically, after the mind-blowing sex, she and/or her partner would inevitably begin to drift apart. The clock started now.

This was when phone calls would cease entirely and texts slowed in frequency. Then it would begin to take longer and longer just to get a response. Plans to hang out, maybe even do the sex thing again, would encounter unexpectedly busy schedules and unforeseen conflicts. All of which conspired, blamelessly of course, to turn a budding relationship into a casual hookup. Then eventually there would be the mutual understanding that while this had been fun...*blah, blah, blah*, fill-in-the-blank reasons. Done.

Ridley, to his credit, even had better excuses than most:

Work schedule very demanding? *Sure. I get it.*

Not over his deceased wife? *Highly plausible.*

In the middle of a pitched custody battle? *Totally understandable.*

Or by far the best one yet: *You live in different countries, Lanie!*

Her heart ached with dread. *Dammit.*

This was entirely self-inflicted. Why had she done this to herself? She hadn't needed to take Ridley's card. She certainly didn't need to call him that first time. God knew, she shouldn't have accepted that first dinner invitation. And what was she even thinking sleeping with him? *Goddamn it, why did I get involved with this man at all?* Her mother was right. Of course she was. She had the requisite experience. The idea of that was sickening.

Lanie brushed past him to get into the bathroom. Inside, she splashed water on her face.

"Lanie?"

She braced her hands on the sink, the cold water running down her face, dripping onto her shirt.

"You okay?" Ridley stood in the doorway a few minutes later, completely dressed. Even his coat and scarf were on.

This is it.

"Yeah." She nodded, smile faltering. She glanced at herself in the mirror. She didn't look like someone who was about to be told, *It's been fun*, and then absolutely fall apart on the D train home. *Good.*

"Did you hear me?"

She shook her head, dabbing her face with a hand towel.

"I said, if you're allowed a plus-one, maybe I can go with you to your cousin Gem's wedding?"

Lanie drew in a breath but otherwise didn't move. "What?"

"You've been incredibly game with the whole thing. But I figure it might be nice to have a little backup."

Lanie blinked. "Ah, okay."

"Okay? Great. Text me the date so I can make sure Therese keeps the day open on my calendar." He checked his watch. "Shit, shit, shit. I don't really need to be at JFK two hours early, do I?"

"During Christmas?"

"Crap, good point. I didn't mean to leave you here. But I have to run. There's nothing to do here. I'll give them the key, just close the door behind you."

"Okay." Lanie nodded, watching Ridley frantically circle the room to make sure he didn't leave anything. "Don't worry, I'll check to make sure we got everything. Just go." She meant it. Sure, he was "making plans" for something two months away, but in the postsex glow they all did.

Yes, just go.

He exhaled, walking up to her. Then smiled. Another big one, dimpled. His kiss was tender but filled with unsaid things. A surprising to-be-continued. Lanie puzzled at it as his mouth left hers.

"It's pretty packed, but I'll send you my schedule for January," he said against her lips.

She nodded, unable to speak. *January?*

"Talk soon."

thirty-seven

Ridley

"Dad! Granddad is going on the intermediate run, can we go?"
Bea ran into the room like a pack of ravenous dogs nipped at
her heels. In reality, it was only her two girlfriends pulling up
the rear.

Ridley sat at the oversized kitchen island–cum–breakfast bar
in Gavin's palatial kitchen, checking his phone. After his text
from the rental car counter telling Lanie he'd arrived safely at
Denver International, other than a quick emoji-laden reply,
he hadn't heard from her. He wanted to believe she was being
mindful of his time here with Bea. *Fair enough.* He smiled to
himself. Bea frowned a little at his dreamy expression.

He straightened. "It's been a few years since you skied. You
think you're ready?"

Bea huffed indignantly as if he'd asked her if she needed her
diaper changed. "Well, Dad," she said slowly, so his addled old

man brain could fully grasp what she was saying. "I don't ski, I snowboard."

Ridley heard a stifled snort. He glanced to his side at the sound of barely concealed snickering, only to see Gavin and his personal chef, Dorothea, trying valiantly to keep straight faces as they huddled over the evening's menu behind him.

"Bea, watch that tone."

Bea hazarded a quick glance at her girlfriends then slid the hand that had snuck suspiciously close to her hip back down to her side. When she opened her mouth next, she sounded a lot closer to her fourteen-year-old self and a lot less like a twenty-year-old. "We've been practicing on the bunny slope since we arrived. And I can do it. Ask Gavin."

Gavin perked up at his name as if he hadn't already been following the progress of the conversation. "They're ready for the intermediate. I vouch for them all."

Ridley didn't really need to consider it. Thyra had said as much years ago when she and Bea used to go with friends to Glenshee in Scotland. But the whole snowboarding thing had been an interest Bea shared with her mother.

He nodded. "Okay. Have fun, ladies. Ask your nan to take pictures."

The girls let out squeals of delight and ran out of the room.

"Sorry for butting in." Gavin broke the silence after Dorothea left the room too.

Ridley placed his phone face down on the countertop and turned to Gavin. Gavin seemed to be working up to something and Ridley realized he could use the distraction. Despite his rationalizations, right now he felt like a spurned lover waiting on a call back from the one he'd given it up to.

Because that's what I am, right? The thought disturbed him.

Had he hurt Lanie? He could tell she was surprised by how amorous he'd been. He cringed inwardly now thinking of how much he'd wanted her. How obvious he'd made that. He'd

probably scared her off being so forceful, and she was too sweet
to tell him so. Or maybe asking to be her plus-one was too forward and he'd made her uncomfortable.

Am I being ghosted?

"Aronsen?"

Ridley perked up, his attention having wandered away again.
"Hmm?"

"I said, I'm trying to, as my therapist called it, 'find the balance between parental figure and friend.'"

Ridley tried not to so immediately bristle at any reference
to Gavin being Bea's parent. If he was ever going to leave her
in Gavin's custody for any length of time, for any reason, the
man would need to learn some "parenting" skills.

Ridley sighed. "As she gets older, it becomes harder for me
to strike that balance too."

Gavin's eyes widened at the admission.

"You're surprised?" Ridley chuckled. "Why?"

"You mean to say King Shit Ridley doesn't always know
exactly how to parent at every moment?"

Even curses sounded absurdly pompous coming out of
Gavin's mouth. So much so that instead of getting angry, Ridley laughed. *Really laughed.* Like, thigh-slapping, gut-busting,
falling-out-of-your-seat laughing. It was almost unhinged
and definitely more than the comment deserved, but Ridley
couldn't stop, as if relieving a pressure valve. Gavin stared at
him astonished. Soon, it became contagious, infecting Gavin
as well. They both howled.

When minutes later their laughter had finally subsided, Ridley could barely breathe. "Is that how you see me?"

"Aronsen, you're joking, surely? You're the perfect man. Perfect husband, perfect father, perfect doctor." Gavin reached into
a mini-fridge built into the underside of the gigantic island-
slash-chef's station and retrieved two bottles of beer.

Ridley took the one proffered and automatically popped off

the cap using his palm and the edge of the countertop, right as Gavin extended a bottle opener to him.

"What the fuck?" Gavin snapped.

"Sorry," Ridley said sheepishly, smoothing a hand along the stone counter, checking for chipping. "I think it's fine."

"Not that," Gavin said, rolling his eyes. "I mean I just finish saying that you're like some prototypical Marlboro Man and then you go and do that?"

It was Ridley's turn to be dumbfounded.

"Can't you stop being a slab of American beefcake for one moment to open your beer bottle like a normal person?"

He'd never thought of himself like that before. He took care of himself, but apart from Lanie openly ogling him for the past two days, it had been years since he'd even thought about his physique. He shouldn't be flattered, he knew, yet he was. "I learned how to do that from an Irishman," he offered. "If that helps at all?"

"It doesn't." Gavin sipped his beer, leaning against the counter. "But do have some respect, this is Van Gogh granite."

Ridley reexamined the turquoise-and-cream countertop, running a finger along the rust-colored veining and shrugged. "Nice?"

"You wouldn't understand," Gavin said superciliously, sounding much more like the guy Ridley knew.

"And that's *your* problem right there. Can you stop being such an overweening prat all the time?"

"Ouch," Gavin said, touching his chest but not looking offended in the least. "The gloves have come off, have they?"

"I don't see why not? Bea's out."

Ridley wanted an outlet for his general annoyance. Since he'd arrived, Gavin had gone out of his way to be a frustratingly gracious host. He said nothing when Ridley turned up on his doorstep unannounced and had seemed almost happy to see him. *The fuckin' dick.*

"Fine. Maybe now you can finally remove that stick from your arse."

Ridley snorted. The gloves were well and truly off.

"Do you know what it's like to exist in the shadow of Ridley the Great?"

"First I'm 'King Shit,' now I'm 'Ridley the Great.' Forget a chip, you've got a boulder on your shoulder, Gavin."

Gavin took a swig of his beer as if working up some courage. "Ever since Harvard, I've had to deal with being compared to you. Do you know what that was like?"

"For a proud, blue-blooded white man such as yourself, it must have really burned." Ridley arched an eyebrow.

Gavin paused with the beer to his lips and smirked. "I don't see color. I wasn't raised that way."

Ridley only rolled his eyes but hearing white people say things like that always made him want to throw up. "I think that fantasy has always been a part of your problem. And all this 'living in the shadow' nonsense could only be about losing Thyra because we weren't ever classmates, and you were born white, male and goddamn rich." He rubbed his thumb and index fingers together. "This is me playing the world's smallest violin for you."

Gavin glowered from behind the brown bottle in his hands.

Ridley heaved an exasperated sigh. "You cheated on her, man! What did you expect her to do? Stay?"

"I loved her!"

"Not enough to keep it in your pants, apparently." Ridley shook his head. "Imagine having a woman so dedicated that she would follow you across an ocean, reorder her entire life, apply for new fellowships and alter her entire specialization to go to the same school as you, and all you can think to do is chase every skirt in the place? I'd have left your ass too."

"And that certainly worked out for you, didn't it?"

Ridley scoffed, though he knew exactly what Gavin meant. "You were younger than us, and a med student to boot, but you got incredibly lucky and stole her away from me. Admit it, you were lying in wait."

He had been. Thyra was magnetizing: older, foreign and more captivating than any woman he'd ever met. Ridley couldn't fathom how a man could treat her like gum on the bottom of his shoe, trying to shake her off as soon as they hit Cambridge. He would have been an idiot to let any opportunity with her pass him by.

"We were friends first," Ridley insisted. "You and I were friendly too, in case you forgot."

Gavin rolled his eyes. "But I saw through you pretty quickly."

"The only thing you saw was the next pretty undergrad you could charm with that accent of yours."

"You make me sound like a predator." Gavin's pride was wounded.

"Technically I guess you weren't, but you were damn unethical. I hope you've had the sense to change since then."

"I am happy to report that I'm currently only dating age-appropriate women," Gavin stated proudly. "I'm trying to be like you, Aronsen. Stable, secure, sensible."

The irony of that statement was like a kick in the gut. But Ridley wouldn't embarrass himself by revealing that to Gavin. How for so many years he'd compared himself unfavorably to Gavin, measuring all his successes against Gavin's. Forever trying to make sure he provided Thyra and Bea some semblance of the lifestyle they might have had if Thyra had chosen Gavin instead. How every achievement and accolade was held up to scrutiny by the light of Gavin's most recent accomplishment at the time. It was beyond laughable to learn now that he thought Ridley was a better husband, father or doctor. He was all of that precisely because he'd convinced himself that Thyra would realize she'd made a mistake in choosing him. It was a burden he'd borne for years—only finally throwing off some of that crushing weight after she died.

Particularly because he refused to give up his parental rights, for so many years Ridley lived in fear of Gavin. Always worried Gavin would swoop in and take back the life Ridley had convinced himself he'd stolen. That's why it felt especially scary, Ridley realized in this very moment, when Gavin returned after Thyra died. And why it worried Ridley to see Gavin and Bea and her grandparents getting along so well on this trip. It was Ridley's darkest fears come to life.

"Truly, Aronsen, I'm taking my cues from you. Not only in parenting but in how to be a better partner this time around." Gavin held up his half-empty bottle in salute. "Here's to fawning, flattery and faithful devotion."

"Whatever." Ridley brushed Gavin's faux compliment off with a smirk, shaking his head. Then he begrudgingly gave Gavin's bottle a little clink against his own. And the impostor syndrome Ridley always seemed to suffer from in Gavin's presence vanished for once. "Oh, and fuck you."

thirty-eight

■ 12-JAN ■ Trans-Continental Airways ■ Flight: 3714 ■
JFK-John F. Kennedy Int'l Airport ► **LHR-London, Heathrow**
Seat Assignment: **11K**

"I'm giving those two seats to my sister Hyacinth and her husband. Otherwise, I'll never be able to show my face at home ever again."

Lanie smirked. With only a month now until the wedding, the seating chart, like a battle plan, was spread across the dining room table for inspection. Gran had been charged with this meticulous logistical job but Lanie was charged with serving Gemma's interests. It amazed Lanie how much all weddings were the same. Somehow, they morphed into your parents' affair that you were merely a guest at.

When and if her turn ever came, she was going to City Hall. She'd already decided.

"You do know Uncle Basil and Aunt Hy are not the only people you can stay with when you go visit Antigua? Or, *gasp*—" Lanie clutched her chest dramatically "—you could stay at a hotel!"

Gran sucked her teeth and cut a glance at Lanie that made her mouth snap closed.

"Wait," Lanie said, "if you put them there we'll be a seat short."

Tulip looked at her blankly and set her mouth.

"Aunt Elliot?" Lanie shrugged. "I don't know. Gemma just told me to make sure."

Her gran nodded with a sigh, smudging out Aunt Hyacinth's and Uncle Basil's names with her thumb to add her absent daughter's. "Now we're one guest short."

Lanie stared at the spare seat for a moment before sucking in a fortifying breath. "I've got a plus-one we could put there, I think."

Gran's head rose from poring over the seating chart. She smiled. "That's the doctor with the nice house in Notting Hill Gem told me about?"

Lanie groaned. *Damn Gemma's big mouth again.* She gave a tight smile as inexplicably her heart double-timed it.

As she had expected, Lanie saw much less of Ridley after they parted at the hotel on Christmas Day. There had been less flying for him as he handled business, details of the clinical trial as well as appointments with his solicitors—so Lanie gave him space. Even on this visit, they'd only managed one brief afternoon assignation after a picnic on Hampstead Heath. But to her surprise, Ridley hadn't disappeared on her. And throughout, more than once, he'd promised to clear his busy calendar to accompany her to the wedding. Though previous boyfriends and purported relationships had never lasted long enough to put stock in plans made months into the future, Ridley appeared to be the exception to the rule. It was time, she supposed, to begin acting like it.

"Yes, Ridley." It felt like her heart expanded in her chest from being able to finally share their changed status with someone. He was not a topic of conversation at home with Ryan, and Narcisa was too guarded to be any fun.

"Tell me about him." Tulip rose to her regal height and went into the kitchen.

Oh shit, Lanie thought, *she's putting the kettle on.*

"I'm so happy for you, my love." Gran grinned, patting Lanie's hand. "But a man with a child? And a widower? You certainly jump in when you commit."

"No committing," Lanie said, alarmed. "This is casual. We're just dating."

"No such thing as 'casual' dating a man with a child, it's not like dating a single person. Each and every decision he makes has to factor in his daughter. You'll come to learn you can't be the center of his world."

"Of course. And I don't want to be!"

Her grandmother gave a barking laugh. "You say that now. But even your father learned that after you came along...part of why he left your mother."

Lanie was stunned silent.

"He wanted to stay the sun your mother revolved around. And early on, Ryan called me, desperate, begging me to take you. But I refused. Instead, I came to New York for a while to help her care for you while she went back to school. Abandoned the cello and got that nursing degree."

Lanie knew the second detail but not the first one. "She wanted you to take me? But you ended up staying with us for four years!"

"You're focused on the wrong part, girl. She didn't want me to keep you forever, just a few months to shore up her relationship with your father. But I could have told her that wouldn't work. That's why I went to her instead.

"By the time you were born, their relationship was already souring. Sending you to me wouldn't have helped. Just unlucky in love, all of us Turner women are." Her grandmother rocked in her seat a little, as if self-soothing. "We choose wrong. Even your aunt Elliot was left to raise two babies when her Leslie disappeared."

A "broken picker," just like Narcisa said. *A generational curse, apparently.*

Lanie knew that whole thing was a scalpel-sharp point of contention among the family. How Gran had left her older married daughter to tend to her younger divorced daughter, only for the married one's husband to abandon her too. Lanie suspected Gran saw choosing Ryan, even briefly, as reparations for leaving her behind in Antigua years earlier while taking Elliot with her to the UK.

Further unacknowledged was the fact that Gran had also done so to escape her own bad marriage. And that her return to England only coincided with her husband's funeral.

"I'm not suggesting a parent can't love. Of course not. Just be careful with this Ridley person. And try not to take it personally if his priorities are not always aligned with yours."

Lanie nodded.

"But," Gran said gleefully, "I have faith. You and Les and Gem have learned from our mistakes! Look at her with Jonah. He's such a sweet boy! Though I always thought—" She caught herself, eyeing Lanie guiltily.

"It's okay. You thought it would be him and me."

Gran shrugged, not unkindly.

"Me too," Lanie admitted, shrugging also. "But things change." Remarkably, the tears she'd expected didn't come.

"I'm so proud of you, Sec," Gran said, seeing her response. "I'll admit I was very worried about how you would handle all of this. I think we all were."

Lanie tried not to visibly cringe.

"Thank you for being so kind to your cousin, so understanding, so helpful. The way you always are, the way I knew you would be. You truly love each other like sisters."

They hadn't been terribly sisterly recently. But Lanie knew

that was her fault. Initially, it was just difficult being around Gemma. Her understandably ceaseless joy had taken a while for Lanie to learn to endure. Still, Lanie hadn't felt that way in months. Not since she'd met Ridley, in fact.

"Thank you," Gran said. "Because I know it hasn't been easy."

Why is she always doing this to me? Lanie's eyes ached. She would not cry just because her grandmother acknowledged how difficult this had been for her.

"And I want to also thank you for coming back and forth." She gestured to herself, stroking Lanie's hand. "Because I know that you wouldn't be doing this if you weren't concerned about me."

Lanie shook her head. "No, Gran. I—"

"Hush now." Gran ignored Lanie's denial, pulling Lanie into her arms and squeezing her tightly.

thirty-nine

Ridley

■ 26-JAN ■ Trans-Continental Airways ■ Flight: 6491 ■

LHR-London, Heathrow ▶ **JFK-John F. Kennedy Int'l Airport**

Seat Assignment: **5A**

Since Christmas, Ridley had found the time he could scrounge together to spend with Lanie to be in short supply. So, he was thrilled when the opportunity to spend a weekend with her in January surfaced. He'd been forced to push his flight home to London back to conduct an on-site interview with a rather elusive candidate for their newly vacated co-PI position in New York. But the delay also gave him the free time he'd yearned for. So, he moved his reservation an additional two days to make sure that happened.

And though when she'd asked him to meet her, he'd had something else in mind entirely—like a lazy afternoon spent in bed—a trip to the New York Botanical Gardens was acceptable too. Still, he couldn't pretend he wasn't a little surprised later on to be walking around her neighborhood in the South Bronx.

"I don't think your cousin appreciates how lucky she is to have you," Ridley said, knowing it was true but also wishing

Lanie would acknowledge how far above and beyond she was going. Every story involving her cousin made the woman sound more and more demanding and ridiculous and Lanie more biddable. "Five months of this is superhuman."

"Whatever." Lanie sighed.

"No, really. Your dedication to her happiness has been commendable."

She snorted. "No more than you always coming back and forth."

"I really don't have any choice," he said in the same exasperated tone he used with Bea at her most obstreperous about this.

"Not to be a jerk but you could've hired someone."

"I *did* hire someone. And yet here we are." Ridley still occasionally wanted to throttle Dash for recommending an old school chum who had clearly padded his résumé, to Ridley's unending chagrin and regret.

"And how lucky we are!" Lanie said, cheerily.

"Oscar Wilde said, 'Sarcasm is the lowest form of wit.'" Ridley's droll delivery made Lanie laugh.

"Everyone butchers that quote. It goes, 'Sarcasm is the lowest form of wit...*but the highest form of intelligence.*' And FYI, I wasn't being sarcastic. We would never have met without it. Plus, you and me, we love traveling, and we get to travel to two of the best cities in the world. We're lucky."

She was right, but thinking of Bea he couldn't help grousing, "You did hear the part where I'm traveling back and forth doing the work of someone I hired to do it for me?"

Lanie flinched visibly. "That was insensitive of me."

"A bit," Ridley said with a sharper edge than he intended. The back-and-forth was starting to get to him. *Doesn't she feel fatigued with this too?*

"Sorry."

"It's okay. If I'm honest, your enthusiasm can be infectious, and sometimes I think it's the only thing that keeps me going," he admitted, taking her by the arm, pulling her closer. "And," he whispered into the side of her face, "and if I didn't have a teenager waiting for me at home, I'd agree with you."

The small frown that had begun to furrow her brow eased. "I truly believe the reason you don't like NYC is because you haven't seen the best parts. I guarantee if you saw more of the whole city, you wouldn't feel this way."

Ridley stared at her knowing he'd already identified the best part of it for him. "I never actually said I didn't like New York. It's just not London. It's not home." *Which is where I need to be,* he thought but did not say. Although from Lanie's crestfallen face, he surmised she'd heard it anyway.

"Look at that!" Lanie pointedly changed the subject.

Ridley turned, following her finger across the wide boulevard then, to an old theater sitting like a stately relic on a busy thoroughfare, dwarfing the businesses to either side: a furniture store and a place that sold something called "cuchifritos." *Which, whatever they are, smell delicious.*

Ridley couldn't tell if the building was in use or not. There was a new banner advertising an upcoming event hanging across the exterior but the rest of it recalled a bygone era. Ridley was admittedly amazed by the magnificent old-school movie theater vibe, with its Italian baroque style: terra-cotta façade, washed pale with age, and stone curlicues framing the blue, red and yellow neon sunrise on the marquee.

"C'mon, then." Lanie gave him a peck on the cheek then pulled him across the wide street at the crosswalk for a closer look.

He checked his watch. "Weren't we trying to catch the Metro-North?"

"Relax," she said as she moved to the box office. "There'll be another train. And it's only one stop anyway."

"Okay, then I'm with you, I guess."

Ridley was from a not particularly nice part of Worcester.

He'd seen his fair share of mistreated, dilapidated and forgotten buildings past their prime. He wasn't that interested in seeing another one in a different city. No matter how infectious he continually found Lanie's enthusiasm.

"Look, you have to see more of New York if you want to know your way around. And as a Black woman and native, it would be wrong of me to let you to do the 'tourist' thing of thinking New York City is merely Manhattan island." She leaned forward at the ticket box and gave the disinterested woman inside an ingratiating smile. "My friend is from England. Could I just show him the lobby real quick?"

She turned to him, raising an eyebrow and giving him a chin nod. Catching her drift and assuming it was his cue, he gave the woman his most affected cockney accent. "I am and blimey! Would you 'ave a look at this place!"

Lanie stifled a snort before resuming her plaintive look at the box office clerk.

The woman sighed. "Sure, honey. We have a concert tonight so the last door on the left is open."

"Thanks." Lanie grinned, taking Ridley's hand again. She threaded her fingers through his and squeezed with palpable excitement.

"When I was a kid, they retrofitted this to be a four-screen movie theater. After my dad left and my grandma moved back to England, it was just me and my mom. Sometimes it was scary. Like, just her and I against the whole world. Back then, we spent so many hours here. So many of my happiest memories are from here. Then they just abandoned it for the longest time. Recently, they restored the original single-screen setup but it's also a performance space now."

Ridley followed her through a low ornate entryway into a foyer that opened up to massive arched vaulted ceilings with heavily gilded baroque murals and elaborate cornices leading to

Corinthian columns. Ridley felt like he'd left The Bronx and the New World completely behind for a European movie palace.

"Wow," he said, looking around agape.

"I know, right?" Lanie was similarly awestruck, as if it was her first time too. "Only architecture buffs and Bronx residents even remember this is still here."

The lobby was almost gaudy in its excess. Impressive gilded chandeliers hung above a dark, round wood-paneled concession stand and ornate balustrades on a plush red velveteen-lined grand staircase. Peeking their heads inside the theater space, it too had walls awash with columns, scrolls, urns and caryatids standing tall along the stage.

"There are only five of these left. They were called Loew's Five Wonders. Technically, only four of them are in the city, one's in Jersey." Her lips curled upward. "This one is the Paradise."

"Very apropos." Ridley lifted an eye to the ceilings again. "I really think you missed your calling on the tourist board. 'Cuz wandering around The Bronx was not on my bingo card for today."

"Oh really? So, what was?"

Ridley gazed at her adoringly before pulling her into his arms. In the empty theater, he tried to keep the kiss he gave her PG but it quickly became a hard R.

"I'm gonna walk you around until you love it," she said when they came up for air.

I already do.

forty

Lanie

■ 12-FEB ■ Trans-Continental Airways ■ Flight: 7446 ■

JFK-John F. Kennedy Int'l Airport ▶ **LHR-London, Heathrow**

Seat Assignment: **29K**

Lanie groaned as she watched Jonah's sister, Charity, flip a penny into her pint. The coin settled gently at the bottom of her glass and the bubbles that fizzed around it mirrored the many dozens roiling in her belly.

Marissa cheered and Shanice, who had been twirling on her bar stool, paused for a moment to appreciate Charity's precision.

"You know what that means, Big Cuz!" Les, the only man allowed on Gemma's hen night pub crawl, gave her a big smile.

Lanie crooked a finger in his general direction—he was shifting slightly in her line of sight as she tried to pinpoint him—then beckoned him closer. He leaned in. "Don't think I haven't noticed that glass of water you've had for every pint of ale we've drunk all night," she whispered.

He smiled conspiratorially. "Babes, I have to get back to Peckham on the night bus. If you think I'm gonna wake up in some dank skip tomorrow morning messing about with you lot, you've got another think coming." He sniffed.

Charity snorted. "A bunch of reprobates, innit?"

"Innit." He nodded, nursing his seltzer unapologetically.

"C'mon then," Gemma commanded. "Drink! Drink! Drink! Drink!"

Her crowd of fellow reprobates chimed in behind her.

Gemma was wearing a slinky, sleeveless rainbow-sequin ASOS dress with a bachelorette's requisite glittery plastic tiara and a giant pink "Bride-to-be" sash. With her normally curly mane flat-ironed bone straight, spider-leg eyelashes and full-face makeup, she looked like an escapee from the pageant circuit.

"So, I'm the only one that thinks it's unfair Les is cheating?" Lanie complained, deliberately stalling. She wasn't sure what number drink she was on. She only knew she hadn't imbibed like this since…damn, since she used to do this bullshit with these same women in her twenties.

But they were *decidedly not* in their twenties anymore. Lanie groaned, thinking of tomorrow's hangover.

"Hey, I'm not drinking either," Fatou offered, as she nursed her virgin mojito.

Lanie waved her off tipsily, nearly spilling her lager. "You don't count. You're Muslim now."

"I was always Muslim," Fatou deadpanned. "What I am now is pregnant."

For one second, there was an impossible stillness among their entire group as they all digested this information. Then through the ambient tavern noises—random conversations, televisions, glasses clinking—came Gemma's eerie squeal at a pitch that probably woke up neighborhood dogs blocks away.

"Oh my God! What? Are you joking? What are you telling me, Fatoumata Gyamerah-Soleimani? What are you telling me, right now?"

Lanie squeezed her eyes closed, bracing herself as the whole world tilted for a moment at the intense noise. Then the rest of the women joined in, screaming and jostling to be closer to Fatou. Someone held Lanie's shoulders steady as people hooted and hollered and moved around her, rattling their side of the solid oak bar so much that the bartender and other patrons turned to look their way.

"Alright, settle." Fatou had to finally raise her voice as assorted women hugged her and Gemma hung from her neck, plying her with enthusiastic but sloppy kisses. "Settle." It was like she was trying to corral a pen of excited puppies.

"When are you due?"

"What did Arash say?"

"How long have you guys been trying?"

"Do you know what it is yet?"

"Do you have a name picked out yet?"

The questions came nonstop. And in her normal, terminally practical Fatou way, she addressed each of them methodically as Gemma looked on, brightly grinning like a high beam.

"I'm stepping out for a cig. You look piqued, love, join me." When Charity spoke directly into her ear, Lanie finally identified the hands that had been holding her steady.

Lanie slid off the bar stool clumsily, leaving the pint and retrieving her cell phone before following Charity out.

In the grip of winter, the nighttime temperatures could be quite brisk, but after the crush of bodies inside, the chill was a relief. Lanie was happy to be outside in the wide-open space and fresh air. She took a deep lungful of it. Next to her, Charity rooted through her stylish snakeskin clutch until she retrieved a pack of cigarettes and a lighter.

"I thought you quit, like, ten years ago?"

Charity popped the cigarette into the corner of her mouth then nodded, cupping her flame to protect it from a breeze that wafted by. "Hmm, yeah." She took a deep drag. "Try being trapped inside with your mum, dad, little brother and nan for two years and only having the back garden to retreat to. See if you don't pick up a few bad habits."

Lanie made a sympathetic noise, opening her cell phone to check her messages. "At least you had a back garden...and that loft extension." Lanie referred to the tricked-out mother-in-law suite Charity lived in above her parents' house. She rushed to open a text that she'd missed earlier from Ridley.

"Innit?" Charity concurred. "I'd have killed my mum if Nan and I hadn't agreed to swap spaces."

RIDLEY:

You dancing on any bars yet?

He accompanied that message with a gif from the movie *Coyote Ugly* of sexy female bartenders line-dancing on top of a bar.

RIDLEY:

If so, send pics. 😊 😈

Lanie giggled, checking the time. It was midnight here, only a little after seven in New York.

LANIE:

That doesn't start until drink #9.
I have 3 more to go.

Is that true? Lanie didn't know. She also didn't know what pub they were at. She turned to read the awning. The White Hart. She groaned. That meant they had two more pubs before they wrapped things up for the night at the Kings Head in Tooting.

Lanie's heart thumped when she saw those wonderful three dots bobbing. She waited.

RIDLEY:

> What are you waiting for then?
> I need pics by the time I get back
> to my hotel. Chug-a-lug.

Lanie snorted at the eggplant emoji that followed.

"That your fella, then?" Charity asked, gesturing to the phone with her cigarette, her perfectly plucked eyebrows bobbing suggestively. "Gem and the girls said he was well fit."

Damn Gemma. The thought both pleased and bothered her. But Lanie grinned, giving Charity a little shrug. False modesty didn't really become her but neither did bragging. And Charity seemed to get it, smiling back.

"Bless." Charity took another deep drag on her cigarette, before breathing it out in a long, exaggerated sigh. She wrapped her arms across her chest, hugging herself as she gazed out at the traffic going up and down Balham High Road.

Lanie didn't think she had ever seen this morose side of Charity before. As Jonah's older sister by two years, they hadn't really hung out much as kids. Particularly since, previously, Charity really didn't care for Gemma, which Lanie used to take as a personal affront. But even as they became adults, Charity was mostly in and out with her own university and work friends.

"You're not getting any younger, Charitha." Lanie startled as Charity spoke, breaking up an extended period of contemplative silence and doing an uncanny impression of her mother, Syreeta. *"Charitha, you and Jonah were in primary school by the time I was your age. Charitha, aren't you embarrassed your younger brother is getting married before you? Think of your poor aachchi, won't you, Charitha, huh?"*

Lanie smiled, finding only mild humor in that. She also sensed the pressure from society at large to pair off. She was already thirty-one, it reminded her, and unmarried with eggs that were shriveling in her womb.

"I always want to say, 'Do you really think I'd willingly subject myself to all the hoops Jonah and Gem are jumping through right now?' Do you even *know* how hard it can be to pee in a saree?"

"Apparently, I'm about to find out," Lanie said.

"Yes, you will."

"Look, Charity. About the sarees…" Lanie glanced around. Their group was tucked away in a back corner inside and no one walking up or down the sidewalk was even remotely interested in their conversation.

Charity frowned, throwing her cigarette to the asphalt and stubbing it out with the toe of her shoe. "What about them?"

"Is it…" Lanie didn't know how to put this.

"Is it what?"

"Is it culturally appor—" the possibly six previous drinks made Lanie stumble verbally "—appropriative for us to be wearing them?"

Regardless of what Gemma said, Lanie still felt deeply uncomfortable with the prospect of donning elements of Jonah and Charity's culture as some form of cosplay on one of Gemma's little whims.

Charity seemed to consider it before shaking her head. "No, I don't think so. I mean I understand what you're asking, thank you, but for one, seeing Jonah wearing a traditional Kandyan wedding outfit will make our grandmother very happy and—"

"What are you two on about out here?" Gemma stepped out of the pub, into the street, shivering immediately. "Come back inside. It's freezing out."

Charity waved a hand with a newly lit cigarette in between her fingers in explanation. "When I'm finished. Mel's just keeping us company."

Lanie held her breath hoping Gemma would go back inside

before Charity continued. But she hung by the door, holding it open. *Waiting*. Exerting silent pressure like she always did.

"Anyway," Charity went on, obliviously. "I think they've been doing a wonderful job of being really respectful, consulting with my mum and nan. And Gem actually looks terrific in her *Osariya*."

Gemma came out of the bar more fully, her arms tightly crossed over her breasts. "Were you talking about the sarees again?" She bristled in irritation. "How did I know you weren't going to let it go? How do I *always* know?"

Lanie felt too drunk to argue. "I just needed to ask, Gem. I think I have that right since I have to wear one too. And it feels, I don't know, disrespectful to me."

"Disrespectful?" Gemma huffed. "Well, *I think* it's bloody disrespectful that you're out here quizzing my sister-in-law at *my* party!"

"Wait, Gem," Lanie started defensively.

She knew all that liquor wasn't helping her comprehension skills, but one look over at Charity's dumbfounded face told her Charity was lost too.

"Hang on," Charity concurred, stubbing out the next cigarette on the sidewalk, then holding up a hand.

"I told you we discussed it already, didn't I? I said we had it under control." Gemma's voice began to rise, ignoring Charity's objections. "We sat down with Nishan and Syreeta and talked about how we had the utmost respect for Sri Lankan culture and wanted to find the most appropriate way to incorporate it into our own ceremony."

"And I asked you that, Gem. You could have just said that."

"You never trust me anyway," Gemma wailed. "Never the benefit of the doubt. Somewhere along the way, you've assumed that I'm just some mug who can't even be relied on to make a simple decision."

Lanie could barely speak, stammering before she could form

a coherent rebuttal. "Just wait! Gem, I've never ever said anything like that!"

"You don't have to say it! I know you think it." Gemma was shouting now and Lanie could see eyes inside the pub nearest the door starting to turn toward the window. "You bloody-well fly all the way to England once a month to check up on us, don't you? What more is there to say? Silly ole Gem, can't even manage to get her own nan to hospital without her *younger* American cousin coming to hold her hand."

"Tell me how you really feel, Gem," Lanie muttered.

"I've tried! And I've tried! And I've tried! But you won't stop and listen, will you? You can't help yourself! You have to show off how smart you are. How capable you are."

"Stop what? What did I do?"

"I can't even get married in peace."

"Hold up, no one forced you to include me. You *asked* me to help you!"

Lanie was genuinely confused. She distinctly remembered telling Gem and Jonah that she didn't want to have anything to do with their stupid wedding and getting roped into every aspect of it anyway.

…*Or something like that. Right?*

"*Help*, not *take over*! We couldn't manage a single decision on our own! There you were in every single element!"

"You couldn't manage a single decision, period. You refused to make any! If I didn't force you, you'd still be picking out cake flavors. And I let you choose things!"

"Let me? Do you hear yourself? It's my wedding! I should've chosen *everything*. But you were always there, weren't you? Butting in—"

"Oh, stop it! Not everything could wait until you or Jonah 'felt' like dealing with it, Gemma!" Lanie yelled. "Believe it or not, getting married in five months doesn't involve wishes or magic *or vibes*. Someone has to do real work and make actual decisions."

"And here's you, always happy to be the one to do it, right?"

"Sorry, someone has to," Lanie said smugly. Even through her alcohol haze and patina of shame, Lanie could still feel the anger brewing within her.

Gemma propped her hands on her hips. "You are so self-righteous. You think that everything would fall apart if you weren't here to pick it up."

Lanie didn't dignify that with a response. She didn't think it, she knew it. She cocked her head to the side, her own arms akimbo now. The fact that their grandmother had been well on her way to developing cirrhosis and had dropped over forty pounds in a few months without raising any alarms said volumes on its own.

Gemma knew what Lanie was thinking by the look on her face and huffed, stomping a foot in indignation.

She's a child, Lanie thought uncharitably.

"You. Don't. Live. Here, Melanie!" Gemma screeched suddenly.

"I know that," Lanie whispered, retracting at that harsh reminder, pulling inward like a tortoise under attack.

But they *did* need her there. She didn't have to say it.

"I don't know how you imagined you and Jonah could've ever been a thing," Gemma said then, changing tack, grasping for any way to wound. And she might as well have pulled a blade out from behind her back because this had gone from a pretty mild argument for them into a bloody street fight in fourteen words. "You live ten thousand miles away."

Lanie rolled her eyes, shielding herself with condescension. "It's more like thirty-five hundred, Gem."

"See!" Gemma turned to Charity, who stared blankly, clearly wishing to be kept out of it.

"What? It's not my fault your relationship to letters and numbers is tenuous at the best of times. Jonah must really be wearing those love goggles thinking you can manage at a uni."

As soon as she said it, Lanie wished she could take it back. Desperately wanted to take it back.

Gemma gasped. Charity turned away, squeezing her eyes tightly shut as if wishing to be anywhere but there. And Les, who had just managed to make it out onto the street, skidded to a stop, eyes going platter-sized.

"I—I'm sorry, Gem."

"At least someone wants me," Gemma said with a sudden, preternatural calm, even though Lanie could almost see the steam rising from her ears and actual tears forming in her eyes. "Someone *loves* me. You're kidding yourself if you think anything will ever happen with that doctor. That he really even cares about you. You? You're a doormat. Like your mother." Gemma laughed cruelly, ignoring the tear streaks that were running down her face, cutting through her makeup.

"At least my mother stuck around."

"Alright! That's enough," Les said sternly. "Both of you!"

"You just can't help yourself. It's Jonah all over again, isn't it?" Gemma shrugged off Les's staying hand on her shoulder. "Chasing after a man who's way out of your league and lives an ocean away so you can blame the distance for why it doesn't work out. You're so concerned with us here? Pay attention to your own life. I know you're a mess back in New York, Mel. I've always known. Nan and Auntie Ryan talk. But you always come here acting perfect, come here acting like...like your shit doesn't stink and you're so smart! Why aren't you back in school, Mel? Huh? 'Cos the truth is you're pathetic. And no one wants you...not even your uni." Her cousin gave her a pitying look. "Still, you can't see it, can you? But aren't you meant to be the clever one of us?"

Lanie bit back a physical reaction to her cousin's words, fighting to remain steady, look unaffected.

Gemma turned to reenter the pub accompanied by her brother, who shot Lanie an irritated glance. Lanie shrugged. *I'm not the one who started this.*

Charity put a hand on Lanie's arm. "She didn't mean it."

"No, she did," Lanie said matter-of-factly, pretending that every one of Gemma's shots hadn't hit their targets, dead center.

Because Lanie knew, in her heart of hearts, *Gem wasn't wrong... about any of it.*

Lanie hung around the periphery of the bachelorette party like a black cloud as it got later into the night. No one said it but she knew she was no longer wanted—*but I organized the party*—so instead of leaving, she floated through the rest of the night on a wave of shots and pints following behind the group until they arrived at the last pub. Replaying what happened in her head, over and over.

"Last orders, ladies!" a waitress came to inform them. A couple of the women in their group jeered drunkenly in response.

By then, Lanie's hand was holding her head, which felt leaden weighing her shoulders down, inches above the bar top. She sat with her elbows on the polished wood surface and scrolled her Instagram and TikTok feeds. Every few minutes, a new photo or video appeared, posted by Gemma or Fatou or one of the other women whose accounts Lanie had unfortunately decided to follow earlier that evening. In a few posts, Lanie even glimpsed herself, a thigh here, an arm there, the back of her head in many. To judge from those feeds, their argument had not even been a blip in Gemma's night.

Why am I still here? She was a glutton for punishment.

It was the only explanation that made sense. She was sulking, wallowing. Why was she even taking Gemma's words to heart? It wasn't like Gemma had been some romantic paragon. Yes, she'd had twice, maybe thrice, the relationship experience Lanie had, but quantity did not equate with quality. In fact, until whatever voodoo or deal with the devil she and Jonah had crafted to fall in love with each other, Gemma had had awful taste. A litany of "dodgy girls and wastemen"—by her own admission.

Gemma had just gotten lucky.

Merely recognizing the potential in Jonah that Lanie had always seen was no feat. And letting herself fall in love with a good guy she'd never previously given the time of day didn't make Gemma some love genius.

Why shouldn't Lanie have that kind of dumb luck too? They were cousins, weren't they?

Lanie closed Instagram and opened her photo gallery. There were tons of pictures of her and Ridley. In London, at Regent's Canal in Hackney, picnicking on Hampstead Heath overlooking the city, and at the Sky Garden with Tower Bridge in the background. She scrolled to pictures of them in New York, on the Staten Island Ferry with the Statue of Liberty behind them. Roaming around the Top of the Rock in Rockefeller Center, of him bending over the railing to check out the "Panorama" scale model of New York City at the Queens Museum.

She smiled to herself. She'd never encountered a man like Ridley before. He was always checking in with her, taking care of her. He liked and respected her and made that fact obvious. She'd never felt she had to do anything special to earn his attention, and with his quiet reassurance, he never asked her to be anyone but herself.

He was someone who genuinely enjoyed her company, and went out of his way to show her that. She'd never been with a man who appreciated her more, or adored her body more, who reveled in all her curves and whose appetite for her was more about his enjoyment *of her* than what she did *for him*. Who showed her in so many ways that her pleasure was his pleasure and vice versa. And the things he did to her, the way he made her feel, in and out of bed…

Lanie shuddered now thinking of their last encounter, after the Botanical Gardens visit, when they'd holed up in a hotel in TriBeCa for the rest of the weekend. Even the way he looked at her made her feel cherished in a way no one had ever before.

That couldn't be faked.

His feelings for her had to be real…because hers were as well.

I love him.

Lanie let out a little gasping hiccup at the realization. The feeling, while itself wasn't new, was newly understood, newly articulated.

She loved him in a way that was infinitely different and vaster than her abiding feelings for Jonah. Like the difference between the light cast by a lamp and that of the sun. She felt a beauty in the way they were together, how happy he made her feel inside. She was suddenly filled to the brim with the immensity of it.

Fuck Gemma and her pronouncements. Forget Mom's prophecies too; she can't see beyond the tragedies of her own love life. And, well, maybe Narcisa just has it wrong. She's never seen us together. She doesn't know how it is. Fuck limerence.

Yes, fuck limerence. Impulsively, Lanie pulled up his number and dialed. It was only nine p.m. in New York and this revelation couldn't wait.

She frowned, slightly daunted when she went straight to his voicemail.

He had to still be up. Lanie shook the setback off, taking a swig from the lonely shot of Irish whiskey that sat abandoned in a row of glasses she'd had the bartender set up earlier.

She was going to do what she had never done with Jonah. She would tell Ridley how she felt so that there could be no confusion. She would not make the mistake of losing him because she was too much of a coward to ever tell him the truth.

She took a deep breath at the tone.

"Ridley? Hey, it's me…"

forty-one

Lanie

Lanie sat on a bench in the lobby of the Royal Mahal catering hall in Tooting Bec. Tonight, the ballroom was conservatively decorated with balloons and streamers for the rehearsal dinner Jonah's family was hosting the evening before the wedding. Tomorrow, according to her explicit directions, it would be festooned with enough cascading foliage and white flowers to look like a garden in spring for the reception.

For now, Lanie cradled her face, her head pounding out of her skull. She could barely think. And when she did, it was about that message she'd left on Ridley's voicemail, which made her head pound even more.

The one where she'd sloppily told him she loved him. And to top it all off, she'd professed that she'd never had a better lover. Said she touched herself—*yes, like the Divinyls song*—when she thought of him.

Oh God. She groaned.

"A-whatis dis? Get up, nuh gyal!" one of her distant relatives said in their strong Antiguan accent, accompanied by a sucking of their teeth. "Eh-eh."

The sound was like nails driven into her skull. Lanie probably looked a mess, dressed up in a fuchsia floral cocktail dress and kitten heels, but nursing a raging hangover. "In a minute," she whispered.

"I've got it, Auntie," a male voice said as someone sat beside her.

Lanie glanced up. Jonah shoved a huge bottle of water into her hands. "I've been handing these out like party favors. What did you guys do? You all knew we had this tonight."

Lanie looked at him again after taking a big swig. As always, Jonah looked dapper wearing a fawn-brown Nehru jacket and matching pants with a pocket square and a black scarf over his shoulders.

"I think we thought we'd sleep it off? But apparently only Gem did." Her cousin was a glowing vision, floating around the banquet hall as if she'd never touched a drop of alcohol last night.

"Well, the rest of you look bound for the rubbish bin."

Lanie did her version of a "bah humbug" noise, sweeping her hand at him in disgust. It was Gemma's fault she felt like this—in more ways than one. It was Gemma's fucking hen night and she'd damn near insisted everyone overindulge. And it was their argument outside the pub that made Lanie call Ridley in the middle of the night to profess her undying love. Now, he wasn't even calling her back. She had no idea if she even still had a date for the wedding tomorrow.

Though historically, men had hightailed it away from Lanie at the first suggestion of anything serious, Ridley seemed better than that, but maybe he'd just been more strung out on the sex than the rest. Because, *yes, Lord*, the sex had been that good. *Really good*. But then she'd had to go say something stupid like I love you. And perhaps now he'd gone to ground.

Tears prickled at Lanie's eyes. She thought all the rest between them was really good, too. Good enough to stick around for.

"Look, Lanie." Jonah turned and took the bottle from her, placing it by their feet before taking her hands in his.

She groaned at the words. *What manner of after-school-fucking-special bullshit is this about to be?*

"We've known each other a long time," he began solemnly. "And you're one of my best friends. And I really love you. I do, you believe me, right?"

Lanie's head pounded, feeling like her brain was about to leak out of her ears. She didn't have the patience for this.

"But you have to grow up and get over me."

She shook her hands free of Jonah's grasp, more annoyed that the motion made her head hurt than by what he said.

Although…how dare he?

"Oh, you think I'm upset about you?" Lanie laughed scornfully, which rattled her brain more. "Get bent, Jonah! It would have been nice if you'd said something like this back when you fucked me!"

"Keep your voice down!" He looked around, alarmed.

"Why?" But she did lower her voice because even alone in the hallway, with this many aunties, uncles and cousins from both sides roaming around, the walls had ears. She grabbed her bottle, ready to move. "Leave me alone, will you?"

"Melanie, wait," he begged. "You're right. I should have been straight with you years ago. But in my defense, we were young."

"Twenty-one is not all that young, Jonah. You had me out here looking like a simp, like you didn't actually tell me you loved me. But I guess that was just pillow talk, huh? Used to tell that to all the girls when you were coming in them, did you?"

He winced and Lanie cringed inwardly at how crude her anger had made her. Impulse control was a real bitch, and Lanie, unfortunately, still didn't know her. She wasn't about to apologize though, because she was still hurt. Twelve years later, it still fucking hurt.

"You know you were my first," he hissed.

Mine too, which made it all the worse, Lanie thought. "What I know is, you made me feel delusional. Like I imagined it."

"I know." Jonah nodded. "And I have no excuse. I'm so sorry,

Mel. I was sorry then too. But I didn't know how to fix it. As soon as it happened, I knew it was a mistake."

"Wow, thanks."

"No, I mean, it was a mistake because *I* was confused. I thought the way I loved you—and I do love you, Mel, so, so much…" Jonah rubbed his temple, struggling. "I thought it was the big way, you know, like you were my one true love. 'Cos I'd watched all the same movies as you: *Love, Actually*, *When Harry Met Sally*, *Four Weddings and a Funeral*, *Sixteen Candles*, *Some Kind of Wonderful*. Most of them *with you*—so I really thought we were Keith and Watts too."

Tears formed in Lanie's eyes as she snorted in amusement. *Guess Jonah suffered from limerence too.*

"It was only afterward that I realized our love wasn't like that. I liked the *idea* of us, but the connection was…different. But by then, I was so afraid I'd lose you by rejecting you that I just freaked out and tried to pretend it hadn't happened at all. Like we could go back to how things were before we hooked up."

Tears streamed down her face, ruining her makeup and making her eyes ache and her head throb more.

"That's your excuse for how you've been treating me the past few months too?"

"Is that fair? You haven't been exactly wonderful either, Melanie."

Well, okay. Recently, as Narcisa might have said, she *may* have been acting like her ass was up on her shoulders.

"You gaslit me, Jonah. For years! Made me look stupid and feel insecure," she cried. "How'd you expect me to act? For me to throw you guys a goddamned parade? And yet I practically planned your wedding anyway. That should have gotten me something."

Her mother was right: all her work hadn't counted in her favor. It might even have made her look more delusional to people. *Muggins here planned a whole wedding of the man she loved to another woman.* She tried to find a napkin or something to staunch the torrent of tears even though she knew saving her makeup was a lost cause. Gemma was gonna kill her.

Jonah handed her his silken jacquard pocket square. "I know. I know. And I am sorry."

"You let *everyone* in the neighborhood think I was some pathetic lovesick dummy…for years! What stopped you from just saying something years ago?"

"Could I have? Would that not have meant the end of our whole friendship?"

Lanie knew how intense she'd been back then. How she still was. *Look at this thing with Ridley.* She put her head into her hands, then straightened again, staring daggers, pointing a freshly manicured finger at him.

"But it would have been *my* choice. And your consequences. You took that choice away from me by stringing me along."

"You're right. And for that, I will spend years—"

"The rest of your *wutless* life!"

He sighed. "The rest of my wutless life, making it up to you."

"Start by treating my cousin like the princess she is."

"I'm already on it." He smiled at that.

"You do know that doesn't mean emptying your bank account, right?"

He smiled shamefacedly. "Yeah, I'm getting that."

"Good."

Jonah reached over to wipe the last stray tears from Lanie's face. "Eek," he said, examining his hands. "You're gonna have to wash it all off and start again."

"Gee, thanks, Captain Obvious," she said snarkily, rising from the bench in search of the bathroom.

"We'll talk again later, yeah?" he asked.

"We better."

"And, Mel. I do love you."

"I know, Stupid. Love you too."

forty-two

Lanie

The morning of Gemma and Jonah's wedding passed in a perfumed whirlwind of airbrushed makeup, safety pins, hair clips and mountains of spray hold. The bridal party had a five a.m. call time to begin a beautification process that involved plucking, shaving, flat-ironing, pinning, curling and primping. As maid of honor, Lanie found that a lot of her time was spent herding people to their assigned places at their appointed hours. They allowed Gemma and Gran to sleep in a little bit but Lanie and Les were up at the crack of dawn like drill sergeants assigned to reveille.

Then, finally, resplendent in their Western gown and morning suit, and accompanied by a far smaller audience than was expected at their reception later that evening, Gemma Turner and Jonah Perera were married during an intimate Catholic mass at Our Lady of Divine Grace at ten a.m. on Valentine's Day.

Lanie exhaled when at last it was done.

The groom had cried, the bride had cried, and even both sets of attendants teared up. Jonah's grandmother, Aachchi, and his parents, Nishan and Syreeta, whooped, which got big laughs from everyone but Father Gary. And through it all, Lanie only glanced at her phone four, maybe five, *six times tops*, waiting for a message from Ridley.

Despite the fact that they had been, at best, cordial for the past two days since Gemma's bachelorette party, Lanie and Gemma silently agreed to a détente. They hugged, kissed, laughed and posed for pictures as if none of the rest had ever happened. And try as Lanie might to fight it, their happiness eased some of the latent animosity that had simmered for the past few months. Watching Gemma and Jonah together, looking perfect, excitedly running down the aisle and out of the church, Lanie understood that ultimately, it was their happiness that had mattered most.

They are still two of my favorite people in the world.

Afterward, the newlyweds hosted a small bruncheon for their church guests at a very swank eatery in Clapham, before adjourning to suites at a hotel in nearby Wandsworth to prepare for the evening's big festivities. There, Lanie stood by the bedroom door of her suite, which was acting as ground zero of bridal party staging, checking her cell.

LANIE:

> I'm getting worried now.
> Seriously, call me. Please.

No reply. No call.

Ridley was MIA.

"Well, this has been quite the whirlwind, hasn't it?" Gran whispered, coming up behind her and pulling Lanie into an encouraging side hug. "I don't think I've gone around the borough this much in years."

"I've noticed. Things are open again. You need to be out more, Gran."

Lanie glanced at her phone again. *Maybe his plane disappeared over the Atlantic?* The thought was both horrifying and comforting. Because he'd need a pretty compelling excuse for his radio silence at this point.

"I know, Sec," her grandmother was saying when Lanie realized she'd spaced out.

"You gave us a real scare."

"Yes. But don't worry yourself. Gemma registered me for Seniors Aerobics at the leisure center."

Lanie dropped the phone to her side and turned. "She did?"

Tulip nodded, with a smile that showed she delighted in surprising her granddaughter. "Les will take me to the first two classes and then Gem will start when she and Jonah return from their honeymoon." Her grandmother kissed her cheek. "See? Nothing to fret over. We're getting back to normal."

"So, you're feeling okay? You have a big part in the ceremony tonight."

"Yes, I know." Her grandmother emphasized, "And I'm feeling good."

She looked good too. For the first time in months, Lanie felt like she could exhale on all fronts. Her grandmother's cheeks were full and flush, looking closer to what Lanie remembered. Tulip wasn't plump anymore, but according to her new doctor, she was approaching a healthy weight for her size and age again. She was finally on the mend.

"And you?"

"I'm great." Lanie nodded, smile affixed.

That's how it was all morning. People commending Lanie on how well she was holding up "under the circumstances" while she busied herself playing traffic cop, directing all the chaos around her. As a result, Lanie was the last at everything: last one to have her hair blown out and pinned up, last into the makeup chair, last one into wardrobe. Even now as Syreeta, Charity and a professional draper hired expressly to help the women into their sarees rushed around making sure everyone was folded, tucked and pinned correctly, Lanie stayed back, waiting to be last. Truth was, she wouldn't have had the time to be upset, even if she was. But interestingly enough, she wasn't.

Not about that at least.

"It's like seeing the old you," her grandmother said then, trying to rub a lipstick mark off Lanie's cheek. "I'm so pleased for you and your young man. Where was he?"

"Don't worry. They're gonna redo my makeup after everyone else is done." Lanie changed the subject rapidly.

Feeling an alert trill in her phone, she looked down. "Excuse me, Gran."

"Of course." Gran wandered back to the couch in her cute pink pastel mother-of-the-bride dress to hurry up and wait with everyone else.

But again, it wasn't Ridley. It was Les.

"Okay everyone!" Lanie's voice resounded through the room, bringing everything to a momentary pause. "Les says Gem will be back from picture-taking in fifteen minutes. We have to wrap everyone else up so that Mrs. Perera and Mrs. Verma can concentrate on the bride when she arrives."

"That includes you too," Gran called back.

Lanie looked down at herself, still in her Western bridesmaid's dress. "Oh. Yeah."

"Hit me with some more lippy, would you?" Gemma asked out of the corner of her mouth, while they stood waiting outside the banquet hall doors. A lush bouquet of white roses, ranunculus and gardenia in her hands prevented them from being of use.

Lanie dug into the left side of her breasts—where the draper, Mrs. Verma, advised her to tuck things—and pulled out the lip gloss the makeup artist had given her for reapplication. At their suggestion, Lanie had deliberately worn the same currant-red color as Gem.

"Ta," she said, puckering as Lanie dabbed Gemma's lips with the lip stain.

"I look okay, then? Not stupid?" Gemma asked for the millionth time. However, unlike in the hotel suite, when Gemma preened while people raved and fawned over her being draped in her white-and-gold traditional Sri Lankan *Osariya*, Lanie could tell now Gemma was unsure. "Not a culture vulture, yeah?"

"No, Gem, I was wrong," Lanie whispered back. "You look spectacular."

And she does.

Adorned with white hydrangeas that circled her bun, Gemma wore a *Nalalpatha*, a traditional Kandyan headpiece. Two long chains with round sun and moon engraved medallions looped by her ears connecting to a middle chain that ran down the center of her head, and all three were attached to a pendant that lay on her forehead. Her gown was resplendent, heavily embroidered with pearls, sequins and crystals. It was a more conservative choice than Lanie would have expected. Fabric obscured Gemma's midsection with draped and folded organza to suggest exposed bits without actually showing any.

Gemma smiled in response, relieved. "Thank you," she said primly, looking straight ahead at the closed hall doors. Then she paused. "...For all your help these past few months. I know what I said the other day but we couldn't have managed any of this without you, Mel."

Lanie's cheeks heated.

"And you and Jonah did a beautiful job with this part on your own. But you know, I've always got you." She put a hand on Gemma's bangled arm. "What I don't know is how you could afford all this jewelry. It looks expensive as hell," Lanie said sotto voce, looking at what seemed like hundreds of pounds worth of traditional Sri Lankan twenty-four-carat gold jewelry that Gemma wore.

"Girl." Gemma gave her the single word and a look in confirmation.

"It looks damn good though."

Gemma was wearing the *Padakkam*, five gold necklaces of various sizes that Gran and Syreeta as her female elders put on her for good luck, an ornate gold choker called a *Karapatiya* and hanging pearl earrings called *Dimiti*, in addition to numerous bangles and a bracelet with five chains attached to five rings on her right hand.

"Tell me you rented all this stuff."

Gemma shook her head. "It was all gifted to me by Jonah's mom and the women in his family. They brought it from Sri Lanka, since they knew I wouldn't get it from my own mother." A dark look briefly transited her face.

As usual, despite being informed, Aunt Elliot was a no-show.

"Well, it's her loss because she doesn't get to see her daughter looking like an absolute goddess."

Gemma smiled, blinking back tears. "Right?"

Les raced out of the banquet hall breathlessly. He was looking good himself in a gold-and-red brocade Nehru jacket with sparkly makeup to match. "Okay, it's time. You good?"

"Honestly?" Gemma looked wide-eyed between Lanie and Les. She looked more frightened now than she had this morning in the chapel. "I'm absolutely brickin' it, fam."

Lanie grasped her arm again. "You already did the hard part, Gem. This is the fun stuff."

"That's right," Les said jovially, switching places with Lanie and taking his twin by the elbow to escort her inside. "'Cos we've already locked it down, haven't we?"

Gemma grinned, nodding.

Lanie beckoned their grandmother over from where she'd been sitting comfortably with Jonah's *aachchi* to stand on the other side of Gemma.

"I'm gonna head in," Lanie said as the Sri Lankan drummers began to play their opening to lead Gemma inside.

At the door, Gemma called to Lanie again and she turned. "If it's any consolation, I think he's gonna show."

Lanie's eyes burned, but she could not ruin this makeup. "Thanks, let's hope so," she managed to croak out, blowing a kiss before disappearing into the banquet hall.

After the *Pirith nool* unity ritual, in which Jonah and Gemma's pinky fingers were tied together by a white thread, the mother's ritual where Gran—in place of Aunt Elliot—was presented by Jonah with an intricately woven white cloth as thanks for raising Gemma, the *Kiribath*, a sweet milk rice confection, was fed to the newlyweds by Syreeta and Gran and then Jonah and Gemma both lit a brass oil lamp to symbolize their commitment to keeping their love burning forever, the Sinhalese *Poruwa Siritha* ceremony was over and the party began.

By nine o'clock, however, Lanie was more than ready to leave. The whole room was thumping with the DJ's remarkably skilled set, and the heavy bass of reggae, hip-hop and R&B made Lanie's brain throb. She was reminded yet again that she was thirty-one years old now, not twenty-one anymore. Getting over a night of hard drinking was no longer a case of drinking a lot of water and popping a couple of pain pills.

"Come dance with me!" Les shouted above the synthy, pulsating beat of 112's aptly named "Dance With Me."

Lanie resisted for a moment.

"You heard them, report to the dance floor," Les declared, dragging her out of her chair as Slim began begging someone to dance with him. "But leave the cell phone."

The dance floor was a crush of hot gyrating bodies. Lanie didn't immediately get into it, but she was in the spirit by the time the singers were instructing people to clap their hands if they were sexy and they knew it. Before long, Lanie had lost time dancing with abandon in her surprisingly flexible saree. She danced with Les, she danced with Fatou and her husband, Arash, she danced with Gran and Gemma, and at one point she even danced with one of Jonah's older male cousins, but had to remove his hands from her bottom twice before she finally gave up and pushed him away.

As the music changed to a slow jam, Jonah approached Lanie and extended his hand. She took it and let him pull her into a loose embrace.

Like Gemma, he was currently sporting his third look of the day, out of the traditional Kandyan outfit with its plush velvet four-cornered hat, elaborately embroidered matching jacket and draped ceremonial cloth wrapped around his waist. Now he wore another dapper white velvet *sherwani* with gold embroidery, *kurta* and pants.

Lanie smiled. *He is too cute.* She reached up to push back some of the stray hairs that had escaped the hold of his slick styling gel before catching herself. She lowered her hand.

"You having fun?" he asked, smoothing his hair back himself as they danced around.

"Sure," she lied.

"You'd have better luck with someone who doesn't know you. Now, what's wrong? And I know it's not about me. Frankly, I'm hurt," he joked.

Lanie gave him a wary smile. "Too soon."

"Sorry." Jonah's face got serious.

"This is your wedding day, Jonah. I'm not involving you in my romantic drama."

"Ah, Les did tell me you'd been seeing someone."

Oh wow. Les too?

"And I apologize for not knowing that already. For not being here for you like I should have. I've just been so caught up with changes at work and Gem." He squeezed the palm he held in

his hand. "But I should always be able to spare time for my best
friend. I'm so sorry, Mel."

Lanie teared up. It had been so long since he'd said something like that to her. She shook her head and smiled. "No, not
tonight you don't. Go find your wife."

They hugged and Lanie made her way off the dance floor
in search of the restroom off the hall's lobby. She knew she'd
sweated out her blowout and she was sure she must have otherwise looked a hot melted mess. Now it was finally time to
find out exactly how hard it was to pee in a saree.

"Lanie?"

Lanie turned slowly to see Ridley standing there in a suit
and tie, holding a bouquet of red roses.

The distinctive wail of Cameo's "Word Up!" filtered out
from the banquet room with its eerily apt interpolation of the
whistling opening strains of Ennio Morricone's theme to *The
Good, the Bad and the Ugly*. The only elements missing from this
impending standoff were sidearms and tumbleweeds.

"Happy Valentine's Day," he said, extending the bouquet to
her once he'd gotten close enough to hear.

"What happened to you?" she asked over the music, ignoring his greeting and the flowers.

It was infuriating that she was still so happy to see him.
That he still looked so dashing, even with his navy suit a little
rumpled, as if he was made for dressing up. He looked absurdly
good in a pair of thick-framed glasses she'd never seen before,
a pink shirt with a navy-and-pink-striped tie and a matching
pink pocket square. His haircut was about as fresh as his shave
and, like his cologne, faintly day-old but still dazzling.

"This is going to sound crazy," he started.

"Try anyway." Lanie refused to acknowledge the roses, waiting to see what he said before deciding whether to take them
from him or thrash him with them.

"I forgot to plug in my cell at the hotel last night. I missed my alarm, then my flight. When I got on the next one and tried to charge my phone battery, the jack was broken. I figured I wouldn't waste time waiting for the phone to charge in a café in the arrivals hall, so I focused on just getting here as soon as I could. I'm so, *so* sorry."

Lanie crossed her arms. On the one hand, he nearly stood her up—after asking to be her plus-one in the first place. But on the other, he still decided to come after what must have been a harried commute. "Did you wear the suit on the plane?"

He nodded. "No time to change once we landed."

"It looks like you were rolling around the aisles in it. So, I guess you really did come straight here."

"Except for the stop to get the flowers." He took a breath and extended the roses again.

She took them this time. "Have you eaten?"

A small smile broke across his face as he shook his head. "Not in about sixteen hours. No time and no food on the flight. I didn't fly back business."

"Ugh, coach sucks." Lanie barely even feigned sympathy, taking him by the hand, but still intertwining their fingers. "I have *no* idea what that's like."

forty-three

Lanie

The black cab pulled up in front of Ridley's house and Lanie looked up at it again. It was so impressive. So symbolic of the sophisticated, put-together man Ridley was. The last time she'd been there she'd been so intimidated by it. Now she was nervous again but for different reasons.

Lanie took his hand as he helped her out of the cab and let him lead her up the front steps as her heart galloped like a wild horse trying desperately to break free of a stable.

Ridley opened the door and pulled her inside. She appreciated his eagerness; she always did. It worked wonders in checking her apprehension. Ridley had a way of making her feel desired in a manner no one else ever had before. She watched him wordlessly from her place in the doorway.

He took off his coat and she followed suit, handing it to him so he could hang them together on the coatrack. Methodically, he loosened his tie, turned on a small lamp and placed his keys in the small glass dish on the nearby console table in the hall. Then he reached past to shut the front door behind her.

"Sor—" She started to apologize for her negligence but stopped, her voice catching as he loomed over her in the entryway, his arm over her shoulder resting against the door.

"Thank you for coming over. Welcome," he whispered.

They grinned at each other shyly in the dim light as if this was their first time. Lanie fought an awkward awareness as Ridley's eyes roamed her face. Easing back, he took his glasses off and deposited them on the table.

"Thanks for the invite." She inhaled as he closed in on her again with intent.

Blocking her body with his, he held her against the wall nearest the door, placing a knee between her thighs, nudging them apart. Sliding his fingers gently along her jaw, Ridley coaxed Lanie into an incendiary kiss that made her toes curl, sucking her tongue into his mouth. He ravished her with a kiss that was heady and flavored with the rum and colas he'd had at the wedding. Lanie's senses were muddled, so much that it took her a moment to feel his other hand creeping past the expert folds of her saree. His impatient fingers sought out her flesh everywhere as his lips left her mouth, journeying lower, skimming her neck and shoulders.

Ridley kissed her chest and pushed up her snug blouse until one breast was exposed. He held the fullness in his large palm, running a thumb over her nipple until it peaked and she mewled. Then he drew it lightly into his waiting mouth, his tongue toying with it. He tugged at her, knowing how responsive the delicious feel of his hot mouth and fervid licks over the sensitive skin made her. Lanie moaned and squirmed against his face, cupping the back of his head, driven to distraction as his other hand reached the flimsy cotton that covered her heated skin.

"You don't need these." Ridley lifted his mouth from her to whisper as he twined the fabric of her panties in his fist to yank them away. It stung as the elastic caught briefly around her thighs before tearing cleanly off, but she was already too eager to care. She needed him inside her.

Pulling her skirt up further, Lanie hitched one leg up on his hip to give him access and pushed against his hand. Understanding, Ridley slipped his fingers between her thighs and feverishly rubbed her exposed cleft until her hips rolled with him involuntarily.

"Relax, I have you all night," he teased, slowing down, waiting her out, infuriating her by forcing her to match his more leisurely pace.

"Please," she panted, her head falling back against the wall as the agonized cry parted her lips.

Ridley held her jaw and pressed kisses along the line of her throat, licking as he went. His other hand moved unhurriedly, stoking a fiery need that soon turned her quiet sighs into loud keening. Ridley's long fingers, one, then two of them, plunged into her slick entrance, working languidly in and out of her until quivers of pleasure in her core became intense spasms that rocked her entire body.

"Ridley!" she cried out as, knuckles deep, he filled all the little spaces in her until she could only whimper. He hit one spot that made her give a tiny sob against his mouth. Then Lanie's knees buckled as the first concussive wave of orgasm overtook her, making her tremble until only his supporting arm kept her upright.

"Steady," he said, grinning with wicked satisfaction, pulling her on wobbly legs further into the house. "C'mon."

"Where's Bea?" she asked, knowing full well that Ridley wouldn't have done what he just did if Bea was anywhere nearby.

"At a friend's for the night," he explained.

The rest of the house was dark, save light from the backyard, illuminating the entire kitchen through the massive windows that made up the whole back wall of the house.

"The foxes are messing with the motion sensor again," Ridley explained as he navigated them through the terrain in the semidark, rushing her toward the freestanding stairs in the living room.

"Ouch!" Lanie cried out, stubbing her toe on the stair tread as they started up.

She tripped upward, flailing, knocking into him as she reached for a way to catch herself. Instead, he fell over too. They *had* both been drinking.

Lanie giggled and soon Ridley did too, out of breath. Neither of them got up, both sitting on the stairs chuckling.

That this man wanted her in any capacity boggled her mind. After seeing what her grandmother, mother and aunt had all endured with the men of their lives, Lanie had been skeptical about ever finding someone like Ridley. She'd struck out so many times. And she thought she'd lost her last hope with Jonah, so her current good fortune was beyond her understanding.

"I—I said something to you earlier on a stupid voicemail that I guess you didn't get," she whispered to him. "But if you did, I want you to know, it's okay with me if you don't say it back."

Ridley was silent for an excruciatingly long moment. Then he reached out, helping Lanie up to the same step he reclined on. He kissed her, sliding her across the step toward him. Ridley reached into her hair and pulled out the last of the clips still holding her now-messy hair in a bun, freeing it of its constrictions. It sprang free, surrounding her face.

"Lanie, I…" he started, looking down into her eyes, but she leaned in, kissing him again hungrily in place of words she wasn't sure she wanted to hear.

The edges of the steps dug into her back as he pulled the voluminous fabric off her shoulder, popping the pin holding it in place. Lanie understood then that before he was done, Ridley was going to ruin her six-hundred-pound saree, so she pushed him off and hurried clumsily up the stairs with him hot on her trail.

"Lanie," he said again, his voice low and husky. "Wait." He

reached her right as she got to the second-floor landing. She giggled, trying to scamper further away.

"Wait. I—I heard your message."

She paused, sighing at his words.

"And I admit, I panicked."

Lanie was disappointed by that and yet still cautiously hopeful.

"At first, I didn't know how to respond and then I knew what I wanted to say but not over the phone. I also knew I couldn't speak to you and not deal with what you'd said, so I avoided calling you back. Then tonight wasn't the right place or time."

Maybe he was about to be braver than Jonah had been and let her down easy to her face. She could respect that.

"I'm sorry I made you wait."

They were always sorry.

Lanie was happy that he couldn't see her rolling her eyes. It didn't matter what he said now anyway; she'd said what she needed to. And there were no take-backs; she knew that now. But he didn't need to reciprocate. It wouldn't affect how she felt about him. Nor would it affect the sex they were about to have or would continue to have for as long as they both remained interested in it. Her experience with Jonah had taught her she could only control her own feelings and behavior, no one else's.

"It's okay," she assuaged.

She couldn't make Ridley feel how she did. She was a grown woman now. Not that misguided nineteen-year-old girl who imagined sex with Jonah meant love between them. Who had allowed herself to be left hanging for years by him and others, concocting fantasies instead of dealing with reality. She understood that now and she would handle it, however Ridley felt.

"No, it's not. Because I love you, Lanie," he whispered, finally. "I do."

Immediately, Ridley's mouth covered hers, preventing Lanie from expressing how flabbergasted she was, how overjoyed.

Then his mouth was on her neck and his large frame was over hers and Lanie tugged at her garments, trying to free herself of the yards of silken fabric and many folds. Frantic, Ridley fumbled with his own clothes, pulling off his tie, tossing off his jacket, opening his shirt to pull out of his pants. They all tumbled to the floor. Suddenly, Lanie didn't care either, fighting valiantly to extricate herself, stripping before at last arriving at her bra. Lying on her back though, it was hard to reach behind and unhook it.

"Flip over," Ridley instructed, then made quick work of unfastening the hooks and eyes of her bra. He hovered above her, as she lay face down on the landing.

"Stay there," he said before delicately kissing her shoulders. He moved from her shoulder blades to her lats. Then Ridley engaged the flat of his tongue to gently tease and linger in the sensitive hollow just below her spine, moving in behind her. He kissed and licked the soft places on her waist, then her full hips followed by the swell of her buttocks, before nuzzling into the part between. "This never gets old." His voice was a low vibrating rumble, muffled between her thighs.

He urged her legs apart with strong palms, tipping her up slightly. Just enough to run his tongue up her center and trace a ring around the swollen, sensitive knot of nerves there. She emitted a shuddering gasp into the soft pile of the runner beneath her cheek at the tingling sensation. Ridley probed her entrance with the tip of his tongue in teasing darts until she saw stars behind her eyelids. Lanie clawed at the carpeting, biting her bottom lip to keep from crying out at the sublime feeling, while still pressing herself into his face to prolong it.

"Don't stop!" she begged, reaching back to cradle his head, holding it there.

And he didn't, not for long minutes, until Lanie thought she would pass out from the intensity of her pleasure. When at last he flipped her back over, after having made her body pliable with her climax, he shocked her by deadlifting her from the floor with ease.

"I do my best work in a bed," he joked, licking his lips.

"Yeah, you do," she concurred to his laughing appreciation. "Though you're no slouch on the stairs."

"I do appreciate the compliment."

In only a few strides he was there, at his bedroom. He pushed the door open and deposited her in the center of a large four-poster bed.

Lanie scooted back toward the headboard, until he caught her foot. Finally, she was able to make out the sharp angles of his face and the long, sinewed lines of his body captured in the moonlight coming through the French doors to his jungle-like balcony.

"You need to prune that," she said.

He looked down at his nakedness. "I think I'm pretty nicely manscaped."

"Not you." She pointed. "Out there."

Lanie wasn't certain but an odd look ghosted across his face before disappearing.

Ridley knelt on the bench at the base of the bed, lifting her foot to inspect her polished toes. "Nice."

"Gemma made us get mani-pedis."

"I like it," he said, kissing each toe then her arch, his breath tickling her sole.

Remaining between her legs, he feathered light kisses up her ankle, calf and knee, nibbling along the way until he reached the soft skin high inside her thigh. Then he dropped onto the bed. Lanie stroked his head and shoulders, spreading her palms flat, moving along the lines of hard muscle that were his magnificent body. She breathed out a hiss as he traced concentric circles with his tongue around the soft flesh of her stomach then inside her belly button.

Ridley took his sweet time, lingering in places until she shivered beneath him. Kissing here and licking there as his mouth wandered leisurely around her body. Lanie held his head between her hands as his five-o'clock shadow softly scraped against the tender tips of her breasts, already peaked from what he'd done to them at the front door. She clenched her molars, her nails digging into his scalp as his teeth on her breast caused pinpricks of exquisite pain, nipping then sucking then licking to soothe. He lavished attention there until moisture seeped from her.

He's so fucking good at this, was her single thought when he finally reached her face, his whole body blanketing hers.

Ridley reached for the drawer in his nightstand, tensing in hesitation, the swollen head of his arousal butting against her entrance torturously.

"You can," she encouraged him, moving her hips. "I'm back on the Pill now."

"You're sure?"

"I am. You haven't been sleeping with anyone but me, right?"

His eyes went dark, fathomless and hard to read in the low light. But she could hear the smile in his words. "Right. In fact…Melanie, I haven't *wanted* to sleep with anyone but you in three years."

Lanie's chest tightened. She hadn't dared ask before, but the knowledge nearly moved her to tears.

"Then yes, I'm sure," she answered in a whisper, wrapping her thighs around him. "I trust you. I love you, Ridley."

"Melanie." He said her name again through an exhale as he entered her with an agonizing slowness that made her body burn. His voice was octaves deeper and suffused with so much desire that she ached at the sound.

He filled her inch by gradual inch until they were notched hip to hip. Lanie gasped at the welcome intrusion, appreciating that each time they did this she swore she wouldn't be able to take it all, to handle the girth of him. And yet every time, she found herself stretched, rapturously full, until he hit places deep inside her that made her quite literally weep from pleasure. She cried out his name then as he seemed to touch her everywhere, his stubble scratching her face, his soft hands skimming her ribs, every sensation making her nerve endings tingle.

Cheek to cheek, she bit Ridley's earlobe and inhaled the salt and spice, the almost earthy mixture of his body and cologne, scents that enveloped her like a haze, musky and enticing. His powerful thigh muscles under hers spread her legs as he grasped the edge of the bed for leverage, keeping an unfaltering rhythm, each stroke driving her into the mattress.

Lanie was completely lost in the feel of him. With one hand wedged against the headboard to brace herself, she dug into Ridley's slick back with the long, talon-like acrylic tips on the other until he hissed. He lapped at the crevice between her jaw and neck as he moved, keeping an unyielding pace. And within minutes, he'd found a blistering stroke that built to a delicious frisson, sending tremors of ecstasy shivering up her spine. Throughout, Ridley continued to hit her unbearably deep. Slipping a hand between them to rub her, he intensified the sensation until it turned her into a weeping, shuddering mess.

"Oh God!" Lanie cried out. It was her last coherent thought as her oncoming climax overwhelmed her.

Her whole body went taut as the orgasmic ripples began to flow through her. Ridley continued to move but soon, as if she'd catalyzed a chain reaction, his orgasm chased hers. He groaned, collapsing on her, panting for air. She held him close, feeling grounded by his heavy body covering hers. She kissed his neck and jaw and listened as their labored breaths evened out, trading filthy praise in amused whispers, until eventually, he rolled away to turn on his bedside lamp.

Bathed in light, Ridley turned onto his side, propped up on an elbow. Lanie moved onto her side too, mirroring him. He leaned in and kissed her sweetly, using his thumb to wipe away the makeup ruined by the film of sweat and tears that covered her face.

"I must look horrible," she said bashfully, flushed and pushing her wild hair out of her face.

"I think you look beautiful."

She grinned at his complete and utter lie. "You're only saying that because you love me."

He grinned back, giving her one of her favorite kind, where his tiny dimple made an appearance. "I do."

forty-four

Lanie

Lanie didn't know what time it was when she woke up but her mouth felt like it was filled with cotton balls and she needed a cup of coffee, immediately. Glancing across the bed at Ridley, she saw she would have to sort herself out. He was dead to the world with even the occasional snore coming from his slightly open mouth.

Sitting up, she surveyed the room. It was exactly what she would expect Ridley's room to look like: highly functional but with a minimalist style. The colors were a masculine slate blue and brown, with steel-gray linens and curtains. Lanie let out a sigh of relief. She'd been terrified to wake up in a room that was either untouched since Thyra died or a shrine to her. And she didn't know how she would have handled either scenario. She hopped out of bed giddily.

As it was, there was only one prominent picture of them as a family and another of Thyra alone. Lanie walked up to the bureau it sat on and picked up the picture frame to have a closer look. In it, Thyra sat out on the balcony relaxing with a sun hat and a book. Lanie had conjured such a complete mental image of the woman—based on nearly nothing, she realized—that actually seeing her now was totally disorienting.

For one, she was better looking than seemed reasonable. If Ridley was normally a solid and respectable eight out of ten on the objective hotness scale, an eleven when he deigned to smile, his wife was well off conventional charts. Absolutely radiant in a totally unassuming way, Thyra Aronsen was a mocha-colored beauty with sexy downturned eyes, high, flat cheekbones and a heavy, luscious bottom lip. She resembled a biracial Liya Kebede, the Ethiopian supermodel, but with a fuller face and a slightly more pronounced forehead. Lanie could now easily envision the stunning woman Bea would grow up to be.

She looked from the frame to the balcony itself. It didn't look so overgrown and unkempt in the picture. Lanie instantly realized she must have put her foot in her mouth last night when she mentioned it. There was no wonder why it was overgrown. Ridley probably couldn't bring himself to deal with it.

"I have a black thumb," Ridley said groggily.

Lanie put the frame down and turned to see his head rising from his pillow. He startled her.

"I have one too." She put both her thumbs up. "In fact, I have two."

"Har, har," he said, rolling onto his side and propping his head up by the elbow. "I mean I kill plants. They're thriving out there on their own. I go out there and they'd be dead inside a month."

"So, I guess it's live and let live, huh?"

"Better than *Live and Let Die*." He smirked.

"Solid James Bond reference."

"Why, thank you," he said, pleased with himself. "You do realize you're standing naked in front of a set of glass doors, right? That my neighbors can see you from their houses?"

"Oh my God!" Lanie hustled back over toward the bed. "Why didn't you say anything?"

"I like seeing you like that…and I thought, maybe if my

neighbor across the street sees I'm finally getting some, she'll stop trying to set me up."

Lanie picked up the pillow she'd used and hit him with it. "Seriously?"

"I'm teasing. I mean, they could see you if they were home but they're out of town. The coast is clear."

"I want coffee," she whined.

Ridley fell onto his back and stared at the ceiling. "I drink tea so that sounds like a you problem."

"Ridley." Lanie hopped back onto the bed and straddled him. "I. Want. Coffee." She sat on his abdomen but could feel him stir under the sheet. She shimmied a little and he groaned.

"My mother-in-law drinks coffee, so maybe you can find something in one of the cabinets. She usually has a cup of something when she's here."

Ridley pulled himself up to the headboard. Lanie shifted a little more to watch him squirm, relishing the feeling before leaning in to kiss him, buttering him up.

"Fine. I suppose if you give me fifteen minutes I can get up and get you something from the café down the street."

"Thank you," Lanie said sweetly, pulling the sheet between them away and kissing a slow trail down his body. She paused at his navel to look up at him. "But you're gonna need more than fifteen minutes."

Lanie padded to the landing, shaking her head. Their clothes were all over the stairs. Before she gathered them up to take downstairs with her, she picked through them and pulled on Ridley's pink dress shirt. She couldn't walk all over the house naked—he had too many windows for that—and without Charity or Syreeta to help, Lanie also wasn't sure she could get her saree back on properly. Of course, the shirt didn't fit properly either, leaving a plunging neckline where she couldn't button it up across her bosom, but Lanie thought that was a pretty sexy look.

Downstairs, Lanie stood in the pivoting glass doorway of Ridley's impressive kitchen and sipped the coffee-flavored swill his mother-in-law left behind. Ridley had gone back to sleep and she needed to be back at the hotel by eleven o'clock to help with checkout. Still slightly dazed from their blissful morning, Lanie heard a sound like the front door opening and whirled around, unsure of what to do.

Oh shit.

She pushed the glass panel shut and had just gotten the cup into the sink soundlessly when Bea rounded the corner from the entryway into the living room.

Oh. Shit.

"Melanie?" Bea asked. "What are you doing here?" Her little duffel bag slid from her shoulder.

"I, uh—" Lanie stopped. Nothing would be the right answer.

"I thought you said you were my dad's friend?" Bea looked her over, frowning.

Friend. Yes. "I am." Lanie nodded, intensely aware that she wore virtually no clothing. She didn't even know where her underwear was after Ridley tore it off.

"What are you doing here?!" Bea bellowed like Lanie was a nude burglar.

Lanie was stunned. Though she'd never envisioned this scenario, she certainly wouldn't have foreseen it going down like this. "Y-your dad invited me over…last night."

Too much information, Lanie.

"But why are you still here?"

Maybe she doesn't understand? Lanie thought, grasping for glimmers of hope.

"Are you *sleeping* with my dad?"

Lanie's brain short-circuited. Her heart began to race. She had not planned on meeting Bea again for a little while, not until after giving this thing between Ridley and herself time to set.

"I think you should talk to your dad—"

"Dad!" she screamed as Lanie stood there nearly immobilized.

Not now, Lanie begged her body. *Not right now.* But she could already feel the lightheadedness coming on. She held on to the lip of the sink to steady herself. Nausea was causing a shipwreck in her gut.

A second later, Ridley flew down the stairs, nearly tripping on the pile of clothing Lanie had left on the bottom step. "Bea!"

"What is she doing here?" Bea said with no preamble, pointing at Lanie like she was a stray cat that had gotten into the house.

Lanie did her breathing exercises, trying to self-regulate. *Inhale: one…two…three…four…*

"Bea." He frowned. "No. This attitude is not okay. Lanie is my guest."

"You said she was just your friend!"

Exhale: six…seven…eight…

"She was—is," Ridley corrected himself.

Before. She was a friend before but now I love her. Lanie finished his sentence in her mind, waiting for him to as well.

"You lied!" Bea screamed, the sound echoing off the tiles in the kitchen. "What about Mum?"

"Beatrix!" Ridley clapped his hands together, making an equally resounding noise, and both Lanie and Bea jumped. Lanie wasn't positive she'd ever seen Ridley angry before. "Uh-uh. We don't do this! Let's calm down and talk."

Bea cried hysterically. Ridley walked up to her and took her into his arms. Then he looked up at Lanie, making a sympathetic sad face. "I think you'd better go."

Lanie was about to say that herself but was completely thrown that Ridley beat her to it.

Excuse me?

She'd just had sex with this man for the third time today and he was kicking her out of his house? Thoughts of Jonah and countless others bubbled to the surface.

He has to deal with his daughter, Lanie.

She's upset, Lanie.

It's not personal, Lanie, the angel on her shoulder said.

Unfortunately, the devil on the other shoulder wanted their say too. And their arguments were far more compelling:

Here it is, what you'd been waiting for, the kiss-off.

And it's only the beginning. There'll never be a moment when you're the one he chooses.

And "I love you" will only mean I love you when you're having sex.

It's exactly as your mother said. You're no one special to him.

She couldn't stop the tears that welled up in her eyes as her mouth trembled. She wouldn't compete with Bea for Ridley's affection. She would only end up looking foolish in that scenario.

Five...six...seven...eight... Lanie exhaled, continuing her exercises, but she could still feel the unrestrained anxiety ratcheting up. If she didn't get out soon, she'd be looking like Bea, who was still bawling into her father's torso.

As soon as she thought she could manage it, Lanie rushed to the pile, pulled out the pieces of her saree and shut herself in the downstairs bathroom to put it all back on.

And to break down in private.

After a few minutes there was a light knock on the door. "Lanie?"

He changed his mind. See, he does want you!

Lanie splashed cold water on her hot, swollen face and squeaked out a hopeful "Yes?"

"Do you need me to call you an Uber?"

Lanie gasped like he'd kicked her in the gut, bracing herself against the wall to prevent collapse. "No," she said, trying to approximate a speaking voice that was not hoarse from crying for ten minutes straight. "I'm okay."

"I want to."

"Fine," she said, resigned.

"It'll be here in eight minutes."

He wasted no time, she thought, crushed. *Guess he was just waiting to press the button.*

"Are we gonna talk through the door?"

She wanted to but opened it anyway.

Ridley was silent for a moment, examining her face. "Oh Lanie," he started finally, reaching for her puffy cheeks. "Baby, I—"

"Save it," she barked back, breaking away. "I understand."

"I don't think you do."

She pushed past him toward the living room, adjusting the fabric on her shoulder. Bea sat hiccuping on a stool but started crying anew when she saw Lanie again. Lanie hurried to the door, feeling Bea's eyes on her the whole way. Lanie was upset that Ridley wasn't trying to stop her from going. Or talking it through with his daughter in her presence.

Grabbing her coat, purse and heels from where she'd unceremoniously dropped them last night, Lanie ran out the door.

"Lanie!" Ridley called when she was by the gate. "Wait, the car will be here soon!"

She ran to the tube station in her bare feet anyway.

forty-five

Ridley

"You said—" Bea's whole body shook with tears that made Ridley feel like his heart was being torn out of his chest. "You said she was just your friend. You lied!"

Yes, he agreed inwardly. But it had been more a lie of omission, a lie he had been telling himself, as well as Bea, was true.

"Nothing had happened then."

"But you wanted it to, right?" Bea's face was red with anger, reminding him of when she would throw tantrums as a toddler that resulted in her getting physically sick.

"Bean, calm down."

"You were planning to get together with her, right?"

"Who I decide to date isn't your business."

Ridley stood between her and the living room so she paced the kitchen back and forth like a caged panther until Ridley had a mind to put her in a seat. He'd gleaned that Bea was not ready to see him dating again, but it frightened him how upset she was now.

"Bean, honey." He sighed. "Sit down."

"Do you not want me anymore?" Her voice, hoarse with tears, cracked completely.

"What?"

"Are you planning to move back to America?"

"Of course not, why would you even think that?"

"Melanie lives in New York. And you're always in New York now!"

"For work, you know this. I'm not moving to the United States."

"Then why are you always spending time with her? She doesn't live here."

Ridley's heart skipped at Bea's speaking aloud a worry that had recently begun taking up space in his head.

"Because I enjoy her company. You said so yourself, honey. You said you liked her. You thought she was cool."

"As a friend! You're not friends. She's your girlfriend!"

He paused. They'd never stated that explicitly. Ridley felt decidedly too old to be someone's "boyfriend" but he supposed he was Lanie's. Especially after last night.

"So, she is?" Bea filled in the blank when he didn't say. "Are you guys together now?"

He nodded. "We are."

Bea's eyes welled with fresh outraged tears. "Why? Why do you need to be with her?"

"Because I love her! I love her and I don't know how that's gonna work exactly but I'm not prepared to lose her because of the distance!"

Bea cringed. Ridley felt ill. He should not have raised his voice.

"You love her more than Mum?"

He sighed, shaking his head. "I love her *differently* than your mom."

"What does that even mean?" She was nearly hysterical now. "You're lying! You're giving up. That's why you sent me to stay with Gavin for Christmas. So you could go be with her!"

"Bea, what are you talking about? I came to Colorado. I came specifically to be with you."

"But you were with her on Christmas? In New York, before you saw me. Right?"

Ridley knew the truth of that whole debacle was more complicated than that, but there was no making Beatrix see the truth through her frustration. *Not now.* And he would not lie. "Yes." All the air left him as he collapsed into a nearby chair. "Because we got laid over. I told you this."

"You are a liar."

"Beatrix! You do not speak to me—"

Before he could finish his reproach, she'd already flown past him. He deflated as the sound of Bea racing up to her room echoed through the house.

"Beatrix Olive!" He tried his stern tone, putting the feared bass in his voice.

That had worked when she was small. Unfortunately, since Thyra had been the primary disciplinarian between them and he was the "fun dad," it had about the effect he expected. As he heard her door slam, he slumped in his seat, defeated. Minutes later, however, there were footsteps on the stairs again and rustling in the entryway.

Ridley realized all at once—but too late—what was happening.

"Beatrix! Do not leave this house!" He rushed out of the kitchen. "Bean!"

Ridley came through the living room in time to catch a glimpse of Bea's teal anorak and slate gray backpack disappearing out the front door. Shirtless, shoeless and clueless, he was in no position to follow.

"*Fuck!*" he growled to an empty house.

The second woman to run out of this house in tears in under an hour. *Great.*

forty-six

Lanie

Lanie dug through her small clutch for the key card to let herself in. The suite was still in a state of utter chaos. There was clothing, makeup and styling products on every surface, and a pile of bridesmaids' dresses on the floor. Not to mention food, drinks, bottles of champagne and empty glasses everywhere. Lanie hoped that she wasn't going to be expected to clean this all up alone. She knew Shanice and her husband, Patrick, had decided to stay in the hotel, calling it "a night off from the kids." Two of the other bridesmaids were sharing another room on this floor as well. Plus, she was supposedly sharing this suite with Les, now that Gemma had moved to the honeymoon suite with Jonah. *Where is Les anyway?*

Lanie made her way carefully to the bedroom, tiptoeing through the mess. It was dark, but she could make out a figure passed out on one of the beds. At least no one was awake to witness her walk of shame.

I mean, it's still a walk of shame if you're wearing a beautiful cream saree, right?

Probably, she decided. *Especially when you didn't know how to rewrap it properly before you got on the Underground and your makeup was smeared from vigorous sex and crying.*

★ ★ ★

"Well, well, well," Gemma said when Lanie exited the bathroom in a plume of steam a half hour later. "Did you leave any hot water for anyone else in the hotel?"

"Might not have," she acknowledged.

To her surprise, Gemma—freshly made up, expertly coiffed and decked out in jeans, a tee and her "Mrs. Perera" hoodie—had used her key to enter and was cleaning up. Lanie joined her in picking things up.

"I guess I should ask you what you're doing here? Shanice said she saw you and your leng doctor duck out last night."

Lanie should have guessed their little cease-fire would have to end at some point soon. It had only been about not embarrassing each other at the wedding anyway. Now that it was over, this was as good a time as any to air their grievances, she supposed.

Lanie snapped, "I could be asking you the same question, no? Aren't you newly married? Why aren't you with your husband?"

"What would you know about it? You disappeared last night before I even cut my cake. Yet you're already back."

Lanie sighed, pausing. "I did not miss you cutting your cake. I saw Jonah put the dab of frosting on your nose and then you smash your entire slice into his face."

Gemma spun on her, dropping an assortment of things. "When are you gonna give this a rest, Mel? Huh? We're married now. How much longer am I going to have to endure your bad attitude? Give me a rough estimate. A year, two? At the birth of our firstborn?"

"Which will be in what?" Lanie dragged her eyes up Gemma's body then feigned checking a wristwatch. "About four months?"

Gemma sputtered, her mouth falling open.

"I figure Fatou already knows, and Les too. How about Gran?"

Gemma's eyes welled with tears, her face crumpling.

"What? You think I'm stupid? I know what you look like

drunk, Gemma. You're barely coherent. During your hen night you acted tipsy but you were swapping drinks with Les—and he had water. At the engagement party, Fatou told me how surprised she was that Jonah proposed so quickly, then you pushed up your wedding date—twice! You're crying at the drop of a hat when you're not eating everything that's not nailed down. Your boobs are getting huge. You didn't want to wear the saree that exposed your stomach, when you love showing off your stomach."

Gemma laughed humorlessly. "Guess that's why you're the smart one with your degrees and your posh schooling."

"Are you for real? Trust me, *this* was not rocket science. How long did you guys honestly think you were going to keep that a secret? 'Cuz that's not how pregnancy works. You're carrying small but your days are *literally* numbered. Do Nishan and Syreeta know?"

Gemma's bottom lip trembled, reflecting the tremor in her voice. "We told them last night."

Lanie shook her head. "Why am I not surprised? I'd expect this from you but I don't understand what's going on with Jonah. And why did I have to figure this out—why didn't you tell me?"

"Because you're so damn judgmental, Melanie!"

"Is this why you guys got married?"

"See what I mean? Fuck you," Gemma barked out. "Do your math, right? He asked me *before* I got pregnant. We sped up the timeline because we knew it would make his parents happy. We were always going to get married. I just got pregnant sooner than we planned." She dropped onto the sofa, pushing various detritus away from her, then put her head in her hands.

Lanie paused. "Gem?"

"Leave me alone, Mel, okay? You got me. Dumb tart Gem, always up for it, falls pregnant finally. Nothing less than what you've always expected of me, what everyone's always expected, right? 'That Gem, she's just like her mother.'"

Lanie closed her eyes to steady herself. *What is wrong with me?* With everything she knew about her aunt Elliot abandoning Les and Gem and them growing up with Gran, why was her head so far up her own ass that she would assume this baby was good news to Gemma?

She sat down beside her cousin. "Hey, Gem, I'm sorry." Her hand hovered for a moment near Gemma's shoulder before retreating.

"Sorry for what? I did it to myself. Fatou told me to get an IUD but I didn't because I heard they hurt."

"C'mon, you're practically geriatric."

Gemma raised her head, affronted.

"For a pregnancy I mean. You're thirty-five. And getting pregnant out of wedlock is not even a thing anymore. Nowadays, it's not a 'shotgun wedding.' Now, it's a 'midpregnancy marriage.' The social stigma is gone."

"Social stigma?" Gemma skewered Lanie with a glare like a red-hot pincer. "What white shit are you chatting right now, Cuz?"

It was true. Relatives, both theirs and Jonah's, would be counting backward as soon as they heard the news.

"You don't have to have it, you know?" Lanie offered. "Or you guys could give it up for adoption. It's no one's business if you're married or single, if you're not ready. You don't have to have a baby if you don't want one."

"Jonah is so excited."

"Fuck Jonah!" Immediately, Lanie couldn't believe she'd said that. And from the look on Gemma's face, she couldn't either.

"That's rich coming from you." Gemma chuckled wetly. "And in any case, I did that already. Repeatedly. That's why I'm up the duff, innit?"

Lanie gave a hybrid cough and chuckle at the off-color joke. "Yeah, I guess."

"You know how it is." She turned to look at Lanie.

"Uh, sure," Lanie said cautiously as Gemma stared at her. "It would have been hard to resist a reliable sex partner while cooped up in the house for almost two years. I certainly don't blame you."

Gemma shook her head. "I don't mean like that, Mel. I mean sex *with Jonah*. You know how it is."

Lanie clung to her feigned confusion, canting her head.

"I know, okay?" Gemma grasped her hand.

Oh Jesus.

"Don't say 'about what' or I'm going to punch you directly in one of those big titties you have."

"How?"

"Come on, Mel. I remember how you two used to be. And I remember when you confided that you weren't a virgin anymore. It wasn't long after that overnight trip to Prague. One of the only times Jonah came along with us." She tipped her head to the side. "You're not the only one who can put two and two together, you know?"

"I'm so sorry." Lanie exhaled the words like she'd been holding them in for the past twelve years. "I didn't know what to say. If I had known you and he would eventually... I mean, I would have said something sooner."

"Sure, to break us up maybe."

"C'mon, Gem, no." Lanie pulled Gemma's hand into her lap and intertwined their fingers. "I would never want to hurt you like that. I was embarrassed. To have spent so many years mooning over a man so clearly not into me, only for him to be in love with you. And he is in love with you in case you're harboring any illusions about him only being with you for the baby. He's had a crush on you since we were kids."

"Oh, I know." Gem grinned like it was the only possible outcome. "He wasn't subtle."

Lanie snorted, then took a deep breath. "I'm sorry, Cuz. We should have told you."

"But I get why you didn't. And then why he did."

"He did?"

She nodded. "One night recently, we were talking about our first times and he started being cagey and vague. Real sus. I figured I knew why, of course, but I waited to see if he would admit it. And he did…eventually. Told me the whole thing, including how bad he felt for how he treated you afterward. Led you on."

Lanie bit her lip. She'd done this already, she wouldn't do it again. "It's water under the bridge."

"It really is, isn't it?" Gemma examined her face.

She nodded. "I know what I must sound like, but I do wish you both the best. I know I haven't always acted that way. I guess I just thought, I don't know, that it wasn't real. That he wanted his dream pinup girl and you liked someone pining after you, adoring you. Just liked the idea of having a guy like Jonah whipped. But I know that's not true. I know you love him as much as he loves you."

"I do." Gemma grinned broadly. "I love everything about him. From his poor clothing choices and preference for sleeping in scratchy wool socks to his collectible action figure obsession and bizarre crushes on female anime characters."

Aww, she knows about Momo and Katara.

Lanie wanted to cry. Only now with true happiness for her cousin and friend instead of jealously.

"I'm sorry. Excuse me." Gemma rolled her neck with attitude. "But shouldn't you know how it feels too?"

"Huh?"

Gemma's eyes rolled skyward. "Your doctor! Dr. Dishy. Ridley, yeah?"

Lanie shook her head, lips sealed shut, desperate not to begin crying at the mere mention of his name.

"Jonah and I watched him from the moment he arrived. He followed you with his eyes the whole night and only danced with you. I know that because a lot of slags tried it. And they're my gyaldem but I had to speak wiv 'em, like, 'Off-limits, yeah? 'Cos that's Big Cuz's man. So you don't fuck wiv 'im.'"

And with that, Gemma closed out her treatise on loyalty. Lanie burst out laughing and crying at the same time.

"Good Lord! What's happened?" It was Gemma's turn to put an arm around her. "You were looking so cute together only last night!"

Lanie broke down and told Gem how her morning had gone. Right down to the walk of shame, because it was a walk of shame—she was sure now—back to the hotel this morning.

"Ohhh." Gemma gathered Lanie up and rocked her in her arms the same way their grandmother had a million times before. "Shhh."

Lanie cried until she was hiccuping and her mouth was dry.

"I don't think anyone has ever loved me."

"Tosh," Gemma said imperiously as if that was nonsensical. "I love you. Nan loves you. Les loves you."

"You're family, you have to."

"I most assuredly do not! And you are so fucking annoying sometimes that you make it difficult. You're a know-it-all and bossy…"

"Okay, okay," Lanie said, amused in spite of herself.

"But you are also brilliant. And you're hardworking, you're funny and so giving. Reh teh teh…" Gemma said as if the list was never-ending. "You would come to Balham for as long as we needed you. I know it. Like, say, you'd even come after the baby is born to help me—"

"No." Lanie sniffed, wrapping her arms around her cousin. "Because you're gonna be very good at this mom thing."

"You think? 'Cos I'm terrified."

"Think about it, your whole calling. The salon, the hair and skin care line—it's always been about nurturing." She squeezed her. "Gem, you aren't your mother."

"Well then, Mel," Gem said, tearily. "It follows, neither are you."

"I'm so sorry, Lil Cuz."

"And I'm sorry too, Big Cuz."

Lanie looked into Gemma's determined eyes. This had been a rough few months, but she was relieved they were finally back on the same page. They wrapped each other up in a hug.

Thank God. This cold war was far too taxing. And over a guy? How embarrassing.

"Plus, I'm convinced you've got Dr. Hot Stuff all wrong," Gemma insisted after a long silence.

"You think?"

"I mean, like, he held your purse all night, Mel," Les interjected sleepily emerging from the mouth of the bedroom with his makeup smeared, wearing only his gold-embroidered *dupatta* and boxer shorts. "I don't know much about love but that's real, fam!"

Lanie couldn't help but smile through her tears as Gemma cracked up beside her.

forty-seven

Ridley

This was the place Clare-Olive told him Bea would be, but as he stood in front of the enormous glass-and-steel eyesore, Ridley still couldn't believe it.

Bea had run to Gavin's. Ridley felt run through. But he'd stayed away as she remained there for three whole days. *Why would she come to him?*

Gavin seemed to be expecting Ridley by the lack of any impediment to entry from the lobby staff. Not that Ridley would have let that stop him, but as a Black man it was nice not to have to worry about the specter of facing the Metropolitan Police or spending time in front of a magistrate on an assault charge.

"Where is my daughter?" Ridley asked as soon as Gavin opened the door, trying to keep the irritation out of his voice.

"Come inside."

He did. But only a sliver of decorum prevented Ridley from shouting at the top of his lungs.

The apartment was humongous. Ridley was certain Gavin could have fit the whole first floor of their house in this apartment about three or four times over. He took a moment to look around. Sleek, impersonal and cold...all aesthetics. Just like Gavin. Ridley could already see that he needed to find his daughter and get the hell out of there.

"Where is Bea?"

"In her room. She's not ready to see you."

"She does not have a room in this house," Ridley retorted.

"Yes, she does," Gavin said with an aggravating calm as he led Ridley through the grand, echoing entryway into an even grander open-concept living room/dining room.

"I did not come here for this, Gavin. Please present my daughter before I do something I'll regret." And he would, Ridley could feel that already. He was just so tired of Gavin and his constant intrusions.

"Are you threatening me, Ridley?"

Ridley was stunned by Gavin's use of his first name.

Of course not. The last thing Ridley wanted was Bea coming out to find two grown men tussling. Plus, realistically, they were a doctor and a med-tech bro. Fisticuffs between them would more than likely just devolve into a slap fight.

Ridley sighed in resignation. So much had already gone wrong in the past few days. He could not add losing Bea to Gavin to that lengthening list. "I just want my daughter and we'll go. I don't know why she even came here."

"Tell me something, Aronsen, why are you giving me such a hard time?"

"A hard time?" Ridley adjusted his glasses in irritation. "Did I swoop in not three months after *your* wife died and try to take custody of your kid from you too?"

"I acknowledge, I—I could have handled that better." Gavin raked a hand through his coppery hair. "But I am not trying to be her father. Far be it from me to encroach on your precious territory. I merely want to know her. To be someone, anyone in her life…"

"She doesn't need anyone else in her life!" Ridley snapped. But as soon as he said it, he knew how juvenile that sounded.

What the hell am I talking about? Of course, Bea needed a village. Like every child did. Why was it so hard for him to allow Gavin a place in Bea's?

"That is not what Thyra thought."

A record scratched in Ridley's mind. "What is it you *think* you know about what my wife thought?"

Gavin stilled, then sighed. "Wait here."

Ridley stood at the enormous windows in Gavin's sterile living room and stared out at the gray sky. Glancing down he saw the HMS *Belfast* on the Thames far below. He stepped back, swaying with the woozy dizziness of vertigo. He could not understand why Bea had sought refuge from him here.

Here! With Gavin? When did I take my eyes so far off the ball?

Maybe she thought he wouldn't brave the heights? Didn't she know it didn't matter where she went, he'd always show up for her? But even as Ridley wondered this, his mind kept straying back to Lanie and how she looked when he asked her to leave. He hadn't shown up for her either. Letting her fly back to the States without clearing the air. Leaving her to think she was low on his list of priorities.

Hurt, unbelieving, betrayed.

He'd take it back if he could.

No. He shook his head. *I would not.* Not if it meant losing Bea in the bargain. *But why are those my only options?*

"Here," Gavin said, sneaking up on him, and shoving papers into his hands.

"What the hell?"

It was a folder of signed and notarized documents. Documents to petition the court to relinquish Gavin's parental responsibility. They were all signed and dated...*from seven years ago*. None had the official seals of His Majesty's Courts and Tribunals Service.

"You've had these for so many years." He looked at Gavin. "Why weren't these filed?"

Gavin bit his lip, looking the most chastened that, in nearly seventeen years of knowing him, Ridley had ever seen. And Ridley knew instantly that whatever Gavin said next would enrage him.

"Thyra asked me not to."

Ridley put a hand against the cold glass of the window to try to steady himself, but that made things worse. The glass seemed to tip forward under his hand and unbalance him. He could swear his vision went black and when it returned there were spots swirling in his eyes. He squeezed the bridge of his nose and blinked a few times trying to right himself.

Gavin bent to pick up all the papers that lay scattered at his feet. Ridley hadn't even realized he'd dropped them. "She what?"

Gavin pointed toward his pewter-colored, ultramodern leather sectional and Ridley staggered over, falling onto it. After pulling out a surpisingly well-worn copy of Layla F. Saad's *Me and White Supremacy* out from under him, the couch was a bit more comfortable than its boxy shape suggested.

"Listen, Aronsen, based entirely on what I managed to glean, I was simply an insurance policy."

"An insurance policy?" Ridley's eyes narrowed. "Against what?"

Based on the dates on the papers, Gavin had filled these out before Thyra had told Ridley she was really sick. To this day, he resented how much of her worsening condition she'd kept hidden from him. Allowing him to continue their day-to-day. Going on as they always had, having petty squabbles and spending days apart. As if their days to spend together, forgive each other and get things right were unlimited. Finding out now that there'd also been these secrets, lies she'd been keeping with Gavin, was too much.

"So, you're saying she told you not to terminate your parental rights? To complicate things for me? To barge back in and create upheaval in Bea's life at this critical juncture when she already feels so insecure?" Ridley skewered him with a gaze as lancing as a hot poker. "Thyra told you to do that?"

"Well..." Gavin shifted in the seat he'd assumed opposite Ridley. "Uh. Not precisely."

"Then make it precise for me, Gavin."

"I'm guessing that there was a reason she wanted me to retain my rights. I just had no idea what it was. Or that she was so ill. And I had no way of foreseeing how complicated my decision to listen to her would make things." He was unable to maintain their eye contact, looking down at his hands guiltily. "But when she did die, well, you see, I became concerned."

"Concerned?"

"That perhaps there was something about your character I was unaware of. So, I sought custody as a means of—"

"Keeping an eye on me?" Ridley guessed. "And that was you 'not seeing color,' I bet."

"That's wholly uncharitable." Gavin gathered a breath and held it, looking for a judicious phrasing of his next words. Ridley could see the cogs turning in his brain. "I wanted to see how you were with Bea and how much you wanted to keep her."

"Keep her?" Ridley exploded, but then reeled his temper back in before he did something rash. "How much I wanted to *keep* Bea? She is a child, Gavin. Not some pawn in a game of one-upmanship! She just lost her mother and because of you, she's in danger of losing her father too!"

"I know that's how it seems, but I had to know that you really wanted her, for Thyra's sake," Gavin said, his voice surprisingly contrite. "And I had to know that you were taking care of her, for my own."

"And this was your solution?" Ridley was incredulous.

"It was the only way I could have gotten access to her to see. Be honest with yourself, Aronsen—had I shown up and just requested visitation with her, would you have consented?"

That question brought Ridley up short for a moment because he knew the answer as well as Gavin did.

"But this way, Gavin? According to my solicitor, no matter how much I fight, you will probably win eventually and I'll be out of the picture. So, what is this, your ego? I mean, I know you're ludicrously rich but do you mean to tell me you have enough money and time on your hands to waste in a custody battle you never really wanted to win?"

"You didn't want me?"

They both spun to see Bea standing in the threshold of the room. Tears streaked her face, before it crumpled completely.

"No, I—" Gavin started as Ridley glared.

If Ridley thought he was angry before, his vision turned entirely red with murderous intent now. When he rose, Gavin did as well, stumbling away impishly before catching himself. Ridley tsked at his cowardice, before rushing to Bea and enveloping her in his arms.

"No, oh no, Bea. I was fully prepared to take you! I bought that house in Colorado specifically with you in mind. Ms. Sandrine and Chef Dorothea, I hired them on to make sure you had a minder and a cook."

Ridley shook his head, hugging Bea to himself. "A minder? C'mon, Gavin. She's not four."

He sputtered hopelessly. "My point was, I was ready, *am* ready to take you if you want, Love. The custody battle wasn't for show—I was very worried about you. But seeing you, I know you don't necessarily need me."

Ridley canted his head in confusion and Bea peeked out at Gavin from over her father's locked arms.

"You are always welcome to come to me. You will always have a place in my house. But I saw you with your dad and your grandparents this Christmas. You're all wonderful together."

That's why Gavin didn't object to Philip and Clare-Olive

coming to Colorado with Bea. And that's why it was his idea to invite Ridley to come too. *To observe.*

Gavin approached them tentatively and Ridley stayed where he was, allowing Bea to decide what would happen next. When Gavin got close, she turned to him. Staying near Ridley, she addressed Gavin. "So, you don't want to take me from Dad?"

Gavin shook his head. "No, and it was never my intention to scare you or your dad. I thought I was doing what your mother would have wanted me to do—look out for you."

Ridley exhaled a breath he hadn't known he was holding. His shoulders fell. He'd known, deep down, that Thyra had long ago wished for some sort of relationship between Gavin and Bea. Maybe this had been her way, albeit faulty, of inciting one?

"The last thing I wanted to do was interfere in the relationship between you and your dad. Even these past couple of days, I allowed you to stay with me because I want you to know you're always welcome. Any home I have, anywhere in the world, is your home too. But—" he lifted a finger in the air "—you cannot use my house as an escape anytime you and your dad disagree."

He winked at Ridley. Ridley snorted against his better judgment at Gavin's obvious nod to co-parenting.

"Do we understand each other?"

Ridley kissed the top of Bea's head and she nodded. "Yeah, I guess."

Ridley had to begrudgingly acknowledge Gavin did well with this small part. His mind strayed to Lanie again, thinking of how much the little girl in her would've loved to have heard her own father say something like that.

How much could those words still heal the little girl inside of her that constantly thinks she's being abandoned?

He nodded to Gavin, thanking him for things he hadn't even known he'd done.

"I didn't intend on you finding out this way. In fact, I have a meeting with my solicitors this week to call off the custody proceedings. I figured having the news come through the lawyers would be cleaner, but in light of everything..." Gavin gestured vaguely with his hand. "I think we can work out a more amicable solution, yeah?"

A few minutes later, Bea walked Ridley into her bedroom and he had to hold his breath for a second. Thank God Gavin decided to drop his case for full custody of Bea.

Spacious and decorated in the more muted gray, teal and blush colors favored by a teen, with vivid floral wallpaper covering the ceiling and a chandelier light fixture, the room was nothing short of amazing. It had a queen bed as opposed to the full one she still had at home. There was an abundance of storage space, a walk-in closet, a chest of drawers and a wide bureau where she could lay all her knickknacks. A large television was mounted on the wall with speakers for surround sound. There was a built-in desk and shelving in the corner nearest huge windows with astounding views of the city below. No doubt a decorator had been given very specific instructions to pick things that matched Bea's sensibilities.

And Ridley couldn't help but be impressed that Gavin even knew what those were.

"This is where you stay when you have visitation with Gavin?"

Bea nodded, grinning. "Wicked, right?"

Ridley nodded back, feeling an incredible sinking in the pit of his stomach.

"It's a wonder you come home. I want to move in here with you." Ridley continued looking around agape.

Bea hopped up on the slightly elevated bed and sank into downy bed linens. "Be serious, Dad. It's nice but it's not home."

Ridley softened. He came and sat beside her. "I love you, my little Bean."

Bea took a deep, shuddering breath, like the kind she used to take as a kid, when she finally calmed down from a hellacious tantrum. Finally, she broke the silence. "I miss Mum so much."

Ridley questioned himself. After these most recent revelations, Ridley felt betrayed. Who was this person who'd held so many things that they should have discussed together so tightly to her chest? Why had she been so secretive? Maybe he could say the same thing about himself?

But Lanie wasn't a secret...or had she been? *Shit.*

It was perhaps time to look at himself and his marriage more honestly and not through the grief-tinged glasses he'd been wearing for the past three years. The truth was the last years before Thyra's passing had not been the best. But he truly hadn't had any clue to the level of dysfunction that had simmered under the surface of their seemingly very placid life.

But, he supposed, that was entirely his own fault.

The very workaholic tendencies that had threatened his custody of Bea hadn't started after Thyra's death. In fact, Ridley knew he was lucky Philip and Clare-Olive had decided to partner *with him* in raising Bea rather than assuming custody themselves. He'd allowed fear of being as impetuous and care-free as his own parents to swing him all the way in the opposite direction. He'd become driven and then brittle. And his insistence on competing with Gavin had turned him into some personification of practical dependability. Someone unadventurous and staid, who was afraid to take risks and was allergic to uncertainty. Someone too busy with work to spend quality time with his family.

It was the truth when he told Lanie he'd turned himself into the person he'd thought Thyra had wanted. And perhaps in those last years, both he and Thyra had begun to resent it.

"I'm sorry, Bean. I know you do."

Bea leaned into his shoulder. "So...now..." She played with her fingers, picking at her chipped polish. "You love Melanie?"

"I do." It was scary to say that out loud. "Do you think that diminishes the love I had for your mother? Or you?"

Bea took a cleansing breath. "In Classical Civilizations class, I read about how the oldest pharaohs of the Abydos Dynasty expected their wives to be buried with them. And I didn't get it. It seemed horrible."

Ridley coughed, looking down and trying to catch Bea's eyes. "Maybe I should have let you drop that class when you asked. Being buried with your spouse doesn't seem horrible anymore?"

Bea shrugged.

"Bea, talk to me. Are you really saying that that sounds reasonable to you now?" Ridley tried to decide whether to be alarmed or not. "That my life should have ended with your mom's?"

"No." She dragged the word out with reluctance.

"Remind me to warn your prospective spouse when the time comes." He laughed.

"It's just that…" She began to sniffle and soon, Ridley could see fat tears rolling down Bea's cheeks. "I can't move on. I can't go get a new mum. It's not fair that you can get a new wife."

Well, what the hell do I say to that?

"While that is true, this is not like a trade-in at the dealership, Bea. No matter what happens between Lanie and me, she will never replace your mother. In your life or mine."

Ridley couldn't believe how untroubled he was by the thought of marrying Lanie. But he also acknowledged the simultaneous truth of what he'd just told Bea. He did miss Thyra. He would always miss her, so much. And there was room in him to hold both things as true.

"I loved your mother and I love her still. That will not change." He hugged Bea to him. "I just love Lanie now too."

"But you aren't going to leave me with Nan, Granddad and Gavin to go off and start a new life with Lanie?"

"What?" He laughed, bemused. "Where'd you get that from?"

"Don't laugh. You promised after Mum died that you would always be honest with me!" She was still upset and more importantly, distrustful. It worried him.

"And I am." Ridley tightened his embrace of Bea's upper arms. "Beatrix. Listen to me, now, okay? I do not plan on moving to the United States. *And* if I was even thinking about it, I would talk with you. That...that's a decision we would be making together."

She leaned away to study his face. "Truly?"

"Of course. I realize now I haven't said this to you in a while, probably not since the day of Mom's funeral, but Beatrix Olive Baker-Smythe, you are as much my daughter as if I had been in the room on the day you were born. And no person, not Gavin, not any new person I start seeing, not even your mother, God rest her, could ever change that. You will always be my daughter. Where I go, you go. Okay?"

She nodded.

"So, if you keep dating Lanie, can we move to New York?"

It was Ridley's turn to pull away. "Say what? I thought you just said you were afraid I was going to move to New York?"

"Yeah, *you by yourself.* I think it would be cool to live there."

"What about your granddad? What about Nan?"

Bea shrugged, wrinkling her nose. "I mean, they could visit, couldn't they?"

forty-eight

■ 16-FEB ■ Trans-Continental Airways ■ Flight 104 ■

LHR-London, Heathrow ▶ **JFK-John F. Kennedy Int'l Airport**

Seat Assignment: **39K**

Lanie lay on Narcisa's couch, where she'd been for the whole weekend.

Coming back from the wedding, Lanie did as she always had. She went home immediately to present herself safe and sound before her mother and then she entered her bedroom and didn't come out again until it was time to go to work. She was a ghost that haunted the rooms of their apartment for half a week, and as soon as the weekend arrived she decamped to Narcisa and Isis's home in Riverdale, an enclave in the North Bronx. Lanie couldn't be in her mom's presence or in her mom's house, because she couldn't bear the gloating.

"You and I both know your mom wouldn't gloat. She loves you." Narcisa had seemed to reach the end of her capacity for coddling around midnight on Saturday. Now, on Sunday morning, she was in normal no-nonsense Narcisa mode.

Lanie shrugged. "Maybe not but I'd feel it anyway. She said this would happen."

Narcisa sighed. "I don't think I agree with your assessment of what exactly happened." Narcisa sat back in the sofa chair across from Lanie.

Lanie shook her head like she was trying to clear it of cobwebs. "What? I told you. He kicked me out of his house!"

"Because his daughter was having a meltdown, right?"

Lanie shrugged to say *more or less*.

"At the sight of her father's new lover damn near naked in her kitchen. Probably to her mind, *her mother's* kitchen, correct?"

Lanie agreed it wasn't a good look—she wasn't that clueless. *Still...* "He kicked me out and called an Uber!"

"Don't put me in the position of defending a man I've never met. He clearly didn't want you to do the precise thing you ended up doing, walking the streets and riding the rails in last night's clothes and no doubt looking like you had the exact type of night you had."

Lanie's cheeks heated, mortified. "Well, he certainly took his time calling me after."

"You also didn't bother picking up."

"Maybe I'm giving him space, Narcisa! Besides, I know where I stand." There was a renewed crying jag to go with those words.

To Lanie's surprise, Isis came and sat beside her, giving Lanie a semblance of what she desperately wanted. Lanie held the woman's slight body tightly as she cried.

When the tears subsided somewhat, Narcisa spoke softly. "You said he told you he loved you. Why do you need to be in competition with his daughter?"

"I don't, of course I don't."

"Because you know what it is to have a father who made everything and everyone a priority above his daughter. And you didn't like that, did you?"

Lanie shook her head, her heart aching at the memory.

"In fact, you wouldn't even want this Ridley guy if you thought he was that way, correct?"

"Yes," Lanie admitted begrudgingly. "But why am I not important enough to *anyone*?"

"Lanie. *Mi amor*, the only person you need to be most important to is yourself. Stop waiting for him, or anyone else, to validate you. Forget them. Find you. Cherish you. Protect you. Care for you. You'd be surprised how much other people take their cues about what's valuable from you. You teach people how to treat you."

Lanie went directly to work from Narcisa's Monday morning. But she finally went home on Monday night. Trudging into the house with her big weekender, she was greeted by the smell of brown stewed chicken filling the house.

Lanie went to her bedroom and flopped down on her bed. She looked around her room, the same one she'd had since she was nine years old. There was no shame in where she lived. With the New York City housing market as it was, most of the people she knew lived with a roommate of some kind—be it a friend, a stranger, a spouse or a parent. Still, it made Lanie feel especially juvenile today that her mom was in the other room. Most likely because she realized she'd been throwing a temper tantrum for days now. Being rejected by Ridley had taught her a valuable lesson. She needed to take her entire life in hand.

You teach people how to treat you.

Lanie took a deep breath, deciding to put Narcisa's advice to good use. Starting now.

She walked into the kitchen with an envelope in her hand. Her mother sat at a small table working on her sudoku. Ryan looked up over her bifocals at Lanie and gave a small polite smile. "So, you're home?"

Lanie knew she meant it in more ways than one, so she

shrugged. Her time flying back and forth to the UK was over but she'd never felt more out of her element in her life.

Ryan's eyebrows rose, bottom lip jutting out, head nodding with faux surprise. She looked like her own mother then.

"Mommy, I have to say this. I think you should be ashamed of yourself."

Her mother took off her glasses, placing them and her pen and pad on the table. "Excuse me?"

Lanie never spoke to her mother like that but it needed to be said. "Your niece just got married. You should have been there. A congratulatory phone call through Gran does not count as an appearance."

"I had work."

"You never take vacation, you have the days. You could've asked for them."

Ryan unfolded her legs, preparing to stand. "You're angry about something and you're taking it out on me."

"No, I'm taking it out on the right person! Maybe I shouldn't have abetted you with this. Had I just refused to go to England, maybe for once you'd have gone instead. Maybe you could have chosen not to put me through the agony of having to do that with a smile plastered on my face. Maybe I could have stayed here and you could have been the one that everyone looked to." Lanie's voice broke as she struggled not to cry.

And then maybe she might never have met Ridley and now her heart wouldn't feel completely shattered.

She presented the envelope to her mother. Dr. Markham's fellowship application. "Maybe I need to move out."

"What?"

"Maybe it's time. Maybe part of my mistake the first time was staying in New York for college. I think we might be too codependent. You and I. You don't do anything because I do it for you. It's like you've given up on life. You go to work, you come home. That's it."

"Is this about Christmas? Lanie, my God, I'm sorry. I didn't mean what I said. Not the way it sounded, at least. Ridley seems like a very nice man but I was only trying to protect you."

"Mom, I don't want to talk—"

"Let me finish," Ryan interrupted. "You know I got pregnant while I was still in conservatory and your father convinced me to drop out. I was alone here in America and it made sense to me. Until I realized what he really wanted was to isolate me further and convince me to take care of him. Not you. Not us. *Him*. So, you dropping out scared me."

"I quit school five years ago. Before Ridley and I ever met."

"I know. It's not him specifically, but when I saw those readmission and fellowship applications sitting on your bed gathering dust while you flew back and forth with this man, I don't know, I panicked. I didn't want you to lose your way. Because without direction, it's easy to be given some by the first man who shows interest. And for him to convince you to move to England to be with him."

"Is that it? You were scared I'd leave? Jesus, give me some credit for having my own mind!"

"No, baby, that's an example. I just don't want you to make the same mistakes I did. You are too talented and beautiful and important to be somebody's plaything. You don't understand how it can be, how very successful men can be. They'll look at you, my sweet girl, and instead of seeing your value ás a person and partner, they'll just see someone they can manipulate and use to prop up their own egos."

"Ridley doesn't think that way," Lanie said but then realized, given the way he'd just cast her aside, who knew?

She did. *That isn't him.*

"Sure, you'll make for a good start until the next one comes along. Lighter, brighter, *whiter*, whatever. And the more successful they are, the quicker they'll be to drop you for the newer, shinier model."

Lanie knew intellectually this was just her mother's pain and resentment toward her father and his wife, but her mother's words shook her nonetheless. No, Lanie wouldn't even consider this, because she knew it wasn't true.

"You're projecting." The words broke from Lanie like a breach in a dam. Ryan looked stunned by her daughter's outburst. "Ridley stayed with his wife until she died and now he's raising his daughter alone because that's who he is. Dad left us because he's a selfish man. That's who *he* is. And it's no reflection on who we are."

Ryan looked as if she'd lost her voice.

"And when you called me 'nothing special' and accused Ridley of using me, it was you who made me doubt myself and feel like I was nothing."

"What do you want me to say?" Her mother cleared her throat, struggling to find the words.

"You could say you don't believe that."

"Of course I don't! I'm sorry."

"Your problem is you've tied your worth up in what Dad thought of you. And you've assumed the same is true for me. Like you don't think I'm capable of discerning Ridley's interest in me or knowing my own value otherwise."

"You know I think you're exceptional. Every day I wonder why you dropped out of grad school. I worry that I encouraged you to do that."

"Mom, no. But when you said I was nothing special I realized you were talking about yourself too, but you *are* remarkable. A caring mother, a skilled nurse," Lanie said. "Losing you was Dad's mistake, not yours. I wish you'd realize that."

At some point in the past two months, Lanie realized that she'd gotten so caught up in what her mother had said to her that she'd overlooked what her mother had said about herself.

"You think?"

Lanie nodded. "I know. How could I be remarkable if you weren't too?"

Ryan smiled. "Look, baby, if he genuinely likes you, believe it or not, I'm glad, ecstatic even. Because I want him to like you."

He loves me.

"And even your grandmother said he seemed to dote on you. So, maybe you're right and I'm projecting, but it's only because you're the most important thing in my life. Naturally I want the best for you."

"I'm the most important thing in your life?"

"You're my child." Her mother seemed confused by the question. "Of course you are."

Lanie bit her trembling lip. She recalled her grandmother's words. *Each and every decision a parent makes factors in their children.* And Bea was Ridley's main priority. But that didn't necessarily have to mean she wasn't important to him too.

"My point is—" Ryan reached across the table to put a hand on Lanie's forearm "—I can admit if I got it—*and him*—all wrong, baby."

They fell into silence until her mother spoke again.

"So, you're really applying?"

She nodded. "I think so. Yeah. Maybe you and I are both ready to get back out there."

"Oh, honey, I'm sorry if I stifled you."

"You didn't, Mom," Lanie said. "I've just been so afraid to fail again. Narcisa says I suffer from a 'failure to launch.'"

"But there's no shame in that. Even NASA has failed sometimes."

Lanie shook her head. "But they've succeeded 166 times."

"That's right, and you've launched dozens of times. Fearlessly. I've watched you. And you'll launch again," Ryan said, patting Lanie's hand. "And you'll succeed too."

forty-nine

"How are we back here again, Melanie?" Professor Skinner paused outside his office to speak to Lanie as she sat at her desk. "I come out of my office and you're back. Not to say I don't enjoy it but I'd gotten accustomed to virtual meetings." He sighed in frustration. "Didn't we talk about this before? Seeing you sitting here every day…again?"

"It's a little weird for me too, honestly. But my cousin is married. I don't need to go anymore." Lanie smiled weakly.

"You know that's not what I mean, Melanie."

"Yes, but—"

"I spoke to Dr. Markham, he said he'd received your packet. He was very impressed," he cut her off and smiled.

"Don't get too excited, Professor Skinner. Frankly, I don't know what I want right now," she said, instead of her usual evasive banter.

His eyes widened in surprise. "Well, you know I think finishing your PhD should be high on that list, but you definitely need to want that for yourself."

Lanie felt relieved that he was relenting…at long last.

He clicked his teeth in resignation. "Anyway, it's great to have you back." Professor Skinner look suddenly glum. "I'd still prefer to see you doing something else. You're a capable woman. I have confidence that you won't allow yourself to waste away behind that desk forever."

She should have known he wasn't done. Lanie sealed her mouth shut and waited. He seemed to realize after a moment, catching himself.

He looked out the window behind her. "Well, ah, it's a beautiful day. And you're going out for your lunch and that's that."

Lanie nodded, smiling. "Sure, okay."

"Lanie."

Her sandwich stopped on the way to her mouth when she heard him call her name. And as always, she recognized his voice immediately.

"I can't believe I found you."

"And saying that will never not be creepy. Stop. It."

Ridley gave her a wry grin.

Besides, finding her was no great feat. Sitting in the central quad near her office, on a campus that was only about sixteen acres of land and buildings, made locating a big Black woman in the predominately white space not exactly hard.

"Can I sit?"

"You can do whatever you want."

"Can I?" Ridley sat beside her, never taking his eyes away from her face. "Can I win you back?"

Lanie gritted her teeth. It had been four *whole* weeks since she saw him last, while fleeing from his house after Gemma's wedding. "That's gonna be a bit harder. Like, maybe even impossible."

"Lanie, I apologize, but I had to focus on Bea. She was going through something."

Guilt ate at Lanie, remembering what Narcisa had said. She knew how important it was for Bea to know Lanie was no threat to her relationship with her father. But it did not stop the ache that bloomed in Lanie's chest remembering how it had felt to be put out of his house. Recalling how vulnerable she'd felt.

"You made me feel disposable."

"I'm sorry. I didn't handle it well. I know."

"Listen, I get it. Bea needed you right then. But you could have asked me to go upstairs. Told me to go get my coffee down the block, said you needed some time. You don't kick me out in front of your kid so she can see I'm just some trash that had to be taken to the curb in the morning. Some chick who didn't mean anything to you."

Ridley grimaced. *Had this not occurred to him?* Lanie clamped her mouth shut so the thought wouldn't slip out.

"You're right. I'm sorry."

Lanie kept her chin up, back straight. She couldn't let him see how much he'd destroyed her with his callousness.

Ridley turned to her fully, propping a knee up on the bench beside her. "Look, I've spoken to Bea and she gets it now. And I get it."

"Do you?"

"I do. I love you, Lanie. I want us to figure this out because we have a much bigger issue to deal with. Namely, this distance. Now that your cousin's wedding is over, I know you won't be coming to England as much anymore. And we've finally found someone to take over the coinvestigator position here, so I won't need to come back and forth quite so often either."

"So, then it's over anyway, isn't it?" Lanie said the words in as casual a manner as she could manage while certain her heart was breaking.

"No, of course not." Ridley shook his head. "Lanie, we love each other. We know this. So, this can't be it. It can't be over."

He reached for her hand and she pulled it away, clasping both in her lap.

"Why? You live there, I live here. That won't change, right?" She turned slightly, facing him for the first time.

He was stunned.

"Right?" she insisted.

"I don't know. I'm not sure what you want me to say," he echoed her thoughts.

Say I'm important. Say you need me. That you want me. That you'll move mountains to be with me. Tell me the things you must have told Thyra.

Lanie waited. Silence surrounded them. The chapel clock high above the quad struck one. That was her cue.

"Between that day and now, I think you've said enough, Ridley: absolutely nothing."

She thought about Narcisa's advice. *I'm teaching people how to treat me.*

"Yes. I think this might be done," Lanie said, barely keeping the tears out of her voice.

She peered down at the rest of her sandwich in her lap as if that might be what she was talking about instead. Lanie rose from the bench as Ridley watched then walked to the garbage and threw that away too.

fifty

Ridley

Ridley sat on the bench, his guts churning, long after he'd watched Lanie walk away, unclear on what just happened.

Had he expected Lanie to run into his arms when he got there? *No. Not really... Or maybe just a tiny bit.*

But he also knew he had a lot to make up for. The days after the wedding had not been his finest hour. It was all still kind of a blur. From gathering Bea in his arms and telling Lanie to leave, to calling after her as she ran to the tube stop. It had all been a shit show.

One he'd caused.

He'd asked Lanie to come home with him because he'd wanted her in his bed, to see her spread across his sheets. Ever since the first time she'd stopped by with her girlfriends and Ridley walked in to see his house full of life again, he'd known it. He wanted her with them, a part of his reality. And Ridley could see clearly now that his infatuation with Lanie had grown into something far more serious far sooner than he'd admitted to her or even to himself.

That's why it had been so amazing to get that voicemail from her, even if she'd clearly been drunk when she left it. It was a five-minute ramble that revealed lots of things he was sure she'd rather it hadn't. He still chuckled thinking about it. But it made him love her even more. And the best part had been learning she felt the same, that she loved him too, when she said so...*seven times*. He'd counted. It had been like hearing the perfect melody played in the perfect key. He'd never admit to her how many times he'd replayed that message, letting it lull him to sleep.

She loved him and he most definitely loved her back. They both knew it. And that was supposedly all that mattered, right? So then, how could shit go downhill so quickly? Ridley was still sitting, immobilized on that bench, trying to figure it out.

His phone rang as he looked around the peaceful and surprisingly quiet campus.

"Did you talk to her?" Bea spoke before he could even answer. "Did you apologize? Did you tell her I was sorry too?"

Ridley smiled despite himself. "I spoke to her."

"Did you apologize though?"

"I did."

"For me too?"

"I did not."

"Dad!" Bea wailed into the phone. "How could you? You promised!"

"Honey, I didn't get a chance. She wasn't in a listening mood."

He didn't know that that was necessarily the truth. It seemed more like there were some magic words Lanie was waiting on but he didn't know what they were. With Thyra, his Rosetta stone had been Gavin and his bad behavior. Ridley had no idea what to do to get through to Lanie.

"Then you listen. What did she say?"

Ridley thought about it. What *had* she said? "That I embarrassed her in front of you and that I made her feel disposable and that we live too far apart."

"And what does that tell you?" This voice was masculine.

"Hello? Bean?"

"That's Gavin, Dad, don't worry. He picked me up from school today."

Ridley gritted his teeth, still not used to the new arrangement that he and Gavin would officially share custody of Beatrix, with Ridley as her primary guardian. "Take me off speaker, would you please?"

"Wait, before you do—Aronsen, think about it. What do all those things tell you?"

"I can't move back to the United States."

"Says who?" Gavin asked.

"Yeah, says who?" Bea chimed in. "But she didn't directly ask you to move back, Dad. She asked you to tell her that you'd consider it."

"I agree," Gavin opined. "Sounds like she asked you to tell her she was not interchangeable, that she was enough of a fixture in your life that you would establish some sense of permanence in your lives together."

She had? How didn't I hear all that?

"Maybe figure out a way to close the distance. Like, I don't know…consider some compromise?" Bea offered. "Like you and Gavin are doing?"

Allowing Bea to travel more freely between his house and Gavin's was hardly the same as him attempting to maintain a transcontinental relationship. "Give it up. We are not moving to New York, Bean," Ridley said.

The sound of Bea sucking her teeth came through the phone.

"Look." Ridley sighed heavily. "I told her I wanted to figure out what we were going to do about the distance because we found our new coordinator."

There were boos and hisses on the phone. His own personal Greek chorus. *Great.*

"What?" Ridley asked defensively.

"You don't lead with why you're not coming back. You lead

with when you're coming next, man! You tell her when she can expect to see you again because you're not going anywhere," Gavin chided.

Ridley hated that this was making some sense. "How do *you* know these things?"

Gavin laughed into the phone. The sound almost made Ridley's ears ache.

"Well, I'm glad you asked. Therapy is this amazing thing I've discovered. But my most foolproof relationship method has always been to think to myself, 'WWAD? What Would Aronsen Do?' And then I do it."

Ridley rolled his eyes.

"So, the question is, where's that impetuous young man gone to?" Gavin concluded.

The very idea that this joker was talking sense took Ridley's breath away. But impulsive moves were his parents' thing, not his. They were antithetical to Ridley's very fiber. To all the ways in which he tried to live his life.

No. His job, Bea's schooling. Their home, their lives. All of those things were in the UK.

"There are too many things up in the air right now for me to do anything as rash as what is being hinted." Ridley didn't even realize he'd said that aloud until he heard Gavin's next words.

"The operative words I hear are *right* and *now.*"

Ridley took a deep breath and held it, trying to locate and then listen to the tiny voice in him that he'd long ago shoved down deep and locked away. What did it say?

Go get her.

"Aronsen?"

"Dad? You there?"

"O-kay," he said to his apparent coconspirators after long minutes of quiet. "Gavin, I think you and I might need to have a little talk."

Bea screeched on the phone.

"Calm down. Don't get excited...yet."

"Too late!" Bea giggled.

"Whenever you want, of course," Gavin said. "I'll happily put you on my calendar."

Ridley rolled his eyes skyward. Thyra'd had one helluva strange plan keeping this guy in their lives...but Ridley could finally see that perhaps there was some merit to it.

"Ridley, go get her."

fifty-one

Lanie

Lanie's heart broke into a million unsalvageable pieces, leaving Ridley sitting in the quad. She understood fully then what the limerence Narcisa spoke about was. "Losing" Jonah had never been as painful as walking away from Ridley. She'd been totally unprepared for that.

Likewise, she was unprepared to find Ridley sitting at her dining room table talking with her mother when she got home.

"What are you doing here?" Lanie asked, stepping fully into her apartment that evening after hesitating at the door in confusion.

"I'm gonna go out," Ryan said, grabbing her coat and keys. "I'll be at the coffee shop across the street, if you need me." With that, Ryan exited.

Lanie turned to Ridley, eyes narrowing. She hated that her rebellious heart raced seeing him there.

"I realized that showing up at your job wasn't the best way to facilitate a good conversation."

"Showing up at my house isn't much better." Her rejoinder was ice-cold.

"Well, showing up on your train route home would have been more logistically complex than I think even I'm capable of." His mouth quirked in a way that suggested he was joking with her.

Lanie didn't laugh, tweaking her ear a little in irritation. "What else is there to say, Ridley? I kinda felt like we reached an impasse. I live here and you live there."

"Yes, but we love each other, right?"

Lanie didn't want to say it again. It felt heartrending every time the words left her mouth. She nodded.

"Lanie." She didn't think she'd ever heard Ridley sound so plaintive, so far off the sure footing he maintained. "Please say it."

The uncertainty in his voice, almost shaky, startled her, but she wouldn't give him comfort at the expense of her own. Those days were done. This was her loving herself first.

"No, because I don't see what difference that makes," she said instead.

"It makes all the difference. It means we don't want to break up, correct?"

"I mean, that would follow." She slid into a chair across from him.

"Well then, we have to make a plan."

"How?" She didn't see how they were going to manage to drag two continents closer together.

"We plan out how we can make this, us, work." Ridley put his hands on the table but did not reach for hers, just left them flat against the surface as if to illustrate his intention to hash it out, like a negotiation.

"Again, you've lost me."

"Let me back up. I told you about my parents, right? How they did whatever they wanted with little regard for the four young children they had at home? Well, growing up like that, the insecurity of it scared me. So, I promised myself I'd never be that way. Never put my children through that. And I made practicality and dependability my mantra. No surprises, no ambiguity, no instability—needless to say, I was a very boring kid."

"You like your feet on the ground literally and figuratively, huh?"

"Exactly."

He grinned and Lanie managed a small smile.

"I craved stability. So, I made a plan for getting into college. And I made a plan for getting out of college. I made a plan for med school. I made a plan for my specialty and then for my career. Right down to where I would practice in Massachusetts." He sighed heavily. "I never planned to leave. Then I met Thyra and all those plans flew out the window. I left the country. I changed my specialty to help her fight her disease. I became a husband and a father when I could barely afford to feed myself. Basically, I turned my life inside out. And I realized I'd done the exact same thing my parents do. I had let my life kind of spin out of control just because I fell in love."

"Out of control? Ridley, you know how in-control your life is? You are the most thoughtful, levelheaded and put-together person I've ever met."

"And do you know how much constant energy it requires *every single day* to try to maintain that? The constant stress of keeping so many balls in the air?" Ridley's voice cracked.

Lanie was shocked.

"The absolute backbreaking work of it, Lanie?"

She hadn't thought about that. Ridley always made his life look effortless. Apparently though, the way he held himself, so reserved and uptight, was not him being stern or unforgiving but him literally and figuratively holding himself and his world together. That was heartbreaking.

"When Thyra died all the little cracks that I was constantly spackling over turned into fissures. Then Gavin showed up and the fissures turned into fault lines and then the study started to fall apart and the fault lines became like tectonic plates shifting violently under my feet and all that control I struggled to maintain began to crumble."

"I'm sorry, but what does this have to do with me?"

"Because at first you felt like another thing in my life that had come out of nowhere and had the potential to upend everything. And you did. But I couldn't resist getting to know you. From the very beginning I was drawn to you, even when I didn't want to be."

"Wow, I sound great. Like a hurricane."

"No, Lanie. You are wonderful. One of the most amazing things that's ever happened to me. You're a light in my life. You became one of the few effortlessly fun parts of my life. Quickly, I began to look forward to the time I got to spend with you. You helped me see that even as everything was happening, it didn't have to mean my life was falling apart—that I could deal with changes. I watched you handle your grandmother's illness and your cousin's marriage with such grace. And even when it was literally turning your life upside down, you still showed up to help the people you love."

"I assure you, I was falling apart inside too."

"Even so, watching how you dealt with your changes helped me realize I was capable of making some adjustment too. And that I could choose not to always take myself so seriously. Leave some room in my life for flexibility and unpredictability and falling in love with an amazing woman."

Lanie rolled her eyes.

"And after you left England, when the idea of you not coming back finally hit me, I had that feeling again."

"What feeling?"

"The feeling that made me follow Thyra across an ocean. That 'Oh my God, I can't let this woman walk out of my life' feeling. That 'I cannot let my "plans" stand in the way of my love' feeling. 'Cuz the thing is, for as impulsive and reckless a decision as it seemed to be all those years ago, I wouldn't have the life I've had if I hadn't done it. And I *really* love my life."

"Won't being with me disrupt that life?"

He nodded. "But not in a way I'm afraid of anymore. I love you, Lanie. And I'm committed to you and to sorting this out."

Lanie gasped, covering her face. She'd waited to hear that from someone for so long.

"The fact that I didn't say that when I first saw you today made you upset, rightfully. And for that I'm sorry," he whispered, taking her hand. "But I spoke with a couple of people afterward…"

"Bea?"

"Among others." He nodded. "And they reminded me that all the things I love about my life are ultimately portable."

Lanie's eyes widened. "What? What are you saying?"

"Wait. Slow down." He squeezed her hand. "Not immediately portable. But with some careful—"

"Planning?"

"See, you understand me."

"I do…" Lanie smiled, slipping out of her seat and coming around to sit on his lap. "Now."

"I can't believe I found you."

"Same here." Lanie didn't realize she was crying until she tasted the salt between Ridley's lips and her own as she moved her mouth over his.

fifty-two

eighteen months later

■ 27-AUG ■ National Airways ■ Flight: 824 ■

JFK-John F. Kennedy Int'l Airport ▶ **SFO-San Francisco Int'l**

Seat Assignment: **8C**

As she moved through the baggage claim, Melanie Turner decided that after this, she was never moving again—it was too much trouble. She was not accustomed to traveling with this much stuff.

The lesson of the day was, clearly, flying was very different when you were taking your whole life with you. *Far less fun.* In addition to her trusty carry-on, she had three large suitcases with her. That didn't even include the boxes that were being shipped freight to San Francisco. And right now, the cart, piled high with her luggage, slipped across the smooth linoleum flooring in the arrivals terminal in the opposite direction of where she wanted it to go. It just seemed to have a mind of its own.

It was like these plans: once they'd been set in motion they just seemed to go. And there was a part of her that still couldn't believe she'd agreed to it all. Of the two of them, Ridley was supposed to be the one who was risk averse, but this had been all his idea. It was Lanie that had taken some convincing. But she admired his bravery and drive to make this happen. To make this life together for the three of them work.

Lanie still couldn't believe it—that Ridley would pick up his life to follow *her*. But he had. It was one of the ways, he'd told her, that he wanted to prove that she was a priority for him. Lanie still didn't know what special alchemy had brought a man that wonderful into her life. But she was grateful for it. *For him*. Because Ridley wasn't kidding when he said it would take some work and time. Nearly two years of it, in fact.

Ridley and Dash had to finish the clinical part of their trial in London before being free to work on the data sets with the new New York coordinator remotely. Then Ridley and Bea had had to sell her house, which incidentally had left Bea independently wealthy at the tender age of almost sixteen. And with enough money to afford the college of her choice. Ridley and Gavin found a high school for her in Piedmont while Ridley searched for a new job. Luckily, San Francisco State University was more than happy to scoop him up when they heard he was on the job market. But overall, it had meant eighteen months of massive change for Ridley and Bea. These two people for whom Lanie had become so important that they had been willing to pick up stakes and make this gargantuan move.

On Lanie's side, there was a shorter move but no less risky a change. In finally applying for the offered position as a teaching assistant in Dr. Markham's Plasma Physics Department, she had agreed to move across the country. And while technically accepting it only meant she was an employee at Cal Berkeley, not a student, as she promised Professor Skinner—and Dr.

Markham reiterated—it also meant she was dipping her toes back into academia. Which was enough.

Baby steps.

Of course, the prospect of her daughter moving away had terrified Ryan. But with Narcisa's help—and an open-ended train ticket—Lanie's mother came to see the change as good and necessary...for the both of them. Still, separation anxiety was an ongoing challenge.

Lanie put a hand up to her face to shield her eyes from the sun's glare as she came out of the terminal doors. She struggled keeping her cart on track as she peered around for the faces she'd recognize.

"Lanie!" Bea bounded up to her and gave her a hug.

After a year and a half of Lanie and Ridley going back and forth once a month, Lanie was grateful she and Bea had managed to get closer too. It helped that Ridley had brought his daughter for that long summer visit he'd promised and allowed Lanie to show Bea all the cool New York places that only she knew about.

"You have a lot of stuff," Bea remarked.

"I lived in New York a long time."

Bea tried to take over but slipped side to side trying to control the unwieldy luggage cart. In the end, they pushed it together.

When he saw them coming, Ridley flagged them down and hopped out of the car at the curb. "Sorry, I couldn't leave the car or they would have towed us." He ran up to Lanie and pulled her into a hug.

It felt like months since they'd seen each other last. It had only been a couple of weeks.

"You're here," he whispered into her hair. "Finally."

"I am." She turned her face up to receive a light kiss.

"We've only managed to unpack the bedrooms without you," he said as their lips parted.

"That's okay."

"You could have left me in the car, Dad. I can drive now," Bea groused as she stepped off the curb to open the trunk.

"Oh, honey, I wish." Ridley shook his head, then adjusted his glasses. "But you don't have a California license yet."

"Neither do you."

"Mine's in the mail, where's yours?" Ridley told his daughter, though his eyes never left Lanie, as if memorizing her face, holding her tightly to him.

"Can we get my stuff in the car please, people?" Lanie laughed easily but she was actually quite tired. It had been a long week of packing her life up to ship across country and then a long flight to get herself there too.

"You ready?" Ridley whispered into Lanie's ear, before planting another kiss on her temple and the car keys in her hand.

She nodded. "My dress is in my carry-on."

"It can fit in your carry-on?"

"It's just a little jersey-knit, sequined thing." She shrugged. "But it's white, which was all I cared about, in case they lost my luggage."

"Now, you're sure about this? San Francisco City Hall is pretty but it's also pretty no-frills. Most people need at least a little pomp. I don't want you feeling cheated later."

"I told you, I've already planned one wedding in my life. I'm good."

He smiled. She'd gotten good at getting him to do that.

"And your mom?"

"Once I showed her that there was a train route that went all the way from Grand Central to Jack London Square Station in Oakland, she was much more willing. I put her on the train myself, she'll be here on Thursday."

"Your grandmother, Gem, Les?"

"Gran and Les are getting in the day after tomorrow. So, I hope we can get the guest bedrooms done by then too. But baby Tori's got an ear infection. No one wants a cranky toddler on a plane for ten hours. So, Gem and Jonah send their love."

"We could wait until they can make it?"

"Uh-uh, no, we can't."

Ridley barked a laugh.

"Hey! I can't do this by myself!" Bea cried out, struggling with the lightest of the three oversized suitcases.

Lanie and Ridley broke apart hurriedly to help. As she watched her fiancé and his daughter bickering playfully, Lanie thought again that it was nice to be home and that perhaps she and Ridley were really done with their traveling. At least for a little while.

Although there were still all those frequent flier miles to redeem.

★ ★ ★ ★ ★

acknowledgments

The irony of ironies is that despite how solitary the act of writing can often be, it's a rare book that exists as the work of one person alone. *Frequent Fliers* is no exception. And I was lucky enough to have many collaborators, supporters and champions.

To Lynn Raposo, my editor, for all you've done, your hard work, patience and diligence. It is a known fact that *Frequent Fliers* would not exist without your guidance, assistance and encouragement. It would also not exist in its current form if you did not rein me in, push me forward and speed me up, LOL! I wouldn't be here, holding a finished product, if not for you. Thank you.

Jill Marsal, as ever, thank you for being the best agent a new author could hope for, and for your unflagging faith in my work.

Tanisha, Tanisha, Tanisha. I am choked up just writing this. Truly, you have been the wind beneath this little writer's wings. I could not have done any of this without your help: your indefatigable support, constant companionship and unfailing enthusiasm. The second book would be hard, everyone said so, but without your faith in me when I had little in myself, it would have been infinitely harder. There are no words, but I hope you know my feels.

Sara Moran, my beautiful, wonderful, wildly talented MSU sister-friend, I am so grateful to have you as my writing peer. Your critique is as invaluable to me as your friendship. Thank you for always giving it to me straight.

Ashley Jordan, as ever, your help with the spicy bits was indispensable. But more than that, your support and friendship have been a gift that I cherish. I cannot wait until the world gets to see what you can do, so I can cheer for you like you've done for me! You're the bar I measure myself against and I still have a ways to go.

Jerneeka Sams, how could I ever thank you for twenty—ahem!—years of friendship? You are my forever ride-or-die and I can't thank you enough for sticking with me through this adventure. Through *every* adventure. ♥

Simone Patterson, I am blessed to have many wonderful and supportive friends, but in the Hall of Fame, you are the GOAT! The #1! You're always there to push me when I can't get out of my own way. And I'll love you forever for it!

Femi Lewis Usanga, Ms. Writer. The OG inspiration. The first professional Black girl writer I ever knew. Your very existence was revelatory. Thank you for always believing in me too.

Amora, Lina, Zandrina and Shalini, I truly believe I wouldn't be where I am without you. I love you so much and I am so honored by all the love you pour back into me. So, even if it doesn't say it, every book I'll ever write is also dedicated to you four fabulous women.

Mom, Dad and Ma'am, none of this would be possible if I didn't have parents like you. You are my foundation. I can never thank you enough for all your love, support…and marketing. I think you guys have sold more of my books than Amazon! I love you.

To my wonderful brothers, Carl, Amin, Cyle. And their

beautiful wives, Felicia and Alyssa. Where would I be without you guys? Thank you for always being there for me, with faith, love and steadfast encouragement.

Regina, Nikki, Tee and Terah, thank you for making room for me. Thank you for tolerating my gloom and being rainbows when my little neurotic skies got bleak. Your advice and insight has been a gift and a balm. And above all, thank you for sharing your time, energy and wisdom with me.

To Andrea DeSilva, with my sincerest gratitude, for being the coolest lockdown neighbor ever and for honoring me with tidbits about Sri Lankan culture.

I am truly blessed to be in the writing community that I find myself in. There are so many lovely, talented people I could and want to thank, but if your name isn't here, please know it's absolutely an oversight:

My mentors—Sami Ellis and Lyn Liao Butler, your friendship, kindness, support and generosity have been invaluable to me all along the way. I can never thank you both enough.

My book "godmother," Ann (A.H.) Kim, thank you for everything you've done and continue to do. I am truly blessed to know you.

Yaffa, Farrah, Naima and Jamie, thank you for your amazing words and deeds of support. You made ME want to read my book, and after hundreds of rereads and edits, that's really saying something!

To Erin, M.K., Harlem, Mia, Tati, Kalie, Meredith, TJ, Kate, Amanda, Lindsay, Lauren, Sarvenaz, Stacey, Kelly, Danielle, Maggie, Ava, Jen, Jess, Ashley, JC, Kaitlyn, Megan, Sandy, Deb and anyone else I've forgotten who has helped, promoted, commiserated, collaborated or just plain had fun with me… Thank you so, so much for being the book community of my dreams. My gratitude is undying.

Special thank-you to my Canary Street Press/HarperCollins extended family: Leah Morse, Diane Lavoie, Alexandra

McCabe, Erin Craig and cover illustrator Poppy Magda, who have gone largely unsung but are as essential to the success of *Frequent Fliers* as I am. You guys rock!

As always to Pat and Brittaney-Belle, Marguerite and Kristin, Yvette and Ada, Shauntae and Leslie, my Bronx family: Auntie Merlyn, Auntie Verna and Jodi, thank you for being there to cheer me on.

S. P., thank you for being my original inspiration.

And finally, to the Cumberbatches of Tooting Bec, my English family. Thank you for making the UK my home away from home. The only place I know I can show up at a moment's notice and be welcomed with open arms, time and again. Auntie Dona, Allison, Daniel, Dawn, Maryam and Uncle Jed Joseph (RIP). I love you to the moon (or the nearest Marks & Spencer ☺) and back!